'A quirky tale of love, work and
the meaning of life'
Company

'A smart, witty love story'
Observer

'Full of laugh-out-loud observations . . .
utterly unputdownable'
Woman

'A chick-lit writer with a difference . . .
never scared to try something different,
Colgan always pulls it off'
Image

'A Colgan novel is like listening to your
best pal, souped up on vino, spilling the
latest gossip – entertaining, dramatic
and frequently hilarious'
Daily Record

'An entertaining read'
Sunday Express

'Part chick lit, part food porn . . .
this is full-on fun for foodies'
Bella

The
Bookshop
on the Shore

Also by Jenny Colgan

The Endless Beach
My Very '90s Romance
Amanda's Wedding
Looking for Andrew McCarthy
Working Wonders
Do You Remember the First Time?
Where Have All the Boys Gone?
West End Girls
Operation Sunshine
Diamonds Are a Girl's Best Friend
The Good, the Bad and the Dumped
Meet Me at the Cupcake Café
Christmas at the Cupcake Café
Welcome to Rosie Hopkins' Sweetshop of Dreams
Christmas at Rosie Hopkins' Sweetshop
The Christmas Surprise
The Loveliest Chocolate Shop in Paris
Little Beach Street Bakery
Summer at Little Beach Street Bakery
The Little Shop of Happy Ever After
Christmas at Little Beach Street Bakery
The Bookshop on the Corner
The Café by the Sea
A Very Distant Shore

By Jenny T. Colgan

Resistance Is Futile
Spandex and the City

The
Bookshop
on the Shore

JENNY COLGAN

WILLIAM MORROW
An Imprint of HarperCollins*Publishers*

For Deborah Schneider,
who is brave, awesome and brilliant

THE BOOKSHOP ON THE SHORE. Copyright © 2019 by Jenny Colgan. All rights reserved. Printed in the United States of America. No part of this book may be used or reproduced in any manner whatsoever without written permission except in the case of brief quotations embodied in critical articles and reviews. For information, address HarperCollins Publishers, 195 Broadway, New York, NY 10007.

HarperCollins books may be purchased for educational, business, or sales promotional use. For information, please email the Special Markets Department at SPsales@harpercollins.com.

Originally published as *The Bookshop on the Shore* in UK in 2019 by Sphere.

FIRST U.S. EDITION

Library of Congress Cataloging-in-Publication Data has been applied for.

ISBN 978-0-06-285018-8
ISBN 978-0-06-291355-5 (hardcover library edition)

19 20 21 22 23 LSC 10 9 8 7 6 5 4 3 2 1

Introduction

When I was very small, I read every single children's book in the small section of our tiny local library (except for the big green book about reptiles and amphibians, of which I was terrified).

I read books about calligraphy, about table tennis, about Brownies (I was a dreadful Brownie and hated it; I only ever got one badge – the reader's badge, yes), books about how to become a spy, and about the Bible, as well as every single story book they had.

I thought that was the point: you read, so you read every book in the world. When I got my adult card, aged thirteen, I lasted about half a shelf of Louis L'Amour before I realised that it probably wasn't going to work out for me (although I got through a lot more Tom Clancy than you might expect in a teenage girl).

So with that out of the way: hello, and thank you so much for choosing *The Bookshop by the Shore* – I know you have a lot of choices. I promise you, I know. ☺

This book isn't a sequel to *The Bookshop on the Corner* or *The Little Shop of Happy Ever After* (depending on where you read it). Here is a funny story: authors don't always choose the titles of their own books, it may surprise you to learn, and long titles were fashionable at the time we chose *The Little Shop of Happy Ever After* but I always found it a bit of a mouthful.

Then my old American editor, whom I adore, said, 'Well, I'm not sure about the UK title. Would you mind if we changed it?' and I said, 'Sure!'

And he said, 'What about *The Bookshop on the Corner*?'

And I said, 'Well, the thing is, it's a travelling bookshop, so it's not really on a corner, is it?'

And he said, 'So, I thought, you know, a bookshop that's handy to you is what I liked about the title.'

And so I said, 'Okay, well, how about I park it on a corner,' and he said, 'Great,' and that is why the only difference between the UK and US editions is the number of times the sentence 'the van parked up on its usual corner' appears.

Anyway, this book isn't a sequel, but it has a couple of the same characters: Nina and Surinder are here, but it's Zoe's story, entirely.

It's also a story too about how if you love books, well, then I always think you have a layer of protection against the world, which sounds strange, but that is what I truly believe.

If you read, I think it means you don't always have to take your own word for it. It means there are more heads to be in, more lives to be lived than simply your own. My son isn't a big reader (nor a particularly precocious child) but I do remember when he read the Harry Potter series he came up to me and said, astonished, 'It's not like a film – it's like actually *being* there, Mum.' And I still believe reading is the best form of direct brain-to-brain communication humans have yet figured out, until Facebook makes us all have implants at least.

Reading can be an escape – I like watching commuters particularly, unaware of the grey morning breath around them, rapt in Thomas Cromwell's England or Michel Faber's Martian worlds or George R. R. Martin's wild eyries.

In the last bookshop novel, I talked a bit about where and how I read, and lots of readers helpfully contributed their own ideas. One of the interesting things that came up was the line between 'real books' and books read on download and audio. Some people – not many – were hardliners, all 'oh there's nothing like a real book'. But what was interesting was how many more love the freedom of carrying a library on their phone or in their pockets, and what I notice more and more is people using their Kindles at a large font, taking away the need for reading glasses – how useful is that?

They're also easy for propping up in the gym and I take mine in the bath every day (I turn the pages with my nose) and haven't dropped it in once, and trust me, nobody is clumsier than me. Also I love audio books as it means you can still be reading when your hands are busy trying to walk the dog.

Although with download, I do slightly miss being able to spy on what other people are reading. I wish they'd put the title of the book you're reading at the top of each page as well; I am constantly forgetting the titles I'm reading and then someone says to me 'What are you reading right now?' and I flail for a bit and they look at me as if to say 'Oh, right, sorry, I *thought* you were a bookish person' which is *very, very annoying*.

Oh and I also got cross at a dinner once when this woman was going on and on about how she would never read on download, that there was nothing like a real book and – I promise I normally am never rude to people but she was being truly insufferable – I said, 'Well, they're really only for people who read *a lot*' which was mean of me but quite satisfying also.

So I think what I'm trying to say is: love whatever you read. Enrich your life with books, of any type. If you aren't enjoying a book, try another – life is far too short.* I'm still trying to read every book in the world. You're a reader. You understand.

Love,

Jenny

x x x

* Except this one, obviously. I will be emailing you personally to check you finished it, and there might be a short quiz.

PART ONE

'The view from up here is different,' said Robert Carrier, extending his wing. 'When you look at things the same way you've always done, nothing changes. When you change perspective, everything changes.'

'But this doesn't look like the city at all,' said Wallace in amazement. 'It's all sky.'

'Quite,' said Robert Carrier, fixing his beady eyes on the slightly grubby boy. 'There are many different types of sky.'

From *Up on the Rooftops*

Chapter One

'So, tell me about the crying?'

The woman sat, kind but formal, behind the tatty scuffed old NHS desk. A poster on the wall suggested a confusing acronym that you would have to remember if you thought you were having a stroke.

The idea that you would have to remember an acronym while also having a stroke was making Zoe very anxious, even more than being there in the first place. There was a dirty Venetian blind just about covering a bunker window that only looked out onto another red brick wall, and coffee-stained rough carpet tiles.

'Well, mostly Mondays,' Zoe said, taking in the woman's lovely shiny dark hair. Her own was long and dark too, but currently tied roughly with something she hoped was a hair tie and not, for example, an elastic band dropped by the postman. 'And, you know. When the tube is late or I can't get the buggy in the carriage. Or someone tuts because I'm trying to get the buggy in because if I don't take the buggy I'll be an hour late even though he's too big for it and I know that, thanks, so you can probably stop with the judgemental looks.

'Or when I'm caught up at work and I can count every minute of how much it's going to cost me by the time I've picked him up and it makes the entire day's work worthless. Or when I think maybe we'll take the bus and we just arrive at the stop and he shuts the doors, even though he's seen me, because he can't be arsed with the buggy. Or when we run out of cheese and I can't afford to get more. Have you seen the price of cheese? Or . . . '

The woman smiled kindly while also looking slightly anxious.

'I meant your son, Mrs O'Connell. When does *he* cry?'

'Oh!' said Zoe, startled.

They both looked at the dark-haired little boy, who was cautiously playing with a farm set in the corner of the room. He looked up at them warily.

'I . . . I didn't realise,' said Zoe, suddenly thinking she was about to cry again. Kind Dr Baqri pushed over the box of tissues she kept on the desk, which did the opposite of helping.

' . . . and it's "miss",' said Zoe, her voice wobbling. 'Well, he's fine . . . I mean, a few tears but he doesn't . . . ' Now she knew she really was going to go. 'He doesn't . . . make a sound.'

At least, thought Zoe, after she'd cleaned herself up, slightly gone again, then pulled herself back from the brink as she realised to her horror that the NHS appointment they had waited so many months for was nearly up and she had spent most of it in tears and looking full of hope and despair at Dr Baqri, Hari now squirming cheerfully in her lap. At least Dr Baqri hadn't said what people always said . . .

'Einstein, you know . . . ' began Dr Baqri, and Zoe groaned internally. Here it came: ' . . . didn't talk till he was five.'

Zoe half-smiled. 'I know that, thanks,' she said through gritted teeth.

'Selective mutism . . . has he suffered any trauma?'

Zoe bit her lip. God, she hoped not.

'Well, his dad . . . comes and goes a bit,' she said, and then slightly pleadingly, as if wanting the doctor to approve of her, added, 'Th-that's not unusual though, is it? You like seeing Daddy, don't you?'

At the mention of his father, Hari's little face lit up as it always did, and he poked a chubby finger enquiringly into her cheek.

'Soon,' she said to him.

'When's the last time you saw him?' asked the doctor.

'Um ... three ... six ...'

Zoe tried to think back. Jaz been gone all summer, truth be told. She constantly told herself to stop following his Instagram feed, but it was like a nasty addiction. He'd been to about four festivals. There were lots of shots of him in different multicoloured hats.

'Well,' said the doctor, who had played a sharing card game with Hari, taught him how to click his fingers, played peekaboo with him and got him to find things she'd hidden around the place, all of which the four-year-old had tried to do, nervously and constantly tearing back to clamber in his mummy's lap, his dark eyes round and scared.

'It's a social anxiety disorder.'

'I know.'

'It's very unusual –' The doctor examined her notes. ' – for a child not to speak even to a parent. Is there anything about the home he finds unsettling?'

They lived on the ground floor of a horrible Victorian conversion on a main road in Wembley. The pipes clanged; the upstairs neighbour often came home drunk and blared music deep into the night. Sometimes he brought friends home who would bang on the door and laugh loudly. Getting the money together for a deposit on a new place – not to mention paying the rent – was a pipe dream. The council had offered her a B&B which she thought might be even worse. Her mum couldn't help – she'd moved to Spain years ago and was finding it more expensive day by day, eking out a pension in sterling and working in a horrible bar with pictures of fried eggs in the window.

Also, since she'd accidentally got pregnant with Hari, Zoe had spent a lot of time pretending she was fine, that everything was okay

9

to her family and friends. She couldn't bear facing up to how serious everything really was. But it was having dramatic consequences.

Dr Baqri saw Zoe's face.

'I'm not . . . I'm not blaming you.'

Zoe's lip started to wobble again.

'You know,' said Dr Baqri. 'You seem well bonded. He's timid, but I don't think he's traumatised. Sometimes – sometimes it really is just one of those things.'

There was a very long pause.

'That,' said Zoe, in a low voice, 'is about the nicest thing anyone's said to me for ages.'

'We normally start on a system of rewards for effort,' said Dr Baqri, handing her wads of charts and lists of goals. 'Nothing but encouragement, of course. Something nice for a whisper . . . a treat for a song.'

Zoe blinked, trying to figure out where money for treats would come from when she was already terrified of what they'd do when it got too cold for Hari to wear his summer sandals every day.

'We could try medication if this doesn't work.'

Zoe just stared at her. Drugging her beautiful boy. This was the end of the line – literally: it had taken them two hours to traipse across London on a boiling day to see a consultant-level speech therapist, the waiting list they'd been on having taken eight months to get them there.

'Do you talk lots to him?' said Dr Baqri.

'Uh-huh,' Zoe said, finally glad there was something that didn't appear to be her fault. 'Yes! I do do that! All the time!'

'Well, make sure you're not talking too much. If you understand everything he needs and wants, there's no motivation. And that's what we need.'

Dr Baqri stood up. Seeing Zoe's stricken face, she smiled.

'I realise it's hard that there's not a magic bullet,' she said, gathering up the booklets.

Zoe felt the lump in her throat again.

'It is,' she said.

It was.

Zoe tried to smile encouragingly at her little boy. But as she sat on those two crowded, noisy buses, schoolchildren shouting and screaming and watching videos loudly on their phones and kicking off, and too many people crammed on, and the bus moving painfully slowly, and Hari having to sit on her lap to make room for other people and giving her a dead leg, and trying to count up what it had cost, her missing another shift, and how her boss Xania was really at the end of her tether, because she kept taking time off, but she couldn't lose this job – everything just seemed so overwhelming. And even when they finally got home, closing the grubby woodchip internal door behind them, Hari stumbling with tiredness, there was a letter lying on the mat in the post that was about to make everything substantially worse.

Chapter Two

'Who did you rent the barn out to? Can't they help?'

Surinder Mehta was sitting in the kitchen of her little house in Birmingham on the phone trying to give constructive advice to her friend Nina, who was doing that usual thing people do when you give them constructive advice – rebutting all of it point by point.

Nina ran a mobile bookshop in the Highlands of Scotland. This was about to become temporarily tricky given that she had also fallen in love with a very attractive farmer, and it had been a particularly long, dark and cosy winter and frankly, these things happen. Up in Scotland, she stroked her large bump crossly. They hadn't got round to putting it on the market.

'They're farmhands! They're busy!'

'There must be someone who can help. What about that girl who used to tidy up for you??'

'Ainslee's at college now. There's just ... Everyone around here already has three jobs. That's what it's like here. There's just not enough people.'

Nina looked out of the farm window. It was harvest and all hands were on deck. She could make out distant figures in the fields, bent low. The light was golden, the wind rippling through fields of barley.

She'd been spared harvesting this year but was still going to have to cater for quite a lot And so she'd come back to the farm to make soup for everyone working late.

'Well,' she said finally. 'Think about it.'

'I'm not giving up my job to cover your maternity leave!' said Surinder. 'That doesn't mean I don't love you, so don't twist it.'

Nina sat in the kitchen after they hung up, sighing. It had all started out so well. She remembered the day: Lennox had been up overseeing the lambing in the upper field; spring had been late and a lot of the lambs had had to show up in harsh conditions, born into lashing sidewinds and in many cases snow. She wasn't absolutely certain of how Lennox would react. He'd been married before and she didn't want him to think she was demanding anything – she was perfectly happy how they were. And he wouldn't want a fuss; bells and whistles were absolutely not his style.

She was so distracted at the book van that day she tried to resell Mrs McGleachin the same Dorothy Whipple novel twice, which would have caused a minor diplomatic incident. She also gave out the wrong mock exam workbooks, likewise, and found herself scrambling *What to Expect When You're Expecting* behind her back every time someone came up the steps to the little book bus, with its swinging chandelier and pale blue shelves, the beanbag corner for children and the tiny desk, which now had a contactless point of which Nina was incredibly proud (when it worked, if the Wi-Fi was blowing in the right direction) and many of the older residents of Kirrinfief denounced as witchcraft.

Finally, Nina had driven the van over the hill, checked the stew she'd left in the slow cooker that morning and greeted the weary Lennox with a soft smile and a deep kiss. 'Book?' she said after supper.

'Och, Nina. I had a bit of a run-in with the coos, you know,' he said. But then he saw her face.

'Aye, all right, just a wee bit,' he said, pulling Parsley the sheepdog over to sit under his arm.

Heart beating wildly, Nina took from the little recycled paper bag she'd used to keep the cover clean the book she'd chosen. It was called simply *Hello* and was beautifully illustrated with a series of slightly impressionistic paintings that tracked the way a baby learned to see, starting in black and white, endlessly fuzzy at the edges, and as the pages turned, coming more and more into focus and going into colour – from the motion of clouds, to the sense of a wind – until the very last page, which was a beautiful executed, very detailed picture of a baby and a mother staring each other in the eye, with just one word: 'Hello'.

Instead of falling off to sleep as he usually did, Lennox stayed stock-still and rigid throughout as Nina's voice quavered, turning every new page. He stared at her as if he'd never seen her before. Even Parsley stayed awake, sensing an atmosphere in the room.

When she'd finished, her hands trembling slightly, Nina closed the little board book with a determined air, casting her eyes down. There was a long pause; nothing could be heard but the ticking of the ancient clock, which still needed winding once a week, on the old wooden sideboard. Tick, tick, tick.

Nina couldn't bear it. Slowly she glanced upwards. Lennox was staring at her with an expression of incredulity on his face.

'You should probably tell me if you're happy,' said Nina quickly.

'Oh!' he said. And in his non-effusive way he said, 'Well, noo.'

Nina looked anxiously at his face.

'I know we didn't discuss it,' she said. 'On the other hand, we didn't *anti*-discuss it . . . '

He nodded.

'So,' he said.

'This is going to have to be one of those occasions we discussed,' said Nina, 'where you have to do that talking thing. I mean, are you pleased? Are you happy?'

He looked at her in consternation.

'Of course,' he said, as if he was amazed she could possibly have thought he'd feel any differently, as indeed he was.

'I mean, we do do it a lot,' mumbled Nina. 'It does kind of follow on.'

'Thank you, yes. I am a farmer.'

She beamed up at him as he reached over for her and pulled her onto his lap, kissing her gently. His hands moved to her tummy.

'That's just me,' said Nina. 'I think it's only a tiny pea.'

'Well, I like this too. So. When?'

'November? I figured nice to have a birthday in a really dull, wet month when there's not much to do.'

He heaved a long sigh and rested his large head on her small one.

'Well,' he said. 'That will be ... that will be ...'

Nina laughed. 'Say *something*.'

There was a long pause as he held her tighter.

'Perfect,' he said eventually, very quietly. 'That will be perfect.'

And they had stayed like that for a very long time.

So, that was fine. Everything else – not so much.

Chapter Three

Zoe called Jaz. She hadn't seen him in weeks.

She wondered, as she often did, how on earth she'd ended up in this situation. How anyone ended up anywhere, she thought.

Oh Jaz. Superstar DJ, here we go. From Birmingham originally, he'd always seemed so much younger than his current twenty-eight years.

He and Zoe had never lived together; she'd never met his family – at which point Zoe knows you will be thinking, 'You absolute *idiot*, why on earth did you get knocked up?' which, let me tell you, is pretty much what her own mum and all her friends said, only in even sharper tones than that.

In a defence that now feels weaker than her bank balance, he was – is – incredibly attractive, with eyelashes that curl nearly up to his hairline, broad shoulders, long legs … Zoe tried. She really did. So did Jaz, for a bit. But being tied down with a child wasn't, he said sincerely, his style, babe.

They rented a hideous bedsit in Wembley and Zoe painted it up as best as she could, even though the wallpaper curled and the hallway smelled of horrible cooking and she couldn't get the buggy past other people's bikes.

Zoe took as little maternity leave as she could get away with (ironically, she works at a really posh nursery – far, far too posh for her to be able to send her own kid there), and Jaz tried to buckle down, took a job in an office and then Hari came along (in a quiet, straightforward kind of a way according to the midwife and, according to Zoe, in a rather traumatic and extraordinary kind of way).

For a short time, they both forgot about the other stuff, and revelled in the beauty of him; how glorious, how perfect he was – his tiny pink fingernails, his father's eyelashes, his sleepy eyes and pouting lips. He was a quiet baby – easy-going; beloved, utterly – and their friends, who were still all young and out clubbing and going to festivals all the time, popped in and brought presents they had nowhere to put and made a huge fuss of them and Zoe's mum visited from Spain and was slightly tearful in a proper *EastEnders* way about everything and for a while, just for a while, Zoe thought everything might be okay.

And then Jaz decided he maybe would go out for a pint or two with the lads, get a bit of DJ practice in, and then he would wake up late for work, and then he wouldn't want to have to deal with Hari occasionally, of course; he was pretty damn cute but the thing about babies, Zoe had realised, is that they're there all the time, every second, and if you stop watching them for even a millisecond they'll probably choke to death or something.

So to stop the fights, Jaz stopped coming home, really, more and more, and it was such a hot summer that year. And there was no outdoor space, nowhere to go and Zoe was staring at all four walls of the bedsit every day, feeling like that woman in the film who was imprisoned in a room.

Except Zoe wasn't imprisoned by anything other than the fact that she didn't have any money to do anything except work and sit; nothing at all. In that London cycle of awfulness, she went back to her job at a very posh amazing nursery, which had organic food and Kumon maths for its privileged children, but only because she left Hari at a really basic childminders', where she thought they just turned the telly on.

17

And if she asked Jaz about the future, he would immediately provoke a huge fight and storm off and not come back for days and Zoe would feed Hari the cheapest mushed-up food she could manage and sit in her one room and wonder what on earth had happened to her, Zoe O'Connell, twenty-eight, promising early years professional, who had been considering doing her masters and even running her own nursery one day. And here she was. Stuck. With Weetabix in her hair and a child who had something wrong with him and now, after two jaunts on a bus to a hospital the other side of town where she'd been told just to basically get on with it by herself, she'd come home to a rent 'reappraisal'.

She'd known. She'd seen it coming. A new organic coffee shop on the corner. A fishmonger. Rumours of a Waitrose. For most of her neighbours, good news. For her, ominous sounds of change. Her landlord, wanting her out and some nice rich young professionals moving in. Indeed, the greengrocers had strung up some white fairy lights outside the shop and painted the place a pale green; the hardware store had remarketed itself as 'vintage'. There were rumours of a Banksy (Zoe wanted to kill him). The grey Farrow and Ball painted fingers of gentrification had stretched out. And now they had come for her.

The letter sat on the hallway table. How something so innocuous could look so malevolent Zoe didn't understand, but she felt afraid even to touch it.

There was no way Zoe could pay it. No way at all. And Universal Credit wasn't going to be much use. If Jaz couldn't pay it, Zoe realised, staring at the paper, she could declare themselves homeless and throw herself on the mercy of Brent Council, which was a horrifying prospect, and who knew where they'd end up. She couldn't. She couldn't be homeless. This was ridiculous. Absurd.

Or go to Spain, live in her mum's tiny one bedroom, find a bar job ... there were plenty of bar jobs. But to move to another country ... Her son couldn't say a word in this language.

Zoe found she was panicking, her heart racing, even as Hari went searching for their old cracked tablet and picked it up.

What could she do? Her hand was shaking. There were plenty of live-in nanny placements, but not one of them would have another child along. None of the day jobs she could find would pay enough. She stifled a sob and called Jaz, or rather WhatsApped him as he never ever answered the phone if he could see it was from her, and insisted that they meet.

Chapter Four

Of course Jaz was late. Of course he was. After it took a million texts to even get him to agree to a time. Zoe had tried saying to him once, what if Hari was in trouble? What if they were at the hospital? and he'd done the usual thing he did of simply shutting her down, shrugging and saying, 'Don't worry – just text me, babe.'

Zoe looked at the board in the café. It was an expensive café, filled with thin blonde mummies and tall handsome daddies carrying their toddlers on their shoulders, buying lavish trays full of expensive cakes and coffees as if the money meant nothing to them, meeting up with groups of friends and Labradors and frisbees.

She perched with Hari on her knee on the end of a big table, not buying anything. More and more people were joining a huge gang of people called things like Fizz and Charlie and Ollie and Fifi and carrying kites and balls and picnic hampers and cool boxes and talking about what a glorious day it was, as the two of them shrank further back into the corner, apologetically taking up the space. She finally bought a cup of tea, the cheapest thing she could think of, and received martyred looks from the skinny blondes parking their expensive buggies up against her stool legs. She concentrated hard on the new Michael Lewis book the library had kept for her.

Books: the one thing that had never let her down. 'All that book-learning!' her mum would say occasionally when she'd had a few, which was fairly often. 'You'd think you wouldn't have ended up knocked up like you did!' And, 'Oh, darling, you know I'm only messing with you.'

Jaz eventually slouched in. He seemed, Zoe couldn't help noticing, to be getting younger. A T-shirt over shorts made him look like an oversized toddler; his over-groomed beard looked a little teenage. Zoe felt she was just getting older every day, the world piling up on her shoulders.

He was still handsome, of course, still had that lovely, weakening smile.

At the sight of him, Hari's mouth turned into an 'O' of delight and he struggled to get down.

'Say "please"!' said one of the blonde mothers to him brightly as if in jest, but in fact deadly serious, and Zoe sighed, but didn't want to get into it at that particular time so instead just put Hari on the ground – feeling them judge her – as he dashed over to see his father whom he adored with every fibre of his tiny being.

'Bro!' said Jaz, pulling him up and swinging him around.

Zoe wished he wouldn't call him that – they weren't bros; it didn't help – but Jaz called everyone that and it was practically a nervous tic.

'What have you got to say to me today?'

Hari said nothing, of course, but beamed down on his father from where he was being held above Jaz's head, those pure beams of love that made Zoe swear, because she was tied to Jaz for ever – and had to be civil about him too – to stop that beam of love ever from flickering or going out. Once Zoe had thought she loved him herself. That was more or less before he was up for making her homeless.

'How's it going?' he said casually. Zoe was now aware they were the centre of attention for practically the entire café. Jaz never minded lots of eyes on him.

'Shall we take a walk?' she said, not wanting to broadcast her predicament to this entire, nuclear, coupled-up, well-off, Boden-smug, mummy-yoga, basement-conversion, minibreak crowd she would kind of like to have hated but instead was desperately jealous of.

'Let me just grab a coffee, babe ... Want anything?'

Out of habit, Zoe shook her head, then watched him spend £9.75 on one vast latte and a huge muffin each for himself and Hari, who stared at it as if wondering if he could eat something so large (he did, and he and Zoe both regretted it later).

At last they escaped the atmosphere of the coffee shop and managed to kick their way through the long grass – past the lazily reading and snogging young people, alone or in groups, with endless leisure time to lie out in a park, letting the sunny day take them – towards the duck pond.

Hari meandered aimlessly, muffin smearing every centimetre of his body so consistently Zoe didn't think she had to apply any sun cream, which was a relief because that stuff cost a fortune.

'What's up?' said Jaz finally; defensively.

'Rent,' said Zoe simply.

Jaz nodded. 'Yeah but, babe ... ' he whined. 'I lost my job.'

He put out both of his hands in a *what you gonna do?* stance. Zoe didn't ask him why. She'd seen him when he'd stayed at the flat. Lying in late. Calling in sick when he couldn't be bothered going in. Complaining about his bosses wanting him to occasionally do a bit of actual work.

'They're going to put the rent up,' she said decisively.

Jaz sighed.

'I'm sorry,' he said. 'I can't do it. I just don't have the money.'

Zoe had thought about it. He could do it. He could get the money. If he told his parents, surely they would help him. They were doing well in Birmingham; they had enough to finance his car. Surely if they knew they had a grandchild ... they might be shocked at first, but they'd come round ...

Jaz's mouth went into that thin line it did whenever she mentioned his parents. Under no circumstances. None.

'It's just for a year,' Zoe said desperately. 'Then he'll be at school and I can increase my hours and it'll be fine.'

'Can't you go to your mum's?'

'In *Spain?*'

At least he had the grace to look embarrassed.

'Hey!' There came a posh voice. One of the annoying perfect dads from the café in pressed chinos and a rugby shirt and immaculate hair. 'Is that your lad there?'

They both turned, and there he was, teetering right on the edge of the sloping side of the pond as a huge vicious-looking duck advanced on his muffin.

And as usual, he wasn't making a sound.

'HARI!' they both screamed.

The child turned around just as the duck grabbed at the muffin and unbalanced him. In a flash, Jaz was there, scooping him up, burying the boy's head in his flashy jacket, muffin smears and all.

'You're all right, little man,' he hummed, as the boy's eyes brimmed with silent tears that fell, staining Jaz's designer shirt as he clasped him tight. 'You're all right. You're all right, my little man. I've got you. I've got you.'

But he didn't. This, thought Zoe viciously, as she turned to head for home. Inconsistent father. Shitty childcare. No money. A developmental disorder. Nothing to do and nowhere to go that isn't sitting in the flat or the library (the kind librarian, incidentally, had been the first to ask if she was worried that Hari wasn't talking).

And now, they were totally stuffed.

Chapter Five

Surinder knew there was something wrong by the way Jaz turned his key in the door after texting her he was coming up to Brum, which was unusual enough in itself.

But she was his sister. She loved him. She knew he didn't have it easy: their two big brothers were both ophthalmologists; she was running an import/export business; Jaz had never quite found his way. Their father had been making a good living by the time he'd come along, and Surinder privately thought he'd been spoiled – cars bought for him, designer clothing. Her parents had worked so hard their entire lives; she knew they enjoyed indulging their handsome baby. But in some ways, it had kept him a baby.

And now, to her utter astonishment, he was sitting at her kitchen table telling her *he* had a baby.

Not even a baby: a four-year-old. With a white woman in London.

He was slumped at the table. The whole room was now sleek and modernist, with a kitchen island and a pastel-coloured expensive food mixer Surinder never ever used. Sometimes she missed the great piles of books that used to drown every surface when Nina was still living there.

'But,' she said, and then shook her head again. 'How on earth . . . how on *earth* have you managed to have a baby?'

Jaz rolled his eyes.

'Yeah, right, well, you take a flower and a bee right . . . '

'Stop it,' said Surinder. 'When were you going to tell Mum and Dad?'

He shuffled uncomfortably.

'Well,' he said. 'It just . . . it just kind of happened, you know?'

'I do *not* know,' said Surinder. 'You don't accidentally just stumble on a baby. Oh my God, I'm an auntie again! Show me pictures! No, don't – I'm furious with you. No, show me. No, don't.'

There was a pause.

'Hand it over.'

He pulled out his closely guarded phone.

'I thought you were weird about your phone because you had a girlfriend . . . Oh, you've got those too, haven't you?'

Jaz went pink to the tips of his ears.

'So why are you telling me now then?'

Jaz shrugged.

'Well, the DJing isn't really taking off and . . . '

Surinder gave him the biggest Paddington Bear stare, which he did his best to ignore.

'Are you here for money?'

'It's really tough out there,' said Jaz. 'People just don't get my vibe.'

'I get your vibe,' said Surinder ominously. She opened the emergency biscuit tin, took one out for herself and didn't offer Jaz any.

'Are you going to tell Mum and Dad?'

'They'll kill me!' said Jaz.

'They won't kill you,' said Surinder. 'They'll be disappointed.'

'That's worse!'

'Oh, for God's sake.'

'I just . . . she needs help . . . '

'Well, you've come to the wrong place. Which you would know if you ever read a paper and had heard the term "Brexit" or "currency exchange" and worked in an import business.'

25

Jaz rubbed the back of his neck.

'What's your plan?'

'I was going to go out DJing on the festival circuit – give it a really big push, you know? Make enough money to sort us out.'

'So,' said Surinder gloomily. 'You're planning on buying some magic beans.'

'You'll be sorry when I'm famous.'

'Where's *her* family?'

'Spain,' said Jaz. 'She's only got her mum really.'

In Surinder's head she saw some big lazy lump of a girl sitting on her arse expecting Jaz to pay for everything.

'You are such an idiot,' she said. 'What's she even like? Have you got a pic?'

To Surinder's horror, Jaz didn't.

'Ah, she's all right,' he said. 'Reads all the time. She's like that old flatmate of yours. Obsessed with it. Books books books. Really boring.'

There was a pause.

'What?' said Jaz.

'Nothing,' said Surinder. 'Just ... oh, I'm sure it's nothing.'

Chapter Six

The harvesting boys and girls had moved on again, but the weather was still soft and golden, the breeze filtering through the now shorn fields. The evenings were still long, even as there was the faintest hint in the clear air that autumn was on the horizon. The geese had started to circle overhead, preparing for their long journey south.

Nina had popped into Mrs Murray's shop in the village to pick up some tarragon to go with the chicken she was roasting that evening, plus four sticky buns of which she would endeavour to keep at least one for Lennox.

'Ooh, look at you,' said Mrs Murray. Nina peered down at her stomach. 'You're huge!'

'I thought I was average,' grumbled Nina, conscious again that she was – as the rather peremptory health visitor kept telling her – quite obvious for how far along in her pregnancy she was.

She had worked out she was pregnant at exactly the same time as a very famous celebrity, and was slightly obsessed with the very famous celebrity, who was showing off a tiny, barely noticeable bump at various hot spots around the globe, while she, Nina, was already having some difficulty leaning down to tie her own shoelaces.

'Well, how many are in there?' said Mrs Murray, who had always been rather direct.

'Yeah, all right,' said Nina, deciding against the buns.

The old woman looked up. 'It is wonderful news,' she said eventually. 'I never thought I'd see that Lennox being happy again.'

Nina smiled, not over the moon to be reminded that she wasn't Lennox's first girlfriend.

'So what are you going to do with yon van . . . ?'

But just as she was speaking, the door to the little shop pinged open and a young girl neither of them recognised came in. She looked tearful. She was slender with high cheekbones and pale hair and spoke with a strong Polish accent.

'Hello?' said Mrs Murray, rather tentatively.

The girl rubbed her face, which was rather smeared.

'When is bus please?' she said.

Mrs Murray frowned.

'Well, that depends where you're going.'

'I don't care,' said the girl fiercely. Mrs Murray and Nina glanced at each other.

'Tuesday,' said Mrs Murray.

'Are you all right?' said Nina gently.

The girl shook her head.

'They are monsters!' she said and Nina was genuinely concerned.

'Who do you mean?'

'Och!' said Mrs Murray, suddenly realising. 'You're up at the hoose.'

'Not any more,' said the girl.

'What house?' said Nina.

'The big hoose!' said Mrs Murray, as if Nina was an idiot.

'You know,' said the girl. 'They are . . . they are . . . '

She looked at them both.

'Wolves,' she spat. 'Little tiny wolves.'

Mrs Murray quietly rang up the bar of chocolate Nina hadn't realised she'd added to her basket.

'I see.'

'I not stay . . . Tuesday?'

'There's a bus for Inverness . . . There's an airport.'

The girl nodded quietly.

'Oh, that hoose,' said Mrs Murray. The girl disappeared, pulling her heavy bag behind her.

'What about the house?' said Nina. She'd only been there a year. She'd got to know a lot of people, but village loyalties were strong and she normally caught gossip second-hand, if at all. Which was fine by her. Every time they included her more – a coffee morning here, a Burns' Night supper there – she felt more and more accepted, on her own merits, as someone who was there for good, not a tourist passing through.

Also, to be fair, absolutely tons of the gossip had actually been about her and Lennox and Lennox's ex-wife. Loads of it. So people tended to shut up, just in case. And also if Nina had thought that the baby was going to damp that down at all she would have been very, very disappointed.

'The Beeches?'

'Oh yes . . . ' said Nina. She was dimly aware of something. 'I think I met him . . . Tall bloke. Hit his head on the van?'

'That sounds like Ramsay,' said Mrs Murray. She sighed. 'It's a bad thing.'

'Ooh, tell me,' said Nina, who wanted to be distracted from the iced buns.

'Wife left him,' said Mrs Murray. 'With the kids and everything.'

'Oh God, really?' said Nina. 'That's awful. How many kids?'

'Three,' said the Polish girl, who had popped her head back in, seeing as there was a rainstorm of the type so sudden and yet otherwise totally normal that even Nina had learned not to comment on it. Scotland's weather was like everyone else's weather. Just a little faster.

'All evil.'

'Come on now there,' said Mrs Murray reprovingly. 'They dinnae have a mam.'

'What happened to her?' said Nina. 'Where is she?'

'I never see her,' said the Polish girl.

'Nobody kens,' said Mrs Murray.

'Seriously?' said Nina. 'Why didn't I know about this? Did he kill her? Is she mad and in the attic?'

Nobody said anything.

'She was a tricky one,' said Mrs Murray finally. 'But naw, she just left.'

'You're *sure*?'

'It's the big hoose,' she said. 'Strange things happen up there.'

Chapter Seven

It was a scorching hot day when Surinder got the train down. Not the kind of fun *let's go to the seaside* kind of a day. It was hot, sticky, horribly crowded and unpleasant on the train. Overheated children moaned and wailed; there was a heavy stench of BO in the carriage. Stepping out of the train didn't cool things at all. The station was mobbed and hot and fretful; trains were cancelled because of over-heated lines and overheated people; and the whole of London felt oddly menacing.

Jaz had begged her not to come, but she threatened to tell their parents otherwise, so there wasn't much he could do about it.

Zoe was incredibly excited and nervous all at once. Was this the beginning? Of Jaz taking her into his life, of building something for them together?

She was profoundly disappointed to see Surinder stepping off the train carriage alone.

She'd dressed Hari up in his absolute best outfit, noticing as she did so that it was already too small for him. She sighed and put him back in the denim dungarees she'd got at the charity shop. He had wriggled and looked put out, even more so when she'd decided to forego the buggy and tried to make him walk the long way to the bus stop. He wasn't having it and she'd ended up having to carry him most of the way, wriggling and struggling hotly, and now she was sweaty and nervous and feeling a mess and this beautiful, put-together-looking girl stepping off the train had to be Jaz's sister, she could see it right away.

Of course he wasn't there.

Zoe put up a hand weakly.

Surinder looked at her – well, not her sister-in-law, but even so. Goodness. She wasn't what she'd have expected at all. Slim – actually, closer to scrawny was putting it better as she wasn't really a type of slim you'd want to be – petite, messy black hair loosely tied back, and shadows under her eyes. She barely glanced at Zoe though before her gaze was pulled to the little boy hiding behind her legs. Her face broke into a smile.

'Hello!' she said. 'Hello!'

She crouched down straightaway. The little boy eyed her up between his mother's legs.

'Are you Hari?'

The child didn't say anything.

'Did ...?' Zoe was conscious her voice sounded nervous. 'Did Jaz explain?'

Surinder straightened up. She was so pretty and confident-looking. Zoe wanted to be her friend immediately. She would never have got knocked up by mistake, Zoe found herself reflecting gloomily. Far too sensible.

'Explain what? Hello by the way. I'm Surinder. Sorry my brother is a dickhead.'

'Um ... that's okay,' said Zoe. 'Did he explain about Hari?'

'What about him?'

'He doesn't ... he doesn't speak.'

'Oh,' frowned Surinder. 'Doesn't sound like a Mehta.'

They stood in the crowded concourse.

'Is there anywhere cool to get a cup of tea?' said Surinder. 'And I don't mean "London cool". I mean, not nine billion degrees'

There wasn't much around Euston, but finally they found a little park with a set of swings. Hari looked at the swings, but didn't dare go near them, and Surinder picked them up tea from a nearby stall.

'So,' she said finally. Hari clambered up on Zoe's knee. Surinder kept trying to interact with him, but he buried his face away.

'He's shy,' explained Zoe.

'I see that,' said Surinder, and they both wondered briefly, shockingly, that if Hari had been a more extrovert child, a charming, chatty boy, whether Jaz might have owned up sooner.

He was, thought Surinder, a beauty though: long, dark eyelashes; flawless skin.

Zoe sighed.

'What's up?' said Surinder. 'Has it been tough?'

Zoe felt tears springing up.

'Oh yes, well, being a single mum ... you know,' she said. 'Well. You don't know. But it's tricky.'

'Does Jaz not help you out?'

'He did!' said Zoe, springing to his defence. 'When he was working, he did. But he just wants to be a bloody DJ and he can't hold down a job until he at least gives it a shot ...'

'You're good for defending him,' said Surinder. 'Look. We want to help. Well, I do ...'

'Your parents?'

Surinder shrugged. 'Jaz is really adamant,' she said. 'I'm sorry.'

'That's okay,' said Zoe. 'Is it because I'm not Indian?'

Surinder snorted.

'God no, they love Angela.'

Then she realised she'd been insensitive.

'My other brother's ... Look. Never mind. Show me where you live.'

As soon as she saw it, with the peeling wallpaper and the mean little electric fire, Surinder made her mind up almost immediately. She knew someone else who hadn't fitted in in the big city. Who'd needed a bit of space to breathe.

'Listen. Do you know much about books?'

'I read a lot,' said Zoe. Then she looked up. 'And I'm ready ... I

33

mean, we need a place to stay. But if you know of a good job ... I promise. I promise I can work hard. I do.'

Surinder looked around. The tiny studio was horrible, but it was spotlessly clean and tidy, as was Hari himself.

'I can't promise anything,' she said, 'but I'll see what I can do.'

She bent down. Hari immediately charged behind Zoe's legs again.

'And next time I see you, young man,' she said. 'I hope you'll be nicer to your auntie-ji.'

Chapter Eight

Nina put it out of her mind – she was fine, she'd be fine, something would present itself, a solution would turn up, Ainslee would come home from college or something. She couldn't take in Surinder's waif – it was ridiculous – when a woman showed up that she recognised dimly from around town. Not a regular in the book van or anything.

'Hello?'

This woman was cross-looking, older, with the beginnings of a humped back, folded arms and a slightly forbidding expression. 'Aye,' she said. 'Can I put a notice up?'

'You can,' said Nina. 'It's £1 a week.'

The woman sniffed.

'Daylight robbery,' she said.

'I'm not forcing you,' said Nina. The woman grumped forward and handed the money to Nina. It was a 'Help wanted' advert: au pair, evenings and weekends, apply to Mrs MacGlone at The Beeches. Nina frowned, remembering the Polish girl. She looked at it again.

'Did somebody called Surinder send you?' she asked suspiciously.

'Whit?' said the woman. Nina looked at it again.

'Are you . . . are you from the big house?'

'Aye.'

'And you need . . . ? Is it three children?'

'Aye,' she said. Nina stared at it.

'And it's a live-in job?'

The woman shrugged.

'There's plenty of space.'

Nina stared at it for a long time.

'Okay,' she said finally. 'Give me the leaflet. No charge.'

The woman handed it over, surprised.

'Can I help you with any books?' she said as the woman turned to leave.

'Och no. Got more than enough of those buggers up at the hoose.'

And she vanished in a bustle out onto the grey cobbles.

Chapter Nine

It was a chilly evening, and Nina drew the curtains – if she left them open, even before it was fully dark, Lennox would peer out of them and fret about his black lamb – lit the stove and made shepherd's pie, Lennox's favourite, in the hopes that it would put him in a talkative mood, or at least a slightly more talkative mood than usual. She brought him tea on the sofa and he looked at her suspiciously.

'Shouldn't I be doing that for you?' he said. 'What are you after?'

'Tell me about the big house,' Nina asked without preamble.

'Why do I need to be bribed by tea to tell you about the big hoose?' said Lennox good-naturedly. 'Is that a Penguin biscuit?'

'Yes.'

'How many Penguins are left in the packet?'

'Don't ask me that.'

Lennox smiled.

'Well. Ramsay is the young laird ... well, just the laird I suppose now ...'

'Yes, I've got that much. Just tell me about whether he killed his wife.'

Lennox half-smiled, sadly.

'Oh God, you got to that story did you?'

'Men always kill their wives,' said Nina, settling down on the sofa.

'No,' said Lennox carefully. 'People very rarely kill anyone.' He thought about it. 'But if they do, it's their wives, yes.'

'So ... '

'I met Elspeth Urquart once,' said Lennox, his voice tapering off into the distance somewhere. 'She was so beautiful. Like a fairy. She was tiny, with this big cloud of yellow hair all around her face. Green eyes. Pointed chin.'

'Cobweb frock?' added Nina. 'What happened to her?'

Lennox shook her head.

'She was always ... not quite there. As if she'd just woken up and didn't quite understand what had happened with her life. She was beautiful, and it was a sudden story I suppose ... '

'What?'

'Well, young Urquart – Ramsay – he was at university in Cambridge when his dad died, sudden like. That was the old laird. And he had to come back and take on the hoose, which was in a right mess ... still is. And he hadn't been back three months when he pitched up with her. Had the children, and then ... she was gone again. I'm not sure she was equipped to live in the modern world. That's what people said.'

'So he killed her?'

Lennox actually laughed. Then he held up his hand.

'Listen,' he said. 'I know. Nobody gets it right when they think someone can't be violent. It's all "oh, he was such a great family man" and so on. But I've known Ramsay since he was a bairn – we went to school thegither. Never known him get a temper, hold a grudge. I know, you'll say anything is possible. But don't you think the polis would have been all over him? There'd have been search parties and petitions and pictures on lamp-posts and appeals and T-shirts and so on and so forth? A beautiful young mother disappears?'

'Mrs Murray reckons it was hushed up.'

'Mrs Murray reckons 9/11 was done by lizards.'

'She does,' admitted Nina. 'What do you think?'

'I think she couldn't handle it. The children came close together.

It can affect women badly, that kind of thing. I reckon either she went away somewhere she could handle it … far away … or she killed herself.'

'Well, why don't people know?'

'Because it's none of our business,' said Lennox. 'Whatever it is, it's a terrible, terrible sadness for the man. His heart was completely broken. You've probably never met him …'

'I have,' said Nina. 'He came in looking for *Up on the Rooftops*. Big bloke. Wife-killing size.'

'Hmm,' said Lennox. 'Well. I doubt it. The polis aren't stupid. It's just a very sad story. Usually fathers leave. But sometimes mothers leave. There's sad things in lots of lives. People get up every day and walk about with smiles on their faces who have been through things you and I could never imagine.'

Nina thought about this, and nodded.

He pulled her close to him, wrapped them both up in the soft tartan blanket that lay across the back of the old couch.

'I don't want anything bad to happen to us.'

'It can't possibly,' said Nina, snuggling into him and holding him close. He rested his large head on her shoulder.

'I agree with you,' he murmured, and they clung together, the light from the fire flickering up and down the room, as Parsley whimpered and turned over in his sleep.

Chapter Ten

Nina was not in fact having the pregnancy she rather thought she might have when she'd first read the line on the box. Instead she was constantly throwing up, forgetting things, sleeping in and being either in tears or running around tidying everything up or in tears again.

And she was so exhausted. She had had absolutely no idea. It was like the baby was eating her from the inside out. Even though she was so happy, even though she felt overflowing with love, she also felt overflowing with nausea, bloating, acid reflux and the need to go to the toilet every five minutes. Lifting the heavy boxes of books was getting to be a problem, even though Lennox did as much of it as he could manage, and there was of course always the risk of her van breaking down. She had forced herself to read the car maintenance books they kept in stock, annoyed but aware of the wisdom of it so she knew how to change a tyre, check the oil and so on – but whether or not she could do this when her breasts were already pushing out over everything she wore and her stomach showed every sign of being about to do likewise was another matter.

She looked again at the CV this London girl had sent. She had fabulous references – but as a nursery nurse, not a bookseller. On the other hand, she seemed honest, hardworking...

She sighed. Outside, they were having a quiet morning, which was odd, as the haar from the loch had lifted and it felt fresh and lovely. This was the thing about the Highlands, she'd realised. It would be a bit miserable and you'd get all used to staying in and then suddenly – although this could happen two or three times a week – the sun would appear, simply to confound and delight you, breaking across the wet dawn dew, popping its head up over the purple mountains ahead, and once again you would forgive Scotland all its wet mornings and dark evenings for the utter glory of how perfect a perfect day could be.

So maybe nobody wanted to clamber inside the van, Nina thought, when the outside world was beckoning bicycles and, for the truly daring (and those in possession of waterproofed rugs), even a picnic, if you could find a sheltered spot that the sun could warm but the wind not spoil.

Anyway. She'd spoken to the woman from the big house, saying she might have found someone for her and the woman had said, 'Is she a criminal?' And Nina had said no, and the woman had said, 'Och, that's a shame,' and Nina had said, did the person she had in mind have to meet the children and the woman had said best not.

Nina picked up the phone.

Chapter Eleven

Surinder liked to think of herself as something of a fairy god-mother for sorting everything out; an amazing, organising angel.

That was not exactly how everyone else thought about it. Everybody else felt they were settling for the best of a very bad job.

Firstly, Zoe had got herself in a bit of a pickle talking to Nina when, nervous and trying to keep an eye on Hari, who was play-ing with his tablet, Nina asked her what she'd read recently and her mind went completely and utterly blank.

The only thing that came to mind was *The Jolly Postman*, which Hari absolutely adored and made her take out every time they went to the library. The fact that Nina was a big *Jolly Postman* fan and sold oodles of them meant that this would have been a fine answer, rather than Zoe stumbling, desperately trying to think of something and somehow landing on a soft-porn trilogy that had been hugely popular a couple of years before. She could practically hear her potential new boss smiling tightly down the phone.

The second interview she barely got a chance to get a word in edgeways. Mrs MacGlone, it turned out, was the housekeeper of the place she was going to stay in. She rattled on in a practised tone. She was there during the day but mornings and evenings would be Zoe's job, in return for which she'd get board and lodging and a small stipend. Meals were provided, but, Mrs MacGlone said, with what sounded like defiance, 'we're simple eaters here.' Mrs MacGlone did the cleaning and the laundry, but would not be doing Zoe's, she made quite clear, and would require help when possible.

'And tell me about the family?' said Zoe, a question she thought was absolutely innocuous.

The long pause suggested this might not be the case.

'Well. Ramsay's the father,' said Mrs MacGlone; she pronounced it 'faither'. 'He's working all hours. You won't disturb him if you know what's good for you.'

'Okay,' said Zoe. 'And Mum?'

'Did the lass no' tell you?' said Mrs MacGlone, grumbling to herself. 'Och, yon English. No idea about things.'

Zoe blinked, wondering what on earth she meant.

'Their mother left. Two years ago. That's why we need you. But no need to talk about it; it just upsets them.'

'Oh goodness. Why . . . ?'

'I said. No need to talk about it. And no' to the maister, he disnae like it.'

'Right. Understood,' lied Zoe, who understood almost nothing. 'And the children?'

'Shackleton is twelve, Mary is nine and Patrick is five.'

'Oh great!' said Zoe, absolutely delighted by the idea of a friend for Hari. 'My little boy is four.'

'Yes, well. Patrick isn't a normal five.'

'Hari isn't a normal four,' said Zoe under her breath in case he heard her. Mrs MacGlone sniffed, as if to say they'd see about that.

'Well then,' she said. 'Six-week trial.'

Zoe was taken aback.

'Doesn't the mai . . . ? Doesn't their father want to talk to me?'

Mrs MacGlone sighed heavily.

'He trusts me.'

'Of course,' said Zoe hurriedly. 'Of course.'

And it was settled.

Zoe may have hated her landlord, who had been making inauspicious noises about the rent for some time and whom she was now leaving, but her gratitude towards him when he took one look round the horrible studio, glanced passingly at the ever-growing damp patch and then, to her utter amazement, handed her back her entire deposit in cash made her want to kiss him.

It had happened so fast. Surinder just had . . . she just had a way about her. She'd swept up all Zoe's objections and worries with the infallible logic that she could hardly stay where she was, could she, and here was a free room in a house, a bit of childminding, a bit of bookselling help – just a tad here and there, she'd be free most of the time – *and* Scotland had free nursery places. What was there to argue against?

And what choice did she have? Jaz had already gone; he was, according to his Instagram, in Ibiza 'picking up gigs' – Zoe didn't know if these were paid or not, and suspected not – and picturing himself against either sunrises or sunsets, wearing a varied selection both of ridiculous hats and young women.

The refund on the deposit was enough for their tickets north – a seventeen-hour coach marathon she was not looking forward to – plus a new coat for Hari and, joy of joys, the supermarket clothes aisle had a sale and she was able to get a couple of jumpers and a cheap knock-off Puffa jacket too. How cold it would be in Scotland was all anyone could talk about. Well, the cold and the Loch Ness monster, seeing as that was where they were going. Every time someone asked about the monster, Hari's eyes went all big and round and he hid himself behind the futon so she'd told people to stop doing it, but it didn't stop anyone. She also didn't really want anyone to know she was going anyway in case she had to turn up again in six weeks, having failed miserably. But she couldn't think like that.

She could do this. She was going to be amazing. Save the wages until she was back on her feet, throw herself into it. And the poor motherless mites! How happy they were going to be that she was there. Obviously she couldn't replace their mum, but she could make things good for them again. It was all going to work out brilliantly. For the first time in a very long time, Zoe was feeling optimistic about things, and she let her imagination run free.

However, she couldn't bear the relief in Jaz's voice when he realised Surinder had sorted everything out. She realised that she had, right at the back of her mind, buried so deeply she couldn't admit it to herself, the tiniest hope, just the smallest, that Jaz would say, 'Hey, I've been thinking. I'm going to give up the DJing and get a proper job and settle down and be a family man and how about we get a nice place together? I'm a changed man.'

But of course he couldn't: he simply couldn't be a changed man. Motherhood had changed her utterly, but it had barely scratched the surface of Jaz, except as, somehow, a cloak of inconvenience; that she and Hari were intruding on the life of an international playboy he had going on in his head.

But no. Even though he was over that weekend, he hadn't even offered to give her a lift to Scotland in his stupid car. He'd muttered something about stopping by to say goodbye, whereupon Zoe had pointed out she was only going to Scotland so he'd still be able to get up and down at weekends and he'd sounded very dubious and she had sounded very cross.

Anyway, he had obviously felt bad because he'd turned up on the last night, when everything was packed away except the duvets and the kettle, with a takeaway curry – a rare treat – and took Hari on his lap and let him play with his phone for the entire evening, and his gentle patience with the boy and Hari's deep silent devotion to his dad broke Zoe's heart all over again.

Zoe looked out of the window one last time, through the grimy net curtains that didn't turn white however much she bleached them, down into the nondescript road with its low-build housing, litter blowing down the street, teenagers yelling and shouting on the corner as they did every hot night, lights streaming down the main drag at the end of the road, which was currently a mishmash of chicken shops, charity shops and fly-by-night vape salesmen, but if her landlord was right, was about to become the hippest thing since Hackney.

It wasn't that much, she knew. In fact, she'd hated it: the dingy room, the tired carpet, the waves of other people's post that piled up by the rackety front door, the sheaves of pizza delivery leaflets and political brochures and general rubbish, and the endless fight for the tiny downstairs space in front of the electricity meters between bikes and the buggy.

But it was home. It was where she had come home from the hospital, accompanied by an anxious-looking Jaz, who kept staring at his phone and holding up his hands and looking nervous and flapping his arms around but not actually doing anything; where her friends, in the first few weeks, had come to visit and exclaim how lovely the baby was, but gradually dropping off as she could no longer go for girls' nights out or hen nights or parties without fussing about a babysitter; where Jaz had come less and less frequently until he'd stopped answering his phone; where she'd sat, after her mother had dropped round for half an hour, bringing a packet of plain biscuits on her way somewhere else, and looked disparagingly at the laundry – how could a small baby even create so much laundry? There was nowhere to hang it; it was draped everywhere, until Zoe felt she lived in an ancient bazaar – then left them to it, just the two of them.

But even this place, with its rattly single-glazed windows, propped open front door, even this place was home. The only home Hari had ever known. And what she was headed into was the utter unknown.

Zoe tried not to feel sick as she put the last box into Jaz's car – he had at least, after much grumbling, agreed to store a few things for her – about what if this didn't work out. Her friends all thought she was mad. Of course her friends all lived in easy-going flat-shares, or had got on the property ladder with their partners.

And she was partly to blame too. She kept up a cheerful countenance on the rare occasions she did venture out; put a smile on her face, said everything was great, saved up so she could pay her share and pretend she didn't notice the money.

She thought back to a couple of nights before where her mum for once had taken Hari and she'd gone down the pub with a few girlfriends to say goodbye. She should have confided more. Told them how hard she was finding it. After a couple of bottles of cheap(ish) prosecco, Tamali had started confessing how she just didn't find her husband attractive after the baby, and Yasmin had said how tedious she was finding motherhood and Cady had started talking about how much debt they were in and for some reason – possibly because she was going away – Zoe had felt entirely overwhelmed by this flood of confessions, face to face, a world away from everyone's perfect Facebook and Instagram babies and lives, and suddenly realised what she had lost, over the last four years, by simply not telling people how lonely she was, how unsupported she felt, just how much harder everything was than she'd ever anticipated. It had never occurred to her that other mothers, whatever their situations, might be feeling exactly the same way.

The evening had ended in a drunken round of cuddles and protestations of love for each other, and Zoe wondered what she was thinking of, leaving these amazing women and swore to stay in touch.

And so she felt thoroughly ill this morning, as well as terrified. Suddenly, ugly grimy London felt safe, and going to the middle of nowhere felt . . . ridiculous. All the girls had said last night how brave she was starting over, which hadn't made her feel brave at all; it had made her feel rather foolish, in fact. But now. Here she was. Jaz was eager to go before the 'parking Nazis' found him, something he seemed more concerned about than the fact that she was moving his son to another country.

Hari loved Jaz's car, and even now was looking tremulous about not being allowed to go for a ride in it. Jaz couldn't look at Zoe. He knew, on some level, that this was both their failures: their failure to manage the most basic of things – to have a child, to stay together, to raise him somewhere comfortable and warm and safe. Neither of them said much beyond promising to see how the six weeks went.

Quite what Zoe was going to do if the six weeks went badly, she couldn't quite bear to think of, not at the moment. She would take it a day at a time.

'Right then,' mumbled Jaz. He was wearing a brown suede tracksuit which looked utterly hideous on him, which meant it had almost certainly cost quite a lot of money. 'See you, bro.'

He punched Hari lightly on the arm and gave a wan smile in Zoe's general direction. She remembered the first night she had seen him in that bar, following a shocking date with someone else, his head back in laughter, white teeth showing. He had seen her on that date while he was with his friends – seen it go badly (the man she was meeting, whose name she couldn't remember, turned bright red with anger when she mildly disagreed with him politically, and she'd trembled as he turned over the bill he expected them both to pay while maintaining a fixed smile and glancing at her watch). When the man had gone to the bathroom, Jaz sauntered over.

'Nah,' he'd said cockily, and Zoe had been so startled and relieved, she'd burst out laughing.

'I got dressed up and everything!' she'd said.

'I see that,' he said. 'But he looks like a slice of old ham.'

'Smells like one too,' said Zoe gloomily.

'Just say bye,' Jaz said. 'Then come join us for a drink.'

He was with a group of friends in the corner. It looked so much more fun than what Zoe was up to. As soon as the man came back, she stood up and smiled as if it were a job interview (which,

48

of course, it had been) and said, how lovely, nice to meet you and bundled him out before he'd had a chance to tell her about his amazing theory about why women should be distributed among men fairly which he'd been planning in the toilets.

Jaz had had a beer all waiting for her. Cocky sod. She'd been so thrilled.

And now, here they were. She'd probably have been better off with the ham guy.

'Bye then,' she said. 'Speak soon.'

'Mmm,' he muttered, glancing up and down the road for traffic wardens. 'Yeah. Right. Cool.'

Then he went to the car. At the very last moment, just as he was opening the door, he came back, quickly, not looking at Zoe, grabbed his son, lifted him up and buried his face in the boy's neat little neck.

Then he put him down again and drove off in a haze of exhaust fumes. Hari waved contentedly. He was so very used to seeing his father drive away from him.

PART TWO

'But how will I know?' said Wallace. 'How will I know they will give me good help?'

'Ask them three questions,' said the pigeon. 'Ask them for a cup of water, a cup of bird-seed, and a joke, and if you get all three, then you will get good help.'

'I don't like bird-seed,' said Wallace.

'Neither do I,' said the pigeon, resting on his cane. 'Ask them for chips. That'll probably be all right too.'

From *Up on the Rooftops*

Chapter One

Some new words Zoe would get to know very well: gloaming and haar.

The gloaming was the evening fog that came down from the hills. The haar was the morning fog that rose up from the loch, often so thick you could eat it with a spoon. On many days, the haar did not burn off but effectively kept on all day until it merged with the gloaming, and the entire world was made of smoke for all the hours of daylight which, in late August, was still most of them.

So it was gloaming Zoe and Hari arrived in, even though they didn't know that yet. They'd disembarked after that marathon journey through which they'd both slept. Zoe hadn't quite realised how heavy the days and weeks of worry – heck, the months – had stacked up on her, weighing her down about money, about Hari, about her job and her flat.

So she might lose a lot: she no longer had a home, except as some stranger's gift, and she was about to take on a job where she knew nothing and nobody.

But right in this present moment, after the miles and the service stations had rolled past, and the road had risen up in front of her, and the cities and towns had grown further apart, and the scenery changed from the manicured fields of the south to the craggy hills and wild landscapes of the north and even further north, there was absolutely nothing she could do. About anything. And there was something about that that felt oddly freeing.

For this instant, at least, it was out of her hands. And the slow motion of the coach had lulled her to sleep, Hari's hot little head against her chest, the two of them against the world, and when she had awoken, in that slightly hungover way of having slept during the day, she hadn't quite known where she was, only that it was foggy and that it felt cold through the seals of the coach windows, and somehow the driver had changed without her noticing, and lots of people had already got off and they were almost the only people left.

She wanted to look out of the window, but it truly was too foggy to make anything out; she got only the impression of cobblestones and bridges and church spires, low and square-set.

'Inverness! INBHERNISH,' said the driver, who wasn't the same one who'd taken them from London. This one sounded ... well, Scottish, she supposed. Zoe told herself to stop thinking that. It wasn't going to be a stand-out.

'Oh yes, that's us,' she said, shaking Hari awake as the coach heaved and set itself down with an exhausted sigh.

The driver got off and opened the side door and, very nervously, and still heaving along an incredibly drowsy Hari, Zoe stepped into Scotland for the very first time.

It seemed incredible they'd only left the boiling stickiness of London behind that morning. A cool wind hit her, underneath the haar that seemed to be settling all around; the air felt damp. She couldn't smell much more than bus station as she grabbed the scruffy cheap old carryalls from the depths of the coach.

All around her, cheerful-looking students and young people were gathering up light bags and waltzing off who knew where. She couldn't handle Hari, who kept slipping out of her arms, and the bags at the same time. Two rolling bags, two coats, one heavy four-year-old, one handbag. She looked around in vain but the driver was

54

already back in his coach, his contracted bag-moving stint over, and everyone else had disappeared into the mist.

'Come on, Hari, you have to walk,' she said more sharply than she intended, and her tone plus the chill in the air – Hari was only wearing a T-shirt – made him start his silent crying and he stood absolutely stock-still, then, very slowly, started to slide down her leg, towards the utterly filthy bus terminal floor. Big blue signs announced INVERNESS BUS STATION on older-looking stone walls, as the fog obscured everything smaller.

'No,' she said. 'No no no no no no, please, Hari, please . . .'

Sometimes, there is no stopping a small child: if they want to lie on the ground, they will lie on the ground, however many bags you have. One bag, over-bulging and over-stuffed, fell down onto the other side of the road, causing the Aberdeen bus to rapidly swerve to avoid squishing it to bits.

'Hari, please, get up get up get up,' she said, without a spare hand and therefore unable to grab the bag lying in the road as it would leave Hari perfectly free to fall into the other side of the road and straight into the path of the next belching bus.

He stared at her, wide-eyed, rolling around, getting dirty, upset and cold, as if this was all her fault – which it was, of course, on some level – and the wind blew right through Zoe and she swore several times under her breath and remembered not for the first time that she was the grown-up. She was the only grown-up, she was in charge and she was just going to lump it if she didn't like it. And here came another bus!

'Please get up, Hari! Please! I'll buy you . . . I'll get you an ice cream!'

Hari's brow furrowed. This would be a very unusual gesture. It was normally his dad who bought him an ice cream. It was practically night time. It was cold. Ice cream was a confusing thought. He lay in the mucky ground, pondering.

'ICE CREAM? ICE CREAM? ICE CREAM?' Zoe was yelling desperately, just as a nice-looking, extremely pregnant, slightly concerned woman appeared suddenly, alarmingly close, through the mist, and stopped short.

Chapter Two

Quickly, Nina went and rescued Zoe's cheap bag from the road, for which the late-running Aberdonian bus driver was extremely thankful, and placed it back on top of the pavement, whereupon Zoe knelt down and gathered Hari, who was now unutterably filthy, covered in diesel and goodness knows what, his hair plastered to his head and his mouth wide open, a grubby finger stabbing in it which meant undoubtedly 'yes, I have considered this, and ice cream would be most acceptable'. The pace of the stabbing motion appeared to be speeding up, and he put his other grubby paw emphatically on Zoe's face, to turn her head towards his.

The other woman stood there. Zoe blinked anxiously.

'Um . . . are you . . . ?' she began.

It was no good. A very long sleep; a very long journey; a small panic. She had completely and utterly forgotten the woman's name she was meant to be meeting. It was in her phone, which was in her bag, which was by her feet, which meant it might as well be on the moon at this point.

The woman didn't rush to fill the silence but instead regarded her with something akin to horror. In truth, Nina had felt very strongly, watching Zoe, that she had got caught up in her excitement at the idea of having a baby, the romance of it, whereas here was the pure grubby evidence of what it was actually going to be like. She was winded, and suddenly very frightened, and unable to think of poor Zoe much at all.

'Um . . .' said Zoe.

'Sorry. I might be mistaken,' said Nina, just in case she genuinely *was* mistaken and had somehow come across a tramp by accident. 'Who are you looking for?'

Hari had now somehow got his hand entangled in Zoe's hair, and was pulling on it, hard and painfully. The bag fell over again. Zoe looked at the Aberdeen bus, and considered getting on it.

'Book . . . book person,' Zoe managed finally and Nina did her absolute level best to smile.

'Hello!' she said. Then she recovered herself. 'Hi. I'm Nina. You must be knackered.'

The woman looking up at Nina seemed far older than her twenty-eight years. Her dark hair was matted where she'd been sleeping on it, she had great shadows underneath her eyes and her clothes were stained. The child was still pulling on her in agitation.

This will be me, thought Nina in horror. This is going to be me.

Oh God, Zoe was thinking in horror. This was exactly . . . She wanted to cry. She thought of the lovely first impression she would have liked to have given: her beautiful child behaving immaculately; looking ready and professional. Unfortunately, she hadn't been able to afford a haircut and had attempted to trim her hair with the kitchen scissors (never do this), plus she hadn't had time when she'd woken up to have a clean-up in the bus toilet. Also, the bus toilet was absolutely and unutterably disgusting and there wasn't anywhere to put Hari down while she tried to tidy them up. She'd gone after them both with a tissue but on balance she'd only kind of rubbed the filth around a little bit and Hari looked crusty.

And this woman, in her purple jumper and short tweed skirt over her bump matching her red hair beautifully ... she just looked so right, part of the landscape, even as she was clearly trying to hide her horror.

Zoe shut her eyes. Well. Too late to back out now.

Nina picked up the bags decisively.

'You'd better follow me,' she said, picking her away along the pavements between the coach stands. Zoe felt bad about letting her carry the bags but didn't see another way to manage it.

Hari sensed immediately that this meant no ice cream, and turned his head into Zoe's T-shirt, stuck his hand down the front of it, a hangover from his breastfeeding days, and silently howled, soaking her top through with his tears. Nina stared briefly, then turned around and marched on, pulling Zoe's tattered bag efficiently as Zoe puffed, trying to keep up with her handbag and an inconsolable and surprisingly heavy four-year-old and his buggy.

'Get in the buggy, Hari?' she whispered and the child shook his head fiercely. Frankly, Zoe couldn't blame him. The fog was heavy and thick on the ground making it very difficult to get a good sense of where they were. Through the main doors of the bus station, she caught sight in the gloom of a large pillared sandstone building boldly proclaiming PUBLIC LIBRARY as Nina headed out towards an extraordinary-looking blue van.

'Well, here we are,' she said cheerfully, then looked worried. 'Oh God,' she said. 'I thought ... ' She looked at Zoe once more. 'I'm so sorry. I thought you'd bring a car seat.'

'I tried,' Zoe attempted to explain. 'But I ran out of hands.'

'Of course! Of course you did. I'm so sorry! Will he be all right on your lap?'

'Of course.'

Nina looked a little longer.

'Or ... hang on.'

She vanished into the back of the van with Nina's luggage and reappeared with three heavy books.

'We could boost him up a bit.'

Zoe looked at the books.

'Oh, don't worry,' said Nina. 'They're books about how to hide vegetables for children. I don't like them. As long as he doesn't pee on them we should be all right.'

And she smiled nervously, and Zoe smiled nervously back.

'Okay, little man,' she said. 'Up you get.'

'He's quiet,' observed Nina. Surinder hadn't mentioned Hari's mutism, considering it just shyness.

'He doesn't speak,' said Zoe. 'Yet, I mean. He probably will when he's ready.'

Nina looked at the little boy properly for the first time. Once you ignored the crumbs and a bit of snot, he was a sweet-looking child. She could see a bit of Surinder in him.

'Does he cry?' she asked, curious.

'Not loudly,' said Zoe, doing what she normally did and pretending to be cheerful to cover up her worries. 'You're just perfect, aren't you, Hari-boy?'

And Hari made a snuffling noise and wiped his nose on his sleeve and looked ready to start crying again and, frankly, anything but perfect, but they decided not to mention this as Nina, her bump touching the steering wheel, set the van to reverse and carefully manoeuvred away from the bus station.

Chapter Three

Surinder, like many extroverts, could never truly understand what it was to be shy. Nina had been an introverted bookworm all her life; moving to Scotland had helped her bring herself out in a tiny community, but she still got nervous around new people. Zoe, meanwhile, was feeling so exhausted and kicked about by life that she felt all her resilience had been knocked out of her and she didn't know where to pick it up again.

It was such a miserable evening's weather too. Nina felt bad about dropping Zoe off at the strange big house. She should take her home, feed her up a bit, look after her. She hadn't expected Zoe to be such a wounded bird (Surinder definitely had been bigging her up).

'So,' she said finally. 'What did you read on the bus?'

This time Zoe was ready.

'*Anna Karenina!*' she announced loudly. Well, she'd brought it. She'd got it from a charity shop, so she was ready. It wasn't that she didn't read – she did – but she'd got out of the habit when the baby was born, and found her concentration afterwards wasn't what it had been.

'Really?' said Nina. 'I find it quite hard to read big books when I'm travelling – amazing!'

Silence fell in the front of the little van.

'Um,' said Zoe. 'Also ...'

She held up a copy of a Jack Reacher novel she'd also tagged along.

'Oh yes,' said Nina, smiling. 'Tell me he's changed his underpants.'

'It's been three days,' said Zoe.

'Oof,' said Nina, and Zoe smiled back at her.

'So the Urquart family ... they're nice?' she said.

Nina winced. She should have, she realised, gone and visited them, made sure everything was okay. But she felt so awful every day now. More awful than she let on to Lennox, who would worry. It was as much as she could do to drag herself to the van, then collapse in front of the fire in the evening.

'I'm sure they're fine,' she said. 'I think it's just ... been a difficult time for them.'

Zoe nodded. The nursery she'd worked at had been posh, full of rich divorced parents. 'It's been a difficult time' vis-à-vis children in her experience meant 'buckle up'.

On her chest, asleep again, Hari snuffled and let out a long sigh.

At last they reached what to Zoe looked like yet another winding road as she checked a printed-out map (the phone reception, Zoe had realised immediately, was rather hit and miss here). But she realised to her horror that Nina had never been here before.

'Just dropping you off,' said Nina, going pink. 'He was at school with my boyfriend,' she added, as if this made it okay.

'Um, okay,' said Zoe, holding Hari tighter. Outside, an owl hooted. They passed two brick posts set on either side of the road where there must have been a gate once that wasn't there any more. A slightly dilapidated sign read 'The Beeches'.

Zoe glanced at Nina, who deliberately ignored it, instead giving out a slightly forced laugh.

'Ha – looks creepy!'

'Mm,' said Zoe, covering Hari's ears, and reminding herself, as the gateposts vanished behind them in the fog, only an owl's hooting penetrating the car, that of course she absolutely didn't believe in ghosts. Absolutely not.

The gateposts, as it turned out, were only the entrance to the house. They weren't actually anywhere near it. There was a long path, which remained shrouded in gloom, and a long gravel drive, somewhat past its best, with rustling undergrowth beside them. They went past dank hedgerows and low-roofed outhouses, before The Beeches finally revealed itself.

It was the spookiest bloody place Zoe had ever seen in her life.

The house was in a style Zoe didn't recognise but would soon learn was common in many of the great houses of the region: a high baronial style. It was grey brick, with numerous turrets sprouting from its high walls, and there was a huge wooden door up a wide staircase at the entrance. The turrets and towers were festooned with windsocks and pointy metal bits, and each looked like a child's drawing of Rapunzel's tower. Windows ran across the ground floor and up the towers, mere slits in some instances, even though the house had clearly been built a long time after there would be any obvious dangers from flying arrows.

It was breath-taking. And scary.

'I . . . I thought it was a house,' said Zoe, shaking her head.

'It is a house,' said Nina. 'It's just a very, very big house.'

The car slowed, crunching on the old gravel. At the front, standing, was the shape of a woman standing crossly with her arms folded, whom Nina didn't need astonishing powers to intuit had to be Mrs MacGlone.

Chapter Four

As Zoe got out of the car, her first impressions of a magnificent castle receded a little. She could see the chipped bricks, the weeds growing up on higher windows, and she wondered if there were more rooms in the house than people ever went in to.

The large woman standing in front of the main door, arms folded, stepped forward.

'Apparently she's not as scary as she looks,' muttered Nina.

Zoe glanced at her.

'Mrs MacDanvers,' she said under her breath, and Nina couldn't help smirking.

Zoe stepped out of the car. A stiff wind blew her dark hair across her face. It definitely needed a trim. And a wash and a blow-dry and a quick root inspection.

Mrs MacGlone looked Zoe up and down.

'Aye,' she said in the manner of one for whom this is not their first meeting with an au pair. 'Zoe, is it?'

'And Hari,' said Zoe, offering up the slumbering bundle over her shoulder.

'That'll be right,' said Mrs MacGlone, watching disinterestedly as

Nina pulled out the heavy bags despite her bump and the two girls brought them up together.

The vast wooden door was peeling and faded, she noticed as she went towards it. Mrs MacGlone frowned.

'We use the other door,' she said, and Zoe immediately couldn't stop her mouth twitching. A servant's entrance! This was Downton Abbey! She looked around and found it was, now that the moon was coming out, just dimly visible behind the thick clouds, impossible to tell what year it was.

There was a heavy piny scent in the air. Now darkness was coming – true darkness, not the phosphorescent gloom of a London street where the trucks and cars never stopped, where everything ran 24/7.

Apart from a faint hooting and rustling, Zoe couldn't hear a sound. And she wondered suddenly if she'd ever been in such silence in her life.

Then, as they were crunching their way to the back of the house (Nina, drooping with tiredness and nausea had rather apologetically driven off and said she'd see her tomorrow; there was a car at the house she could use), Zoe heard the huge front door creak and saw a light glow inside. There was a quick flash of something white, and a slightly eerie cackle of laughter. Zoe turned her head sharply, but there was nothing there. Mrs MacGlone showed absolutely no signs of having noticed a thing as the silence returned.

The back door – a simpler affair with four panes of glass – did not creak: obviously it was always open. It led them into a flagstone corridor with a large room on the right-hand side filled with wellingtons and walking sticks and raincoats.

'Leave your jackets in the boot room,' sniffed Mrs MacGlone. Zoe blinked. She had never actually heard of a boot room. Hari's eyes were wide; he had woken up and was now staring around him in wonderment. Zoe felt rather the same.

Mrs MacGlone bustled on into a large low-ceilinged kitchen with a long servants' table down the middle of it. The room was cold (there were no rugs on the floor) and rather dank, with a large butler sink. The only sound was a very loud old fridge buzzing away. There was, Zoe couldn't help but notice, absolutely no smell of food or cooking in the air at all.

'This is the kitchen,' said Mrs MacGlone helpfully. 'I don't cook.'

'But ... what does everyone eat?' said Zoe.

'Och, we do all right.'

'Well,' said Zoe, who was beyond exhaustion. 'Perhaps you could show me everything tomorrow? I'd quite like to put Hari down ...'

Mrs MacGlone looked at the child, as if a four-year-old being asleep at eleven o'clock at night was a peculiar sight, sniffed again, then carried on through the narrow corridor and led them up a twisting flight of stone steps, Zoe banging the luggage on every single one of them, and through a hidden door underneath the old brown staircase into what was obviously the main hallway of the house, leading to the wide front door.

Everything was polished wood and smelled of beeswax. There was an overwhelming sensation of dark brown as well as the heavy tartan-patterned carpets which were secured with heavy gold stair-rods on the wide brown staircase with its carved pinions and banister. A large grandfather clock sat on the landing, actually ticking. Zoe didn't think she'd heard a working one before.

Once again, she caught the shadow of a distant laugh.

'Did the children want to stay up and meet me?' she asked, hopefully.

'Git to bed!' Mrs MacGlone yelled up the stairs, and they heard nothing more.

'Right,' said Zoe. 'Well. And Mr Urquart?'

'He isnae here,' said Mrs MacGlone.

'Goodness,' said Zoe, genuinely surprised. 'Just as well I showed up then.'

Mrs MacGlone sniffed, as if it was certainly too early to be sure about that.

Chapter Five

Zoe carried on dragging her bags and following Mrs MacGlone. There was, as it turned out, another set of back stairs, through a hidden door next to the one they'd emerged from, which twisted up and around three flights to a long corridor in the attic.

The first door was open and inside was a tiny room with two single beds and a small sink. It looked not entirely unlike a cell. A high window looked out onto pitch-black. Regardless, hugely relieved, Zoe put Hari on a bed, where he immediately turned over, snorted and fell fast asleep. There wasn't a duvet, just a rough blanket, and she covered him up with it. The room was chilly.

'Where's ...?'

'The bathroom's at the end of the hall,' said Mrs MacGlone. 'I'll show you everything else tomorrow. I'm off.'

'You're off ... somewhere else?'

'I've been doing night shifts since the last girl left,' said Mrs MacGlone. 'I'm sick of it. I'll be back in the morning. Bye.'

Zoe watched her go, realising to her horror that she didn't know where the end of the hall meant exactly – the corridors seemed to go on for ever and could absolutely possibly get lost. Or killed by ghosts, her subconscious said, but she ignored that. Mostly.

Also, she was starving hungry. On some level, she realised, she'd been hoping to arrive ... Okay: honestly, Zoe had hoped she'd turn up to a lovely warm Scottish house, with fires burning and something traditional – haggis maybe? She'd never had that. Maybe a nice big bowl of soup and lovely children so pleased to see her and a nice dad saying thank heavens you're here, and a cosy room and ...

The tap on the sink dripped solemnly. Something in the depths creaked. Zoe turned on her phone – no signal, but she could still put some music on and, quietly, she did, just to feel less utterly alone.

She delved into her handbag and triumphantly found half a packet of semi-chewed rice cakes right down the bottom. Together with a glass of water – surprisingly clean and refreshing from the old brass tap – that was going to have to make a meal, she supposed.

Well. She looked around at the bare beds, the empty, ancient wardrobe, the tiny window. Look on the bright side. It was ... different. She felt as far away from anything as she ever had in her entire life.

She sat on the bed. The mattress was so thin she could feel the springs beneath it. How long would she have to look on the bright side? Well. Tomorrow would be better. Wouldn't it?

Chapter Six

At first, opening her eyes as she customarily did – at 5.30 a.m. with a small boy on top of her indicating that she take him to the toilet – as Zoe struggled into wakefulness, she didn't quite realise where she was, or what had happened.

Then it struck her.

Quickly, without thinking, she bustled out of the room with Hari, unsure as to where the toilet was – there were eight doors on the corridor, any of which could lead to anything, but most, as she found out, were locked. Argh, this place was *sinister*, especially when you were freezing and desperate for the toilet.

The loo was right at the very end, annoyingly, as they sprinted up the linoleum. It was a single old Thomas Crapper toilet with a long chain and enamel handle, and a huge, ancient clawfoot bath, but no shower. Zoe screwed up her eyes. After her long journey yesterday, she could absolutely do with a blisteringly hot shower, but there didn't seem to be anything like that at all.

While Hari went to the bathroom, she experimented with turning on the bath.

Yellow gouges of water shot out from the mixer tap – it obviously hadn't been used in some time – and Zoe groped around for the plug and grabbed the tiny, hotel-sized bar of soap by the sink. It hadn't occurred to her, she realised, to bring shampoo. She supposed, when she was trying to compress their belongings to the smallest size possible, that she'd just collect and buy that stuff up here once she'd got settled, that she'd be able to borrow some things when she got here, or pop out to the shops.

She couldn't recollect seeing anything on their journey from Inverness the previous evening that looked like a shop.

The hot water continued until it had covered about two inches of the bottom of the enormous bath, then turned cold abruptly. Zoe stared at it in consternation. Was that it? Did people really live like this?

On the other hand, she needed to wash, that much was clear. On the first day of a new job, it was kind of recommended.

Reluctantly, and shivering on the cold tiles of the unheated room, she stripped down and took Hari out of his pyjamas, even as he wriggled and bodily protested. They stood and she soaped them both down with the tiny bar of soap as well as she could, which wasn't very. She didn't dare risk attempting to wash their hair. That would just have to stand.

Hari was pointing at his mouth.

'I know,' she said. 'I know you're hungry, baby. We're going to unpack all our clothes, and then we'll go get some breakfast, okay?'

Hari wasn't remotely pacified and started to look as if he was going to cause trouble, even as she pulled an old towel, which had been washed and dried many, many times, from a small stack in the corner of the room, and wrapped up his shivering body, holding him close to her.

'Don't worry,' she whispered in his ear, although she was talking to herself as much as she was talking to him. 'I know it's new. And strange. And different. And that's okay. Sometimes life just turns out that way. And it'll be all right. I promise.'

It struck her forcibly that this weird house, with its weird corridors and odd number of staircases, and mysterious children and the mysterious parent . . . it suddenly struck her, with some horror, that

69

the house might not have a television. That the soothing power of *Hey Duggee* and his assorted cubs might not be able to exert their soothing power; that *Octonauts* might not distract him utterly when he needed soothing and calming down. She grabbed his ancient tablet when they got back to the room. Just until he felt better. They could plug it in downstairs.

The house was silent as they descended the stairs. In daylight, she could see how derelict it was, dust and cobwebs everywhere except in the polished hallway, which remained pitch-dark, the huge door closed. It looked like a drawing room led off it, but that was shuttered. Also, the ground floor of the front, public section of the house was the first floor of the back; the grounds sloped round to the back of the house.

The chilly kitchen was a more attractive sight in the morning, with large dirty windows letting weak sunlight pour in. There was also a kitchen door which led on to a small flagstone terrace, overgrown with wild grass, and then straight onto the lawn, which stretched down to the wall of a kitchen garden, with a thin gravel path running straight through it.

There was no sign of an electric kettle, but there was a big old black steam kettle on top of the ancient electric oven, and Zoe figured she could work with that for now. She filled it with water – it weighed a ton – and propped it up.

Warning Hari not to go near the stove – he was clutching his tablet like a religious talisman; they'd found a plug, and he patently didn't want to come with her – she pulled her jumper further round her and found herself stepping out into the fresh morning.

The grass was damp with dew, but the heavy mist which had sat around the house the previous evening, while not entirely gone, was lifting; you could see it swirl and move like a living thing. Zoe had never seen anything like it before; it was like being in a cloud.

Just above, however, she could see the very first rays of sun doing their best to poke out from their thick grey blanket; here and there, a shard shot through, turning the drops of moisture on the grass stems into twinkling diamonds.

Zoe took a great, deep breath and pulled the fresh air into her lungs.

It was intoxicating. So pure, with an edge of fresh cold and a hint of sunlight; with a mossy scent of grass and leaves and a high note of ancient fir trees and the ghosts of millions of bluebells and snowdrops and daffodils, taking their turns, year after year.

Zoe took another deep breath. She felt it could make you drunk; it was so rich and fierce. She opened her eyes, glancing back into the kitchen to make sure Hari was all right. She could see him through the open door, hunched, completely immersed in whatever he was watching, in a world of his own.

'Come on, Hari!' she called softly, but he barely glanced at her before he shook his head.

The long, beautiful lawn was a little overgrown with daisies and wildflowers, but not necessarily the worse for that. An ivy-covered brick wall led to a walled garden with fruit trees bursting over the top of it. The house was behind her; the turrets, here and there, catching the sun on their spires and weather vanes. And to her left, the grass ran down over a mossy terrain which led down – to Zoe's absolute shock and surprise, as she had noticed nothing like this the previous evening – to a small cove, right there in front of the house, where an old rowing boat, in desperate need of a sanding down and a coat of paint, was sitting – and beyond, a great shimmering expanse of green water, patches of sunlight glinting off it here and there. The loch itself, Loch Ness. Zoe had known it was near, roughly. Just not exactly *this* near.

'Hari! Hari! Come see!' said Zoe, clanging back into the kitchen. The kettle was making a loud whistling sound, and she poured it into a cup with a tired-looking teabag she'd found in an otherwise empty cupboard.

'Well, you should maybe say hello or perhaps good morning,' came a voice.

Zoe whirled round, almost spilling the boiling water. The voice – definitely a child's voice – had appeared out of nowhere. For some ridiculous moment, she had thought it might be ... No. That was ridiculous.

71

Standing in the kitchen door was a small boy with brown hair sticking straight up, wearing very old flannel pyjamas that were too short for him. Despite his odd appearance, his stance was confident.

Zoe blinked. Then she realised, and put on her biggest smile.

'Hello! Are you . . . ?' She couldn't remember which kid was which. 'Are you Shackleton?'

'No,' said Patrick. 'Yuk. That would be absolutely disgusting. I'm Patrick.'

'Oh yes! Hello, Patrick. I'm Zoe.'

The tiny boy frowned.

'Well,' he said. 'I absolutely don't want to remember that. You are . . . '

He glanced at his fingers.

'Our number seven nanny. I shall call you Nanny Seven.'

'Just call me Zoe please,' said Zoe. Patrick padded over and jumped up carefully on one of the kitchen stools which were rather too high for him.

'I don't think so. Toast, Nanny Seven!'

Zoe stared at him. To her amazement, Hari put down his tablet, got up and padded over to the newcomer. This wasn't like him at all.

'Who are you?' said Patrick.

'This is Hari,' said Zoe. 'He's living here too.'

Patrick regarded the boy with some suspicion. Hari glanced over at Zoe worriedly, but she smiled at him as if to say it would be all right.

'Hmm,' said Patrick eventually. 'You don't talk too much. I like that. I like to talk A LOT. Do you like dinosaurs?'

Hari nodded.

'Okay,' said Patrick carelessly. 'Two toasts, Nanny Seven.'

'Well, hang on there just a second,' Zoe was starting to say, when she spied another figure walking nervously towards the kitchen door.

'Good morning!' she trilled. She wished Mrs MacGlone was there. It was too weird to have to do this all by herself. A scary thought hit her – that Mrs MacGlone had now left for good and she'd never see her again and would just have to get on with it – but she put it to the back of her mind.

The girl looked to be about ten, not showing any hints of puberty but growing long and tall, like a reed. She had long, dark hair that desperately needed washing and an incredibly pale face with a long, pointed chin. It wasn't a pretty face, necessarily, the first time you saw it. But she looked interesting and inquisitive and different. She was wearing a pale white nightgown that trailed behind her; the effect was rather sinister with the dark hair.

'I'm Zoe.'

The girl sniffed, stared rudely at her and didn't reply.

'That's Mary,' said Patrick. 'She's horrible.'

'Shut up, tyke,' said the girl. She had a strong local accent.

'See,' said Patrick.

She went into a cupboard Zoe hadn't noticed before and drew out a box of cereal. Then she went out of the door altogether and came back with a carton of horrible UHT milk.

'So, I'm going to be your new au pair.'

'I'm nine,' said Mary flatly. 'I don't need an au pair.'

'You quite absolutely do,' said Patrick. 'You're in-CORR-igibile.'

'You don't know what that means, tyke, so just shut up.'

'I do actually. It means horrible and mean and nasty to brothers.'

'Oh well, in that case it's a good thing,' said Mary, dumping half the milk on her cornflakes, flooding the bowl all over the table and not bothering to do anything about it.

'I like your house,' said Zoe vaguely. Mary shot her a look that made Zoe amazed she was only nine and not fourteen and full of hormones.

'You can pay to come round it four times a year,' she hissed. 'Why don't you do that instead?'

Hari stood up with a ragged old piece of blanket he liked to carry round in emergencies crammed up against his face, his thumb in his mouth.

'And this is my son Hari, who's going to be staying too.'

Mary completely ignored Hari too – which made Zoe incredibly

73

angry – pulled out a phone and started to tap into it in a very ostentatious fashion. It was an unexpectedly modern thing for the girl to do in such an old house.

After a moment, Patrick did the same thing, and the two of them sat absolutely buried in their phones while Zoe tiptoed around the table, fetching some of the cereal for Hari – Mary shot her a look at this, as if she were stealing – and moving dirty cups and plates out of the way. To her horror, there didn't appear to be a dishwasher. How on earth could a family survive without a dishwasher? She sighed. The sun was still coming through the windows. She took Hari's hand and set his tablet to one side.

'Let me show you this,' she whispered.

Chapter Seven

Even in her short time back in the kitchen, the weather had changed, and the haar had burnt off even more, and there were more and more patches of sun on the grass. Hari looked around him in astonishment. Zoe had taken him to Brighton once or twice, but it had always been absolutely crowded with people everywhere and a rough stony beach that wasn't any fun to lie on.

This, on the other hand . . .

They wandered down to the little sandy cove. The beach was golden – a colour Zoe couldn't have imagined. These people must own their own beach. What an extraordinary thing, to own your own beach! She shook her head in amazement.

The lake – the loch, she supposed – was absolutely vast; it seemed to go all the way to the horizon. She couldn't see an end to it in any direction except straight ahead, where great mountains loomed out of the fog, but how far away they were she couldn't tell.

Apart from that, there was just the lapping of little waves onto the shoreline, next to the abandoned boat. She knelt down and put her hand in the water. It was frightfully cold and clear. You could probably drink it, although she wasn't minded to do that right now. She took a sip of her coffee. Even black instant coffee without any milk in an old chipped mug, she realised with some surprise, tastes absolutely delicious when you're standing on a beach at the water's edge, on an utterly glorious – if chilly – morning.

Suddenly a hand clasped the bottom of her nightgown frantically.

'What? What is it?' she said, crouching down. Hari was pointing frantically out into the middle of the loch. 'What is it, Hari?'

His trembling finger held fast, pointing furiously somewhere, but there was obviously nothing there.

She looked out. Birds were circling over the water.

'I know,' she said. 'Look at the birds. Aren't they beautiful?'

Just as she was thinking this, she heard a loud screeching noise and jumped half out of her skin. Hari gasped. They turned round, hearts pounding, only to be confronted with a gigantic peacock, feathers distinctly downwards facing, hard little black eyes staring at them and pointed beak wide open.

'CAAAAARK!'

'Oh bloody hell!' said Zoe. 'You gave me a shock, Mr Peacock. Here.'

She retrieved the bread she'd picked up as she'd left the kitchen. 'Try this.'

She threw a couple of bits in the peacock's direction and gave a slice to Hari to do the same, stopping him from holding onto it to tempt the animal to come closer; it looked as if it could bite off his fingers.

'CAAAARK!' The bird seemed to be warning them that it wasn't particularly mollified by the offerings they'd brought – while gobbling them up anyway – so they sidled round it carefully back to the safety of the kitchen.

'It's beautiful out there!' said Zoe, still in shock. Patrick sniffed.

'They all say that AT FIRST,' he observed darkly.

Finally, another figure clumped downstairs. He was physically as different from the other two as chalk and cheese: large, lumpy, sandy-haired. He was just on the brink of puberty and looked as though he didn't know what to do with himself. His feet and hands were huge, massively out of proportion to his body, and he sat down in his seat with a sigh, after putting on six slices of toast.

'Um, good morning.'

The lad looked her up and down.

'Nanny Seven!' prompted Patrick.

'I don't need a nanny,' said the boy, and Zoe had to admit he had a point: he looked more or less ready to play in the Six Nations.

'Good because I'm not one,' said Zoe. 'Hello. I'm Zoe. I'm here to be your au pair.'

'Shackleton,' grunted the boy, and it was such an unusual name in a young person that Zoe had to ask twice.

'Don't ask him his name, he HATES that,' informed Patrick. 'If I'd been born first, I'd have had it. And the estate,' he pondered thoughtfully.

'You're welcome to it, small fry,' shot back Shackleton.

'I shall,' said Patrick. 'And none of you can come. NEVER NEVER NEVER.'

'I shan't leave,' said Mary. 'So there!'

'You WILL! You WILL leave my house, you WILL, you stupid girl!'

Patrick suddenly dived at her in a fury. Out of instinct more than anything else, Zoe stuck her hands out and hauled him off.

Patrick went rigid as soon as she touched him.

'Leave me alone!'

'Yeah, all right, just ... leave your sister alone.'

'Yeah, leave *me* alone,' said Mary, sticking out her tongue, even as Zoe felt the little boy trembling in anger.

'Who wants more toast?' she said, looking hopefully at the toaster, but Shackleton had already laden all six slices with butter half an inch thick and most of a pot of marmalade, and was chewing through them stoically.

'Sorry,' he said, his mouth full and crumbs spitting out. 'Think I finished it.'

Chapter Eight

Zoe couldn't have anticipated how pleased she was to see Mrs MacGlone when she turned up on the dot of 8.30. None of the children even looked up as she entered and put on cleaning gloves.

'You've met then, I see,' she said.

'Well, yes!' said Zoe, following her out into the hallway. Mrs MacGlone turned round with a sigh as soon as they were out of earshot.

'Yes, Mary is always like that. Yes, Patrick has a very high IQ. No, you may not smack them.'

'I had no plans . . . '

'Oh, believe me, you'll want to.'

'Why aren't they at school?' said Zoe.

Mrs MacGlone sniffed.

'Mary got excluded. Then Shackleton fought someone who made fun of his sister for being excluded, so he got excluded too. Patrick isn't meant to start till Christmas.'

Zoe blinked in astonishment. It hadn't occurred to her to ask before. What on earth did they do all day?

'How long are they excluded for?'

'I think the headmistress will decide that.'

'And what do they do?'

'Search me,' said Mrs MacGlone, who was starting to polish the banister. It became clear there was obviously one area of the house she considered her concern, and it wasn't the back kitchen.

Shackleton started up a very loud and noisy computer game. The sound travelled all the way from the kitchen, which answered at least one question.

'Bleeping things,' said Mrs MacGlone ominously.

Zoe looked around the rest of the large hallway in the daylight. There were ancient oil paintings on the wall, some hung tapestry and a large stag's head with shining eyes. Mrs MacGlone pushed past her and opened the large handle of a huge heavy wooden door and pushed it open slowly. It creaked obligingly.

The room was dark, with the shutters drawn. Mrs MacGlone tutted. 'I do not have time to do this today,' she said. 'I have the west wing, and the laundry, and the children's wing, and the two staircases ...'

She moved stiffly, and Zoe wondered just how old she was.

'You have a lot to take on.'

'You can say that again,' she mumbled.

'He's been at it again,' she continued, heading towards the windows and pulling them open. Bright sunshine flooded the room, showing the motes of dust floating on the rays. Dazzled, Zoe turned her head then slowly looked up to take in the space.

It was actually a lovely room, stretching out right into a huge bay window at the front of the house – but it was filthy. The most arresting thing about it was that every square inch of the wall space was completely covered in bookshelves, old wooden ones that had been moulded to fit the walls. The ceiling was wood-panelled too, making the room look very brown.

But the books! Zoe had simply never seen so many in one place, nothing like. Hundreds and hundreds, perhaps thousands. There were great big old leather-bound volumes, ancient bibles and encyclopaedias and what looked like spell books. There were gold-bound books, and ancient manuscripts delicately held together. Carefully behind glass, there were several scrolls and – Zoe couldn't help but gasp to see it – an illuminated manuscript. A real one, in somebody's home. She took a step forward, fascinated and oddly moved by the tiny painted figure of a monk and the wildly overwrought S, tangled with vine leaves and fruit and the tiniest of meticulous decorations in ink that had dried centuries and centuries ago.

There were shelves of orange Penguin Classic spines and shelves of black Penguin Classic spines; vast atlases piled up from every period of history; neat hardbacks in many different languages; old James Bond originals as well as an ancient, cloth-covered collection of Dickens that Zoe wanted to touch, then decided it was better not to.

There were huge volumes of art history, some extraordinary German-looking children's books and endless other volumes, stretching right across the room and back again.

The only furniture were two armchairs in front of a vast fireplace, and a large green leather desk with an old rotary dial telephone on it as well as two pens, some blotting paper but nothing else.

'Oh my goodness,' said Zoe, almost forgetting what it was she wanted to say. 'A library.'

'This isn't the library,' frowned Mrs MacGlone. 'Nobody uses this at all. No point.'

'Really?' said Zoe, thinking of the three children crammed into the kitchen, attached to their devices. 'I'd have thought it could be quite handy.'

'Would you now?'

The voice was low, booming and, of all things, sounded amused. Zoe whirled round, startled.

A very large man was standing there, taking up all the space, it seemed. His head was too high for the door frame; he was almost comically too tall.

'Just showing the new girl around,' said Mrs MacGlone. 'We'll get out of your way, sir.'

'Just keep her out of my library.'

'Of course!'

There was a slight pause, then a loud noise.

'DADDY!'

Patrick launched himself from the hallway like a bullet from a gun. Mary hung behind.

'MARY is being horrible! And Shackleton won't let me have a turn! And he finished the marmalade because he is absolutely QUITE HORRIBLE.'

'*Daddy!* Stop Patrick! He's being a clype and he's just awful and *I hate him.*'

'We don't ... we don't hate anyone, Mary,' said the tall man, holding out his hands in what was clearly meant to be a conciliatory manner.

'*You* might not,' said Mary snidely. '*I* do.'

And she looked straight at Zoe.

'Good, good,' said the man distracted.

Zoe found herself uncharacteristically nervous. This was the guy whose wife had left him. Ramsay Urquart. What had happened? Was he cruel?

'And!' said Patrick. 'There is a baby in the kitchen that doesn't know its own name.'

'*Is* there?' said the man. 'Well.'

'This is Zoe,' said Mrs MacGlone unenthusiastically.

Zoe overcame a stupid urge to curtsey.

'Hello,' she said. 'And that's my baby in the kitchen.'

'I see,' he said. 'So you are ...'

'Nanny Seven,' said Patrick helpfully.

'Right. Good, good,' Ramsay said again. Zoe frowned. 'Well, welcome I suppose. Do try and stay a bit longer than the others! Ha!'

'I'd like to, sir,' said Zoe. 'Just ... you tell me what they like and I'll try for us all to have a fun time.'

He grimaced.

'Fighting, mostly, as far as I can tell,' he said. 'I just ... well. I have a lot of work to do.'

'What do you do?'

'I'm an antiquarian bookseller.'

Zoe looked puzzled.

'I buy and sell old books. Very old books. I travel a lot ... around the country ...'

'It's important he's not disturbed,' added Mrs MacGlone.

'It is absolutely important,' agreed Patrick, although he was still hanging onto the bottom of his father's trousers.

'Leave him alone then, creep,' hissed Mary.

'SHUT UP!' howled Patrick.

'Now, now,' said the man. He looked at Zoe.

'So, um ... try your best ...'

'Of course,' said Zoe. She'd met his type before, although they were normally slightly smoother men, never off their phones, or aeroplanes; who saw their own children as faintly irritating interruptions to their highly important lives, and she didn't think much of them.

'Is Shackleton on that computer still?' he asked Mrs MacGlone, who nodded. He sighed. Then he knelt down and took both the children in his arms, patting them awkwardly on the shoulder. Zoe wondered if it was for her benefit, something that was confirmed when she heard him whisper to them, 'Please be nice to her. Please. We can't keep going through this now, can we?'

Neither child said anything, but Mary's face was stony. He straightened up again.

'Great! Wonderful! Mrs MacGlone will show you the housekeeping box, tell you what's what. Just one thing ...'

Patrick wandered off looking cross.

'This will absolutely be about the library,' he muttered to himself as Zoe watched him go.

'Just ... well. Yes. Keep them out of my library.'

Chapter Nine

Zoe made her way back into the kitchen. It looked like a bomb had hit it. Mrs MacGlone was scurrying around picking up plates and putting them in the sink. Hari was, to her surprise, wandering towards Patrick, who had commandeered Hari's tablet and was showing him facts about dinosaurs on it.

'Don't you have a dishwasher?' she said. Mrs MacGlone looked at her sternly.

'I don't really get on with new-fangled things,' she said.

Zoe blinked.

'Wouldn't Laird Urquart want to make your life easier?' she said.

'Ha,' said Mrs MacGlone. 'Ramsay hasn't the slightest idea how his dishes are cleaned.'

'And the children help you?' said Zoe, risking another one of Mrs MacGlone's looks, which she duly got.

'I don't know what fancy ideas you're bringing up from London,' said Mrs MacGlone, which was rather ironic as the children at Zoe's fancy nurseries had never cleaned up a thing in their lives, except their mothers referred to 'au pairs' rather than 'servants', 'but we do things traditionally here.'

Zoe shot a side glance at Shackleton, who hadn't even taken a plate for his toast and marmalade and had managed to make an almost perfect circle of crumbs around himself while he played his computer game. A knife sticky with marmalade and butter lay face down on the table. Her own mother would have had a coronary.

Zoe mentally added it to her list of things to worry about later.

That was becoming a very, very long list.

'So,' concluded Patrick, 'that is how dinosaurs invented television.'

'You're so pathetic,' sneered Mary from her seat at the side of the table.

'Well, you're a stink pig.'

'Takes one to know one, stink pig.'

'Oh, so you admit it, stink pig.'

'Can I help you?' said Zoe, starting to clear up around them, including Mary's filthy feet which were fully propped on the table. Well. This would have to stop pretty soon. 'Then, I'm going to see Nina.'

Mrs MacGlone's face softened.

'She runs that book van, doesn't she? Ask her if she's got any new Barden Towers books in. *He* doesn't deal in that kind of thing. Only fancy books.'

'Oooh, I *love* Barden Towers . . . ' started Zoe, who was indeed a massive fan of the nineteenth-century-set serial about the humble scullery maid in the great house who worked her way up and eventually fell in love with the lord and . . . ah. Zoe let the sentence taper off.

'Um, I've got *The Triumph of the Staircase* if you'd like it,' she said shyly. Mrs MacGlone blinked. 'Well. Well. Now.'

Zoe could tell Mrs MacGlone didn't want to say yes and look like she was trying to be friendly in any way as it would be a clear sign of weakness, so she didn't press the issue.

'I'll leave it downstairs,' she said, as if it would be all right if they didn't actually have to meet each other for the handover.

Mrs MacGlone sniffed.

Zoe glanced around. 'Well, okay . . . bye then.'

Patrick and Mary were kicking each other under the table.

Shackleton was now pouring sugary cereal into a bowl. Bits were going everywhere. Hari looked at her expectantly.

'You're coming with me,' she said, grateful to get him out of that environment.

Rather oddly, he gazed at Patrick briefly and shook his head.

'No, you're coming,' said Zoe.

Hari shook his head more abruptly.

'I think he absolutely wants to stay with me,' said Patrick airily.

'Well, he can't,' said Zoe shortly. Hari looked like he was about to screw up his face, gesturing madly to the show they were watching about dinosaurs. He scowled as she scooped him up and headed to the door, Mrs MacGlone reluctantly handing over the car keys to the 'nanny car'.

Just as she stepped out, she turned round to say goodbye. Shackleton was buried in his phone. Mrs MacGlone had disappeared. Mary, however, was standing in the door frame.

'We don't want you here,' she hissed. 'We don't need you and we don't want you. So why don't you just *stay away*.'

Chapter Ten

The 'nanny car' turned out to be a tiny scuffed-up green Renault that seemed older than Zoe herself. The insulation was more or less stripped out, so you could see the metal of the roof, and the heating was definitely idiosyncratic, but it started eventually and Zoe figured she could get used to no power steering if she absolutely had to. Although she couldn't deny it: she rather wished she didn't have to. Mary had shaken her up, even though that was ridiculous from such a small child.

Zoe sighed and swung around the non-working fountain in the courtyard of the house a few times just to get the hang of it, sparking up gravel as she went.

'Oof,' she said, then glanced at Hari, who was on an ancient, deeply stained booster seat in the back. He looked up, concerned.

'It's fine,' reassured Zoe, swinging round again. 'Just having fun!' Her voice sounded hollow, even to herself.

She went around the fountain a few more times. It was a very long time since she'd had a car – there was no use for it in London really. She'd gotten a second-hand one way back when she'd passed her test; it had been so exciting. They'd driven to music festivals and round the M25 and down to Brighton and done all sorts of things with friends, hanging out, smoking out the windows, playing the music loud in the scorching London summer sun.

They were good days, she thought. In her memories they were totally golden. And very, very short. Was it possible, she wondered with fear, that she'd only had about three good days? And now they'd gone? The car had gone long ago, sold to buy baby stuff. So much baby stuff.

Zoe glanced up at the side of the dark, crenellated, imposing grey house. On the second floor, there was, strangely, a huge stained-glass window. It looked totally out of keeping with the rest of the house. As she was staring at it, she thought she saw the shadow of a person, and suddenly realised she had been circling the fountain for quite some time and should probably get a move on.

Her second thought was, ridiculously, was that a person at the window or . . . ?

But when she glanced up again, the figure was gone.

The green Renault turned left out of the entrance to The Beeches, then bounced down the single-track road for what seemed like hours. It was a pretty straight shot to Kirrinfief, the town where the van plied its trade.

There were rows of pines, so many trees, and then suddenly they stopped and to Zoe's utter surprise, she saw a huge car park. It was mostly empty, but there were a few cars here and there, with people getting out of them, many in macs, and a few huge coaches belching smoke and picnic tables and rubbish bins, and a big old gabled house with 'Ness Centre and Café' written on it in faded writing. Zoe blinked. After the vast silence of The Beeches, it was like accidentally wandering past Piccadilly Circus.

She glanced at her watch. Nina had said tenish, but it was only nine o'clock; Zoe had felt so awkward in the kitchen she had got them out of there as fast as she could.

She pulled over briefly.

The sign was in English, French, German, Japanese and what looked like some fairly recently added Russian and Chinese underneath. It was rather tatty and faded.

There was a medium-sized red sandstone house, with peeling green gables, and, in the window, a fairly tragic selection of dusty old Nessie soft toys. Zoe hauled Hari out and stuck her head round the door. A nice-looking woman came over, looking anxious.

'Hello,' said Zoe cheerfully. 'I was wondering if you did take-away coffee?'

'Oh. No,' said the woman, as if it had only just occurred to her. 'Should I, do you think?'

'I don't know,' said Zoe. 'But there's a lot of people out there who look as if they've been on a bus for a long time.'

'Oh yes,' said the woman, whose name was Agnieszka. She perked up. 'But we do sandwiches at lunchtime! Cheese or cheese and ham!'

'Okay,' smiled Zoe. 'Thanks!'

They headed back outside.

The mountains rose up high above the water line, reflecting back into the loch so it was a perfect mirror, and the sun, with the chill wind beneath it, felt kind and soft in the deep autumn light.

Zoe felt sorry for the tourists desperately looking for some stupid monster that wasn't there – after all, look what *was* here: the glorious vista, the fresh winds, that heavy scent in the air.

Zoe blinked to herself, even as Hari was pointing ferociously at the Nessie toys in the café window and pulling her firmly on the arm. Then he pointed out to the loch, then pointed to the toy another child was carrying behind them, dragging it through the sandy rushes.

'I'm not buying you a toy, Hari – I'm not your dad,' she said, kissing him full on the cheek. 'I promise, there'll be lots of toys to play with at your new nursery.'

She felt him stiffen in her arms. Well. It had to happen at one point.

'Come on, let's go.'

And then it was the oddest thing: they backed away from the colour and the clamour of people with different foreign tour groups, all speaking different languages and wearing brightly coloured cagoules and mackintoshes while coaches settled and cars vroomed and boats out on the loch pulled on their motors and everything was hustle and bustle – then before they'd gone twenty metres down the road, all was quiet again; nothing but birds gently lifting off across the road, or the glimmer of what might be deer in the woods, as if there were never any people there at all.

Chapter Eleven

'We're going to a farm next!' Zoe said excitedly to Hari. Sometimes she felt as if Hari was blind; that she was narrating the world to him as if he couldn't see it.

But it was so hard to know what he understood and what he didn't. What he liked and what he didn't: that much was plain. But otherwise she was just filling the space. Or, as people had occasionally said, with utterly breath-taking cruelty, oh how nice for you, a quiet toddler, wish mine was like that.

'Cows, sheep, chickens!' Zoe added, as a chicken did in fact march out in front of the little car and stop bolt upright, fixing its little beady eyes on them as if it were a border guard.

'Hello, Mr Chicken,' she said as she opened the door. 'May we pass?'

The chicken didn't move. Zoe lifted Hari down carefully.

'Um, hello?' she shouted.

Lennox wouldn't have answered her even if he had been there – no farmer can be found at home in the daytime – and Nina was, sad to say, fast asleep. She'd got up at 4.20 with Lennox and made him tea while he went out and did the milking – it was a freezing morning and he was so glad of her kindness that she was happy to do it for him.

Unfortunately, the bump had slightly overwhelmed her so she'd taken her own cup of tea back to bed, just for a few minutes, just until he came back in, just a few pages of *Emma*...

And then she'd immediately dropped off again and hadn't even stirred even when Lennox had stomped in, showered, changed and stomped back out again to see what the lads were doing down at the lower meadow and why they weren't doing it any faster.

Lennox had looked at her lying there, pink-cheeked and dreamy and absolutely ridiculously vast – every time he thought she couldn't possibly get much bigger, she appeared to get massively and instantly bigger – smiled to himself about how much he'd love to climb back in there and nuzzle deep into her neck, then shook himself and went to find his dry stone wall tools.

So Zoe stood alone in the muddy farmyard, being eyed by an evil chicken, Hari gazing all around him as if she'd transported him to the moon, feeling somewhat bamboozled.

Eventually, she persuaded Hari to stomp through the mud in his new yellow wellington boots (a gift from her old nursery friends) so they could circumvent the chicken, which continued to eye them suspiciously, turning its head incredibly far around while they squelched along. Zoe wondered briefly if the chicken had actually got stuck.

Her attention was soon distracted, however, by the sight of the blue van which had picked her up the day before. Not one job, she thought to herself, a trifle ruefully – two!

In the broad sunlight, it was actually rather lovely, a vintage old bus, painted a pale blue.

She tried the back doors, which were unlocked, and pulled them open. Then she gasped.

It really was extraordinary, just how much you could get inside what didn't look that big from the outside; it was like a little book TARDIS.

Looking straight ahead, firstly the pneumatic steps unfolded to greet you, though there was also a ramp Nina used for wheelchairs and buggies when she needed to, as well as for rolling boxes of books in.

One side was fiction; the other side non-fiction. The far right corner was covered in bright cushions and had a tiny table and was the designated children's zone.

The deep blue shelves had cord running through the centre of them, to hold the books in when the van swung round corners, and at the front, bolted to the floor, was a little cupboard for stock, paper bags, the till, card reader and a little seat for whoever was serving.

There were more high shelves built for stock at the back of the van and a beautiful tiny carved chandelier with stags' heads hanging down from the centre of the roof. On the floor of the van were several old Persian rugs Nina had to vacuum each day, and was sincerely looking forward to not having to.

There was a gap between the main part of the van and the roof, which had tiny thin windows so light could get in, as it did from the open doors. The entire place was quite enchanting.

Zoe took a further step inside the van as Hari ran straight to the children's section at the back, his eyes wide.

'No!' said Zoe. 'Sweetie, you can't touch the books. You can't. They're for sale; they're not for you. I'll read you a book tonight.'

He looked at her, then defiantly held up a book he'd spied about dinosaurs.

'Oh, well, be careful then.'

The stock wasn't massive of course – but oh, it was beautifully put together, carefully chosen so that if you were in the mood for a psychological thriller, or a great sweeping historical romance, or a modern state-of-the-nation book, only the very, very best were represented; not always the newest – although there was a good up-to-date selection on both sides of the aisle – but a perfectly curated miniature snapshot of the very best books you could find anywhere. And every book Zoe had loved throughout her entire life, it seemed, was here.

Here was a full hardback Chalet School series her mother used to let her borrow from the library; a complete set of immaculate Shardlake novels; all the great mountaineering tragedies she'd briefly got obsessed with as a teen; more Philip Larkin than you'd expect to find in a bookshop smaller than most people's front rooms; and a large schoolbook section.

The fact that there were so many of her favourites there made Zoe immediately think that anything else on display must also be what she liked, as if the person who ran the shop had already reached inside her mind and figured out what she would enjoy. It made her think too that however intimidating she'd found Nina so far (Nina would have been wildly surprised to hear herself referred to as intimidating), surely someone who liked as many good books as this – look! There was *The Hitchhiker's Guide to the Galaxy*! And *Knowledge of Angels*! And Pat Barker, and Kate Atkinson, and Andrea Levy and Louis de Bernières and all the good things – had to be a good person. It was a very odd concept – that you could become friends with someone simply by examining their bookshelves – but nevertheless Zoe believed it fervently.

She grabbed a racy biography of Princess Margaret, and an old but beautifully well-kept Antonia Forster, and quietly joined Hari on his pile of cushions on the corner.

Chapter Twelve

Nina realised she'd overslept when she woke up, the sun high, the bedroom in disarray; the tea next to the bed stone-cold. Cursing, she jumped up, remembering that the new girl was starting today. Where was she? Hadn't she woken her? Couldn't she have come in and gotten her? What was she doing, sitting outside like a lemon?

Nina was cross with herself. Looking in the mirror, she could see already her hair was an absolute midden. Her breasts had been kind of hilarious to begin with, and Lennox had certainly, in his quiet way, been firmly appreciative, but now they seemed to be taking on a life of their own, as well as pointing in completely different directions. And she felt absolutely awful. She was meant to be in her second trimester, for goodness' sake; she was supposed to be glowing like a goddess, gliding munificently through life. Instead she felt utterly awful all the time.

'Oh, for *goodness*' sake,' she hissed, jumping in the shower, then reminding herself not to do anything in a hurry because if she fell down – she nearly slipped – she wouldn't be able to get up again.

So it was in a thoroughly bad temper that she approached Zoe's little green Renault to find nobody in it, and the door of the book bus thrown open to the elements. She stomped up to it, intending to say a few things about how keeping chickens out of bookshops was something she genuinely wanted to encourage. She couldn't help but be slightly struck, though, by the sight of the girl and the tiny lad curled up on the children's cushions in the corner, both utterly engrossed.

Nina cleared her throat.

'Um.'

Zoe jumped up, feeling as if she'd been caught doing something she shouldn't.

'Uh, hello,' she said, carefully smoothing the book down and putting it back on the shelf as if she hadn't been seen. 'Um, sorry. I was just ... I didn't know where ...'

'Why didn't you ring the doorbell?' said Nina, still cross with herself but somehow finding herself taking it out on Zoe for the simple fact that Zoe could still see her own toes.

'I wasn't ... I didn't want to ... I mean, isn't that your house?' stammered Zoe, her face a picture of misery.

'Well, obviously.'

'I didn't ... I wasn't sure what the right thing to do was.'

'You didn't phone?'

Zoe held up her cheap pay-as-you-go phone. 'I haven't got a signal here, I'm sorry ... I really am sorry. I didn't ...'

Nina shrugged.

'Don't worry about it now. Let's get moving. Have you been to see the nursery yet?'

'No, I thought ...'

The fact was, Zoe was terrified of visiting the nursery. Having to explain everything. Getting a doctor's note. Whether Hari would be unbearably miserable and she wouldn't be able to help or do anything about it at all.

As she looked out over the fields and the low threatening clouds, though, she felt incredibly alone.

'I thought we'd settle in for a day or so ... is that okay?'

Nina sniffed and looked at the little boy.

'Just ... no food in the van, okay?'

'Of course,' said Zoe quickly. 'Honestly, he's very good. I'll keep him out of the way.'

'Okay,' said Nina. She sighed. 'I suppose I'll have to work it out myself soon. But I'm sure I'll just be able to bring the buggy and stick it in the corner.'

Zoe couldn't help it: she let out a little laugh that she desperately tried to turn in to a cough.

'What?' said Nina, suspicious.

'Nothing!' said Zoe. 'It's just ... it can be quite tricky when they're in their buggies.'

'They just lie there, don't they?' said Nina.

'Well, some do,' said Zoe. Nina felt prickly. She was being helpful here; she didn't need Zoe being all superior about her motherhood experiences.

'Well,' said Zoe, after a slightly awkward pause. 'Can I get started?'

Nina drove them down to the post office, where several new boxes were waiting. She smiled broadly.

'Oh yes,' she said, looking up. 'A nice house clearance. Lots of new books bought but never read.'

She sighed. 'It's sad really.'

'You're bringing them back to life,' said Zoe, trying to be encouraging, and because she felt they'd rather got off on the wrong foot.

'I hope so,' said Nina. 'But it's still sad ... thinking you have all the time in the world to read!'

'You're about to have even less!' said Zoe merrily, then wished with all her heart that she'd bitten her tongue as Nina's face clouded over again. She'd only been making a joke; Nina seemed to think that instead she was giving her childrearing advice every two seconds.

'Although,' Zoe added quickly, 'you know you can read while you're breastfeeding.'

Nina blinked.

'Really?'

96

'Totally! You need a pillow, then it's a cinch.'

'You don't lean the book on the baby's head?'

'No!' said Zoe. 'Well. Only kind of resting at an angle. They'll be eating; they won't mind.'

Nina frowned again and they carried on unpacking in silence. Ignored, Hari climbed inside one of the boxes and pretended to be driving a boat. He was highly disappointed to be near water and not going on one. It was his dream. He'd never been on a boat. Only the bus, and when they would cross from north to south London from time to time, he would stare down at the busy river, fascinated.

Zoe was completely unaware of this. His pictures of boats just looked like long outlines. In fact, she thought he was doing lovely drawings of snakes and worms and had instead taken him to a discount day at the butterfly park where he had been draped in snakes and photographed without looking particularly pleased or distressed about it either way.

Nina perked up as she unearthed more treasure in the box: untouched hardbacks and a beautifully illustrated *Peter Pan*.

'I get half my stock like this,' she said, expertly repacking the books she didn't want to send on to a second-hand dealer. 'Then the rest is new books from wholesalers. You'll need to unpack and check them off the box. It's tricky because we order so small, but they're really good. Do you think you can manage that?'

Zoe nodded, then as she was lifting the discarded box away she frowned and fished something out. It was a small, rather plain pale pink cloth-covered novel in beautiful condition, with no title save a little pair of ballet shoes on the front.

She opened it carefully. Sure enough, it was a very early edition of the Noel Streatfeild classic, complete with full colour plates and line drawings. It smelled very faintly of old polish and deep wood, but it was in flawless condition. There wasn't even a badly scrawled name in the frontispiece, but rather a beautiful gold ex-libris plate inscribed, 'To Lady Violet Greene, best wishes, Mary.'

The book was utterly beautiful.

'Um, Nina,' said Zoe, not wanting to get above herself. 'I mean, just so I'm sure about how you organise things and so on … I just don't quite get it … sorry, why don't you want this?'

Nina looked up, ready to explain a few things to Zoe about the book business.

Nina was not a vain person in any way shape or form, but the one thing she did know, the one thing she was sure about, was books. Books she loved. Books that changed her. Books that may not be the best written, but stayed with her. Books that would leave people cold with fear, or stir the blood, or make sad people laugh and forget their troubles just for a little while. She knew books. So she was going to have to explain to Zoe that it was something deep in the bone; a feeling, a sense you had for what books would come into your life one day and be your friend for ever.

'Well,' she began. 'The thing you have to understand is …'

Then she saw what Zoe was holding.

'Oh,' she said. And she took it with reverence. 'Oh, look at this.'

She unfolded the first page and gasped.

'Oh my goodness,' she said. 'I must have baby brain. I must …'

She was furious with herself.

'I think … You know Noel Streatfeild's real name was Mary?' she said. She googled quickly and sure enough, the handwriting was the same.

'Signed by the author!' she said, whistling through her teeth. She looked up at Zoe, feeling embarrassed.

'Good catch,' she said.

'I loved it so much,' said Zoe.

'Me too,' said Nina, wishing she could take it with her, head back to bed, sleep even more and start the day over again.

Chapter Thirteen

They pulled up into the centre of Kirrinfief, seeing as that was where they were expected most Wednesday mornings and it would be a chance for Zoe to meet the customers and maybe pop into the nursery. Zoe went round with the duster – she'd vacuumed the van back at the farm, and Nina was already aware of how helpful this was going to be, especially as Zoe stretched up to get to the top shelves that Nina had been finding more and more difficult. It felt like every time she remembered where her centre of gravity was, she lost it again.

Zoe suddenly felt terribly nervous. Despite the fact that she'd had a baby a few years ago now she hadn't exactly gone back to her old wardrobe. The odd thing was, she *weighed* the same. It just seemed to be distributed in totally different places. And it was tricky, not working as well as not having any money. She'd gone to Primark and bought a plain black top and black trousers and was trying to accessorise with a floaty scarf of her mother's, but was definitely thinking she was not a floaty scarf type of person, and if you're not a floaty scarf type of a person, all a floaty scarf does is annoy you and get in your way, sometimes even getting in your mouth or sticking to your lip gloss, so eventually she took it off and Hari snaffled it to use as a captain's scarf on his boat.

'Oh look,' said Zoe. 'He's pretending to have his own pet snake. He's obsessed with them.'

Nina smiled politely.

'Do I look all right?' said Zoe. Nina glanced up. She'd had to change her wardrobe considerably after moving to Scotland, and everything generally now consisted of several thin layers piled up and then occasionally dragged off in a tearing hurry when the sun came out, topped off with a bright yellow mackintosh she adored and Lennox thought was hilarious. Although he liked it as, even when he was up striding on the hills, he could spot her from miles off. Now it was the stretchiest T-shirts she could find, all of which were incredibly stretched. The mac still just about fitted though.

She glanced up.

'Yes, you look fine,' she said, barely looking up. Then, spotting Zoe's face, said, 'You'll be fine. Honestly, everyone's really nice.'

Zoe smiled bravely.

'Good!' she said, and Nina opened the back door of the van.

Outside, the clouds were scudding across the sky, and Zoe briefly paused just to watch them. In London, she never noticed the sky. It was full of cranes, of towers that appeared out of nowhere, great big empty glass boxes in the sky, waiting for goodness knows who to live there.

Here it looked as if the sky was perpetually washing itself clean; as if completely changing itself was as easy as shaking an Etch A Sketch. Every time she looked up, it seemed completely different. She felt her fingertips tingle. She glanced back. Hari was fine in the cab, looking at the book that was almost certainly going to come out of her first wage packet. Well. Here she went. She took a deep breath as Nina put the blocks on the wheels, pushed open the door and changed the closed sign to open. She shot Nina a look, hoping to get an encouraging smile, but Nina was already looking down the road.

The first customer advanced slowly, at a steady pace. She

was an older woman, with tiny bifocals attached to her by a long chain around her neck, and she wore a slightly disapproving look on her face.

'Um, hello,' said Zoe as she mounted the steps. The woman looked at her, then looked at Nina.

'Who's this?' she announced loudly.

Nina sighed. Of course the first customer would be the trickiest. Of course it would. Mrs Wren, feared matriarch of Wren Dairies, who ran it with a rod of iron and gave fairly short shrift to super-markets, milk drinkers, lactose intolerant people, local shops, juice drinkers and in fact pretty much everyone in the world who wasn't a cow. She pretended to only like books about cows but in fact could easily be directed to the most raucous bodice-rippers Nina had at any time and Nina kept a stock of these in for just this reason, even though, had anyone else looked inside them, they'd quickly have realised they'd actually have been better off under the counter.

'Hello, Mrs Wren,' said Nina. 'This is Zoe. She's going to be helping me out while I have the baby.'

Mrs Wren snorted loudly.

'Cows just pop 'em out,' she said. 'Pop 'em out and get on with things.'

Seeing as the two things cows had to get on with was eating grass and giving milk, and the things Nina had to get on with numbered in the several hundreds, Nina didn't answer this, but smiled nicely.

'Ah well, you know,' she said non-commitally.

'Hi,' said Zoe. 'Nice to meet you. Do you know what you're looking for?'

A frosty silence descended. Zoe blinked. She wasn't quite sure what had gone wrong.

'Do you have,' said Mrs Wren finally, 'any new books in? About cows.'

Zoe looked at Nina. She hadn't seen any on the shelves. Inspiration struck her, and she took down a book called *We Are All Completely Beside Ourselves*.

'You might enjoy this,' she said. She had, very much. 'It's not about cows though. It's about a monkey. About a girl who has a monkey for a sister.'

Mrs Weir looked at her fixedly.

'A girl. With a monkey. For a sister,' she said eventually, as if Zoe had recommended a 'How To' book about killing puppies.

'It's very funny,' mumbled Zoe. 'And sad. And it's just ... it's very good.'

Mrs Weir turned to Nina.

'A girl with a monkey for a sister.'

Nina raised her arms. 'Or!' she said, and stretched to an out-of-the-way spot on the very bottom shelf, puffing slightly as she removed a black-coloured book illustrated with an extremely buxom, rather shocked-looking young woman with cascading hair wearing a corset and an enormous pink skirt, being eyed cruelly by a man in period soldier costume. 'I have ... *The Billionaire Earl's Impossible Passion*.'

Zoe screwed up her face.

'Has it got cows in it?' asked Mrs Weir fussily, getting out her wallet.

'He's a billionaire,' said Nina. 'He's got everything.'

'Are they all like that?' said Zoe after she'd gone.

'Nooo,' said Nina rather too quickly, as she'd just spotted Colonel Gregor marching up the street. A spry and well put together figure, he also liked to buy expensive tomes of military history – ideal for Nina; hardbacks were good sales for her – then come along and explain why everything was wrong, sometimes with the help of moving about the stationery she kept on her desk. It was worth it to keep him as a very good customer but Nina wasn't quite sure how to explain this to Zoe.

Instead, she stood watching as the colonel replayed the Peninsular War with her paperclips standing in for the Bourbon soldiers while Zoe hovered awkwardly, which made Nina feel awkward too, until the Crombie twins, Bethan and Ethan, came in and immediately started causing havoc, particularly when they found a small boy in the back of the van.

'CAN WE KEEP HIM?' shouted Ethan when Hari declined to answer their original question.

'I don't think they sell boys,' said the weary but sweet Kirsty Crombie, who taught at the local school. 'Hello! Are you new? Is he yours?'

Zoe grinned. 'Yes, he is.'

'Ooh lovely, always nice to see a new face. Hello, little man. What's your name?'

Hari blinked appreciatively.

'He's a late speaker,' said Zoe quickly, as usual.

'Oh right ... Will he go to school here?'

'I don't know ... It's all a bit new.'

'Okay! Where are you staying?'

'Up at The Beeches.'

A deathly silence descended.

Kirsty looked at Nina, who pretended to be very busy looking for Kirsty's usual, which tended towards manuals about how to get out of teaching, life after teaching and who needs teaching anyway. If you asked Kirsty if she liked being a teacher, she would say she absolutely loved it, apart from the kids, the admin, the marking, the other teachers, the government, the hours and the money.

'Um ... whose idea was that?'

Zoe glanced at Hari, but he didn't seem too upset being inspected in his box.

'Oh, Nina set me up there.'

'*Did* she?' said Kirsty, as Nina went bright puce. 'And how are you finding it?'

'Well, I've just arrived ...'

'Kirsty's the headteacher,' said Nina, trying to deflect attention.

'Oh!' said Zoe. 'Why aren't they at school? When can they go back?'

Kirsty sighed.

'They're excluded. Until half-term, I'm afraid. The daughter got in ... well. Of course I can't really discuss it.'

'MARY URQUART BIT AND KICKED STEPHANIE GILLIES!' shouted Bethan from the back of the shop. 'SHE HAD TO GET STITCHES!'

'AND SHACKLETON TOO!'

'SHE is SO mean,' said Bethan, looking like a tiny old lady passing gossip over the garden fence. She shook her head sadly. 'Mean, mean, mean.'

'It's ... everybody realises it isn't easy for the Urquart kids,' said Kirsty. 'But I've sent plenty of work home. Um. Good luck.'

'Thank you,' said Zoe awkwardly as Kirsty bought *Topsy and Tim Go to Hospital*.

'Stephanie Gillies had to go to the hospital,' observed Bethan loudly. 'For all the stitches.'

They were still discussing it as they headed down the street.

Zoe turned to Nina.

'You knew about this?'

'I genuinely didn't,' said Nina. 'I'm sorry ... I knew they were troublesome but ... '

'Hari is only four,' said Zoe. 'What if she bites him?'

Nina cringed.

'It's a big house,' she said. 'Maybe keep them apart?'

'Oh good,' said Zoe. 'Perhaps I can lock him up in one wing.'

Chapter Fourteen

There was a distinct *froideur* in the van after that, and Zoe was quite happy to escape to go examine the nursery, her mind working furiously. Lots of kids bit, she told herself. Perhaps not nine-year-olds but ... She thought of the look of terrible disdain on Mary's face for a moment. Well. At least Hari never liked being out of her sight, that was one thing. And perhaps the nursery would be amazing ...

She followed Nina's directions. It is hard to get lost in Kirrinfief. There is the central cobbled square, with Wullie's pub and the war memorial and the irregularly frequented bus stop and a little park with wildflower beds (the council ordered it to try and save some bees. Every year a child gets stung and there is a bit of a kerfuffle about bee management, but so far the bees are winning out, and the wildflowers do look very pretty).

Four streets go off the square – two up, two down. Downwards leads south towards the loch, and much of the housing – mostly single-storey grey cottages connected to each other in the old style, even if their thatched roofs are long gone, and many have dormers – go up in zig-zags, higher and higher up the side of the hill, so that nearly everyone has a view over the loch and down into the ever-changing valley with the long shining railway line. It also means everyone has a bit of a clamber to get home from the shops, but that can't be helped and is probably doing you good.

The nursery, however, is downhill, just next to the school. It was a small low building originally built as a community centre that now spends most of the day as the centre of a small typhoon, and is used in the evenings for a variety of purposes, including puppy training classes. Not a few mums and dads arrive late for pick-up and wonder why they can't use some of the puppy training rules on their own offspring.

The centre is run by a woman called Tara, who was a type Zoe knew very well from childminding herself: commanding of voice, elaborate in her condescension to very small children and almost completely ineffectual at all times. She was wearing a purple pinafore and a bright pink scarf with dangly silver bits tied round her hair.

Sure enough, inside the nursery was havoc; a blur of tiny people charging up and down.

'YOU'RE ENGLISH!' boomed Tara. 'WELCOME! I *sound* English, but my heart and passion are here, in the bonny Highlands of my homeland.'

She did, Zoe thought, sound very much like she came from Surrey.

'Now, here, we like our children to have freedom to express themselves.'

Out of the corner of her eye, Zoe saw a boy of about three – but very large and sturdy – expressing himself by hitting another child repeatedly on the head with a toy car.

Tara gave Zoe a pitying look and knelt down to the child's level.

'Now, Rory,' she said in what she plainly felt was a very charming voice. 'Are you feeling bad today? Is that why you're using the car in a non-kind way?'

Rory simply growled in response and snatched back the car.

'Would you like to just hand me over the car and let me keep it for now?'

Rory would not like to do that. Meanwhile, the child who had been whacked was still crying quietly and being completely ignored as Tara wheedled with his tormentor. Zoe closed her eyes and

106

contemplated whether or not a village the size of Kirrinfief was likely to support another nursery.

She concluded: not.

Hari was clinging onto her hand in a way she knew meant 'get me out of here at once'.

'Well, I shall let you have the car just the once, my darling,' said Tara to a still mutinous-looking Rory. 'As long as you promise to be nice with it!'

Rory promised no such thing as Tara swept on.

'We do painting over here,' she said, coming to a corner that was utterly covered in paint splashes. A harassed-looking younger woman looked up, shadows under her eyes.

'Ah, Tara, have you got a minute ...?'

'Just showing round a new parent!' trilled Tara. 'Showing them our wonderful community spirit! And happy environment!'

There was definitely an echo of a warning tone underpinning Tara's words, and the woman went back to trying to separate some girls who were splattering each other's hair with poster paint.

Zoe would have run out of there in a minute; in a second.

But then she glanced out of the huge window at the back of the building. It overlooked the garden.

There was something they called a garden in the nursery in London, but space was at such a premium, it was really a tiny terrace with a few tricycles and a strip of grass that occasionally yielded one snowball if it snowed, which it never did. Sometimes they would bundle the children up in rows of triple buggies and take them across the road to the neglected little corner park, constantly terrified in case any of them got hit by a car or stolen, all of them in tiny hi-vis jackets. And that had been an expensive, exclusive nursery.

Here, there was a vast lawn leading to a high stone wall at the end. Even though the day wasn't particularly warm, a clutch of small children was charging around, being nominally supervised by a young woman staring at her phone. They were jumping, laughing and throwing themselves in and out of a huge sandpit with complete and utter freedom. Two little girls were sitting, trying to make daisy chains. One boy was halfway up a low tree, swinging upside down on his little legs, laughing uproariously.

Zoe froze, staring at it, then looked back at Hari, who was hiding behind her knees in absolute terror.

It felt awful; almost cruel. But he needed this. He needed it.

Tara led Zoe into a large, well-proportioned office at the end of the hall and shut the door.

'This is where I come for a little peace and quiet!' she tittered. 'Not that I don't love the little things. Each and every one of them. Now. Do you have your council papers?'

Suddenly she was all business. Zoe had emailed her in advance, cutting and pasting the information from the outpatient letters about Hari's diagnosis.

'You have to fill this in so the government can reimburse us. We're *so* excited he's disabled! Does he have a SEN?'

'No,' said Zoe. 'But he has elective mutism.'

Tara donned a pair of bright red spectacles and tilted her head to one side.

'You know,' she said. 'We don't call it that any more.'

'I realise that,' said Zoe stonily. 'But he's not selectively mute. He never speaks at all.'

'Well, we'll have to write selective mutism on the form.'

Zoe curled up her fingers very tightly and pasted a fake neutral expression on her face.

Hari stared at her. Zoe's heart dropped at the thought of having to leave him to the mercy of every other child running about. But then, she thought, all parents felt that way leaving their children at nursery. They must do. Surely.

'And,' whispered Tara confidentially, 'I believe I already know your address. Am I right?'

Zoe nodded. Tara's face lit up.

'Tell me,' she said. 'What's it like? What's he like? Have you seen

Ramsay? How is he doing? That poor man. Such a disaster when she ran off. Left everything. That big house. Those lovely children. I mean. How *could* you? As a mother?'

'I've only seen him briefly,' said Zoe.

'Such a tragedy. Well, so they say. I mean, nobody knows. I mean, are her *clothes* still there?'

Her head was still tilted. 'And how are those little mites? You know they never came here. I never understood it – why they wouldn't be better off in a wonderful creative environment like the one we have here. *We* could have loved them as a family. I love all the children here like family.'

Zoe smiled.

'Well,' she said. Then she decided the best thing to do would be to lie. 'Everything's fine,' she said. 'When can I start Hari?'

'Tomorrow morning will be fine,' said Tara. 'It's strange, you know, we seem to have lost some children recently. Well, these things do happen!'

And they walked out, through the chaos, Hari squeezing her hand so tightly it hurt. Zoe thought how she had to now head back to the big house, with its apparently violent inmates, and attempt to cook everybody supper.

It had been a long day already.

Chapter Fifteen

Zoe couldn't believe it when she walked into the kitchen. It was as if nobody had moved all day. The place was a mess. Shackleton was grunting into a headset and playing an ancient food-spattered Xbox at high volume. His language was . . . colourful. Mary was screeching about something down the phone, and Patrick was reading out loud from his tablet in a voice meant to cover up the noise of the other two. The radio was playing at an absolutely punishing volume and she couldn't see Mrs MacGlone at all. Then her vision cleared a little and she saw that there was someone in the laundry room pulling down a heavy and peculiar pulley system that had clothes drying on it.

'Um, I'm back,' said Zoe.

Mrs MacGlone let the laundry pulley drop with a thud.

'Thank the lord,' she said, pulling on her coat and arranging her scarf and hat. No 'good to see you' or 'how was your first day'.

'How are they?'

Mrs MacGlone shrugged.

'That's not my job,' she said, and was out the back door before Zoe had her own coat off.

'Good riddance, you old witch,' shouted Mary behind her, and the other two laughed.

'Oh good,' said Zoe, who would have given a lot of money right then to be back in her horrible bedsit, unpleasant as it was, getting ready to eat own brand beans on toast and cuddle up with Hari in front of *Paw Patrol*.

She could cook – her own mum had been a good household cook; a single mum like herself, she'd had to make a little go a long way and was convinced her daughter should learn likewise – until, of course, her daughter went to university, got a fabulous career and hooked a wonderfully rich man. Sadie had done her best, from Spain, never to betray how sad she was about Zoe's circumstances. But she hadn't had to: mother and daughter could read each other perfectly.

And heading back to bed wasn't, Zoe thought, how Sadie would have tackled things. She'd have unleashed the frying pan and said 'come on, me luvvie, let's see what we got 'ere' just as she was now doing for holidaymakers in Spain who wanted a full English, and were even happier when it came from a proper cockney.

She marched into the kitchen and started peering into cupboards.

There was absolutely nothing there. Not that the cupboards were bare; far from it. They were well stocked, just not with anything she would call dinner. There was jam, lots of bread, packets of crisps, rice cakes. There was fruit in the fruit bowl, and boxes and boxes of cereal. Nobody was starving the children.

But. There were no stock cubes. No tinned tomatoes. No onions, no mince, no pasta. Nothing she would consider to be dinner material.

Maybe there was another kitchen? The house was definitely big enough to have two.

'Um, Shackleton?' she said, but he only grunted, and she realised she should ask Patrick. 'Patrick, where's all the food?'

Patrick looked at her.

'That is absolutely all the food, Nanny Seven!' he said.

'What do you mean?' said Zoe. 'What do you eat?'

Patrick frowned.

'Toast' he began, counting out on his fingers. 'Apples. Bananas.

Sausages. Peanut butter. Tomatoes. Ginger biscuits. Bran flakes. Rhubarb. Crisps. Celery.'

'That can't be true.'

Zoe stared at them in disbelief. Patrick furrowed his little brow.

'Um,' he said. 'And . . .'

Mary rolled her eyes.

'You forgot *cheese triangles*,' she hissed.

'Cheese triangles!' said Patrick triumphantly. 'The end.'

Zoe shook her head in disbelief.

'But Mrs MacGlone . . .'

The children all made gagging noises.

'NEVER eat what Mrs MacGlone makes,' intoned Patrick in a deadly serious voice. 'It's poison, Nanny Seven. Poison.'

'And what about the other nannies you had?'

'They were mostly crying.'

'Or they just let us eat toast, they didn't care,' said Shackleton stolidly. 'Which is fine by us. We should just do that.'

Zoe blinked. On balance, their diet, she supposed, would just about keep them from scurvy. But beyond that . . . what on earth was their father thinking?

'Well,' she said. 'Why don't we make that change today?'

'Because toast and peanut butter is very nice, Nanny Seven?'

Zoe almost jumped in and asked what their mother had cooked for them before and managed to stop herself just in time. Just before she'd got back to The Beeches, she'd googled the family madly and found nothing beyond a piece on a music event that had been held in the grounds ten years ago. She'd gazed at the tiny, low resolution photographs for ages and had thought she might have spotted a woman with a baby in her arms, but it was truly impossible to tell.

'Well,' she said instead, rolling up her sleeves. 'Let's get started. Have you got any cheese that *isn't* triangular?'

Eventually she rounded up some fish in the freezer that 'Wilby brought us in the summertime' which was going to have to do, with some very old breadcrumbs at the back of the store cupboard, some old, soft potatoes that could have oil poured on them and crisped up as wedges and some frozen peas, literally scraping the bottom of the barrel, or in this case the freezer.

Then she tried to work out how to turn on an oven that seemed half electric and half gas, and needed to be lit with matches in a terrifying *whoof.*

'I'm not eating any of that,' Mary had said, arms folded.

'You don't know what it is yet,' said Zoe patiently.

'Well, you've touched it, so . . . '

'I'm just making some toast,' said Shackleton.

'No, don't do that please,' said Zoe, her face going red. 'I think you've had quite enough . . . '

'Who cares what you think?'

'Please I will absolutely have some toast.' Patrick popped up and Zoe realised to her exasperation that Hari was standing right next to him, nodding his head and pointing to his mouth quite emphatically.

'Nobody is having any more bloody toast!' said Zoe, conscious that the fish was burning on one side while still looking frozen on the other. The smell was not fantastic.

'Oh, so you're just going to let us starve?'

'I don't think you'll starve,' hissed Zoe, concentrating.

'Ouch!'

They all turned round, as the large shape of Ramsay appeared at the kitchen door. He had bumped his head on the door frame. Zoe squinted. He couldn't come in the kitchen very often if he didn't know how high the door frame was. She mentally went over what she'd just said. She thought she might have threatened to starve the children to death. Not ideal. He stood there, looking awkward. And he was absurdly tall – how did he even get about? Zoe blinked. She was all alone in this house with a man she didn't know, whose wife had disappeared, whom Nina didn't appear to know anything about . . .

'DADDY!' yelled Patrick, flinging his arms around the man's knees. He wasn't a small child, but he only came up to just above knee height.

'Hello, little man,' said Ramsay, bending down and rubbing his head. 'What is your best fact about dinosaurs today?'

'Dinosaurs could reach the length of seven London buses,' said Patrick promptly. 'What's a London bus?'

'Long story,' said Ramsay, hauling the boy up. 'Hey, Mary,' he said, coming forward to the girl and tentatively putting his big hand on her hair. She immediately stiffened and pulled away, looking in the other direction. Zoe watched.

'Where's Mrs MacGlone?'

'She's gone home,' said Mary sulkily. 'She just left *her*.'

'Don't say "her",' said Ramsay instinctively. 'Say ...' It was no use: he had completely forgotten.

'Say Nanny Seven actually!' said Patrick.

'No, don't say that either,' said Ramsay.

'Sorry, I have to ask ...' said Zoe, cutting this line of conversation off, 'what do you eat?'

'What, me personally?' said Ramsay, as if she'd asked him if he ate grass.

'Well, all of you.'

'Oh,' said Ramsay, looking slightly shifty. 'Is this about the peanut butter?'

'She going to try and change things,' said Mary. 'It's always funny, this bit.'

'Mary, hush,' said her father. He ran his hands through his hair. 'Mrs MacGlone says not all battles are worth fighting.'

Zoe was already of the opinion that Ramsay was not fighting a single battle, but certainly wasn't going to start in on that.

'Something is most absolutely smelling bad bad bad,' came a small voice, and she dashed over to the cooker.

She looked at the fish in the pan. It was completely ruined.

'Oh no. I'm sorry, there's no tea.'

'We've run out of tea?' Ramsay looked confused. 'There's money in the ...'

'She means supper,' said Mary loftily. 'She doesn't know what it's called. She calls it "toilet" too.'

Zoe flushed.

'I'm ... this oven is really hard to work, you know?'

114

Now it was Ramsay's turn to looked embarrassed.

'Uh . . . oh. Is it?'

Shackleton got up wordlessly and headed for the toaster. Patrick cheered and Hari joined him in cheerfully jumping up and down.

Ramsay hadn't stayed for long. He seemed, Zoe thought, oddly disconnected from the children, as if he'd just come across them living in his house. He'd taken some fruit on a plate and vanished again, back into the deep silent hallways of the house; she wondered where he went. In the front wing, she supposed, whereas of course she was confined to servants' quarters.

She cleaned up the crumbs as best she could and picked up a visibly drooping Hari.

'Do you have bedtimes?' she said, already knowing the answer. Mary simply snorted.

'No!' said Patrick. 'Good night, Nanny Seven.'

And having had absolutely enough of this peculiar little household to argue, she waved vaguely in their general direction, left them to it and headed to bed, laying down Hari and dreaming of nothing more than a hot bath then total oblivion. She kept both her bedroom door and the bathroom door open. She would be utterly amazed if Mary had ever been up here, but she wanted to keep on the safe side, even if it was a little eerie taking her clothes off with the pitch-dark corridor outside and the pipes gurgling.

Zoe had been – was – poor. Proper poor. She'd fed her electricity meter with a top-up card; she'd had to think about every kettle she'd ever boiled.

But she'd been able to have a bath more or less whenever she wanted. As the cold, clear water trickled out of the tap, it was the final straw. She collapsed by the side of the bath, muffled her mouth with a towel, and cried and cried and cried.

115

Chapter Sixteen

You can't cry for ever, although Zoe had a pretty good try. Eventually she was simply too exhausted and lay face down on the bed next to Hari, whose steady snuffling breaths she fell into a rhythm with, until she too drifted off, utterly wrung out and worn out.

She woke without knowing where she was once again. It was just so quiet. You couldn't hear a single thing; it was like sleeping underground. Hari had stirred. She picked up the little boy and took him to the bathroom. He must be starving too.

The old curtains were heavy with dust – the place needed a good sweep out, it weighed you down. She pulled them apart and grinned wryly. Everything may feel terrible – no, she corrected herself. Everything *was* terrible. She was in a strange country with strange people and couldn't do a single thing about it and nobody liked her and some actively hated her and she was working two jobs, neither of them particularly successfully so far.

There was also the odd patrons of the bookshop; Nina's slight awkwardness, which rather put paid to Surinder's insistence that Nina was absolutely desperate for her to come and help; and oh my God, today she would have to leave Hari at that nursery. Zoe screwed up her face.

But out of the window – which badly needed washing but even so – the view was, she had to admit, utterly and completely beguiling.

The morning haar off the loch made the sunrise look abstract and pastel, hazily smudging the pink and gold on the horizon, giving everything the soft outlines of a watercolour. Zoe suddenly found herself wishing she could paint. She pulled Hari up in his fireman pyjamas, which were far too small for him, and showed him the window. His mouth opened in a round O and he pointed to the water.

'Isn't it beautiful?' she said to him, leaning his dark curls against her face. Even with everything else gone, she still had this. 'Isn't it beautiful?'

Nina was eating her second breakfast, feeling exasperated.

'No, she's nice,' she was saying, as Lennox looked perturbed at her bad mood.

'So . . .' he said.

'So . . . oh, I don't know. She's just so *London*. I don't know if she's going to understand how people are here.'

'Well, you could say you were very Birmingham,' said Lennox, smiling.

'Hmmm,' said Nina. 'Anyway, I don't think we're the problem. I think maybe that other job is a total nightmare and she's going to leave us and it won't matter whether or not she understands what people want in the bookshop and I'll be even more stuck than before.'

She sighed. She felt absolutely awful this morning, but Lennox had enough to do and she wasn't going to worry him. Lennox took her in his arms and looked down on her, smiling.

'Well, we'd figure out something else,' he said in the reliable slow way she generally adored, except this morning when she was irritable and not very good at being placated.

Nina buried her head in his chest.

'Why does everything have to change?'

Lennox gesticulated outside. 'Because life changes. The seasons change. The world turns round. Old things become new . . . '

He stroked her bump.

'New things . . . good new things.'

'I know,' said Nina crossly. 'I know all that. I just feel so . . . *lumpy*.'

'You've never been lovelier,' said Lennox honestly. 'But everything changes.'

'Except you,' said Nina, somewhat comforted.

'Aye,' said Lennox, still standing there holding her, steady as a tree. 'Except me.'

Chapter Seventeen

At least if you woke up early enough, Zoe was to discover fast, you finally got the hot water. Feeling not remotely in the mood to be generous, she filled a bath as deep as she could manage and sat in it for ten minutes on her own, breathing in the scalding steam and luxuriating before it cooled enough for Hari to be able to get in it.

After that, she felt slightly better. Then bad for taking so much of the hot water. Perhaps Patrick could use the bath after her (she suggested this to Patrick, who was very much of the opinion that in fact not having a bath at all was the kindest thing to do for Patrick).

Mrs MacGlone was back, thank goodness, looking surprised to find out nobody had burned the house down at night.

'You shouldnae use that stove,' she said. 'It's no' safe.'

'But how can I cook for the children?'

'Och, they dinnae care. Perfectly happy with bananas.'

She took off her coat.

'Right. Better get on. It's a chandelier day, and I've got the ball-room fireplace to sweep.'

Zoe watched her go. She guessed – rightly, as it happens – that Mrs MacGlone had been there a long time (she underestimated the time frame however: Mrs MacGlone had been there since she was fourteen years old) and that she might as well try to change the weather. The housekeeping money was kept in a biscuit box – Zoe was to help herself for shopping, then she'd get a cheque at the end of every month to get paid. Zoe hadn't seen a cheque for years. She'd suggested direct debit and Mrs MacGlone had looked at her as if she'd suggested being paid in bitcoin, so she'd said that a cheque would be fine, even though she appeared to be an extremely long way from the nearest bank.

The children were still in the kitchen, still in tatty clothes, still attached to their devices, and Zoe wondered if they'd been to bed at all.

She was picking up the heavy kettle when she nearly got knocked off her feet by something gigantic and shaggy that appeared to have materialised out of nowhere. She got more of a fright than she realised and might have made a noise out loud – Mary sneered spitefully as she jumped.

'Porteous!' yelled Patrick, leaping up from his chair and bounding over to the Hairy Maclary-style beast, a dog who had so much fuzz in front of his face it was hard to tell which way his head was looking, and some rather splendid dreadlocks tumbling down the back of his enormous head. Zoe blinked. It couldn't be, but he rather looked like he was bouncing about in a black cloud of dust, like Pig-Pen. Mrs MacGlone seemed completely unperturbed.

'Thanks for coming back, Porteous,' said Patrick cheerfully getting a reasonably white T-shirt substantially un-white again.

Hari leapt up and clung to Zoe's knees in an unwieldy fashion.

'Is this your dog?' said Zoe. 'I didn't know you had a dog.'

She wasn't very used to dogs and moved back a little bit. Her neighbours had had a large angry-looking Staffie and she was permanently just a tiny bit frightened of the dog running up the stairs and tearing Hari limb from limb despite the owners insisting that

Sabre was perfectly friendly and just wrestling and having a bit of a jolly tussle whenever he saw the baby.

Zoe had tried to believe this and was sure it was true and had heard lots of good things about how Staffies were just wonderful dogs and she normally liked dogs, but she couldn't deny that at the base of it, she saw the dog's incredibly powerful jaws, and how it growled whenever they passed in the hall, and couldn't help, even subliminally, showing her fear to her son. Hari therefore was totally and utterly terrified of all dogs, however much Zoe tried to encourage the patting of clearly benign pups in the park; the sweet greyhounds down the end of the street; her friend Mindy's cockerpoo. None of this worked. Hari started to shake at the very sight of a tail. It was, Zoe often reflected, yet another way in which she appeared to be failing her own child.

'Of course!' said Patrick. 'He is absolutely my dog.'

And he thrust his hands around the beast's neck, who sat there, panting happily. Zoe noticed that he had toast crumbs around his chops. This was ridiculous. The entire household was addicted to gluten.

'He's *not* your dog.'

Mary was looking dramatic this morning, her long dark hair fluttering behind her, wearing her little white nightgown. Zoe thought that little girls living in big houses shouldn't wear white nightdresses. It was just spooky, especially with the dark shadows underneath her eyes and strained expression.

'Morning, Mary!' said Zoe, trying to start with a blank slate. 'Did you get some sleep?'

Mary looked right through her and walked into the kitchen on silent bare feet which didn't in the slightest make her look less like a ghost. She stood by the back door, then passed through it into the misty morning beyond, her feet leaving wet footprints in the overlong dewy grass out into the back meadow. Zoe watched her go sadly.

'Well,' said Zoe. 'Hmm. Is she going to meet friends?'

'We haven't got any friends,' said Patrick loudly, not sounding remotely bothered. He bent down. 'Except Porteous who loves me.'

'Get that beast out of here,' said Mrs MacGlone. 'He's mucky.'

'So he's not your dog?'

'He belongs to Wilby, the gardener. Patrick got the wrong end of the stick and now ...'

'I LOVE YOU SO MUCH, MY DOGGO.'

Hari inched forwards.

'Would you like to meet my doggo?'

Patrick had reached up to the table and grabbed another piece of toast, which Porteous was slobbering over. Hari took another step forward. Zoe watched, fascinated and slightly amazed. Hari still had one hand on her jeans, but his other was stretched out.

'He's the BEST doggo,' said Patrick. Hari blinked as Patrick handed him a bit of toast to offer him. Everyone in the kitchen went quiet as Hari very slowly, and with a trembling hand, extended his little fingers with the toast in it.

Zoe held her breath as Porteous turned his mighty shaggy head and, with a great gulp, swallowed up the slice with a lick of his tongue and a smacking noise, and Hari jumped with surprise, and then – a very rare sound indeed – made a little barking noise that Zoe alone recognised was a laugh. She gasped and picked him up and kissed him on the top of his head, even as he wriggled to get free.

Chapter Eighteen

'You know,' Zoe said, still buoyed as she got ready to leave, 'I could probably put Patrick in the nursery too. I'm sure they have places.'

It would be nice for Hari to have someone, she thought Mrs MacGlone shrugged.

'I don't think the maister would hold with that,' she said. 'Too much . . .'

Zoe blinked. She didn't know what Mrs MacGlone meant.

'Too much . . . speculation.' Mrs MacGlone said the last word very quietly, shooting a warning look at Patrick. 'We've already had enough trouble at the school.'

'Well, they'll have to go back to school,' said Zoe. 'Can I ask . . .?' she continued, deciding to launch into it head on. Patrick and Hari were now chasing Porteous round the kitchen table, making the most extraordinary racket. Shackleton would occasionally put a leg out and try and trip Patrick, who would kick him fiercely.

'You may not,' said Mrs MacGlone, pursing her lips. 'I don't encourage gossip or speculation, Miss O'Connell. We have enough chatterboxes through this house.'

She marched out of the kitchen carrying a tin of Brasso and a pile of old newspapers.

'It upsets them,' she said as she passed Zoe. 'Can't you see that? It would upset anyone. And the maister won't like it. Not one bit. You want to stay here, you mind your business.'

Still, Zoe's spirits were still higher than the previous day as she bounced down the road with Hari, even after they passed Mary in the long grass, wandering along by herself, down to the foot of the water. Zoe watched her. It would never occur to Mary, she knew, that a terrible grown-up such as herself could understand exactly what she was going through – loneliness and loss. She watched as the girl picked up a stone, and hurled it, a perfect arc in the misty air, landing in the absolutely motionless loch with a splash she couldn't hear above the noisy little engine of the car.

Driving on, past the coaches pootling into the Loch Ness car park, which made her think that if there was a monster that had survived for hundreds of years, the one thing it would have learned to avoid was a car park full of noisy people looking for it.

To distract herself, she made up silly songs for Hari about dogs that matched the songs playing on the radio. Today she was going to be on point, tidy, helpful and more open with Nina to try and somehow convince her that hiring her hadn't been a terrible case of misguided charity.

She glanced at Hari.

'You're going to love nursery,' she said, feigning an enthusiasm she didn't really feel. 'Honestly. Everyone is going to be so nice to you. I'll make sure that big boy doesn't hurt you.'

Hari looked at her. She couldn't read his expression at all.

'Aha!' shrieked Tara, rushing over. 'It's our beautiful boy who's *so* nice and quiet.'

Zoe grimaced.

'I've sent through the paperwork,' said Tara. 'We'll be getting that extra help in no time! Come in, come in, we've got a coat hook for you ... oh, no, it appears that we don't. Never mind!'

Hari was standing stock-still. Zoe knelt down.

'My darling,' she said, her good mood evaporating. This was ridiculous. People sent their children to nursery every day.

But still. Since he'd been born, he'd been hers, petted and played with. She hadn't had to share him with anyone; only Jaz when he could be bothered to pop in. The rest of the time he had been hers alone, through the good times and the bad – more bad than good, admittedly. But now all she could remember was cosy nights wrapped up reading *Each Peach Pear Plum*; his lazy smiles on cold winter mornings; him sitting up in his high chair sticking his paws out for more pureed plum, or shutting his mouth up tight like a gimlet when it was the turn of broccoli; the way he bounced up and down on the tube; his delighted face when she bent down to rub his nose when he was in the buggy; his tiny snow boots her mother had sent in the coldest winter, which he loved and wanted to wear long after he had grown out of them; the mittens which he had repeatedly pulled off with his teeth, that stretched the elastic as they rolled under the wheels of his buggy.

The whole exhausting, charming, whirl of babyhood they had left behind as surely as they'd got rid of the potty and the second-hand Bumbo they never used and the muslins and the big metal pinging tins of follow-on milk; the tiny plastic spoons and soft cotton hats; the Sudafed and the baby wipes and the sterilised bottles boiling hot from the dishwasher; the tiny sheets with hedgehogs on and the little towel with the hood, where she could wrap him up like a baby bear and play peekaboo, lying in front of the two-bar fire on the cheap rug, blowing raspberries underneath his arms while he giggled and giggled and had no idea at all that the world outside the tiny warm ring of the two of them was a cold place.

'You just have a good cry, dear!' boomed Tara irritatingly, although actually it was a little helpful as Zoe did in fact instantly feel a bit less like crying. He was just ... so little. And defenceless.

As she was thinking this, Rory the monster child stomped up to him again. He was holding a toy boat. Hari stretched his hand out to get it. Rory whacked him with it.

'Rory!' said Tara. 'Here at the Pure Tots Nursery, we don't behave like that towards others. We talk about our feelings and express ourselves.'

'Do you know what?' said Zoe. 'Why don't we try again another time?'

'But it's meditation class this morning!' said Tara.

Zoe felt awful and utterly torn. Then she stared out of the window again, to the garden. This was the right thing. She knew it. She couldn't leave him with those unhappy children at the big house and she couldn't drag him to work every day. She couldn't keep him tethered to her, much as she wanted to.

'Go outside,' she whispered. 'Go outside and play, my darling.'

And so she had to leave without looking at his face, and cried the entire way up to the farm.

Nina, who was feeling rather unwell, was waiting for her anxiously, mostly because she didn't want to do the vacuuming. She frowned.

'How was nursery?'

Zoe grimaced and side-stepped the chicken who didn't appear to have moved from the previous day and ruffled its feathers at her quite aggressively. Zoe quickly rubbed her face with the back of her hand and looked around her. A tall figure was marching up the hill ahead, whistling as a dog bounced about his heels. That must be Nina's other half. How lucky she was.

'Busy day ahead?' she said, shaking herself out of it.

'I hope so.' Nina frowned. She really could have done with another lie-in. 'Normally we go down to Farr, but it's not really season yet – there's a hillwalker's convention in a month or so; we do well with the Wainwrights.'

126

She indicated a pile of walking guides, and Zoe brought them down and started dusting them.

'How do we get tea?' said Zoe.

'Yeah, they're a bit weird about burning water in a moving van,' said Nina.

'Oh yeah. Maybe they *do* have a point,' said Zoe.

'That's okay – the pub lets us use theirs. But I hate herbal tea. I figure I've given up coffee, alcohol, Lemsip and raw cheese; the baby is going to let me have a cup of tea.'

'And sushi,' said Zoe.

'Yeah,' said Nina. 'Not much of a call for that up here.'

'Right,' said Zoe. 'I couldn't afford it anyway. Ooh, have you read ...?'

'Yes,' said Nina.

'You didn't know what I was going to say.'

'I know,' said Nina. 'Just saving time.'

Zoe smiled.

'You didn't know!'

'I did! *Sushi for Beginners*.'

'It wasn't ... oh. Yeah. All right.'

Nina sat up behind the driving seat of the van, stretching her hands out as usual to get them round her bump. Then she thought about it. It wasn't raining, and Lennox didn't have the tractor round. There was room in the yard. She shouted at Flossie but as usual the chicken was too stupid to move, so she got out and picked her up, stuck her muddy claws on what remained of her lap after she'd climbed in the passenger side.

'Okay,' she said. 'You have to learn to drive this thing at some point. Might as well do it now.'

Zoe gulped.

'Really?' she said.

'Well, you just drove here, didn't you? I mean, you clearly *can* drive.'

'I passed my test,' said Zoe, starting to gabble. 'I mean, you know, it's hard to do in London. Well, I couldn't pass it in London actually.

I ended up going down to my friend in Kent because I knew the traffic wouldn't be so horrifying and awful and I wouldn't have to worry quite so much and, okay, it took me a few times and obviously I couldn't really afford to have a car in London, there's no point really, ha, there's so much public transport and . . . '

Nina blinked.

'Please. Tell me you can drive this van.'

'Probably,' said Zoe. 'Do you really have to watch?'

'Yes,' said Nina a little stiffly. 'In case you reverse it into my house.'

'And the chicken will be watching me,' said Zoe, her voice tailing off.

'The chicken isn't watching you,' said Nina. The chicken continued to fix Zoe with its beady eyes. 'Okay,' she conceded. 'It is, but it has absolutely no idea what you're supposed to be doing.'

'That makes two of us,' said Zoe, clambering up into the driver's seat. She seemed very high off the ground. She glanced in the rear-view mirror. There wasn't one.

'There's a full van of books between us and the road,' explained Nina. 'Use your side mirrors.'

Zoe glanced down at the gear stick. It was a huge thing with a white knob on the top.

'That's the gear stick,' said Nina and Zoe tried not to bristle.

'Okay, okay, give me a minute . . . mirror, signal, manoeuvre.' Zoe tried to look in the non-existent rear-view mirror again, then cursed herself.

'I really am flustered,' she said.

'I'm sorry,' said Nina. 'But you'll need me in here to show you where the lights are and stuff.'

'It's really the chicken.'

'Forget about the chicken!'

'Bork!' agreed the chicken.

Going bright red, Zoe tried to chunk the heavy gear stick into reverse. She wasn't quite sure what happened, but it didn't engage and instead the vehicle lurched forwards, bouncing up and down. There was an ominous dropping noise from the back. Nina tried her best not to wince visibly. Trying again, Zoe lurched forwards, deeper into the farmyard mud, causing the back wheels to lose their grip and start to spin.

Nina tried to remember how hard she'd found it herself to drive the van when she'd first got it, and to be more understanding, and then slightly belatedly remembered that when she'd learned to drive it, there wasn't a precious cargo of beautiful books inside it. She blinked hard as Zoe revved the engine even more and a slight smell of burning pervaded the atmosphere.

'Just let me quickly reverse it,' she said, ponderously unbuckling her belt and starting to climb down. She opened the door a little.

'No, it's all right, it's all right, I can do it!' said Zoe, panicking a little. She thrust the gear stick finally into reverse, gunned the accelerator and applied some pressure to the massive steering wheel, which caused the van to jolt backwards and twist itself along the back, which in turn startled the chicken, which in turn fluttered through the half-open window, which in turn made Zoe go 'SHIT, THE CHICKEN!' and pull the wheel around again, which resulted in the van firmly ensconcing itself deep in the mud, and that mud covering itself all up the side of the van.

On the plus side, the chicken was absolutely fine.

Chapter Nineteen

The chicken was fine. Alarmingly, Nina wasn't. Zoe jumped out of the van once she'd finally shut the damn thing down, and charged around to the other side of the vehicle. Nina was looking very pale.

'Oh my God, are you all right? I'm so sorry! I'm so sorry!' said Zoe.

'It's . . .'

Nina screwed up her face a bit.

'Sorry, I just . . . I just . . .'

Nina quickly threw up out of the side door of the van, narrowly avoiding Zoe's shoes, which was a relief as they were the only smart ones she had.

Zoe held her hand.

'You look . . . you really don't look well,' she said. Nina was utterly pale and sweaty-looking. Zoe felt for her pulse. It was racing.

'Could you . . . ? Can I take you to the doctor's?'

'You've stalled the van.'

'I've still got the car,' said Zoe.

'Oh, I'm sure it's nothing. No. Don't . . . don't . . .'

Nina threw up again.

'I just . . . I feel very, very unwell,' she muttered as Zoe handed her a bottle of water. 'I just need sleep, that's all.'

'Probably just a bug,' said the practical Zoe. 'But worth getting checked out.'

'I'm really, really hot,' said Nina. They both stopped for a second as the chicken started to peck at the spew, and Nina groaned deeply. 'Don't get the doctor.'

Zoe was already googling.

'How long have you been feeling bad?'

Nina sighed.

'A while,' she said quietly.

'Why didn't you tell anyone?'

'Because ...'

Nina didn't like the answer. Because she wasn't ready to give up the van. Because she couldn't help resenting Zoe turning up with her cute little perfectly behaved child and taking over her job and her life and had no problem fetching and carrying and had obviously breezed through her own pregnancy while Nina felt she was so clearly and visibly failing at it.

Because she'd been jealous, and because everything she'd had with Lennox had been so perfect, and she couldn't bear it not to be. Because of stupid reasons.

She didn't say anything.

'Well, I'm here now,' said Zoe. 'Do you want me to call your boyfriend?'

Nina shook her head. 'I don't ... I don't want to worry him.'

'If you're not well in your pregnancy, worry everyone!' said Zoe, attempting a smile. 'Seriously. Raise hell.'

Zoe helped her down and was surprised by how shaky and wobbly Nina was.

'I'm sure it's something I ate,' said Nina, feeling sick and panicky and horrible and just desperately wanted to lie down. 'Can I just go to bed? My own bed.'

'Will the doctor come out?' said Zoe, who thought this probably was the best plan of action.

'She will,' said Nina in a faint voice. Zoe led her into the farm-house. Like everyone who went there, she was surprised by how modern and cleanly it was decorated. Nina never had much cause to think kindly about Kate, Lennox's artistic ex, but she always appreciated her wonderful taste.

Feeling slightly odd – but then again, feeling odd and trespassing in other people's houses did seem to be more or less everything Zoe did these days – she helped Nina into bed, found her a pot to throw up in, which Nina immediately obligingly did, made her some proper tea she couldn't keep down and called the local GP's office. She was put through to the doctor, then Nina was put on and after that things moved with fairly alarming speed.

The local doctor, Joan, was an extremely practical woman with short hair, clogs, a peremptory attitude towards humans and a dogged devotion to all animals. She turned up in her dirty hairy SUV with a dog in the back – surely against NHS guidelines – washed her hands, took one look at Nina and called 999.

Then both the girls got very frightened. Nina grabbed Zoe's hand, forgetting entirely that they weren't actually that close, and told her to go and find Lennox, he'd be in the upper field; there wouldn't be a signal.

'Of course,' said Zoe, not even thinking about her shoes. She ran to the door then turned back.

'What does he look like?'

'He's the really gorgeous one,' said Nina her face pale and sweaty.

'Um, okay,' said Zoe.

'Lanky lugs with sandy hair,' said Dr Joan, who had picked up the chicken and was patting it gently and interrogating the girls as to precisely how much sick the poor creature had eaten.

Zoe dashed outside.

The wind was high, pushing the clouds against the sun so it felt like the world was moving beneath her feet – sun, shade, sun, shade – as she ran; it buffeted her, making her eyes sting. Her feet sank into the newly empty furrows of the autumn fields, and she remembered – from her devoted readings of *Swallows and Amazons* rather than any actual farm experience – to shut the gates behind her. She found herself running through fields of sheep which in any other set of circumstances she would have wanted to stop and look at.

Instead she just shouted 'Lennox! Lennox!' on the wind until a farmhand came out and stared at her curiously.

'Lennox?' she said. He shook his head and pointed to a barn so far away it was only a tiny shape on the horizon. Zoe had mud up to her ankles. She dimly remembered now a line of wellingtons at the door of The Beeches that vastly outnumbered the people who lived there, and now understood why. It was too late anyway: her shoes were ruined. She glanced at them. They belonged to a life from quite long ago.

She caught her breath and started running again, finally appearing at the door of the barn, realising she hadn't run that far in years. If it hadn't been so awful, there would have been something freeing about running up a sunny clear hill at full pelt; about being totally winded and spent. Something different.

'Sorry, where the fuck did you spring from?' came a not unpleasant voice.

'Are you Lennox?' she gasped, shocked at how raw her throat was.

'Aye.'

He looked at her, in the middle of helping a sick ewe he did what he did every day; focused entirely on the job in hand to the exclusion of everything else, including whatever Nina might be up to. (This exceptional focus generally drove both Nina absolutely mad and turned her on something frightful.)

'It's Nina,' she barked. 'You have to come.'

His face changed immediately and he leapt up, forehead furrowed.

'What ... what is it?' he said, charging out. He stuck her on the back of his quad bike – Zoe had never been that close to one in her life; neither of them wore a helmet – and tore down the hill at top speed, bouncing across the ruts, practically surfing the grassier patches. Zoe didn't have a chance to catch her breath at all. Once again, if things hadn't been so grave ... she might have loved it.

Joan was waiting to meet them; the ambulance was still a way away.

133

'What is it, Joan?' he said, running indoors, leaving Zoe to get herself off the bike.

'You know pregnancy toxaemia?' said Joan.

Lennox stood stock-still in the doorway. His hand started to tremble. He took a step forward.

'Aye,' he said. 'Jesus. That kills sheep! It poisons them and it kills them.'

'No, no, it's not so bad, honestly. Bad example,' said Joan. 'It's not so bad in humans. They can fix it if they catch it in time, and we've caught it. We will catch it.'

She glanced at her watch.

'How long have you been feeling bad?' said Lennox as he went in to see Nina, pale as a wraith on the bed. How hadn't he noticed? Bloody harvesting. 'Why didn't you tell me?'

Nina's face creased.

'Because you were busy, and I was busy and . . . I thought it was . . . I thought it would be better than this . . . '

She really did start to cry now and he leapt to the bed beside her and gently stroked her hair.

'Hush now by,' he said soothingly. 'Hush now bye' exactly as if she was one of his sick ewes, and even realising this, she leant into his muscular side, and felt comforted.

Chapter Twenty

There was no book selling that day. (In fact, in all the drama, they both completely forgot to mention the stuck van to Lennox, which meant that when it rained that evening, it plugged the van into a gigantic mire that eventually turned to quicksand and became a five-person job to pull the damn thing out again, including hiring a digger, which Lennox kindly put down as a farm expense and never mentioned to Nina again.)

Nina was feeling nothing but relief. Pre-eclampsia was diagnosed, quickly and without fuss, in a way that implied the staff had seen it a million times before, even though the doctor lowered her glasses and her voice before imparting the terrible information that Nina would have to stay in hospital, possibly all the way to her due date, keep quiet and move about as little as possible.

Nina had blinked.

'Seriously?'

'I'm so, so sorry,' the doctor had said. 'You're going to find it terribly dull.'

Nina frowned.

'But I can read, right?'

'Oh yes!'

'It won't harm the baby?'

'Not at all.'

Nina sank back against the pillows.

'I think,' she said, Lennox holding her tightly, 'I think that will probably be all right.'

Zoe meanwhile sat next to Lennox in the Land Rover, staring into space as he drove.

This wasn't at all what she'd thought it might be like. She'd hoped that she'd be working with someone in a cushy job in a bookshop. She'd fantasised about a cosy corner of a lovely house, not a servants' room with iron beds and a cold-water bath. That hadn't been it either.

Zoe smiled ruefully at the picture she had had of herself, calmly reading all the new books and bringing light into the lives of some adorable motherless tots and generally helping people out in a sticky spot, some kind of combination of Julie Andrews and Supernanny. There had been very little in that fantasy, she thought now, of her watching a chicken eat sick. A lot of dreams in her life hadn't turned out exactly as she'd expected, she reflected.

Behind her a car slowed down and honked loudly. She turned around, startled, wondering who it was honking at. Everyone stared. It was Joan, the doctor.

'GOOD WORK TODAY,' she hollered out of the window at Zoe. From the back of the car, several dogs joined in a barking chorus. 'YOU WERE ABSOLUTELY RIGHT TO TAKE IT SERIOUSLY. ABSOLUTELY BLOODY RIGHT!'

Then she wound the window up and drove off with a screech of the gears and a splatter of mud on the spring road. The car, Zoe noticed, was absolutely filthy. She hoped Joan didn't have to do much surgery.

Lennox turned to her, as if just realising she was there, dropping her off next to the little green car.

'Aye,' he said gruffly. 'Aye. Thanks. Thank God for you.'

Zoe got out of the Land Rover. The chicken stared at her meanly, without blinking.

'Yeah. Thank God for me,' she wanted to tell it. And when she got into the Renault to drive away, she realised that someone had left her a basket of fresh eggs, some still warm, some with feathers still stuck to them, on the passenger seat.

Chapter Twenty-one

Zoe was worried about Nina, obviously – she had had a friend with pre-eclampsia and knew what a terrifying experience it was, as well as a rather lonely and boring one, stuck in hospital and denied the pleasures of late pregnancy (which were, though, she recalled, mostly people prodding you without asking and wondering if you had twins in there and how could you possibly stand up without overbalancing and other less than helpful theories) and in fact it basically boiled down to sitting in the bath and feeling like a desert island and she had rarely felt lonelier than having nobody to help her put on her own socks.

Anyway, she was worried, but glad Nina was safe in hospital. As she bowled along in the stuttery green car, past the great smoke-belching coaches leaving Loch Ness for the day, under the lengthening shadows from the mountains on the coast, the flash of a white tail of a deer disappearing into a forest, and rounded the bend of the long drive where she could see the great house ahead, she felt something inside. She wasn't quite sure what it was at first. But there was the tiniest possibility it felt like . . . a tiny bit like optimism. Like a little bit of hope. Like something – the tiniest seedling was, after so long in the gloom – starting to push its way out of the earth.

Something could have turned disastrous that day. But it hadn't. And she had the added bonus of a disconsolate-looking Hari charging towards her in delight when she turned up at nursery. She snuck a sideways glance at him now in the car, staring out of the window at the house, looking delighted to be home. She had asked Tara how the first day had gone and Tara had looked awkward, and elsewhere, but she had him now, and that was enough.

Zoe's good mood lasted as long as it took to get through the back door. She could hear the yelling from miles off. It was actual, full-throated screaming.

The noise was horrific. It sounded like somebody being murdered. The sun went behind a cloud, casting the great house into shadow suddenly and Zoe dumped the car, told Hari to stay in his seat, exactly where he was and looked around for something to hit the murderer with. There was fortunately a hardback copy of *The Hobbit* lying in the back of the car, and she took it stealthily, heart beating, and advanced, carefully holding it up to the door, her heart in her mouth . . .

Zoe peered round the door frame. The screaming was getting louder.

'Hello?' she said, trying to make her voice sound low and threatening rather than, as it came out, loud and querulous. 'Who's there?'

The screaming stopped, abruptly, and Zoe felt her arms prickling.

'WHO'S THERE?' she yelled, and burst into the kitchen, her arms aloft.

All three of the children on the floor immediately burst out into howls of mocking laughter at the sight of her, white-faced and shaking, holding *The Hobbit* above her head. Even Mrs MacGlone, who was at the sink, turned round and Nina saw her lips twitch.

Mary, who'd been lying flat on the ground, her hair tumbled out around her, sat up from the position in which she'd been vigorously trying to kick Shackleton on the chin.

'What are you going to do, elf us to death?' she asked in ringing tones.

'Bore us to death more like,' said Shackleton. 'Couldn't you at least have used *The Watchmen*? It's in the downstairs loo.'

Patrick gazed up at her severely.

'Actually we were only playing,' he said.

Zoe's fear turned to fury, as it so often does.

'That's not playing!' she said. 'Look at you!'

Shackleton had a huge bruise on his chin from where Mary had kicked him; Patrick had scratch marks on his face.

'Are they allowed to do this?' she demanded of Mrs MacGlone, whose face turned to stone.

'I'm just the housekeeper,' she said stoically. 'Nothing to do with me.' She glanced pointedly at her watch.

'It was Shackleton's fault!' yelled Mary hotly. 'He started it!'

'Shut up, you little vixen! It wasn't, as if I could care what the hell you're doing.'

'You're a lying prig and you can just shut up!' screamed Mary, working herself up into a state.

'You are both the stupidest people actually IN THE WORLD,' yelled Patrick, careful not to be left out. All three started screaming abuse and insults at each other.

Zoe, still bristling, stood up on the nearest chair, and dropped the heavy book onto the flagstone floor.

The noise was extraordinarily loud. All three stopped temporarily.

'RIGHT,' said Zoe, in a voice that brooked no argument. 'That is absolutely enough.'

'But,' said Mary.

'Shut it,' said Zoe. 'Right now.'

'Or what?' said Mary. 'You'll leave? Fine by us.'

''Fraid not,' said Zoe. 'In fact, I found out today that I'm going to be here for a long time, whether you like it or not.'

They did not, and made this clear.

'Right,' she said. 'In my car, there is a cake and some sausages.' There were. The woman serving at the tiny village shop had stared

140

at her in rude, open-mouthed silence for so long Zoe wondered if she had a disability. Zoe went on: 'I brought them back for supper. I will make supper with those things. But there are a few things that are going to happen first.'

'You're going to bribe us with sausages?' said Mary in a tone of utter disdain.

'Sausages!' said Patrick gleefully.

'I'm not bribing you,' said Zoe. 'I'm feeding you. As soon as you all get up.'

Shackleton reluctantly got up off the floor. Mary aimed a good kick at his kneecaps as he went.

'Oi,' said Zoe.

She had them standing up, and then got down from the stool to go to fetch Hari, who came in shyly.

'You help Mrs MacGlone put the cups away.' She pointed to Patrick. 'You –' This was aimed at Shackleton. '– sweep this room; it needs it. You –' to Mary '– put the laundry piles in everyone's room.'

'No,' said Mary. 'That's not our job actually?'

'Actually,' said Zoe. 'From today it is. From today jobs are everyone's jobs. Because when you guys are just lying around you get in to trouble. So I'm going to make it my mission to keep you busy.'

Patrick padded over to the sink and obediently picked up one cup at a time.

'Suck-up,' said Mary.

'You don't need to have either sausages or cake,' said Zoe mildly.

'Good. They stink.'

'But you do need to put your laundry away.'

'No, I *don't*.'

Zoe picked up the pile of Mary's laundry from where it had been drying by the fire. They really had to get the kitchen sorted out; it was a mess, and uncomfortable and unproductive.

'If it doesn't get taken away, it gets binned.'

'You're not serious.'

Mary looked at Mrs MacGlone.

'Mrs MacGlone, she's completely crazy.'

Mrs MacGlone could not deny it. She loved the motherless mites, in her way and did the best she could by them, but they were totally out of control and she was not the person to control them. If this – the seventh attempt – if this peculiar person could manage it, then so much the better. Ramsay was scared of his own children, and she wasn't much better; too wary of Mary's whiplash tongue; too aware of the housemaid she had always been, and the place she'd always known.

Mrs MacGlone looked scary, but wasn't. Zoe looked mild as butter, but wasn't.

Zoe threw a sock of Mary's onto the fire. Mary watched, absolutely outraged and horrified and secretly slightly impressed.

'I hate those socks,' said Mary. 'I'll go without.'

'Put your laundry away!'

'Shan't!'

The entire room was silent now, everyone watching incredibly closely to see what the outcome was going to be. Zoe really wished she knew herself.

Well, she was in it now. This was the crux of it. If she backed down now, she might as well pack her bags. And she really, really couldn't afford to do that.

Be consistent was the message, wasn't it? Along with be firm? Was this too firm though? Burning socks? It wasn't the most dignified situation Zoe had ever found herself in.

Mary was watching her with her arms folded, a smug expression on her face, as if daring her to go further.

'There's a sleeper train back down south you can catch tonight,' she said saucily. 'We won't miss you.'

Suddenly the mist descended. Zoe couldn't help it. She couldn't manage like this, not with everything that had to be done. She cast around on the laundry pile and extracted a small cardigan – it had to be far too small for Mary; she must have grown out of it anyway. It had little foxes stitched into it. Zoe picked it up and advanced towards the fire.

The scream that Mary emitted now made the earlier noise seem like laughing.

142

Chapter Twenty-two

Mary leapt for Zoe like a crazed animal. Zoe was fairly convinced that if the article of clothing had actually gone into the flames, Mary would have gone in straight after it, so distraught was she. She snatched the cardigan from Zoe's hands and pulled it to her, tucking it under her chin like a much younger child, tears streaming down her cheeks.

'Her mother made her that,' said Mrs MacGlone quietly from the side of the sink. Zoe swallowed. Oh God. That was awful. So awful. She felt dreadful.

She looked up at Mary, all the anger drained away, leaving only a vast well of pity.

'Why would you leave something so precious strewn about?' she said in a soft voice. 'Wouldn't you want to keep it safe?'

There wasn't a sound in the kitchen. The traumatised child froze for a second, then finally nodded sharply and angrily.

Zoe moved forward very carefully and slowly, as if she were approaching a wild animal – which she was. Mary backed away.

'Come with me,' said Zoe gently. 'We'll put everything away together.'

Her voice was as soft and lulling as she could make it, almost as if she were singing. She could see the internal fight on Mary's face; the desperate desire of the girl to continue to defy her, to force her away; the sheer weariness in her face. It must be so tiring to fight and to fight and to fight against the world; to be so angry and frustrated, every single minute of the day.

She didn't touch Mary, simply picked up the laundry pile and handed half of it to her. Mary didn't speak, didn't capitulate in any way.

But she took it.

Still treating her as if she was liable to attack and bite at any moment, Zoe pushed open the door to what she'd worked out was Mary's bedroom. It was dim; the curtains were closed tight and didn't look as if they'd been opened in some time.

It was a large room and absolutely no concession had been made in the decoration that it was for a child. The walls were wood-panelled, with old oil paintings hanging on them. The curtains were a heavy burgundy tartan which was copied on the bed covers. Persian rugs covered the dark wood floor.

There were a few toys; things for very little girls. A doll's house – a beautiful one – had had the front pulled off and the furniture scattered all over the ancient rugs. A few books, their spines uncracked, lay scattered higgledy-piggledy. The bed was made but nothing else had been touched, presumably on Mary's instructions. Clothes were strewn all over the room.

'I wish,' said Zoe, keeping her tone light. 'I wish I could do that Mary Poppins thing and snap my fingers and make everything tidy itself up. If I had a superpower, that would be what it would be, don't you think?'

Mary looked about and frowned. But she spoke.

'That's the stupidest superpower I've ever heard.'

'Well, what would yours be?'

'Dematerialisation, obviously.'

Zoe blinked. Well, this was progress, of sorts.

'Okay,' she said. 'Now is there a place for things, or shall we make one?'

Mary shrugged.

'How about . . . pants and tights up here?'

She opened a heavy old wooden chest. The other clothes in there – she was amazed – were all tiny, toddler girls' things. Beautiful, hand-smocked dresses, little Liberty prints. It looked like the wardrobe of a girl from a hundred years ago. But everything was so very small.

Zoe looked at the girl again in her grubby nightgown.

'Mary,' she said softly. 'Do you need new clothes?'

The girl shook her head.

'I like my clothes,' she said.

Zoe looked again at the cardigan. The little foxes worked into the wool were exquisite.

'They are beautiful,' she said. 'It's all beautiful. But wouldn't you rather some things that fitted you better?'

Mary shook her head fiercely.

Zoe walked over and opened the curtains. Evening light flooded into the room suddenly, lush and golden. It showed up the dust everywhere. She opened a window too. The room didn't smell bad, just a little old. A little sad. The fresh autumnal air, chillier than it looked from the sunshine, came in.

'That's better,' said Zoe. 'I always feel better when I can breathe.'

She looked around.

'Okay,' she said. 'Let's arrange your clothes, see what we have, shall we? Make sure everything is organised and kept as well as it can be.'

Mary looked for something she could disagree with in the state-ment but didn't seem to find anything, so she shrugged.

'I'll make us sausages later,' Zoe said, hearing the door slam below and realising Mrs MacGlone must have left. 'I really must teach Shackleton to cook something.'

Mary half cracked a smile. 'Shackleton couldn't cook anything! He's so incredibly stupid.'

'You don't need to be smart to cook,' said Zoe, not wanting to contradict her. 'A dog could make a shepherd's pie.'

'No, it couldn't!'

'It could! It would have to bite the carrot chunks off though. *Ruff!*'

And that is how Ramsay saw them, as he walked down the passageway in search of a cup of tea and hoping not to encounter too much chaos: the little girl and the new person, two dark heads leaning over a pile of clothes and folding and hanging them up. He stopped in the door frame for a while until Mary turned and saw him, and he was surprised as, for once, she wasn't either screaming at someone or clinging to his legs.

'Hello, *liefe*,' he said softly. 'Can I come in?'

Mary nodded. Zoe moved backwards as he came and folded his long unwieldy body down on the floor. It was like putting up a deckchair. His legs shot across the rug.

He caught sight of the cardigan Mary was still clutching furiously underneath one arm.

'Oh,' he said softly. 'The fox cardigan.'

Mary went bright red.

'It's beautiful,' he said. 'Does it still fit?'

Mary wouldn't answer.

'Maybe we could let Patrick wear it.'

Zoe winced. This was exactly the wrong thing to say. And so it proved, as Mary screwed up her face.

'Oh God, no way! He'd ruin it! He's not allowed to touch it! He ruins everything!'

'Ah, right, okay,' said Ramsay hurriedly, shifting his position. He looked altogether too big for the room, even though the room itself was large. 'Um.'

'Here,' said Zoe quickly, grabbing the first thing she found. 'Look at this I found stuffed behind the cupboard. I bet it would still fit you.'

It was a bold stripe T-shirt with a big lion's face in the middle.

'For when you want to roar,' said Zoe with a smile. Mary's face lit up. 'My lion T-shirt!' she said. 'I thought it was lost. I thought Patrick stole it.'

She frowned, obviously remembering some terrible punishment she'd dished out to Patrick.

'I think,' said Zoe carefully, 'I could let the hem down a bit and that would totally still fit you.'

Mary dragged it on – it was covered in dust – over her nightie, and sure enough, it did just about fit. She almost smiled.

'Well done,' said Ramsay to Zoe, who looked at him.

'Don't say that yet,' she said, looking at her watch. It was way past Hari's bedtime and she still didn't know how to use the stove and she could smell the once delicious but now ominous scent of toast rising up the stairwell. 'There's no dinner yet.'

'I don't want any,' said Mary promptly.

'That's okay,' said Zoe wearily, getting up. 'That's okay.'

Zoe didn't know what time she woke up. Hari wasn't stirring, but the entire house was still. Except . . . except . . .

She listened. It sounded like it was coming from right outside her door. A loud sobbing. Confused, her heart racing, she checked Hari again. Then she jumped up.

'Hello?' she ventured. The sobbing continued. 'Mary?'

There was no answer. Carefully, she tiptoed towards the door over the linoleum. The wind was moaning through the trees outside the window. She realised she was absolutely terrified and tried to tell herself not to be ridiculous.

'Patrick?' she said. 'It's okay. It's okay, Patrick, I'm coming.'

Steeling herself, she threw open the door . . .

The crying ceased immediately. There was nothing and nobody there. She looked up and down the empty hallway but there was nothing.

'Hello? Hello?'

But the house did not reply.

Chapter Twenty-three

'Thank you,' Zoe found herself saying again. It really *was* a terrible palaver getting vans out of the mud. The morning was fresh and dry. She had managed – had forced herself – to believe last night was all a dream.

'Mmm,' said Lennox. Zoe was quickly realising nobody had been joking when they said he didn't say much. She'd brought Hari along – she'd think about nursery later. After all, it wasn't the worst thing for him to hang out with someone who was obviously doing all right but also didn't feel the urge to talk very much.

Zoe couldn't deny it though. There was a bit of her that thought that changing scene, starting nursery, something new in his life – she'd thought that would prompt something at least. Some noise from the little boy. It was all she thought about as she drove down the long roads. It felt, as she came to know the area more and more, that every day there was something new. She heard a woodpecker out in the woods, battering away. Fish leaping in the loch. She wanted more time to explore; but there was just so much to do.

'How's Nina?' she asked. Lennox's brow furrowed.

'I want to say, having a bad time,' he said. 'But I'm not sure I can. There's a new delivery in – could you pick her out something?'

'I don't think there's anything she hasn't read,' said Zoe.

'Yup,' was Lennox's only response.

'I'll definitely have a look. Might be time to revisit some old classics.'

Lennox had washed down the whole van; it was gleaming.

'You're sure you know how to drive it?'

'I just need to practise . . . without anyone watching me,' said Zoe decisively.

Lennox definitely smirked.

'And don't do that, sunshine! That man smirk thing. That makes it worse!'

Lennox put up his hands.

'Aye, all right.'

He backed away. Then he stepped forward again. Hari wasn't paying attention; he was crouched down attempting to pat the chicken, who waddled away every time he got too close.

She smiled, watching him chase the chicken. She had slept incredibly well the night before. It was, she thought, something to do with the coolness of the air at night – London retained its heat; the very buildings gave it off.

Here the breeze was cool and when she lay in bed with the window open a crack it was an absolute luxury not to have to worry about being woken by burglars, drug deals, sirens, helicopters, shouting Ubers or fights outside the window.

Even though everything in her life was in limbo – and she still wasn't a hundred per cent sure there wasn't a mad woman bricked up in the attic of the house she was staying in – it felt strangely safe. The cool air; the gently sleeping Hari; the occasional hoot of an owl or a squawk of something else on the run from the owl; the scent of berries on the night air.

She had gone to back to bed after the disturbance of the previous evening, emotionally exhausted, and had expected to toss and turn and worry about everything. Instead, she had lain down for a moment, just to feel lulled by the night sky she could see through the open curtains, the blazing stars unobscured by night pollution, and had made a half-turn to pick up her book, but then found herself, just as she grabbed it, lightly dropping off the shelf into the deepest slumber, tumbling down like Alice, and had awoken, completely refreshed, to a piercing draught and a cold ray of liquid sunshine penetrating the unclosed curtains and, as usual, a small boy sitting on her chest.

Perilously and painfully slowly, Zoe pulled the van away from the farmyard gates. She stuck in second gear, figuring that would be fine until she figured out what she was doing. Lennox watched her go, worried. This was Nina's pride and joy; her life. She was under strict doctor's orders not to have any stress at all. He really hoped Zoe wouldn't mess this up – crash the van, or destroy the stock or the business. He sighed. They couldn't really afford it but he'd get in an extra shepherd for the season; he had to be at the hospital. They didn't chat much – he'd read the farming press; she'd beat him at Scrabble – but it didn't matter. He was there, and that was the only thing that mattered.

Zoe decided not to make a right turn onto the village square so she could get to the corner plot, but instead go all the way round the left-hand route and end up there eventually. She could probably, she suspected, do this with everywhere she went from now on.

The little village looked beautiful this morning. The cobbles were polished by recent rain; the rows of small whitewashed cottages had smoke coming from the chimneys. Children were out playing, making the most of the holiday, and Mrs Murray's shop had a bright display of buckets and spades and towels outside it for those heading to the shores of the loch.

Nervously, Zoe took up the pitch, turned the little sign from closed to open, propped up the latest intake and pushed open the doors with a hopeful grin.

The morning was busy, but not particularly lucrative. Everyone but everyone wanted to ask about how Nina was getting on. They loaded Zoe down with cards and presents that she ended up having to pile in the passenger seat; homemade marmalade and chutneys; home-brewed gin ('Tell her not to have too much,' said old Mr Dennis, who didn't think it had done his mother much harm when she'd drunk it during her pregnancy, and also didn't think much was wrong with being five foot three inches tall). Zoe eyed it carefully and wondered if it would be wrong to purloin it and drink it by herself at night when everything got too much.

Yes, she concluded reluctantly. That would be very, very wrong.

It was lovely that everyone was giving her things. Unfortunately what they weren't giving her was money in exchange for books.

'Nina said she was getting that book in for me,' was a common sentence, followed by complete blankness when Zoe asked them what it was.

'I'm after that book with the red cover.'

Or 'You know the one? It's got a doctor in it. A *bad* doctor.'

The worst of it was, as she desperately tried to recommend things, she knew Nina *would* know. She was trying to listen to Lennox's instructions and not call her every second – the one time she had tried (someone was almost exactly positive that Nina would know if their book about walruses had come in and Zoe turned the place upside down and actually it might be seals), Nina's phone was engaged and Zoe concluded correctly that she was talking to her mum.

She was exhausted as she parked up the van carefully, trying to keep out of the muddy area and the stupid chicken's way. Lifting Hari out bodily in his car seat even though it weighed a ton – why, she wondered frequently, didn't she have the most amazingly toned Thandie Newton arms given the amount of four-year-old lifting she did? It didn't seem fair – she hauled him into the little green car and nearly squashed another neat basket of eggs that was sitting there.

She put Hari on the ground.

'Ooh!' she said. 'Look! That could have gone *very* wrong, huh?'

Hari blinked.

'Well, that's supper sorted,' she said, and she glanced around to see if Lennox or anyone else was there to thank, but the farmyard was totally deserted. So she thanked the evil chicken, before carefully driving around it.

Chapter Twenty-four

Mrs MacGlone was pulling on her coat.

'I've got bingo,' she said, sounding almost cheerful for once. 'With Thea Newton. Who cheats. Always. I spent the day giving the grand piano a proper going-over.'

'How can you cheat at bingo?' said Zoe, confused, but Mrs MacGlone had already gone.

The kitchen, as usual, was covered in crumbs and Shackleton sat placidly eating his way through a jar of marmalade, eyes fixed on the screen.

'Oh, for heaven's sake,' said Zoe, irritated. 'Enough. Come on! Get up! You're going to help me make supper.'

She was going to do a big shop. Just as soon as she found out where there was a big shop.

Shackleton looked at her sideways.

'You're all right, ta.'

Zoe blinked. Then she went behind the cooker – it was absolutely disgusting back there – and, taking a deep breath and closing her eyes, she pulled out the tiny ancient internet plug.

Shackleton leapt from his seat and she suddenly remembered just what a large chap he was.

'Oi!' he said. 'Put that back.'

Zoe folded her arms.

'Neh,' she said. Mary looked up, blinking; she looked pleased it appeared to be somebody else's turn for getting it in the neck from Zoe today.

'Nanny Seven, you are ABSOLUTELY QUITE TERRIFYING,' came a small voice from the ground.

'You can shut it. Now, give me that back.' In dirty old tracksuit bottoms and unwashed hair, overweight, pasty-faced and truculent, Shackleton was an unappealing prospect.

'You're going to learn to cook something,' said Zoe. 'Help out a bit. Get you doing something.'

'No!'

'Okay,' said Zoe, weighing up the plug in her hand and wandering over to the sink with it. 'Fine.'

Shackleton stuck out his large lower lip.

'I'm telling Dad.'

'He's not here,' said Zoe. 'Where is he, anyone know?'

The children shrugged lethargically, and Zoe felt cross with him all over again.

'So. Help me and you get the internet back.'

'That's against my human rights,' said Shackleton.

'Also, I don't know why you're teaching him to cook – he's already too fat,' said Mary.

'We don't talk like that,' said Zoe. 'Not about your brother, not about anyone.'

Mary rolled her eyes. 'Yeah, in made-up land.'

'No, in real-life world. Land,' said Zoe somewhat awkwardly. 'You may have to catch up with the outside world a little.'

'Why?' said Mary. 'It's horrible!'

Zoe opened her mouth and then shut it again as she wasn't exactly sure she could argue with that.

'Right,' she said, raising up the basket. 'We have fresh eggs. Can you make an omelette?'

Shackleton looked at her and tutted.

'Does that mean yes or no?'

'It means he doesn't know what an omelette is,' piped up Patrick.

'Shut up!' said Shackleton.

'That can't be true,' said Zoe. The children looked back at her blankly.

'Oh lord. Have you got any cheese?'

'We've got the triangles,' said Patrick.

'Yeah, okay, any cheese that doesn't have a picture of a cow on it?'

The children looked dubious. Zoe investigated the fridge carefully and dug up an old piece of blue cheese. Well. She would have to assume it was mouldy in the first place, that was the point of blue cheese, wasn't it? It wouldn't kill them, would it? *Would* it? She could google it. Oh, except she couldn't because she'd pulled the internet out and wasn't a hundred per cent sure that just plugging it in again would make it work and it would also completely defeat the point of the entire exercise.

'Okay,' she said. 'What else have you got?'

'Peanut butter,' said Patrick.

'Hmmm.'

She pulled the normal butter out and wiped it round a heavy black pan, then dug around until she found a whisk that looked older than she was and started whisking the eggs together with salt and pepper. There wasn't a herb to be seen. She couldn't imagine what Mrs MacGlone was thinking. Then she thought about the miles of ancient carpet that needed hoovering, the endless shelves that needed dusting, the house that once upon a time would have had a raft of servants cleaning and polishing, and now had one faithful retainer with dodgy knees, and it began to make more sense.

But why didn't their dad feed them? Perhaps he didn't eat either.

'Okay,' she said, handing the bowl and whisk to Shackleton, who stared at it as if she'd just handed him a dog's tail. 'Go on, move your arm around.'

He shoogled the whisk up and down a little.

'You can remember to make omelettes and scrambled eggs

differently by remembering omelettes *om*-it the milk, *omelettes,*
*om*it the milk, you see?'

She looked at them. They did not see. In fact, they were all still
quite surprised by the way she'd cracked the eggs.

'We'll get to scrambled eggs later,' she said. 'Keep whisking,
Shackleton! Try and make it frothy!'

Patrick crept up and stuck his nose over the side of the bowl.

'Eggs!' he said in amazement. 'Can I crack some, Nanny Seven?'

Zoe glanced back at the basket. There were a few left over.

'You may all have a shot at cracking them in a bowl,' she said. 'Just
one each though.'

Naturally Patrick made a catastrophe of his and bits of shell and
yolk ended up half on the bowl and half on the floor. However his
bewildered face turned delighted when, out of nowhere, Porteous
shot in through the left-open kitchen door, panting, with his tongue
out, and neatly scooped up every last piece of egg, shell and all. It
was so fast and unexpected, they all burst out laughing, even, just
for the tiniest instant, Mary who, as soon as she saw Zoe looking
at her, immediately clammed up and reassumed her habitual sulky
expression.

Hari, Zoe was pleased to see, moved forward with his little hand
out, as if to stroke the huge creature, who immediately lurched
round and knocked him straight off his feet.

There was that quiet moment when a small child falls down and
everyone – including the infant – has to gauge how dramatic the
fallout is going to be.

The room was briefly silent. Then Hari let out a curious gurgle,
which sounded almost like a giggle, and Patrick dashed over.

'SO FUNNY!' he shouted. 'He knocked you over! Hahahahahaha!'

Hari himself blinked several times, clearing the tears that were
threatening to form, then Patrick helped the little boy to his feet and
the two of them immediately started trying to crack another egg to
repeat the experience.

'Oi!' said Zoe. 'No wasting eggs! Anyway –' She took a sly glance
to the right. '– it's Mary's turn.'

Mary had been sitting at the table, torn between refusing to engage, in however small a way, with whatever Zoe was doing, and an obvious interest in what was happening. The butter was sizzling on the pan and letting off a delicious smell – Zoe realised suddenly she hadn't had any lunch and was absolutely starving.

Once again treating Mary like a nervous wild creature, Zoe held out the whisk. The girl looked at it. Then, with just a tiny movement, she shook her head.

Zoe didn't take it as rejection. She took it for what it was: Mary recognising her existence without being aggressive towards her.

'Okay, Patrick,' she said. 'Your turn.'

And she sat him up on the counter. Hari instantly looked so downhearted she put him up too, and they companionably moved the whisk together, while Zoe shooed out Porteous, who good-naturedly shuffled back to the gardener's house.

'Okay,' said Zoe finally, when the mixture was extremely frothy. 'Stand back . . .'

She poured the first batch into the pan as everyone watched her with rather more attention than she'd expected. Patrick ooed as the mixture hissed and popped.

'Right,' she said, as she spread it around with an ancient blackened spatula. 'Cheese!'

She pulled out the blue cheese.

'That smells bad bad bad,' muttered Patrick and Hari put his hand on his nose and they both laughed and Zoe laughed too, and just for a moment – just for a tiny moment – it felt like a normal kitchen. And upstairs, even though he had Wagner blaring as usual, Ramsay stopped what he was doing, just for a second, turned down the music, and listened for the echo of the distant, chiming laughing sound he hadn't heard for so long, like a long-lost whisper of bells.

Chapter Twenty-five

The weather was coming in in earnest. Zoe had been reasonably confident that it was going to go to crap every single day. All she knew about Scotland was that it was freezing and full of drug addicts that only ate deep-fried Mars bars. She was explaining this to Lennox, who was thoughtfully bringing in large boxes of books she couldn't lift up at the farmyard. She filleted them quickly, Lennox blinking in confusion. He'd honestly thought Nina was the only person in the world who could do that with books. His ex had been able to do it with shoes.

'How do you do it?' he said.

'It's easy,' said Zoe. She picked up and discarded books rapidly. 'Look! Obviously a knock-off. Trying to pretend to be someone else with the font. Has a small creepy girl on front.'

'What's wrong with books with a small creepy girl on front?'

'They're all terrible,' said Zoe stoutly. 'Except for *Flowers in the Attic*, and we're not allowed to stock that any more.'

Lennox blinked.

'Why not?'

'You don't want to know,' said Zoe with a shiver. 'It's not *all* bad you never read as a child.'

She efficiently tipped out the rest and gathered what she wanted.

'Only the best,' she said, checking where the books fell open.

'What are you doing now?' said Lennox.

'Checking for dirty bits,' she said.

'Oh.' Lennox screwed up his face. 'You want those or you don't?'

'You have to read the customer.' Zoe sighed. 'Of course that's where I have trouble. I don't know anyone. Here.'

She handed Lennox a book.

'*Anne of Green Gables?*' he said, looking puzzled.

'For Nina,' she said. She added an Agatha Christie, *The Hotel New Hampshire*, the short stories of Saki, a *Peanuts* treasury and a collection of David Sedaris essays.

'Comfort reading. Send her my love.'

Lennox nodded and picked the books up.

'Oh, and ask her if she can't make a full list of characteristics and quirks of every single person in the village,' Zoe shouted after him, but he'd gone, nodding gravely to Hari, whom he liked immensely.

But going on in the little bus, there was still a lot of curiosity disguised as concern, and not a lot of book buying. When Zoe timidly introduced the subject and tried to direct people to new things, there was a bit of a tendency to look at her and say, 'Well, the thing is, Nina knows exactly what I like' as if Nina had magical powers that she, Zoe, in no way could possess. Also, there wasn't much point in asking people straight out what they liked, as sometimes they would lie, or they simply didn't know.

In short, she wasn't selling many books. Not many at all. People asked her whether she was bringing children's storybook hour back, and she supposed she'd have a go, but when? She could barely get it together as it was; barely had a second to plan anything. Adding something new at the moment felt like a push too far. She didn't realise – and Nina had a lot on her mind so we can't really blame her for not mentioning it – that Tuesday morning children's story time was vitally important: all the mothers on the whole would buy the books after the reading, and spend time chatting them over with the children. It was a real boost to the shop's income for the price of a quiet half-hour on the cushions, a few cheap cups of coffee and a variety biscuit box.

Instead, she dusted, tidied and pushed out the new hardbacks, but in vain. It wasn't taking. Not hanging around at the nursery probably didn't help; she could see all the mothers standing outside it, chatting, but she couldn't join in, she was always in such a rush. And she had to pluck up the courage. When she went there or into the local shop, everyone fell silent and she felt more of a stranger than ever. It was odd: when she had started work, she'd thought she'd be less lonely, getting out of the house, meeting people in a small community. But apart from Lennox, who treated her with the same quiet politeness he treated everyone, it was very hard to meet people.

'How do people meet people around here?' she'd finally asked Lennox awkwardly. He'd simply stared at the question. People requiring a social life was a mystery to Lennox.

She'd even asked Mrs MacGlone of all people, who sniffed and said everyone round here was awful and to steer well clear, and *not* to talk about the big house, that's all they wanted to know, sticking their nose in everyone's business and Zoe had said, well, it was just as well she didn't know anybody's business then and Mrs MacGlone had sniffed once more and said, well, quite, wasn't that what she was always saying, and she had mothballs to stitch. And Zoe had been about to say, had she heard anything odd round the house – she kept feeling not quite alone in her room, she couldn't understand it at all – but she didn't. It was just so strange.

'So,' Zoe had said as casually as she dared. 'You know how there's millions of huge bedrooms here and mine is tiny?'

Mrs MacGlone had fixed her with a look.

'Yours,' she'd said, 'is a *staff* bedroom. You're no' a guest.'

And she'd stalked off witheringly, and Zoe couldn't find the words to say that she knew she wasn't a guest – she was just slightly concerned she had an uninvited one.

Chapter Twenty-six

One Sunday, Zoe woke early, wondering what on earth to do. Mrs MacGlone wasn't in, and neither was Ramsay: it was just her, and the children and Hari, all day.

She was in a strange place and she had very little money. She should go and see Nina, but she assumed on a Sunday, correctly, that she'd have a lot of visitors and so decided to leave it to a quieter day.

It was sunny and chilly outside, but nobody was stirring. Downstairs on her own, she found herself looking at the long hallway with its chandelier, festooned with spiderwebs, and suddenly found herself overcome by a longing to do something; to make a change.

She heard Mrs MacGlone every day; running the old cranky twin-tub washing machine, using the old hoover, washing plates and dishes by hand and vanishing on far-flung jobs in the depths of the house. It wasn't that she didn't work hard: she did. But the sheer amount there was to do for one person was simply terrifying. The house ran, but only just.

Zoe went up to the huge main front door. The thick old wood towered above her, and she inspected the two bolts and a snib with a rusty old key left in the lock. She drew back the incredibly stiff bolts, which hadn't been oiled in for ever, and twisted the key with some difficulty using her entire weight. The old key protested and finally gave way, Zoe worrying briefly that she might have broken it and it might be some old chieftain's key and she'd owe Scotland a billion dollars for ever kind of thing.

Hari was standing behind her suddenly. She was used to him creeping up silently; she knew other people found it startling. He was still wearing his little fireman sleep suit with the feet that he was getting too big for – normally she'd just cut off the feet, but she'd rather hoped that her circumstances might change enough that she wouldn't need do that. He couldn't have grown in the short time they'd been there. Surely not.

He was clutching, she noticed, an old bear made of stiff-looking hair. It looked older than Zoe herself.

'Where did you get that?' she said, going towards him for a cuddle. The thing was ancient; an antique. It smelled of old wooden boxes and sawdust and horses, for some reason. Its eyes were real glass and it wore a faded tartan ribbon around its neck. Any label had long gone.

Hari pointed upstairs, unhelpfully.

'I'm not sure that's yours,' she said in a gentle tone of voice. 'I think we'd better check with Patrick's daddy that it's okay for you to play with that.'

Hari eyed her fixedly and shook his head, then cuddled the bear closer as if to show how vehemently he didn't agree with her take on things.

'It's not ours,' said Zoe, sighing. 'Nothing here is ours, sweetheart.' Hari blinked, then turned away, hiding the bear from her. Zoe bit her lip.

'Well, you can hold on to it for now,' she said. 'While we're in the house. Just . . . don't forget: it's not your bear.'

Surely if it was a priceless family heirloom, Mrs MacGlone would point that fact out in about five seconds. Until then, she'd just have to keep half an eye on them both. And he did look very cute, like a little Christopher Robin with an original Pooh Bear.

Using both hands, Zoe pulled open the great door, which made a vast creaking sound on its hinges.

It was a revelation. Cold bright light streamed in from outside. Birds were singing and chattering; the trees were blowing in the stiff breeze on the other side of the gravel driveway. It was dazzling.

It showed up the old hallway in all its shabbiness, but also the beauty of its ancient wood panelling and the good quality of the dark twentieth-century oil paintings and even the stag's head – which Hari hadn't noticed before and made him jump – and the elaborately carved banisters of the main staircase.

Wanting to see more of the house, Zoe opened the door to the downstairs sitting room with its old piano she'd glimpsed on the first day, the shelves crammed with books, and opened the old shutters and the heavy curtains there too. More and more light fell into the room, revealing heavy old maps and piles of paper everywhere, dust swirling in the air, and odd bowls and vases that didn't seem to have a place.

'Right,' said Zoe cheerfully. There was nobody here to judge or forbid her to do anything. The children still weren't up. She went through into the kitchen and found an ancient, flour-spattered old radio and moved it around the house until she found a signal. She just needed something jolly and uplifting, and sure enough found a rusty poppy channel that was playing the kind of music that fitted her mood.

Under the huge old butler sink in the kitchen were acres of cleaning materials and polish, and she put on Mrs MacGlone's big old apron and brought them all through and started to go through everything in the overstuffed room. She filled black bags with what was patently rubbish – old envelopes, year-old junk mail and broken plastic spoons and old rags. She found an empty drawer and started putting things she thought you might need into that drawer, then got caught up and started emptying all the drawers.

It was mindless, busy and satisfying work, and Zoe didn't realise how loudly and cheerfully she was going at it and bustling around, the sun blazing in, the music at top volume, spraying and cleaning and packing and moving, Hari dancing and 'helping', until she got the sense of movement behind her and turned around to see all three children standing on the landing of the staircase, gazing at her. Mary was wearing the lion T-shirt.

'See?' Patrick was saying. 'She has gone quite absolutely mad.'

Zoe stood up, annoyed that she felt guilty and caught out. She was the one who'd been dumped here and told to get on with things. What right did they have to be judging her on trying to make their environment nicer?

The music was still blaring. Shackleton went down and turned it off. Mary stepped forwards. She was utterly pale and shaking with rage.

'*What* are you doing?' she said.

Zoe glanced around. The entire place was so much better already: it smelled fresh with the wind blowing through it, and the windows and shelves were gleaming. The umbrella bucket now had every umbrella she could find in the house in it, rather than them being scattered on every available surface. She'd made it through to the boot room to the left as you came in, which now had shoes and wellingtons neatly arranged in a row, and all the hats – some with feathers, some from the last century; many completely mad – lined up on the rack or piled neatly on a shelf built for that purpose. The mirror in the room had been cleaned, and the curtains opened, so you could actually see what you were wearing.

'Cleaning up,' she said. 'It doesn't seem like Mrs MacGlone gets the chance for a proper spring clean. Or an autumn clean!' She stepped forward. 'Want to help?'

Mary glared at her.

'Why did you *move stuff*?'

'Because,' said Zoe sensibly, 'everyone has to live here. Isn't it nicer if it's a nice environment?'

Mary gazed at her, eyes full of hatred.

'This is how it's *meant* to be,' she said. 'This is how it's *meant* to be. You're ruining it! You ruin *everything*!'

And she charged off through the front door, and vanished into the garden.

'She does that a lot,' said Zoe with a sigh. Patrick came forward.

'Well,' he said in a voice too practical for his years. 'You know. You are absolutely moving stuff Mummy put there. And Mary absolutely does not like it.'

It was the first time Zoe had heard any of them volunteer information about their mother. She moved forwards and knelt down.

'Don't you think,' she said as gently as she could, 'that your mum would maybe have liked the house to look nice? And clean and lovely for you all?'

Patrick shrugged.

'I don't remember,' he said in the tiniest voice imaginable, and Zoe went to take him in her arms. It was a completely natural gesture, but the boy flinched backwards immediately, almost stumbling in his rush to get away from her, and she cursed herself for attempting to move so fast.

She turned her head.

'Hari,' she called quietly. The little boy stepped forwards.

'Do you maybe think you could lend Patrick your bear?'

Without question, Hari came forwards holding out the moth-eaten old antique, and without looking up, Patrick took it and buried his face in it. Zoe announced she was going to make everyone pancakes for breakfast in the jolliest 'everything is totally fine' voice she could muster, expecting Patrick to follow her through at least out of curiosity, which he did, and had stopped being upset enough to recover his appetite by the time the pancakes had arrived.

Most curious of all was Shackleton. He was standing in the kitchen and came forward to watch as she cooked. Then he cleared his throat – he was at the age where his voice could jump from deep to high and back again within the space of the same sentence – and said, carefully, 'I'd like to help.'

Zoe whirled round. She hadn't been expecting this.

'You mean it?'

165

Shackleton shrugged, his mouth full of pancake.

'Might as well,' he said, shrugging. 'Have you fixed the Wi-Fi yet?'

'Um,' said Zoe, who didn't know how to make it work again. She'd tried, but no joy.

'Soon,' she said. 'If you help me clean out the house, I'll totally definitely fix the Wi-Fi.'

Chapter Twenty-seven

So they spent the rest of the long, breezy Sunday hauling things out, dusting, cleaning and, for Patrick and Hari, mostly chasing spiders. Mary came back in from time to time to make sure they weren't moving anything, and Zoe gravely showed her the large chest in which she was saving anything – keys, broken watches, sole earrings, random scarves – that looked like it might be important, and displaying the bin where she was getting rid of everything else – old paintbrushes and tennis balls, odd socks, junk mail, Christmas cards, broken crayons and unstrung rackets.

Mary didn't say anything, just kept a beady eye on proceedings. Zoe wondered, as she watched her go, whether it would have helped had Hari been a little girl; someone with whom she could have played, or petted, or taken at least an interest. Zoe looked at her again. The poor thing, her bedraggled hair spilling down her back, could barely take an interest in herself. Zoe quite sternly set her to washing windows so she didn't have to come inside with them if she didn't want to and, after clearly considering a stand-off, Mary finally set to it in as grumpy and half-baked a manner as she could which was still, Zoe thought, getting things done, so there was that.

Patrick fell with delight on a huge dark chest of old toys that had somehow been kicked behind an ancient sofa in the living room – why did they never go in there? Zoe wondered – and pulled it open, and within two minutes, Patrick and Hari were marauding around in cowboy outfits, shooting toy pistols at each other. Patrick was making the *peow peow* sound, and Zoe listened carefully just in case – but, nothing. They had found utterly ancient old horse heads on sticks with wheels and were galloping about, getting in the way. There was a gradual but absolutely definite improvement in the lower rooms as Zoe whipped off all the cushion covers and ran them through the washing machine. The sheer amount of grime to be found in the shelving was quite disturbing, and all of them got dirtier and dirtier, with smuts of grime on their faces, and Shackleton was, amazingly, being incredibly helpful, climbing ladders and getting through endless cloths with vigorous energy and good humour. Zoe smiled; she wouldn't have thought he had it in him.

'I think doing without the Wi-Fi is doing you good,' she teased, and he shook his feather duster at her in a joke-threateningly way.

Ramsay was returning from London, feeling unutterably weary and washed out. It had been a very difficult couple of days. He carried the new Sotheby's catalogue, full of work he couldn't afford and hoped to find something rather nice that he could sell but wouldn't be very sorry to part with.

Of course it wouldn't be enough. It was never enough. Not with what the house needed. What the children needed. His father's ancient lawyer had suggested he consider selling part of the estate, that they'd received interest – it would make a nice luxury hotel apparently – but he couldn't. He just ... No. He couldn't. They'd find a way through somehow.

Why did he have to be the one who hadn't taken a proper job, unlike those idiots he'd been at university with who'd all gone and made a fortune in the city? He'd always loved books, that was all. Hadn't really thought too much about money really, which, he allowed, was totally his own fault for growing up in privilege. Not that they'd been so well off – his father had never had any money either. Growing up in a house like The Beeches was supposedly its own reward – or burden – and it took absolutely everything just to keep the lights on.

He'd hoped, once upon a time, to make it a happy place; transform its dark spaces and tired decor and make it somewhere wonderful for his family to grow and run wild, just as he had done with his friends when he was younger – fishing, wandering every day for hours down to the water or paddling across the loch or building tree houses. That was why he'd agreed to keep it on, take over the sacred trust. And then his father had died and he was kind of stuck with it.

And, when his father went, so did the glorious haven he had dreamed of building for his own children, just as it had been for him.

That, he sighed, as he did whenever he thought about it, had been very much derailed.

As he came up the driveway in the old Land Rover, however, something struck him, and for a moment he couldn't figure it out. Then, he realised. The front door was open. At first, he was worried – had something happened? Had someone been there? Had someone come?

Then he realised that the shutters in the downstairs drawing room were pulled back too, and that you could see into the room for the first time in ... well, a very long time. Was that Shackleton up a stepladder? And, oh goodness, was that Mary with a sponge in her hands?

Rubbing his tired eyes with his large hands, Ramsay did his best to take in the sight. He parked and slowly got out of the car. There was ... music, and was that Patrick laughing? Wilby's stupid dog had got free again and was gambolling about the place.

'Daddy!' shrieked Mary and ran to him, burying her head into his tummy as she always did, climbing up him in that slightly desperate way he knew well.

'Hello, sweetheart,' he said, lifting her up even though she was – was she getting heavier? He was so used to her being as light as thistledown. Well, that would be a good sign. He held her in his arms and she clung on like a baby monkey.

'What are you up to?' he said.

Zoe's heart had been pumping in her chest as she heard the car draw up over the noise of the radio. Would he be cross? Furious? Indifferent? It was so difficult. She was used to parents having lots and lots of very precise opinions over what they wanted their children to be doing. This was all new. She had absolutely no idea what was going on in his head.

She needed to have a word with him, she knew she did. This wasn't benign neglect. Letting children eat toast all day ... not go to school ... wearing clothes that didn't fit them. This was perilously close to actual neglect. She needed to talk to him about it. She was absolutely definitely going to.

Her first thought was how exhausted he looked. This annoyed her for reasons she couldn't put her finger on; it wasn't fair, if he'd just driven a long way. But how hard could fiddling about with old books be really? He wasn't even trying to sell them to people like she was. And he was hardly doing the heavy lifting with the children.

She hadn't thought for a second how utterly filthy she was until she saw him staring at her face and suddenly realised she was just covered in muck. She rubbed her nose, which had a large black stain on it, wondered if she'd made it worse (she had) and then wondered whether to take the old scarf out that she'd tied to keep her hair back, or whether that would look odd too.

'Um,' said Ramsay.

'Daddy! Come see!' said Patrick, wearing the cowboy outfit with a princess dress thrown over it – exquisitely made, not supermarket nylon at all – which must have been Mary's, long ago. It looked handstitched. Mary caught her staring at it and turned her head into her father's shoulders.

'WE DID CLEANING!'

Ramsay looked at the little chap and, for the first time, smiled. It changed his face, Zoe thought, and realised how relieved she felt. There had been the chance that he might turn up furious and start screaming at her for touching his things. She had no idea who this man was, nor why his wife had left him. But she couldn't bear it, truly; couldn't bear living somewhere so utterly grim. So.

She realised she'd folded her arms and must look like a rather cross Mrs MacGlone, give or take a few decades. She unfolded them straightaway.

'I see that,' he said, and passed into the hallway, with the floor scrubbed clean and shining, the coats neat in a row, the paintings dusted and straightened, the walls washed down and the windows sparkling (after Zoe had gone over everything Mary had done).

'Goodness,' muttered Ramsay. Then they showed him into the drawing room and he turned away.

He remembered suddenly, with piercing clarity, the day he'd brought her home ... It had been a bright breezy day too, with the promise of summer on the air, the seasons turning, and everything then had been sparkling, or felt sparkling and new, and everything was full of possibility and hope ...

'You don't absolutely LOVE it?' said Patrick, puzzled. Hari had dived behind the sofa and was hiding there. Tall men scared him.

Ramsay blinked, looking at something that simply wasn't there.

'I ... I do,' he said. 'I ... I do like it.'

He looked at Zoe. 'Thank you ...'

'Nanny Seven,' supplied Patrick helpfully.

'Um ...' Ramsay searched his brain. Goodness, she really was grubby. Did she know how dirty she was? What was her name again? '... Zoe.'

'You're welcome,' said Zoe. She looked around. They were nearly finished. Ramsay and Shackleton could move the furniture back as she stretched the covers over the old cushions and straightened up the sofas neatly. She looked at the old curtains which had been hoovered but really now looked shabby compared to the rest of the room.

'These could do with a clean too.'

Ramsay moved forward to have a look, then his large foot slipped on the wet, now polished floor and he went straight over onto the sofa and landed, looking very surprised, on Zoe's newly plumped cushions.

Zoe watched him carefully. It was the kind of thing – a loss of dignity – that would make many men cross, and find it essential to cover up. Men that really were scary, that really did mean harm, couldn't bear to be funny.

Ramsay burst out laughing to find himself in such an awkward position. Then he squinted.

'Did you ... clean the chandelier?' he gasped in amazement, and was then even more amazed when Zoe indicated that it was Shackleton who had managed it.

He grinned even more broadly. 'Well, I'm glad I tripped over my stupid big feet then,' he said, screwing up his eyes. 'Because I am telling you, everything is looking a *lot* better. Especially from this angle.'

Patrick jumped up on his father's chest.

'Can you stay there and be a horse?' he yelled. Zoe looked at Ramsay, his curls falling back off his tired face, his gentle expression, as his eyes closed briefly before he said, 'Of course,' and as Zoe went off to get the tea ready she was surprised to see Hari peek out from behind the curtain – not joining in, but certainly watching the fun.

'You know,' she said in a voice she tried not to make sound bossier. 'It's really good when you hang out with the children. You really ought to do it more often.'

Everyone froze. Ramsay stood up very slowly.

'Thank you,' he said, his tone now icy. 'Thank you for your advice. I'm so glad we hired an expert on my family.'

And he turned and walked away.

Zoe cursed to herself: she had hoped Ramsay might join them for supper so she could ask him about a dishwasher, a thing they most desperately needed. But they didn't see him again all evening.

Chapter Twenty-eight

Mrs MacGlone, of course, was absolutely furious.

If, up until then, Zoe had managed to keep on fairly neutral territory with her – mostly because Mrs MacGlone didn't expect her to stay; didn't expect anybody to stay and deal with Shackleton's sloth, Mary's unbelievable rudeness and Patrick's non-stop chattering (she could not have known how bittersweet but still welcome a noisy child was around the place to Zoe's ears) – this was like a declaration of war; on Mrs MacGlone's turf, no less. She'd let Shackleton touch the chandelier!

Of course she realised she wasn't able to keep the house up to the standards old Laird Urquart would have found acceptable. There were three housemaids in those days, a cook, a laundress, a housekeeper and a butler as well as the garden staff. That's what it took to keep things straight, whatever thing this slip of a girl thought she was doing. Suppose she thought she was very smart, showing up Mrs MacGlone as lazy or sloppy, which she most certainly was not; it was everything she could do to keep the kitchen, bathrooms and bedrooms more or less straight, the carpet vacuumed and their clothes clean, doing everything the way she'd always done it, since she was not much older than Mary was now. By the time she'd sorted out food and done the shopping, there wasn't a second left to spare.

She had quite the furious speech all ready to make to Ramsay the following day so it was doubly annoying when, as was his wont, he shut himself up in his library all day and was nowhere to be seen.

And if young missy thought she was going to get round those children with fancy food and pancakes and filling them with all sorts of nonsense, she had another think coming. Bribing them would never last for long; she'd seen it before. Maria-Teresa had tried to bribe them with all sorts of sugary junk which had ended up in Patrick losing a tooth because she didn't supervise teeth brushing, and Mary refusing to eat anything at all and a stand-up row between all of them that had ended, inevitably, with Maria-Teresa and her bag at the end of a drive. Sometimes the girls hitchhiked out. Maria-Teresa had, not altogether unstylishly, driven the green Renault to Inverness station and ditched it with the key in it. Nobody had stolen it by the time Ramsay had got Lennox to drive him up there to fetch it.

She approached Zoe early in the morning before they entered the kitchen.

'What's been going on here then?' she sniffed.

'Oh,' said Zoe, smiling nervously. 'I thought we could give you more of a hand round the house?'

'So you don't think I'm up to it?'

Mrs MacGlone's mouth was a hard line.

'That's not what I think at all! I think you do an amazing job!' said Zoe. 'I just thought it might be good for the children to ... help?'

'So you've been here five minutes and you know what's best for them?' said Mrs MacGlone. Zoe bit back the retort that little could be worse than the huddle of awkward people she'd stumbled across, like a tiny lifeboat of stragglers left after a shipwreck, washed up, clinging to the kitchen tiles.

Mrs MacGlone stepped up to her.

'People come and go frae these children's lives,' she said in a voice made more threatening by its low tone so nobody could hear her.

'They come in, they faff about, they make *nothing* better – and then they leave and we're right back where we started. The less you do and change, the better, missy.'

'Maybe I'm not like that,' said Zoe, her voice quivering.

'Och aye, *you're* different,' said Mrs MacGlone. 'Here you come, on your holidays frae that London, dragging that wee laddie, looking for a free bed. You'll be here and as soon as you're back on your feet, you'll be off again, back to *England*.'

She said 'England' as if it were a swear word. And the children slouched past on their way to breakfast and didn't bother saying good morning and it was like nothing had changed at all.

Chapter Twenty-nine

Zoe was so cross heading out that she didn't notice the clouds damping high over the mountaintops. As a Londoner, she was used to the weather being mild variations of the day before; there weren't dramatic changes normally. She didn't even check the weather forecast. Now, however, as she tuned in the radio – it was definitely helping her understand the local accent so she tried to keep it on all the time, plus Hari liked the music – she heard them talk about storm warnings and power lines and to take care, but she was only half listening. Instead she was lost in her head, cursing herself for being such an idiot. Thinking she might be able to make a difference.

Mrs MacGlone knew exactly what Zoe should be doing: keeping her head down, being grateful for the roof and the food and the money until she left the children again as they had been before, in their too-small clothes and all-toast diet, utterly cut off and isolated from the world.

But she was wrong. Why didn't he see? She was thinking about Ramsay, furiously, as she drove on. What was it with fathers? Hari barely knew his. But Ramsay was there, with three traumatised children who desperately needed him. How could he be so thoughtless?

Was it because he was posh? Or some kind of crazed sociopath, something his ex had found out, to her cost?

Well, maybe she couldn't change things, she thought, just as Mrs MacGlone had said. But she wouldn't stand by and do nothing. Someone had to look out for children. Even horrible ones. Although she had unavoidably developed something of a soft spot for Patrick. Anyone who was nice to her child was guaranteed her eternal fealty.

She glanced at Hari in the back.

'Okay!' she said in her jolliest voice. 'Nursery today!!!'

Hari gave her a level and entirely disgusted look.

'Aha!' Tara had exclaimed when they showed up again. 'Excellent, Hari! We were just about to sing a song about how much we value ourselves. You like to sing, don't you?'

'Actually . . .' Zoe had started.

'Oh *yes*,' Tara had said as Hari's face started to crumple. 'Not to worry! We'll put you at the back, just outside the circle and you can clap!'

'I'll only be a couple of hours,' said Zoe desperately. 'It's just a little bit, Hari. Just a little bit. You can play outside.'

And she did it: she somehow managed to harden her heart again and turn around and walk away from her little boy. It's for him, she told herself. It did not help her believe it.

In tears, she picked up the book bus, noticing the high grass in the fields bending right over, but thought little of it, even as the reeds were flat on the ground. All the cows and sheep in the field were sitting down, but that meant absolutely nothing to Zoe. She hoovered, straightened up and, with slightly more practised abilities, carefully drove in a large circle around the central point of the unmoveable chicken and trundled off down the hill.

Lennox had been outside making sure his haybales were carefully strapped down when he saw her and charged out of the barn, waving his arms uselessly behind the disappearing van. The forecast was appalling, and certainly there was no place for taking out high-sided vehicles. He didn't know what she was thinking; Nina wouldn't have gone out today in a million years. In fact, maybe best not mention

Zoe had taken the van out in an amber warning. If she pootled down to the village then came back he could probably just about paper it over. He tried Zoe's number. Nothing, of course. There were plenty of mobile black spots on this road, and the heaviness of the incoming clouds didn't help either.

In fact, Zoe had decided to go further afield that day. She had, she felt, rather exhausted the curiosity of the people of Kirrinfief once they found out a) that Nina was grand; no better nor worse, b) dropped off some knitting for her – this was, Zoe surmised, going to be the woolliest baby of all time – and c) they weren't quite sure what kind of book they were in the mood for; they'd just wait for Nina to tell them, thanks. She always knew.

Running a bookshop sounded so civilised, so simple. Not just looking blankly at a nice old woman who had asked her very loudly and repeatedly to give her something she definitely hadn't read but would like, and every time Zoe suggested something, would shake her head and say, no, not that type of thing at all.

Nina had left her some notes about little villages around and where she could park from time to time, generally on Tuesdays and Thursdays to match the farmer's markets. She'd also left a map, as trying to get your phone 4G to work in the Highlands was a thankless task at the best of times, and Zoe was trying to drive and work out the route at the same time.

There wasn't any thunder – it wasn't that type of storm – but there was suddenly rain – crashing, drenching rain, hurling itself against the windscreen – and when you looked outside, you could see the trees bending over, pushing their leaves towards the ground. Zoe blinked.

Should she be worried? Everyone said it was bad weather up here; that was practically the first thing anyone ever said about Scotland. You just expected it to be this bad, didn't you? Probably everyone just got on with it and didn't bat an eyelid. The van skidded a little bit here and there on the road and she pulled the big wheel back towards the central line, her heart going in her chest a little.

She'd got, she realised, much more conscious of her own worth since Hari had been born. Before – and many of her friends could still do this – she could be almost careless of her own life. Drive too fast, stay up too late, do slightly crazy things, be reckless. Because it was just you.

Now it wasn't just her, and that was the biggest change of all. Suddenly it was vitally important that she didn't crash the car, or vanish, or do silly things when she'd had a little too much to drink, or anything like that. The idea of leaving a small child motherless, no matter what she was like, or how she was doing as a mother, was just too dreadful to bear. She could easily make herself cry just by imagining the circumstances in which someone would have to explain it to the lad; how his little face would screw up in confusion; how the police officer explaining it would be doing their best to be kind … How awful must the situation of the Urquart children's mother have been? What could possibly have broken her enough that she could leave her children? What – or who?

At any rate, she slowed right down on the road, checking her mirrors conscientiously and doing everything absolutely right, which would have been fine had not slowing down on that bend right there – just as she came to the strait along the lochside, with the turn-off to the visitor centre – meant that she was precisely placed for a charging coach, pulling out and getting caught in a crosswind because frankly it was travelling rather too fast, to immediately start barrelling down the road in her lane, and to miss her, as she smashed into an overhanging branch, bringing it straight down through her window.

Chapter Thirty

The noise was unbelievable. Suddenly, as soon as the window smashed, with ear-crashing volume, the crazed howling of the wind outside the van, like a malevolent dark rising force, smashed into her.

Zoe gasped, her mouth pulling backwards to scream as the branch bounced straight off her window; it tumbled underneath the van's wheels and a sharp smell of asbestos from the brakes hit her as the tyres stalled and the huge great edifice started to turn in on itself, onto the other side of the road, where the large coach from the loch-side continued to barrel towards her.

Zoe held up her arms to the side, desperately reaching for her baby, then realising he wasn't there.

In the split-second that elongated endlessly, she thought that this couldn't possibly be it, and of Hari and Hari's face, and somehow, before hysteria and blackness overcame her, she managed to lift her foot off the brake and put both hands on the wheel, pulling them furiously one over the other until the terrible trajectory of the vehicle righted itself and in fact, with an instinct somewhere deep inside her, she did exactly the right thing by pulling the steering wheel hard to the left and slamming her foot on the accelerator. The van shot forwards, smashing through the wood on the ground, puncturing both front tyres, but moving, nonetheless, on the left side of the road, where she desperately tried to control the motion of the five-ton vehicle, and saw the left turning for the visitor centre up ahead.

Praying there was nothing else coming, she screamed past the coach, broken glass all over her hair and her clothes, oblivious to the cuts and bruises on her face, and shot the van round into the access road, finally putting on the brakes and bringing it to a halt, Meanwhile the coach driver ran the entire coach off the road and into a ditch with a sickening thumping noise.

Zoe sat in the vehicle, the engine of which was ticking and clucking and very unhappy as it cooled down. She stared straight ahead, even as the wind blew right into her face, trembling and not realising what was trickling down her face and onto her T-shirt: blood.

After a few moments – which felt like hours – of total silence, the people at the visitor centre came charging up, yelling and concerned, along with lots of tourists in many different languages. Zoe still didn't move; just sat there, stock-still, staring into space.

'Are you all right?' The voice was low and gruff and penetrated Zoe's frozen state.

'Hey! Listen to me!' it said, slightly starker and rather more cross. 'Listen to me. You have to listen to me. You need to get out of the van.'

Zoe lifted her hands and looked at them dispassionately as if they weren't hers.

'Blood,' she said.

'Your windscreen blew in,' said the voice. 'You have to get down so we can see you're all right.'

Zoe could hear the voice and understood what it was saying, but it didn't seem to have any relevance to her. She didn't feel the need to do anything. She had her seatbelt on. Maybe she'd just stay there.

The next second – or minute, or hour, she had no way of knowing – strong arms were lifting her out of the cab and holding her
up on the ground. Glass spiralled down onto the stones of the
car park. The wind was absolutely howling through the bending,
swishing trees.

'Come on, get her inside before something falls on us,' said a voice.

'The books!' gasped Zoe, suddenly panicking. Everything was
back there. 'What about the books! What if the van blows up!
Someone save the books!'

The same low voice she'd heard before laughed.

'Well, I don't think that old rust bucket would have it in her to
blow up. But trust me, if it doesn't – which it won't – there's no way
I'd risk having someone inside saving some bloody books when it
happened.'

And a set of hands half pushed, half carried her into the large
building ahead; there was obviously a hotel of sorts next to the visitor centre. The nice-looking receptionist Zoe had met once before,
Agnieszka, who didn't serve coffee in the mornings, was standing
beside the large open fire and had her hands at her mouth when she
saw her, then immediately summoned someone from a back room
who came charging out with a large roll of multi-purpose blue paper.

'Sorry,' she said. 'But would you mind terribly standing on that?'

Zoe didn't mind anything; she couldn't see or think straight.

'And first aid kit!' the receptionist trilled. 'Oh, my poor dear, are
you all right?'

Zoe didn't have a clue, and let Agnieszka lead her over in to
the bathroom.

'There there,' she said, as Zoe stared at a bleeding face she
didn't recognise, then glanced at her blood-spattered hands. She
was trembling.

'You had a little accident,' said Agnieszka, sizing her up expertly.
'But I think – I *think* – you're going to be all right. Does anything hurt?'

Zoe looked herself up and down in the mirror again, swallowed
hard. 'I don't think so.'

'Hang on,' said the woman and disappeared, reappearing with some brown liquid in a small glass.

'Sit down,' she said. 'Drink this.'

Zoe did as she was told, then spluttered and coughed.

'Ah, there you are,' said Agnieszka nodding her head approvingly. 'That'll get you.'

Tears sprang to Zoe's eyes.

'It's blended,' said Agnieszka mysteriously.

Whatever it was, gradually Zoe felt herself coming back together.

'Oh my God,' she said, swaying a little. 'Oh my God.'

'I know.' said the woman. 'It's absolutely wild out there. Thank God you're all right.'

Zoe started washing her arms.

'You *are* all right?' said the woman anxiously.

'I think so,' said Zoe, still shakily. 'Oh God … a tree. A tree attacked me. Oh God. I need to … I need to contact Hari. No. No I don't. Nobody tell him anything. Oh God. Oh *God*. I leave him for *one day* and nearly get killed. *One day.*'

'Is there someone you want me to call?' asked the nice lady.

Zoe stared at herself in the mirror, and a tear trickled down her face. She realised, horribly, that there really wasn't anyone that needed calling. Her mum would fret and was too far away. Jaz wouldn't care. Nina would only worry about her precious van. She suddenly felt very upset and very alone. She splashed water on her face, started washing away the blood.

'I'm fine,' she said eventually. 'I'm absolutely fine.'

'You don't look fine,' said Agnieszka. 'You're white as a sheet. Come through and have another whisky. Although I'll probably have to charge you for this one.'

Zoe walked back into the lobby which was now full of similarly shell-shocked if not quite as scratched and banged-up tourists, bustling round the bar and asking in heavily accented English for whisky and tea. The woman smiled at her apologetically, pointed her towards an empty sofa, and slipped behind the bar. Zoe wobbled towards it. A tall man came up to her.

183

'You okay?'

Zoe blinked at him.

'I . . . I brought you in a second ago?'

He swam in and out of focus a little bit. Broad. Solid-looking. Dark curly hair. Large jumper.

He put out a hand.

'Murdo. Hi there. Are you okay? You looked a bit shocked.'

'I'm . . . I'm fine,' said Zoe, looking round at all the people and the noise and the friendly smiles of all these strangers, and she passed out on the carpet before she could take another step.

~ ~

Dr Joan was holding up a rather large shard of glass to the light, but Zoe had not the faintest idea where she was.

'Look at this!' sniffed Joan. 'This is like when I took an entire spool of barbed wire out of a horse's stomach.'

'What, for fun?' someone else was saying and Joan was pointedly not answering them.

Zoe blinked and glanced at her arm.

'*Ouch!*' she said.

'Yes rather,' said Joan. 'Unfortunately you were unconscious so I couldn't ask your consent for an anaesthetic. But I just took it out anyway.'

'Owww,' said Zoe as the pain flooded her. 'I feel *very strongly* that this wasn't my fault.'

'Yes, Nina's always had trouble driving that van,' said someone else sagely.

'I wasn't having trouble!' said Zoe, suddenly feeling very alert. 'The coach was having trouble! It was driving straight at me.'

'It's a very big van for a very wee lassie,' said someone else. Zoe turned round.

'I swerved to stop the coach crash!' she said. 'Everyone should be telling me how brave I was and how I saved everyone in the coach by not crashing into it.'

184

People's heads turned to a short chubby man wearing a clip-on tie and a short-sleeved shirt with tinted bifocals – clearly the coach driver. He lifted his hands up.

'Bad stormy day for everyone, aye?' he said. 'Och, wee lassie, I'm glad you didn't do yourself a mischief.'

'You nearly did me a mischief!' said Zoe loudly, furious.

The landlady hushed her. 'It's okay,' she said. 'You've had a shock.'

'I've had two!' said Zoe. 'First I had to crash my van and now the bus driver is telling big fat lies about it!'

'I'm just glad you're no' hurt,' muttered the coach driver. 'When you crashed your van.'

'I *am* hurt,' said Zoe, brandishing her arm.

'You know,' went on the coach driver. Someone had brought him a snifter of whisky as well and he appeared to be turning into quite the hero of the hour. 'The last girl with that van – you see it everywhere, it's a menace –' To be strictly fair to the coach driver, sometimes it *was* a menace. '– the last girl nearly got run down on the level crossing.'

He smiled benevolently at Zoe. 'I'm so glad I managed not to hit you.'

'Yeah, well done,' said a couple of bystanders.

'It's hard for yon English,' said a voice. 'They don't know the roads, do they?'

There was a mutter of general agreement at this, that English people could not in fact possibly know the roads. Zoe would have contemplated threatening to sue, except it seemed increasingly likely that the coach driver would find 250 people who thought they were all genuine eye witnesses and would testify on his behalf. She glanced at her sore arm.

'Oh, for goodness' sake,' she said. 'I just want to go home.'

'Good,' said the man called Murdo. 'Looks like you're thinking more clearly already.'

'I am,' said Zoe frowning at the small coach driver, who was now being comforted and clapped by his passengers like some kind of hero. 'I am thinking this is all nonsense.'

The van was a mess, books everywhere, the windscreen

completely gone. Someone had already kindly removed the broken glass though. But what now?

Well, the best thing to do was to call someone. But Nina was in hospital and the last thing she could do was have a shock. There was nobody at the big house she could call – what would Mrs MacGlone do, after all? She sighed, and stared at her phone.

Behind her was the man who'd helped, heading towards what appeared to be a boat on the shore.

'You all right?' he said.

'I don't know what to do,' said Zoe, trembling.

'Well, call someone, I suppose,' he said, looking at the empty windscreen.

'Do you know who to call?'

He did.

～ ✕

The mechanics were stuck behind a few fallen trees en route, but if she could sit tight they'd get there. The same went for the coach. Inside, Agnieszka was going pink with excitement about how many lunches she was going to have to prepare. The choices were sandwiches with cheese, or sandwiches with cheese and ham, so she was going to be busy.

Zoe went out into the road and started picking up the books that had scattered when the van had careered from side to side. Some were dusty and a little damp; some had more or less got through unscathed. Perhaps, she thought, she could have a sale.

Murdo came out next to her and picked up a copy of *The Terror*.

'What's this then?' he said, looking at the ship on the cover with interest.

'Oh, the *Erebus* and *Terror*,' said Zoe. 'Two ships went to try and find the Northwest Passage and were never seen again.'

'And this is what happened to them?'

'It's an idea,' said Zoe. 'It's pretty gruesome, incredibly dark and very, very long.'

She mused.

'A near-perfect book in fact. The warmer you are when you're reading it, the more you'll enjoy how miserable everyone else in it is.'

Murdo carried on looking at it.

'I might take this.'

'You can have money off if it's damaged,' said Zoe.

Murdo didn't mention that he thought – having picked her bodily up off the floor and saved her from potentially dying in a fireball then calling the garage – he probably ought to have it for free, more or less.

'Okay,' he said. 'I'll take it. I'm a sailor myself.'

'Oh yes?' said Zoe, looking at him. He was solid-set, running mildly to fat, but in a comforting rather than unattractive way. His pleasant bluff face was ruddy and he had very humorous, sparkly dark eyes, she couldn't help noticing. Then she reminded herself what had happened the last time she'd noticed a pair of sparkling dark eyes.

'Whereabouts?'

Murdo indicated the loch in front of them, lapping on the narrow shore. 'I take the tour boats out,' he said. He tapped the book. 'It's not quite the Northwest passage,' he smiled. 'Although it does get a little tasty from time to time.'

They both looked out on the choppy waters. 'Bit too much today,' he said. 'Not for me,' he added quickly. 'I mean, for the tourists.'

'You take people out to look for the monster?' said Zoe.

'You crash vans full of books into buses?' he said.

'I do *not*!'

'Okay,' said Murdo. 'But everyone's got to make a living.'

'Have you ever . . . ?'

'Maybe.'

'You didn't know what I was going to ask.'

'You were going to ask if I'd ever seen the monster. Because that's what 99.99 per cent of everyone asks me and the other person was very, very drunk.'

Zoe smiled.

187

'Well, I'm glad I'm a very boring person and we can get it out of the way. What do you mean "maybe"? Is that what you have to say, otherwise nobody will come out on your tours with you?'

'Maybe,' said Murdo again, infuriatingly.

'I thought it had all been disproved anyway,' said Zoe. 'Science and that.'

'Science and that,' said Murdo contemplatively. He scratched his mop of thick hair. 'Uh-huh.'

'Oh, that's good,' said Zoe. 'Kind of a mystical schtick going on that doesn't quite answer the question. Very good.'

They wandered back towards the hotel. Several bus passengers were milling around. The bus wasn't going to get fixed any faster than they were, and they peered into the van curiously.

'Have you got any books on Loch Ness?' said one woman wearing a Pac A Mac against the still-howling wind.

As it happened, Zoe had two, one for adults and one for children, and she immediately sold both of them.

'You'd think,' said Murdo, who should have been doing repairs and maintenance on his boat in down time, in a storm, and as a result was much happier hanging around and talking to this dark-haired girl. 'You'd think that someone running a bookshop around Loch Ness would probably carry a few more books about Loch Ness.'

'I *know*,' said Zoe, who was rapidly coming to this conclusion herself. 'I think I'll have to get some in.'

Agnieszka emerged from the hotel, a tea towel thrown over her shoulder, a happy look on her face.

'This is the busiest we've been in months,' she said happily.

'You should crash more tour buses,' said Murdo. 'Set them up, like pins in the road.'

Agnieszka hit him playfully with the tea towel.

'You be quiet.'

She turned to Zoe.

'It's hard. The official visitor centre is round the other side. They get most of the business – they've got a cool museum and everything. We get what's left.'

'It still seems lots,' said Zoe, thinking of the coaches in the morning.

Agnieszka sighed.

'Oh, they come, they take a picture, sometimes they buy a sandwich, they use the toilet, then off they go again. In fact, I'm losing money just in how much toilet roll they get through.'

'Can't you charge them?' said Zoe.

'Seems a bit . . .' Agnieszka screwed up her face.

'Don't they catch the boat here?'

Agnieszka shot Murdo a cross look.

'Oh no, *some* people moor out of the visitor centre. Even though they live practically next door, they go right to the other side.'

Zoe looked at Murdo. 'You live next door and you take the boat away every morning?'

He looked back at her.

'You haven't been making a living in the Highlands long, have you?'

Zoe had to turn away to serve a few customers, who were buying anything Scottish they could find – she even sold a mint edition of Waverley novels (which was going to cause Nina's eyebrows to rise. It would also raise the eyebrows of the airline check-in staff who loaded planes by weight, and those of the lady's Canadian grandchildren, one of whom would devour the entire series in one gulp and grow up to become Newfoundland's foremost Sir Walter Scott historian and an internationally recognised expert with an incredibly fulfilling career as a television academic).

'Maybe,' she said, musing. 'Maybe I should come down *here* more often. Especially on rainy days.'

'You know the coaches are heading back to Edinburgh or to London?' said Agnieszka. 'I think there's a lot of people would like something to read. Bring some large print.'

'And some translations?' said Murdo. *'Per favore seduti.'*

'That's quite impressive,' said Zoe.

'ボートに座ってください,' said Murdo.

'Okay, now you're freaking me out,' said Zoe.

'He can speak six languages,' said Agnieszka, looking at him fondly.

'I can,' said Murdo. 'That was "Please don't stand up in the boat".'

'I'm still impressed,' said Zoe.

'*Et vous pouvez manger bien dans notre retour au centre*,' he said. 'That's the bit, Agnieszka, where I tell them to eat at the visitor centre.'

'That place is horrible,' said Agnieszka.

'Yes,' said Murdo patiently. 'But they can get more than a sandwich with cheese or a sandwich with ham and cheese.'

'Everyone likes ham and cheese,' said Agnieszka.

The storm, as they'd been talking inside the van, had started to die away and there was even the occasional watery ray of sunshine peeping out from behind a cloud, as if the sun was apologising shyly for all the tempestuous fury that had come their way just moments before. Zoe couldn't get used to it at all: surely there couldn't be anywhere else in the world where the weather changed so fast and so entirely. The stones beneath their feet were already drying out.

They emerged as the crowd thinned, and looked at the little brown hotel. The gutters needed cleaning and the window frames repairing and repainting. Agnieszka sighed.

'You could do it, you know,' said Murdo.

'Would you start your boat from here if I did?' said Agnieszka. Murdo shrugged.

'Maybe.'

He turned to Zoe. 'Will you bring your van back?'

'I don't know,' said Zoe. 'Will there be an evil coach driver ready to jump out and run me off the road?'

'It's all right to admit it when things haven't quite gone your way,' said Murdo.

Zoe gave him a hard stare, just as the welcome sign of a large AA van finally trundled up the road towards them.

Chapter Thirty-one

Nursery had not, Zoe gathered, gone well today. Not at all. There appeared to be a bruise mark on Hari's arm that Tara insisted had been utterly accidental.

But she couldn't bear to think about what would have happened if she'd had him with her. What if a shard of glass had cut right through him? Hit him in the eye? She felt caught between a rock and a hard place.

Still though, here was something undeniable: as they turned back up the gravel drive, Zoe having driven the entire route at twenty miles an hour, Hari started bouncing up and down in his seat with excitement, and as soon as she stopped the car and unbuckled him, he dived down in glee and charged off round the back to find Patrick.

The idea of Hari doing anything on his own happily was completely new to Zoe, and she watched him for a while as he went, then carefully and tiredly got out herself. It had been a big day and she didn't feel ready to face the kitchen just yet. Mrs MacGlone came charging out and vanished without as much as a wave.

Zoe took her time. It was now a deep golden-stained afternoon, only the shaken leaves and fallen branches everywhere any reminder that the storm had existed at all.

She lingered in the forecourt and stared up at the engraving over the front door. She hadn't noticed it before; the letters were so ornate she'd assumed it would be in Latin or something poncey she wouldn't be able to understand.

But now she could see there were small repeated designs – a fish, a sheaf – and the words, cut in an angular font into the grey sandstone around the door frame: 'Speuran Talamh Gainmheach Locha'.

She was staring at it when she heard a crunching of heavy feet on the gravel and turned round to see Ramsay coming up behind her. His face was rueful.

'I ... I wanted to apologise.'

'No need,' said Zoe. 'I've been told not to stick my nose in.'

He rubbed his hand along the back of his neck.

'I appreciate it may not seem like a conventional set-up.'

Zoe blinked.

'You can say that again,' she said.

He sighed and kicked the doorstep.

'I have ... I have to work very hard to keep the lights on here.'

Zoe nodded.

'It ... well. Things can ... anyway. Sorry.'

'I'm sorry,' said Zoe. 'I spoke out of turn.'

'No, no. I know what you mean ... They're not being too horrible to you?'

Zoe decided it was prudent not to mention the fact that she was fairly sure things were being moved around in her room, and that morning Shackleton had dropped an entire bag of flour on the floor and watched her clear it up as Mary had laughed in her face.

Instead she changed the subject.

'I hadn't seen the thing carved over the door before. What does it say?'

'I never look at it myself,' confessed Ramsay. 'But I know. "Sky, sand, loch, land".'

'... loch and land,' said Zoe.

'Actually it's pronounced *locchhhhh*,' said Ramsay making a slightly spitting sound.

'I know,' said Zoe. 'I'm not going to try it – I'll sound like an idiot. I'm from Bethnal Green.'

'You'll sound like a *correct* idiot, who's making an effort!'

'I am making an effort! Look!'

She held up the dripping plastic bag. Lennox had left her some venison steaks.

'What's that?'

'Venison,' said Zoe. 'I'm to fry it up with some cloudberries.'

'Where did you get it?'

Zoe glanced up.

'Why? Did someone steal it off you?'

Ramsay ran his hands through his hair. 'Oh, generally speaking. Still, at least you're in the supply chain. Can you really cook venison?'

Zoe shrugged.

'Well, someone on YouTube can, so I'm taking it from them.'

There was a slight pause, then Ramsay said, 'Right, yes, I see,' in a way that made it instantly clear to Zoe that he didn't have the faintest idea what she was talking about.

He grimaced.

'Am I . . . ? I mean, there's enough cash in the kitty, isn't there? You're not having to poach to feed the children or anything?'

'Oh no, it's fine,' said Zoe. 'Well, if you have any spare?'

His face looked worried and she looked back at the inscription.

'So. Sky, sand, loch, land. Is it basically just reminding you that you own absolutely everything around you? That you're the master of all you survey?'

Her tone was lightly mocking.

Ramsay blinked in surprise. The four words were burned into his make-up really; he'd always heard them, repeated as if a grace, and their Latin translation made up their crest of arms. *Caelum lacus harena terra.*

'No, quite the opposite,' he replied, a trifle irritated. 'It's to remind you what's actually all about you, that you're merely a trespasser on what has always been here and what will always be here. It's a reminder to treasure it and to look after it, and that worldly things – houses, cups, jewellery, all of that stuff – don't last and don't matter.'

He warmed to his subject.

'And also, it's even better than that – it's not like a skull and a goblet and a pile of rotting fruit. It's hopeful. It's saying, you will come and you will go, but these things that go on for ever are all around you; look how beautiful and wonderful they are. Sheaves from the field, fish from the loch, light from the sky and glass from the sand. Every day.'

Zoe looked at him. He was quite different when caught up in speaking. She was so used to him being distracted and distant; never quite there or at one with the children or the house or her. He caught her looking and his oversized hands started to fiddle awkwardly with his buttonhole.

'I see,' she said. She looked beyond him, down the gravel drive and into the garden. The evening sun was descending, and the shadows of the trimmed hedges were long across the grass.

'We used to have topiary,' said Ramsay, who was looking the same way as her. 'That's bushes cut into shapes.'

'I know what it is, thanks,' said Zoe chippily.

'Oh yes, of course. Sorry.'

'I'm not actually on the house tour.'

He went quiet after that, put his large hands deep in his pockets.

'Oh, I'm only teasing,' said Zoe, cursing herself for being so out of practice at talking to new people. 'What topiary did you have? A monster?'

He gave her a look.

'No,' he said eventually. 'Not a monster. We had roosters one year though.'

'I bloody hate chickens,' said Zoe automatically. Ramsay gave her a strange look.

'Well, I hate this one chicken,' said Zoe. 'This one chicken who had got it in for me.'

'I don't think chickens can have it in for people,' said Ramsay.

'Well, you explain how it keeps pooing in my wellington boots.'

Ramsay frowned.

'Perhaps move your wellington boots?'

'I did!' said Zoe. 'It found them. Because it is a chicken of evil.'

'We also had fish,' said Ramsay hastily changing the subject. 'Beautifully trimmed. They were lovely.'

'Can't you still have them? They'd look lovely in this light,' said Zoe. The sun was golden and huge, going down in the sky.

'I know,' said Ramsay regretfully. 'Cutbacks, I'm afraid. Again.'

'You should train up the children to do it.'

Ramsay gave her a sharp look. 'I'll add that to my list of things I'm getting wrong, thanks.'

There was a tricky silence.

'Right. I'd better get on. I might let Shackleton loose on the venison.'

'That,' said Ramsay, 'is not a phrase I ever thought I'd hear.'

And he followed her into the house where, in short order, a very pleasant roasting scent started to emanate on the autumnal air, followed briefly by a rather less pleasant burning smell, but one that was soon rectified, and there was so much it didn't really matter that some of the edges had to get chopped off, and anyway Porteous turned up at a perfect time and slipped in and out like a leftovers ghost, whisking any spare food away, and Ramsay, sticking to his word, actually popped in for half an hour, and there was a conversation instigated by Patrick about dinosaurs and why it was very unfair that they didn't have some way of watching more films about dinosaurs as the television was broken and Ramsay had frowned and said he hadn't realised they had a television and Zoe had said, you guys are living in the 1920s and Ramsay had said he didn't see much wrong with that and she said, well, you will when you have to get glasses for Patrick because he's trying to watch *Jurassic Park* on my phone and Ramsay said he would try and deal with it and Zoe said he should, they were practically giving tellies away these days and Ramsay said, quite right, they were only fit for the dump and Zoe said, I have now lived in this house for six weeks and I can tell you I'm not sure about your knowing what's fit for the dump abilities, and the children, of all things, actually laughed – they actually laughed – and it had suddenly occurred to Ramsay, as it hadn't for a long time, that perhaps he should nip down to the cellar and get one of those lovely bottles of red his ancestors had stored down there – why ever not? – and there was light and noise and chatter in the kitchen for the first time in such a very long time, and he felt a quick stab of guilt, then decided he could probably squash that down too with the red wine, when there came a sudden and decisive knock at the back door.

Chapter Thirty-two

Everyone turned their head round, Shackleton letting his mouth fall open. Zoe hissed at him to close it, then smiled.

'Hellooooo!' trilled a loud confident voice, clear as a bell. Zoe blinked. Nobody visited. That was kind of the deal, as she understood it. It was just them, Mrs MacGlone, Wilby the gardener and the occasional lost tourist pretending they needed directions in an attempt to get in to have a look round. Zoe had been quite amazed by their boldness. But they always came to the front door. Whoever was attached to this voice had been here before.

A tall, slender blonde sidled in. She was heavily and fully made-up in a way that made it difficult to tell her age – she could have been anywhere from about twenty-eight to a very well preserved forty – wearing an expensive coat that wouldn't have lasted two minutes in Lennox's courtyard and bringing with her a strong scent of fine perfume. She reminded Zoe immediately of the women who dropped their kids at the nursery she used to work at; the ones to whom she was utterly invisible.

Her first striking thought was that it might be the children's mother; her thin face wouldn't be a mile away from Mary's pinched look. She blinked. It couldn't be, could it? But then again, surely the children would be reacting, rather than sitting still, staring at their food glumly.

'RAMZER!' the woman yelled. Ramsay's brow furrowed at first, then his face relaxed slightly.

'Rissie,' he said finally. She barrelled over.

'Darling,' she said, embracing him. She ignored everyone else in the room. 'I'm back. I know. Ages. You know what it's like.'

'I do.'

'Oh God,' muttered Mary under her breath. Zoe shot her a look but Mary didn't return it; she didn't want an ally. Instead she stood up.

'Hello, darlings,' said the woman, looking round. 'Oh, look at you all, beautiful and gorgeous as ever! Aren't you amazing!'

All three children stared at her stonily.

'Here, I brought presents!'

She produced three boxes of Turkish delight from her bag, smiling slightly nervously.

'I've been in Istanbul and I thought . . . '

The children took them sullenly, without thanks, and immediately ripped them open and started eating them, disregarding the dinner already on their plates. Zoe was horrified by their rudeness.

'THANK YOU,' she said loudly. 'I think that's what we all meant to say.'

Mary shot her a look.

'Um, don't mention it,' said the woman. She smiled hopefully at Ramsay. 'They're such dear little things.'

Zoe couldn't think of a word less suited to Shackleton, who was practically grunting as he scarfed the sweets, sugar around his mouth and a bit of spittle on his chin. She glanced at Ramsay with her eyebrows up and he said, "Children, say thank you to Larissa.'

'*Thank you, Larissa*,' said Mary in the most sarcastic tone imaginable.

'You're so welcome!' said the woman. 'Are you the new nanny?'

'Hello,' said Zoe, putting her hand out. Larissa looked surprised as if acknowledging her was about as far as she could be expected to go, but took it, smiling graciously.

'They're just such gorgeous kids, aren't they?'

Mary snorted loudly. Hari was behind Zoe's knees, and she patted his head encouragingly.

'I'm going upstairs,' Mary announced, and walked off, leaving her plates behind her and scraping her chair loudly. Normally Zoe would have called her back, but she wasn't in the mood for a Mary shout fest that evening in front of this glamorous person, so she left it.

'Do you fancy coming out for a drink, sweetie?' Larissa was saying to Ramsay. 'You look like a man who needs a bit of fun.'

Zoe was slightly annoyed that Larissa was obviously right about this as they swept out, Larissa saying once again how lovely it was to see the wonderful children, who stared at her glassy-eyed.

'Well,' said Zoe. 'That wasn't very nice behaviour.'

'She's absolutely not nice,' agreed Patrick.

'Not her! She was super-nice! I'm talking about you guys!'

Shackleton methodically carried on with the Turkish delight, chewing without much enthusiasm. He shrugged.

'She is Daddy's SPESHUL FRIEND,' Patrick said. 'She told us that.'

'She isn't,' said Shackleton scornfully. 'She wishes.'

'She is!' said Patrick. 'She told me she is very, very SPESHUL.'

'Very, very ANNOYING,' said Shackleton. 'She is all sweet sweet sweet.'

'What's wrong with that?' said Zoe. 'What's wrong with someone being nice to you?'

'AND THEN!' said Patrick with a flourish.

'And then what?' said Zoe.

'AND THEN! FOR SURE!'

'What are you talking about?'

'Not "for sure", you absolute plank,' said Shackleton. 'Brochure. She brought brochures. We weren't meant to see them.'

'What kind of brochures?'

'Prison,' said Patrick.

'Prison?'

'Boarding school,' said Shackleton. 'She thinks we should be in boarding school.'

'Ohhh,' said Zoe. 'Really? And you definitely don't want to go to boarding school?'

Shackleton gave her a look. 'She wants rid of us so she can marry Dad and ... '

'Ugh,' said Patrick.

'She seems nice,' said Zoe mildly.

'She pretends,' said Patrick. 'It's not real.'

'Sometimes people pretend to be nice until things are nice,' said Zoe. 'And it works.'

Patrick looked unconvinced.

'No,' said Shackleton. 'People pretend to be nice until they've packed other people off to boarding school and they never have to see them again.'

'Prison,' said Patrick and his little face looked so sad Zoe suddenly felt her heart go out to him.

Normally at night she went to bed before the children, absolutely exhausted. Tonight, however, she could see how rattled they were.

'Look, you can't be rude to people in the house like that. It was naughty.'

The boys looked at her.

'But if you help me clear up ... would you like a story?'

She was electrified by the change in Patrick's demeanour.

'I DO!' said Patrick. 'I ABSOLUTELY WANT A STORY! Please please please! I never ever get a story!'

'Doesn't Daddy ever read you a story?'

'He's always working. Or in the ... LIBRARY.'

He said the word like he might have said 'dungeon'.

'What about your other nannies?'

'"We most absolutely do not read English, Patrick",' recited Patrick. '"Mary has been absolutely most naughty, Patrick, and nobody deserves a story". "Go away, Patrick, I am very busy with my crying at the moment".'

'Well,' said Zoe, her lips twitching unavoidably. 'You go and get in your pyjamas and I'll come up and brush your teeth and we'll see what we can do.'

'Do you have to brush your teeth *every* day, Nanny Seven?'

'Yes,' sighed Zoe, clearing away the rest of the plates. 'I'm afraid so.'

Even she was surprised when she got up there and found, lined up in front of the sink in the bedroom, in a room very like Mary's but with two beds in it, both of the younger boys in identical ancient flannelette pyjamas with well-darned tears.

'Oh, look at you two,' she said. 'Did you get dressed all by yourself?'

Hari nodded solemnly.

'I perhaps absolutely helped,' said Patrick.

'Okay then,' said Zoe, and took out her old Kindle with *Up on the Rooftops* on it. It had been her absolute favourite as a child.

'What is going to happen?' said Patrick, sounding nervous. And Zoe's heart went out again to the child who never got read a story.

'Well, first we get nice and cosy,' said Zoe. Hari was already sitting up patiently. He was too young for it, she knew, but it was the soothing quality of her voice as much as anything else when she put the two boys either side of her on Patrick's bed.

'Can Hari sleep here?' he asked eventually. Sure enough, just like Mary's room, the bedroom was absolutely vast and quite spooky, with tree branches waving in the wind outside the huge windows. She would never hear a sound. Not that Hari would ever make a sound.

'Would you like to do that, Hari?' she said. She was a little worried. They'd never been separated for a single night before, not ever. She didn't even own a baby monitor. She'd never had enough space to use one.

And. The ghost.

Hari, however, nodded, delighted.

'Are you sure?'

It wasn't a case of her being just in the same house. She was out of the huge bedroom, down the passageway, up the back stairs, and along the west wing where the servants' quarters were. He could scream and she wouldn't hear it. Mary could bite his leg off and she wouldn't know until the next day.

'I'll look after him!' said Patrick, not entirely setting her mind at rest.

'Do you know how to get to my room?' she said, and Patrick screwed up his face. 'Maybe?'

How, thought Zoe, raging inwardly, had this worked before? Who put children so far away from their caregiver that nobody could hear them if they cried at night? What on earth were they thinking? Were they just left to cry it out?

'Well, maybe not tonight,' she said.

'I can get Daddy,' said Patrick. 'Daddy is close. He likes it when we come in.'

'Oh,' said Zoe. 'Well.'

She hadn't thought of that. That he would want them close to him. But then, he was away so often . . .

She started reading anyway, trying to figure out what to do.

So they started out on the perilous (that means 'dangerous') *journey through the rigging, desperate and terrified as they saw, looming ahead, their destination* (that means place you're going to, Hari) – *Galleon's Reach. The wind was picking up again, and Wallace saw the weather cocks on the roofs around them, ships in full sail, spinning and spinning.*

'It's getting worse,' he muttered to Francis. 'We're going to have to find safety until the storm passes.'

'Fish!' said Francis, and Wallace rolled his eyes.

'Stop going on about fish,' he said. 'The pigeon mentioned it, that's all. Pigeons eat fish. I think.'

'I CAN SEE FISH!' Francis was shouting now and wobbling up and down in a way that Wallace didn't like. One slip was all it would take ...

He followed Francis's trembling, dirty finger, pointing south-east towards the river. And then he saw it ...

'No,' he said, his face white. 'No ...'

She found Patrick was grabbing at her arm.

'What's going to happen?!' he demanded. 'Why is the boy point-ing at fish?'

'Well, we'll find out,' said Zoe. 'This is what stories do. They start at the beginning, then things happen ...'

'Bad things?'

'Yes, usually bad things. Good things happening don't really make for very interesting stories.'

Patrick thought about this for a while.

'This,' he said eventually, 'is why I only like things about dinosaurs.'

Zoe considered it prudent at this point not to tell him what had happened to all the dinosaurs.

'You don't like stories at all?'

He shrugged.

She ventured an arm around his shoulders, which he shrugged off immediately.

'Well,' she said. 'Bad things happen.'

'This is a very bad thing happening,' said Patrick, point-ing to the illustration on her Kindle. 'Look! At Belin's Gate. Who's Belin?'

'An old warrior king,' said Zoe. 'He's there to protect the fish.'

'But they're only children!' moaned Patrick. 'They ABSOLUTELY cannot fight him.'

'Yes,' said Zoe patiently. 'But don't worry. There's lots of the book to go. It'll probably turn out fine ... it *will* turn out fine.'

Patrick looked at her unconvinced.

'Do things turn out fine?' he asked in a quiet voice, and Zoe suddenly found herself a little short of words and with an unexpected lump at her throat. She glanced at Hari, who had fallen fast asleep.

How could you tell a child without a mother that things turned out fine? If you were a child without a mother, did things turn out fine? Would lying help?

Zoe wanted to take him in her arms and hug him. But she couldn't.

'It's a long way to the end of the story,' she said.

She lifted Hari up.

'Can't he stay?' said Patrick, looking tiny in the big bed.

'One day, maybe,' said Zoe, and stood up. They regarded one another.

'Would you like a goodnight kiss then?' said Zoe casually, as if she didn't care one way or the other. There was a pause, then a tiny voice said, 'Absolutely I would,' and she bent down, Hari over her shoulder, and kissed Patrick very lightly on the forehead, and he did not shy away.

Chapter Thirty-three

Zoe did it. She ordered as many books on Loch Ness as she could find in the catalogue and started taking them to the visitor centre. She didn't even always take the van back to Lennox's, partly because it was further away and partly because she didn't want him to ask any suspicious questions about why she had a new windscreen. And partly the chicken.

Also, by the hotel was a small, slightly dilapidated children's playground, and while the autumn weather remained crisp and fine, she could take Hari along and pretend it was okay for him to be skipping nursery, and soon it just made sense to take Patrick along as well, and the two of them kicked leaves and climbed the climbing frame and absolutely loved the fact that the choice was either ham or cheese or ham and cheese sandwiches.

Murdo would bring his boat over from time to time and Agnieszka would come out and chat, and it was so pleasant to have adult company for a change – particularly adult company that wasn't constantly keeping secrets or looking annoyed – that Zoe could sit down on the benches overlooking the loch in between coach visits, and hear the children crunching in the leaves, and watch the sun sparkle off the water, and drink a cup of tea – she'd persuaded Agnieszka it might be a good idea to buy some paper cups and start serving it, and sure enough it had been a clear hit right away – and she'd take a breath, and look at the cash box and feel, just for a moment, rather pleased with herself.

The following Sunday, Zoe took Hari with her to the hospital for a visit. Nina was looking tired, but otherwise well, her bump vast and swelling over her loose-fitting pyjamas.

'How's it going?' said Zoe.

'Thanks for these,' said Nina, indicating the line of about four hundred Agatha Christie books Zoe had fed her in a tearing frenzy the previous week.

'I'm cutting you off,' said Zoe. 'Otherwise you're going to start accusing randoms of murder.'

'It's always the people you least suspect,' said Nina. 'Did you find out what happened to Ramsay's wife by the way? According to Agatha Christie, she is definitely dead, and it will definitely be somebody unlikely.'

Zoe shrugged.

'Okay,' she said. 'The gardener.'

'Oh no, it's always the gardener,' said Nina.

Zoe unloaded another pile. 'Okay. Start on Rebus. The murders are a great deal grittier.'

'I'm not sure if that's better or worse.'

Nina sighed and shifted slightly uncomfortably.

'Okay, let's have a look at the accounts then.'

She didn't have high hopes of the accounts at all, had been dreading it in fact, telling herself as long as it covered the petrol, the stock and the wage, it was all she could hope to keep the show on the road.

So she was to find herself pleasantly surprised – pleasantly surprised and undeniably slightly jealous.

Nina was proud of her ability to find the right book for the right person; to know instinctively what would suit people – where they would find comfort, or solace, or laughter, or thrills. Moods for books changed like the weather. Sometimes you wanted something profound to lose yourself in; a completely different world. Sometimes you wanted a romp. Sometimes you undeniably just wanted to read about something utterly awful happening to somebody who wasn't you. It was part of being a reader, that books chased your moods, and it was Nina's great skill to match them, like a sommelier matching a wine list to a menu.

'I can't believe you've managed to suit so many people to books.'

'Um. Yeah. Just luck I guess,' said Zoe. She felt obscurely guilty about the fact that so much of what she was selling were colouring books and silly stories about the Loch Ness monster being real – tartan tat, she knew Nina would say – and there was on some level a suspicion that Nina was right.

On the other hand, Zoe thought mutinously, she was making money. She wasn't sure Nina had ever been poor. Not properly poor. If there was money out there to be had, it was absurd to pass it up. That was how she justified it to herself. Plus, she'd had the windscreen to pay for.

'I've sent you the order papers,' Zoe said quickly. Nina hadn't really looked at them, having been particularly engrossed in the new Robert Galbraith.

'Fine,' she said.

'And I've been going up to the visitor centre . . . '

'At the loch?'

'Yeah . . . not the main one, the other one.'

Nina was furrowed her brow.

'What,' she said, 'are you selling there?'

She was instantly suspicious.

'Have you turned the van into some tartan touting tatty tourist shop?'

'That's a lot of Ts,' said Zoe. 'And no! I'm just . . . getting stuff in people seemed to like!'

'People like refined sugar and heroin,' said Nina. 'Are you selling that too?'

Zoe bit her lip uncomfortably. She had genuinely thought that she'd come up with something good and profitable. The coach parties cooed over the lovely little blue-painted van, bought souvenirs to take home and everyone was happy. Also she was considering selling tablet, which was by absolute definition refined sugar.

'So while you're at tourist places all the time, what's happening to all my regulars?' said Nina. 'I've spent two years building up clientele all round this area. They rely on me. If the van goes, they'll just go back to getting stuff other ways ... or not reading at all!'

'I know that,' said Zoe. 'Because they keep coming in and saying to me, "I want that new red book ... Nina will know the one I mean." Didn't you write any of this stuff down?'

'Yes,' said Nina. 'I totally wrote down everything I expected to happen when I had to get turned upside down and made to lie on my back unexpectedly for three months forty miles away from the place I actually live in.'

She couldn't help feeling a bit teary at that and Zoe went and sat on the bed next to her. She knew what it was like to feel lonely when you were pregnant.

'Sorry,' she said, opening her bag. 'Here. I brought you ...'

She pulled out a copy of *The Nanny Diaries* and *Rosemary's Baby*. Nina gave her a look.

'What?' said Zoe. 'It just helps to know that however badly you do, someone else will be doing worse. I've got *We Need to Talk About Kevin* too.'

'Oh, I've read that.'

'Yes. Well. Read it again, trust me. You'll feel quite differently about it.'

Nina took them with a smile.

'Thanks. But ... I'm a bit worried about what you're doing.'

'What, looking after your job and making money?' said Zoe flatly.

'I just ... I'd just rather it was the way it was.'

Zoe blinked.

'Right. On it.'

But as she left the hospital, she couldn't help feeling slightly mutinous. She was doing well for the van. Why couldn't Nina see that?

Chapter Thirty-four

It was the most glowing autumnal day. Everything was bright yellow and orange, the trees slowly beginning to turn. Zoe had got herself a cup of coffee and walked outside, wearing a vast old jumper over her nightie. She relished a few moments by herself as Hari picked his way through cereal indoors with Patrick chattering away to him as usual; Shackleton was half-listening, half-reading, and Mary had yet to emerge.

Some curling fronds of mist were lifting from the garden, but the sun promised to be warm and there were few clouds left in the sky. The trees rustled and swished enticingly ahead of her, and she watched to her utter amazement as a large bird – and how she wished she knew more about them – landed on the lawn and started ferociously tugging at a worm in the grass as the peacock bustled away, squawking. The air was scented with gorse and there was a feeling in the air that even in London Zoe could remember from her childhood: bonfires in the air, fireworks and Halloween coming in, all the feasts and treats of autumn with Christmas at the end. Such a wonderful time of year.

She had also had a good morning. She'd got up early and seen Shackleton sitting there, disconsolately prodding at his disconnected computer game.

'Come on,' she said. 'Nobody else is up. Help me make muffins.'

'Make what?'

'Just do it,' she said. 'Come on.'

And she'd made him weigh out the flour while she'd fiddled with the temperamental oven, and mix in the butter and the salt and the little bits of cheese and ham and onion they'd found around the place, and he'd watched them rise up, golden and fresh in the oven and smelling absolutely delicious, while she had completely enjoyed the genuine pleasure Shackleton had taken in it.

'I think you have a knack for baking,' she said to him, and he looked pleased. 'You should do this more often.'

'Can I eat them yet?'

'Absolutely not, you—'

'OW!'

'Well, there you go. I was about to warn you.'

He smiled.

Zoe went over to boil the kettle as he still tried to get the too-hot muffins out of their moulds.

'Mum would have liked this,' he said suddenly, and Zoe had to stop herself from turning around. She stayed staring at the kettle.

'Oh yeah?' she said, her heart beating fast, trying to keep her voice light.

'Well, she wouldn't have eaten them,' he said. 'But she would have liked the smell.'

'What was she like?' said Zoe, but as she turned round again his face was a picture of concentration getting the muffins on the cooling rack, and he didn't bring the subject up again.

'Well done,' Zoe said to him again later as they all sat around eating breakfast together, and Mary scowled, but Shackleton beamed and his big awkward face looked almost handsome.

It made Zoe think, looking at him, that the children really ought to be getting back to school; September was nearly over, and nothing at all had been mentioned. She'd need to talk to the headteacher, Kirsty, about it. Oh – and the children, and their dad.

But today was just glorious, and possibly one of the last nice days they'd have. She was determined that they were going to go out and enjoy it. It was absurd, she thought, that they hadn't even seen all the way round their property yet. Imagine living somewhere so large that you hadn't actually walked to the end. It was ridiculous, it really was.

She'd come indoors, refreshed, ready to round them all up. They were going on an outing!

She turned on the radio and found something suitably rousing and turned it up loud.

'What is happening?' said Patrick suspiciously.

'We're going exploring,' said Zoe.

'Oh good!' said Patrick. 'Whereabouts please?'

'Your garden!'

Ramsay, turning up rather exhausted from Larissa's that morning, saw the little party out at the far end of the garden and felt a pang. He jumped out of the car and hurried over to join them.

'Are you taking a walk? Can I come?'

Zoe wanted to give him a bit of a telling-off for not ever suggesting to take the children anywhere themselves, but the fuss she'd had dragging Mary and Shackleton out against their extreme protests made it rather more understandable, if not forgivable, and now that they were all out, she wasn't going to spoil it. The children were running among the golden trees, all having sticks, and Porteous had joined them and was leading them on a squirrel hunt, or a dinosaur hunt, depending on how old you were.

'You can come' said Zoe. 'Just as long as you get us a dishwasher. There isn't enough in the kitty.'

Ramsay walked closer. A low branch hit him on the head and he tried to brush it away. He couldn't seem to get anywhere without hitting something.

'Are you telling me,' he said eventually, 'that I wouldn't have got through six au pairs if I'd had a dishwasher all this time?'

'And good broadband and a microwave,' said Zoe. 'And a half-decent coffee machine. But apart from that, probably.'

Ramsay frowned.

'Why didn't any of them say?'

'They were probably too astounded,' said Zoe. 'Assumed they were being mended or something and were just waiting for you to appear with them.'

'It never even occurred to me,' said Ramsay, pushing his hair out of the way. Zoe rolled her eyes.

'Why are you rolling your eyes?'

'Because you consider this stuff below stairs!' said Zoe. 'It's absurd! You're not some Edwardian duke!'

'I think I am actually,' said Ramsay. 'Debrett's thinks so.'

Zoe stared at him.

'But we're the people,' she said. 'We're the people spending the most time with your children. Your children, the most important people in the world. Don't you think we're worthy of consideration?'

Ramsay flushed.

'Yes,' he mumbled. 'I'm sorry. I've been so distracted. It's all been such a ...'

Zoe waited for him to explain, but his voice tailed off.

'I'm sorry,' she said. 'I feel like I'm always lecturing you.'

'No, I'm sorry,' said Ramsay again, scratching his head. 'I get the feeling I need it.'

They walked on, the sunlight dappling down through the trees, the only sounds the children far off, running and laughing – even Mary's voice laughed at one point, the sound like low music exhumed from a faraway place, and they both paused together to listen to it.

Zoe was desperate for him to tell her. Just ask, she told herself, her fingertips digging into her palm. Just ask. She wanted – she desperately wanted – to like him. No, that didn't matter. She wanted him ... to be a good father. To be the kind of dad the children deserved; all children deserved. She needed to know.

She even opened her mouth to ask, to say something. It was ridiculous. These days, there were no secrets. Everything was out in the open. People talked. People asked about things.

'Ramsay . . .' she started but he was already talking.

'Your boy,' he said. 'Has he always been like this?'

Zoe was taken by surprise and looked up at him. His face looked nervous.

'He's never spoken, no,' said Zoe, wondering if they were confiding in one another, even as the tables had turned. They strolled on; for all the world they could be chatting about flowers, or bicycles, or something completely and utterly innocuous.

'He cried when he was younger, and laughed but . . . less and less now.'

'And what do they professionals say?'

'They say . . . he'll talk when he's ready,' sighed Zoe. 'That it's anxiety and he'll grow out of it. I really, really wish he was ready. Mostly so I could stop having this conversation.'

She smiled, though, to show she wasn't angry with him, just the situation.

Ramsay smiled back.

'I know,' he said then looked startled, as if something had slipped out that shouldn't.

'Oh . . . were you like that?' said Zoe, curious.

'Oh no,' said Ramsay, slightly flustered. 'That's not . . . that's not what I meant. I just . . .'

Zoe left a silence for him to finish.

'I know what it's . . .'

But he still couldn't seem to get it right. He took a deep breath and walked on slightly faster.

'Well. Anyway. There we are,' he said eventually. Zoe blinked. 'He's a nice little chap,' he added, looking at her. 'You should be proud.'

'Patrick has really looked after him,' said Zoe. 'So should you.'

Ramsay grimaced.

'Oh, that's nothing to do with me,' he said, his forehead low, and then the children came bursting out of the trees, laden down with conkers and holly and huge baskets of brambles and smeared sticky faces, and Zoe couldn't help looking at them all together and being happy to see them.

Larissa turned up again just as they were making jam. The two older ones were taking it in turns to stir the pot, and there was more music on the radio. Ramsay was by the fire, feet up on the grate, reading his book. Normally he'd have shut himself away in his library. Zoe looked at what he was reading; it was a beautiful hydrographical study of the loch from 1854, with full plate illustrations.

'I could sell that,' she said, not taking her eyes off the children stirring for an instant. They didn't realise quite how hot the jam was or, as was always possible in the case of Mary, had decided that if Zoe had said it, it absolutely couldn't be the case and was just pushing it to see.

'What? This?' said Ramsay, looking at it. 'I don't think so. It's completely out of date, totally archaic and some of it is downright wrong.'

Zoe couldn't help it. Her lips twitched.

'What? What is it?' he asked.

'Nothing.'

He looked at her. Shackleton laughed.

'She means you, Dad!'

'I most certainly do not!' said Zoe. 'Little pitchers have big ears. Come on.'

Ramsay looked a little awkward at first, as if he hadn't quite realised she was joking. Then he tried to smile, even as Shackleton burst out laughing.

'Well, you couldn't sell it.'

'I bet I could,' said Zoe. 'Why do you like it?'

'Because it's beautiful,' said Ramsay. Patrick pattered over to stare over his shoulder and Ramsay hoisted him up on his knee for a closer look. 'Because it tells you about a previous age, when people had only sail to go out on the loch or their two arms to row, and what they saw when they were out there, and what they thought it was. And how they lived – look.'

Zoe glanced over as he pointed out a line illustration of a row of tumbledown buildings.

'Look at that. The crofts that lined the shoreline. They would collect oysters, kale; they used seaweed as insulation. It would have been so commonplace to the artist, they don't even mention it. They didn't even know that in twenty years' time the clearances were coming. Everything they had, everything they knew, their entire way of life was about to be swept away. You could walk down there tomorrow and if you were lucky you might find a stone or two, buried deep in the ground, that used to mark their homes there; homes of people who lived for generations. And in an instant, they were gone and everything was wiped out, but without even realising it, they're memorialised here. There's still a place where people can see and remember them. And that's why I like it.'

It was quiet in the room for an instant. Then Mary yelled as the jam started to bubble and boil over and there was panic for a few moments as Zoe quickly stirred the jam together, then got them to empty and dry the jars from where they'd been boil-washed in the sink.

Ten minutes later, everything had been poured and sealed and nine jars of varying shapes and sizes were pleasingly full of the dark purple liquid sitting on the table and Zoe was despatching Mary, Patrick and Hari to a pile of stickers on which they were to date and label the jam jars. She looked fondly at the bent heads, then turned back to Ramsay.

'I can sell it,' she said again. 'And if I do, will you buy us a dishwasher?'

Ramsay looked at her and looked at his beloved book.

'I hate to give things up,' he said.

'Well, perhaps you're right and I won't be able to sell it,' said Zoe, her eyes dancing. Sighing heavily, Ramsay handed it over.

216

'Let's see,' he said. 'And don't get jam on it.'

Zoe rolled her eyes, placing it down carefully and wrapping it up in brown paper.

'Yes, thank you, I realise that. Tea? And bread and jam?'

Ramsay was thinking there wasn't much more he'd like than a huge cup of tea and some fresh bread and jam when Larissa appeared at the door.

'You left at some speed this morning!' she said, brandishing an ancient-looking, absurdly oversized waistcoat that clearly belonged to him. 'It's beautiful. An absolute classic. Ooh, doesn't the kitchen look gorgeous! Yoohoo, everyone! It's great to see your gorgeous faces.'

Mary sniffed.

'Hi, Larissa,' said Zoe. Larissa gave her a momentary cold look – she hadn't liked the domesticity of the scene she'd arrived on – then put her smile back on.

'Oh hello! You're doing a brilliant job here, well done! And I love what you've done with your hair.'

Zoe's hair was so windblown it had a stick in it.

'Darling Ramsay, I hate to take you away from the lovely children, but you know it's the hunt ball on Saturday? We were going to discuss it?'

Ramsay sighed.

'Well, honestly, I don't really want to go, so I feel there's no need. People just gossip and—'

'Oh no, everyone's so lovely! They're not gossiping; they just miss you! Want to know how well you're doing with the business and everything.'

Ramsay let out a hollow laugh. 'Well, that will be a pretty short conversation.'

'Oh, sweetie, you can't lock yourself up for ever, can he, Zoe?'

Zoe blinked.

'Well . . . no. No. You shouldn't.'

Although she genuinely felt exactly the opposite; that any time he did have, he should be spending it with his children.

217

'Really?' Ramsay looked at Zoe, as this was very much what he had thought she had meant as well, and he felt rather injured that she hadn't noticed he was trying to improve.

'Come on,' Larissa said to him. And once again, 'You deserve some fun, darling!'

The Urquart children looked up at that, instant fear in their faces, as if the day they'd spent in the woods had not in fact been fun for their father after all.

Zoe moved over to the sink so her face didn't betray her mood. Ramsay glanced at her and saw she'd moved. Larissa noticed and tried her most appealing smile.

'Pleeeease?'

'Yes, yes, all right,' said Ramsay, getting up. 'I'll come.'

'Plllleeeeeeeeasssssssee,' imitated Mary nastily as soon as they were out the door. 'Plllleeeeeeeaassssseee marry me and get rid of your children. Plllllleeeeeeaassssssseee!'

'Mary!' said Zoe. 'None of that. I mean it.'

'Maybe you'd be glad to be rid of us too,' said Mary. 'Everyone else is.'

'Well, I'm afraid you're rather stuck with me,' said Zoe. 'Especially now the ghost has left.'

There was a sudden silence. The three children all looked at one another and Zoe, who had taken a calculated risk, suddenly felt oddly relieved.

'Um, what ghost?' said Mary innocently.

'We told you to stop it,' said Shackleton crossly. 'Just … just *stop it*.'

'STOP BEING A STUPID GHOST!' shouted Patrick. 'I absolutely don't want Hari to go!'

'I don't know *what* you're talking about,' said Mary, marching out and slamming the door.

'Has she really stopped?' said Shackleton. 'It's a good sign if she has; she did it to all the other nannies.'

'Not quite,' said Zoe, thinking of the occasional swishing noises that came up and down the corridor at night. It was amazing just how much relief she felt, even as she told herself how ridiculous the whole thing had been. 'But hopefully she will now.'

Zoe looked at Shackleton, who was still wearing a pensive expression following Larissa's departure.

'You know,' she said. 'I mean, you will have to go back to school at some point. Why don't you just go to the school in Kirrinfief? Or Inverness?'

Shackleton turned on her almost viciously.

'Ooh, where's your mum, Shackleton? Why have you got such a funny name? Do you have ghosts in your house? Mah mah mah. All bloody day. No chance.'

'They are absolutely mean,' agreed Patrick from where he was illustrating a very complex sign for Dinosaur Jam. 'Why do you think you're so absolutely clever, Patrick? Are you always showing off?'

Zoe smiled at that.

'I like it when you show off,' she said, tousling his hair.

'I'm NOT showing off,' said Patrick crossly. 'I am just absolutely clever.'

'You're not that clever,' pointed out Zoe. 'Mary's got all the hot water again.'

'Oh no,' said Patrick happily. 'No bath for me.'

Chapter Thirty-five

The weirdest thing was, Zoe had genuinely thought things were getting better.

She hadn't realised, truly, that it was often when people were feeling things were getting slightly more cheerful, that was when everything started to go pear-shaped, when you let your guard drop.

The season had worn on, each day only exacerbating its beauty. The sun had stayed well into September, and for the first time ever, Zoe was watching the seasons change day by day; the leaf patterns you could almost watch turning golden and orange. She pointed out the changes to Hari, and it was the strangest thing: she went from being annoyed at their tiny attic room to loving the way it put them right up among the tree tops, almost as if they were in their own little nest, listening to the swishing as the leaves fell and watching the great clouds of birds take off on their long journeys south. Zoe had heard of bird migration, dimly in a classroom somewhere, but she had never seen it, the great concatenations of squawking creatures rising, one and a multitude, each with the hidden knowledge inside them, a collective instinct that would take them all the way to Morocco. They watched them and marvelled, partly at the sight, partly at the idea that she was becoming a birdwatcher. Her cleaning up efforts had uncovered several pairs of binoculars and she had felt very little guilt at annexing a set – after all, how could it, she told herself, be stealing if she didn't take them out of the house – and Hari could sit, once she'd taught him to stop fiddling with the knob, for hours watching the eagle come back and start picking worms out of the ground, stalking around like a gang leader in a pub as if to warn off any other birds.

She found some beautifully illustrated bird spotting guides and stocked them. Once again, they weren't popular in the village, where people had grown up with the land and didn't need someone to tell them the difference between a crow and a starling. But at the visitor centre, they did absolute gangbusters. You could see if you were quiet – the herons sit, watchful, glorious, as if utterly scornful that any other creature could approach their beauty and ballerina grace, then unfold their magnificent wings, extend themselves, take off over the loch like Nureyev.

With a four-hour drive for many of the tourists back to Glasgow or Edinburgh, the spotter's guides were a huge hit, and once more, Zoe made a reorder without telling Nina exactly what she was up to. She realised yet again this was going completely against her instructions, that she was flagrantly disobeying her boss, who was in hospital, but that was just going to have to wait, because she had ninety million problems on top of that one and for the moment, the fact that she was making money and actually successfully running the business was so much of a high she couldn't bear to think about it.

But The Beeches, if not exactly a haven of peace and happiness . . . it felt settled. There was order, routine. The children had to get out of the house, that was the new rule, so they weren't just sitting around giving Mrs MacGlone trouble. They also had to clean their own rooms and bring down and take up their own laundry.

There had been various fulminations and some swearing on this issue, but Zoe was unbowed. There may have been six au pairs before her, but few had had to deal with quite as much intransigence as a childminder at a London pre-prep, and she was resolutely unfazed, figuring also, with every day she stayed, that the family would be less and less likely to want to find someone else, however much Mrs MacGlone disliked her.

And however much Mrs MacGlone disliked her, it didn't really matter as the effects made themselves known. Freed of following the children round the kitchen, she had time to keep the public rooms cleaner. The shutters now being open year-round left the dust harder to ignore, and the amount of rubbish that had been removed made it easier to get into the nooks and crannies. The entire house was looking better, more lived in, cheerier.

And, best of all, Zoe had won her dishwasher. She had brought the receipt for the book home triumphantly, along with Ramsay's not inconsiderable cut, sticking her tongue out at him when she met him in the hallway.

He had looked at first pleased and then crestfallen.

'What is it?' said Zoe. 'Don't know what a dishwasher is? Worried you'll have to ask for one and point at a washing machine by accident? A washing machine is somewhere you put your dirty clothes ...' she went on.

'Yes, yes, you've made your point,' said Ramsay. 'No, I was just thinking ... I loved that book. I hope it went to someone who appreciated it.'

Zoe didn't say that a girl from a party of Korean-American students had bought it for her grandmother back in Seoul, who didn't speak a word of English but liked 'old things'.

'Why yes,' she lied furiously. 'It was someone who had traced his family roots back to those original crofts and desperately wanted a memento.'

'Really?' said Ramsay, looking delighted. 'What was his name?'

'Mac-something,' said Zoe quickly. 'Can we have our dishwasher now?'

And true to his word, Ramsay had someone sent round and plumbed one in and that had made such a difference to the family – Patrick thought it was magical, and kept trying to turn it on with only one cup in it – that Zoe was now considering how to lobby for the microwave, even if she knew, deep down, that what she would really, really like was a coffee machine. And things were feeling not too bad. Which is probably why it all started to go so wrong with Mary.

PART THREE

'What happens if I look down and fall, Wallace? What if I can't stay up?'

'Well, don't look down then, Francis. Be positive about it.'

'So you can fly if you think you can fly?'

'You are the stupidest person I have ever met. But maybe. A bit.'

From *Up on the Rooftops*

Chapter One

Zoe had been a cheerful, bookish child, not much given to intro-spection. If she had a bad day at school, she'd read the Famous Five, where friendship was assumed and never questioned. If she'd had a good day at school, she'd read *Charlie and the Chocolate Factory*, where untold treats and wishes came to good, unspoilt children. If she was feeling sorry for herself, she'd read *What Katy Did* and imagine the horror of being trapped in bed. If she was feeling in a positive mood, she'd read *The Magic Faraway Tree*, and make up her own lands.

In short, she self-medicated with books.

(By the way, as the author of this novel, and one who has herself always self-medicated with books, I cannot rightfully attest or deny whether this is a better way of dealing with 'real life' than any other. In fact, as a reader (all writers are just readers one step to the side), I'm not actually sure I believe in this 'real life'. I know it is a terrible betrayal to say this, but come on, aren't books – whisper it – quite a lot better in real life? In books, baddies get blown up or chopped up or sent to prison. In real life, they're your boss or your ex. In books, you get to know what happened. In real life, sometimes you don't get to know what happened ever. They're not even sure they've found Amelia Earhart. So. Books are absolutely the thing in my opinion, or as the old saying goes: whatever gets you through the night (which I should say is also books. Books get you through the night).)

So. Zoe hadn't really had much experience with truly troubled children – children who might be upset for very good reasons, like not having a mother and having what Zoe considered at times to be an almost cruelly distant father. All the children she'd dealt with were cossetted – worshipped, some of them – which made them tricky but not disturbed.

She didn't see the warning signs; wouldn't have recognised them. Mary being rude and dismissive wasn't exactly new behaviour, so that mild autumn day had started like any other. Zoe had got Shackleton baking. He just got better and better. His stolid face was looking less petulant and more cheerful by the day as he carefully measured out raisins and used his phone to look up recipes. Zoe had told him he was improving so much that she was considering offering some of his baking to Agnieszka in the visitor centre to sell, or getting him a couple of shifts in the kitchen down there, and he was going to it with a will that surprised them both.

'Almost as if there's a world beyond toast,' Zoe had remarked when passing him that morning as she went to put long socks on the little ones who were both insisting on wearing shorts (they liked to dress the same every day), before they went charging into the trees, the route to which necessitated a shortcut through a nettle patch and much screaming despite Zoe's daily warning about the connection between exposed knees and nettle stings, and their daily surprise about how dock leaves didn't actually work immediately like magic.

Zoe had been in Kirrinfief and in between not selling any books, had managed to catch up with Kirsty the headteacher, or rather, Kirsty had popped in as soon as she'd seen the van.

'Haven't seen much of you around here,' said Kirsty breathlessly.

'Ah,' said Zoe. 'Really? No, I've been here loads, you've just missed me.'

Kirsty looked around.

'Loch Ness monster books?'

She frowned.

'I think you'll find there's a bit more to Scotland than that, Zoe.'

'Yeah, *I* know that,' said Zoe.

'Anyway, did you get the letter?'

Zoe shook her head.

Kirsty sighed.

'Oh, for goodness' sake. Ramsay is absolutely useless. Anyway. There's a restart date. After the October holiday. There's a voluntary anger management session. And then they can both come back to school.'

It had almost certainly, Zoe thought, gone with the rest of the post to the mysterious 'library', and never been seen again.

'Well,' she said. 'That's good news. I suppose.'

Kirsty frowned.

'I know he doesn't care,' she said. 'Could you ... could you maybe help, Zoe? I think you're a good influence.'

'You're flattering me,' said Zoe.

'I am,' said Kirsty. 'It's a total pain in the arse from every conceivable angle if they don't turn up.'

'I am surprised we don't have social services crawling all over us,' said Zoe wonderingly.

'You would if you lived in a council flat,' said Kirsty, and they both pondered whether this statement was true.

'Anyway!' said Kirsty. 'The second of November: that's when we're back. That's your deadline.'

'Jings,' said Zoe.

Kirsty laughed.

'I'm not sure that quite works on you,' she said. 'You sound like you're in *EastEnders*.'

'I know,' said Zoe. 'I was just trying it out.'

'Well, now you know!'

'Do you want to buy a book before you go?'

'I would!' said Kirsty. 'Unfortunately I have twins, a full-time job, a husband who picks his nose and two excluded pupils to worry about.'

'It would all be better if you just read ...'

But Kirsty had already bustled off with Bethan and Ethan.

'Bring them in!' she hollered. 'I'll be nice, as long as there's no biting.'

Everything seemed relatively calm in the little kitchen, and Zoe thought she might as well have a shot as, presently, Mary entered.

'Hello, love,' said Zoe. 'Hey. Look.'

She thought back to Larissa the other night.

'Shackleton and I were talking about school.'

Shackleton sniffed.

'Yeah, right, whatever.'

'I just wondered if you wanted to come with me next week. To have a chat with Kirsty. I mean Mrs Crombie. The headteacher.'

'I know who she is,' said Mary, who had gone watchful and still, her voice a monotone.

'I mean, it's the October holiday soon, and then in November ...'

'I'm not going back.'

'Well,' said Zoe. 'You kind of have to. Otherwise they'll put your dad in prison.'

She'd meant it to be light-heartedly, but the way it came out she realised that wasn't how it sounded at all. It sounded all wrong.

'They won't,' said Mary, looking terrified.

'No, I mean ... I was exaggerating, obviously, I mean. But ... darling, it's the law. Children have to go to school.'

'Can't we be home-schooled?' said Shackleton.

'Who by? Mrs MacGlone?'

'You could do it.'

'I can't do long division,' said Zoe. 'One. And two, I already have two jobs, thanks.'

'And three, you'd be *rubbish*,' burst out Mary suddenly. 'Rubbish and terrible and horrible and *hate you!*'

And she fled out of the room in tears, banging the door.

Zoe watched her.

'Yes,' she said to Shackleton. 'And also for those reasons.'

Shackleton looked relieved, as if worried that she might be upset.

'I think,' said Zoe measuredly. 'Perhaps just on this occasion … some toast?'

She also found herself thinking how much less Mary's outbursts upset her these days.

'I made bread!' said Shackleton surprisingly.

'Seriously?'

The boy showed her where he'd been leaving it to rise.

'I watched a YouTube tutorial.'

'Shackleton, I could hug you!'

He looked concerned.

'I won't,' she added reassuringly. 'But aren't you clever.'

He grinned, and she turned the oven on for him.

Presently, Zoe decided to take a bunch of laundry up to Mary, who had in fact been much better at fetching it herself recently, but school talk had obviously put the kibosh on that.

Zoe did knock – she went over and over it in her head later when trying to work out if she had done the right thing – but the rooms of course were so large and the doors so thick and she was carrying a large pile of washing and …

Nonetheless. She pushed open the heavy white door with her shoulder, her chin on top of the washing pile, still half-smiling at Shackleton and his baking and marched sideways into the room, dappled with pale green and pale yellow light from the trees, only to come across Mary, the child, the little girl with the pale face and the long dark hair, carving a long thin snaking line into the back of her leg with the edge of a razor, the blood dripping against the pale white skin like a horror movie.

Chapter Two

At first, the thought that flashed through Zoe's head was that Mary had started her period – could she though? Or was she too young? But then girls did these days, didn't they, things had changed . . .

All of this went straight through Zoe's mind until she realised that the simple, normal reason was not the right one; that the tiny thing flashing in Mary's hands was a razor blade.

The gorge rose in Zoe's throat, but she knew there was no time to show her shock. The girl's face was paler than ever, but defiant too; a purple pulse at her slender throat.

'See,' she was saying, without speaking out loud. 'See what you made me do?'

Zoe turned her head and put it out of the door not to startle anyone.

'Ramsay!' she shouted, trying to sound business-like but not panicky. 'Ramsay. Can you come here . . . would you mind, please?'

Nobody heard. Stupid stupid *stupid* big house. She charged down the stairs and along the corridor and banged furiously on the huge, forbidding library door, screeching, 'COME UP TO MARY'S! NOW!' then ran back to Mary's side, fiddling with her phone to call 999, trying to get a signal.

She grabbed the first thing she came across – an old shirt of Mary's – but the child immediately screamed at her until she picked up an old towel.

'Come here,' she said. 'Darling. Please. Give me the blade. Please.'

Mary was staring at the blood on the floor, quite horrified and surprised, as if she'd never seen it before. Please, thought Zoe. Please let it have been the first time.

'Just give it to me. Right now,' she said quite snappily, putting out her hand. To her surprise, Mary automatically dropped the blade to her, still catatonic.

Zoe moved as slowly and carefully as she could and wrapped the towel around the child's legs, moving her in towards her own body, ignoring the blood going onto her jeans until she could find a way to staunch the flow.

Patrick appeared in the doorway and Zoe, as calmly as she was able, hissed, 'Patrick, get your dad? Mary fell down.'

At that, Mary started, her huge eyes looking up at Zoe wonderingly. Zoe rubbed her back in what she hoped was an encouraging manner.

'Ssssh,' she said. 'We'll get you all cleaned up.'

Mary's mouth opened, and she started to cry in great gouting tearing sobs, as the blood continued to drip onto the floor below.

Chapter Three

At last, Ramsay appeared at the door, blanched and immediately disappeared. For a terrible moment, Zoe thought he might have left – just turned and gone. He couldn't have, surely.

He was back in a few moments, though, carrying a first aid kit which was in a wooden box and looked as if it might have been left over from any of the last four wars.

'Mary,' he said, going up and caressing her head as Zoe washed her hands at the bedroom sink and prepared to take a look. 'Mary, Mary, Mary.'

The girl wept on.

'I can't ... I am so ... I wish ...'

Zoe got down to practicalities. She washed the wound quickly. Most of it was surface, but at the thigh it was deep.

'You're going to need a stitch,' she said. 'I'm sorry, sweetie. It won't stop bleeding without one. You really got yourself.'

'I'll call Joan,' said Ramsay. Zoe stood up.

'I think no,' she said, shortly. 'I think maybe she needs to be in hospital.'

'But you said a stitch ...'

Zoe shook her head, even as the girl sobbed harder.

'She needs to be assessed, Ramsay. You can see it. I'm sorry. I feel for her, and I have done since I got here. But she needs help. Don't you think?'

'It's not her fault,' said Ramsay miserably.

'I never said it was,' said Zoe. 'Don't you see? It's because it's not her fault is why she needs to see someone.'

She knelt down.

'This bleeding isn't stopping,' she said. 'I think you should call an ambulance. If she's nicked an artery, we'll have to be quick.'

Ramsay fumbled out his phone and called straightaway. Zoe managed to tie a reasonable tourniquet thanks to a first aid course her old job had made her do. But as she was trying to clean Mary's leg, she noticed something much more worrying – underneath the bright new wound, a faded, old patch of hairless white, an old scar. She glanced up at Ramsay, who looked away. Immediately she realised. He knew. He *knew*. She burned with a white fury on the little girl's behalf.

As they waited for the ambulance, Mary with her head buried in her father's shoulder, Zoe's brain was racing. How long had the child been self-harming? Ramsay had seen that scar before, she could tell.

What had he been doing? Ignoring it? Hoping it would all go away? What the hell kind of a father was he? What was he *thinking*?

Mrs MacGlone was summoned to babysit and they stuck to the story that Mary had fallen over and cut herself, and so they were taking her to get her seen to.

'Are you going to the hospital?' said Mrs MacGlone sceptically. Zoe had already decided. She wanted to be there, see what Ramsay told them there. This was a duty of care issue.

'Yes, I am,' she said shortly. 'If you could keep an eye on Hari, that would be helpful.'

It wasn't a suggestion.

At the hospital, they waited nervously as Mary was triaged and taken away to get stitched up. She clutched Ramsay's hand as the nurse worked expertly and quickly and then said, as Zoe had known she would, we'd just like someone to come in and have a few words with Mary on her own as to how this happened, okay?

Ramsay and Zoe sat two chairs apart in the waiting room. Everything seemed to be taking a very long time. Zoe went and got them two horrible cups of tea from the vending machine but was too angry to start a conversation.

Eventually the receptionist came over.

'Which one's next of kin?' she said, her face looking from one to the other. Zoe wondered what she thought they were – an estranged couple? Two people who'd fallen out? Divorcees?

Ramsay stood up, looking as usual ridiculously over-tall in the low-ceilinged A&E. His head hit the light fitting.

The receptionist looked up at him as she prepared to write something on her clipboard.

Chapter Four

Zoe found herself twisting round, staring at Ramsay. He was bright red. She raised her eyebrows at him but he point-blank was refusing to meet her gaze.

At that moment, the young doctor emerged from the side room Mary was in and beckoned them forward.

'Can I come?' said Zoe, still burning and absolutely not letting this go ahead without her as a witness. Ramsay shrugged and she tagged along behind. Mary had been moved to a ward, so they now had the room to themselves.

'Now,' said the man, looking at the two of them. 'I can't do anything without your explicit consent to this. You're her legal guardian?'

Ramsay nodded.

The doctor frowned.

'Her only guardian?'

Ramsay nodded swiftly again, as if he had absolutely no need for ridiculous discussions on the subject. His patrician air made the young doctor more nervous than he seemed to be already. He consulted his notes and cleared his throat.

'Well, we've sutured the wound but it nicked an artery. Potentially a very harmful injury.'

He looked up, eyes wide behind his glasses.

'Potentially lethal if you hadn't found her.'

'Jesus,' Zoe couldn't help saying under her breath. Ramsay simply closed his eyes.

'We've patched her up,' he said. 'But I'm afraid by law we have to keep her under observation. Just in case this was a ... '

'Suicide attempt,' said Ramsay, and the doctor flushed, looking relieved he didn't have to actually use the words.

Ramsay blinked. His fingers were clenched very close into his fists.

'Whereabouts?' he demanded. 'Here?'

'No,' said the doctor. 'We have a facility attached to the hospital.'

Ramsay clenched his jaw.

'I don't want her to go there. She's not going to that ... asylum.'

'It's the best place ... They have the facilities ... We can't ... '

Ramsay's face remained absolutely stony; there was none of the normal, equivocal gaze about him.

'No,' he said. 'She's not going there.' He got up. 'I'm going in to see her.'

All three entered the small antiseptic room together. The hospital was quiet at that time of day, not at all like the noisy bustling places Zoe used to take Hari to. It was almost restful. Mary was sitting up, scowling.

'My darling,' said Ramsay, going over to the bed and putting his arm around her. 'My sweetheart. I'm so sorry.'

Ramsay looked at Mary and framed his large hands on her tiny peaky face.

'Tell me you weren't ... '

Mary's huge eyes filled with tears. She shook her head.

'I wasn't ... I wasn't trying to kill myself. I promise. I *promise*!'

Ramsay engulfed her in a hug.

'It's okay, sweetheart, it's okay.'

'Don't make them put me in the nuthouse! Please! Don't let them put me in the nuthouse!'

'Don't ... don't call it that,' said Ramsay. 'All we want to do is make you less unhappy, sweetheart.'

'But I just ... It was just a little cut.'

'But ... but why?'

Ramsay's voice was so sad, so full of tenderness, as if he already knew there wasn't an answer. Zoe looked at him, wavering.

'To try ... I thought it might help.'

She said the next words so quietly it was almost impossible to hear.

'Where the scar is.'

Ramsay turned his face away and couldn't speak. Instead he pulled Mary closer to him as she whispered in his ear.

'I miss her.'

'I know,' he said, rocking her like she was a lot younger than her nine years. 'I know you do. I know.'

'I'm doing my best, sweetheart.' Mary lowered her head. 'I'm doing ... me ... and Zoe ...'

'Oh, you and Zoe,' she said, her tone dripping with sarcasm. 'Oh yes, I forgot about "wonderful Zoe".'

'Who found you,' chided Ramsay gently. 'Before you bled out all over the floor.'

Mary pouted.

'You should probably be grateful.'

'Why?' said Mary.

'Because!' said Ramsay, his voice suddenly raised. 'Because I can't lose another person! I can't lose you, Mary! I can't! I'm your dad!'

Tears came to Mary's eyes and she nodded.

'Yes,' she said in a tiny voice. 'You're my dad.'

'I'm your dad!' said Ramsay. 'I'm your dad! And I love you! And I will try to make things right as well as I can, Mary ... but you have to ... you have to stay with me. You have to. You have to try. Even when you don't want to. Even when it's hard. Even when you feel it's all my fault ...'

239

Her face whipped round, and Zoe realised he'd hit a nerve.

'I know you think that,' he went on. 'I know you do. I can't ... There's nothing I can say or do to change that. But please believe me. I am trying.'

Mary shuddered in his arms, and let the tears run down over his shirt.

'I wasn't trying to ...'

'Hush now,' said Ramsay. 'I'll stay,' he decided. 'Doctor, I can stay, right?'

'Well, she'd really be better off in—'

'No! She told you. It was a small cut that hit the wrong place. It was an accident. We're staying here.'

Zoe stood up. Her anger had dissipated, replaced by a deep pity and a sense that Mrs MacGlone, of all people, had been right: she was intruding on something deeper than she understood; on things that were not her business.

'I'll go and sort the others,' said Zoe. 'Get tea on.'

She came over.

'I hope you're okay.'

Blinking, Mary looked up at her. And for the first time said something Zoe wasn't expecting:

'Thank you.'

Chapter Five

Back home, Zoe was instantly set upon by everyone. What was wrong with Mary? Shackleton was perturbed.

'Is she attention-seeking?' he asked intently. 'Or is it ...? Was it ...?'

The kindness in his voice again was unusual.

'He is asking,' said Patrick. 'If Mary is most absolutely dead.'

Zoe glanced down.

'She is most absolutely not dead,' she said, trying to make her voice sound light. 'It was just an accident; she had a bit of a fright. She'll be back tomorrow and we will all be very, very nice to her.'

In fact, she realised as she walked into the kitchen, the golden autumn light heavy through the windows, even though today had felt like it had lasted about a hundred hours and she couldn't believe it was still daylight and not the middle of the night, there was something different.

It was heavy with great coils of ivy and acorns. The boys had decorated it. It looked beautiful. And on the stove was a simmering pot of stew, with red berries and wild mushrooms carefully collected by Porteous's owner. It smelled heavenly.

'Did you do that?' she said, turning to Shackleton, who smiled bashfully. 'That's amazing! Gorgeous.'

'She's not coming home tonight?' he said, worried. 'And Dad?'

'No,' said Zoe, shaking her head. 'I'll stay home tomorrow and hopefully I'll be able to go and pick them up then. Would you like to come?'

Oddly, both the boys shrank back.

'I don't ... Not hospital,' said Patrick, uncharacteristically quiet on the subject. They both looked terrified.

'Okay,' said Zoe. 'Hari and I will go, won't we, sweetie?'

And the little boy looked up, beaming.

Zoe was trepidatious driving in the next day. Hari was bouncing happily in the back, his eyes following the bright red and orange falling leaves, swirling and dancing across the windscreen.

'There's so many,' said Zoe wonderingly. 'Where do they all even go?'

The big – huge – relief was that they were going to discharge Mary. The paediatric psychiatrist had accepted her explanation that she was self-harming rather than trying to commit suicide. Not that that was necessarily okay in itself; they had to contact all sorts of authorities and phone numbers, which Zoe saw Ramsay glance at in a fairly cursory manner and made a mental note to herself to grab the list and make a plan of action. They would also join the CAHMS waiting list. Without exactly saying so, the psychiatrist implied that this might take some time.

But they weren't going to admit her to the inpatient facility. Ramsay's patent relief was overwhelming, as Zoe pulled up in front of the hospital to find them both waiting there for her.

Ramsay had shadows under his eyes – he couldn't have slept and seemed to have aged five years in one night – and when Mary baulked at being pushed in a wheelchair, he carried her into the back of the car himself. Hari waved his hands about, grinning happily to see her. As usual, Mary disdainfully ignored him, but he was never bowed. He was just pleased.

Zoe and Ramsay regarded them in silence, as Zoe took the wheel again without Ramsay saying anything about it, even though he could barely contort himself into the front seat of the little green car. He looked absolutely beaten up and she was happy to drive through the long golden roads, utterly empty, in silence, which made it a pleasure in itself, the long rolling fields ahead full of gathered wheat in huge round – not square – bales, and every so often catching a glimpse of sparkling sunlight on the loch, or a tractor tootling along one way or another, or a motor caravan pootling up the middle of the road that Zoe would daringly overtake.

She was waiting for the two in the back to fall asleep which, lulled by the drone of the engine, they soon did so she could ask Ramsay a few very serious questions.

But by the time they had slumped over in their seats, Mary's face in the mirror still chalky white; her leg up in the middle of the seats, heavily bandaged and supported, Zoe glanced to the side . . . and saw that Ramsay was asleep too, his head leaning against the window, the sunlight burnishing the sandy curls on his large forehead, the tension at last drained out of his face.

She couldn't bear to wake him, and so she let him sleep, let everyone sleep, and nothing broke the silence save the occasional bump in the road and the occasional cry of the birds cycling higher and higher in the updraught.

Chapter Six

Zoe put Mary to bed without her waking up, carefully changing her into pyjamas, then went out to find Ramsay.

She found him eventually down by the old abandoned rowing boat, staring out across the water.

'She's on a waiting list,' he said eventually, as if knowing what Zoe would say before she even opened her mouth.

'But what about privately?' said Zoe. She couldn't deep down believe that Ramsay didn't have any money, whatever the state of the gardens; the house made it simply impossible.

Ramsay heaved a sigh.

'I'm . . . I'm not a . . .'

His hand went to the back of his neck.

'We tried. Before. It didn't work out well.'

'What happened?'

'She refused to talk other than to call the therapist a . . . name I wouldn't like to repeat.'

'Oh,' said Zoe. The question was on her lips and she couldn't ask it: why was she like this?

'They wanted to drug her. Give her really serious drugs.'

'I think medication can help a lot of people.'

'Dosing my little girl ... when she didn't want to take anything. She's just sad. She has ...' Ramsay's gaze was very distant. 'She has good reason to be.'

He turned to Zoe, his expression imploring. 'Being sad because you miss your mum ... I mean, that's normal. Not a medical condition that should be drugged into submission. Don't you think?'

Zoe considered it.

'Yes, but if she's hurting herself ...'

'I know, I know, this changes everything.'

He ran his fingers through his hair and had obviously no idea it stuck up in all different directions afterwards. Then he turned his face away and it took Zoe a couple of moments to realise suddenly, with an odd shock, that he was crying, and trying with all his might to pretend that he wasn't.

'Let me talk to someone at the school,' said Zoe, going towards him. Had it been someone else, she'd have put her hand on them, given them a cuddle. But with Ramsay this presented two problems: firstly, he was so enormous that she would end up putting her arm around his hip or something equally awkward, and secondly, of course, he was her boss. But standing there doing nothing felt bad too. She ended up flapping her arms rather weakly, and he quickly rubbed his face with the collar of his shirt and stood upright again.

'Sorry,' he said.

'Don't ever be,' said Zoe, and looked at her watch to make it look like she was very busy and had something to do. 'But I could see what Kirsty offers ... They must have a counsellor.'

'No, don't ...' Ramsay winced. 'I don't want ... gossip and social services and everything ... It just makes her worse. If we're going to get her back to school.'

Zoe nodded. 'Okay. Well. I might talk to the headteacher privately then. We're friends.'

He winced again.

'Okay. Well. Maybe casually. Just to see what they do have.'

Zoe turned.

'If it helps ... I don't think she's alone. In this cutting thing?'

Ramsay's face was so sad.

'Christ, really?'

Out on the lake, there was a quick splash as a salmon bounded up, glistened like silver in the sunlight and vanished again.

'Oh,' said Zoe.

'What?' said Ramsay.

Zoe stared at the sun gleaming off the shiny hide of a seal who was staring at them so intently it was impossible to think it hadn't recognised them. The expression on its face was like someone trying to place you at a party.

'It's just so beautiful here.'

The seal hopped along the rock.

'Hello, fat seal,' said Zoe. 'It's just me.'

The seal hopped along its rock a little bit more.

'That looks painful.'

'They're very thick-skinned,' murmured Ramsay.

Zoe watched as he bent down and picked up a stone to skim. She found herself musing on how very far it was from the bottom of his body to the top and wondered if he thought it was strange, then realised what a ridiculous thing she'd just asked herself.

She looked around her, from the water through the woods and the gardens to the house, cold air catching in the back of her throat.

'You know, where I grew up ... we had one room. My dad ... he wasn't really around. Was involved with ... '

She tailed off.

'Bethnal Green ... stuff. Before Bethnal Green was all nice and posh and full of furniture shops and things like that. We didn't have anything. No grass, no trees, not really. Just traffic and exhaust fumes and a little flat in a council block with "no ball games" written up everywhere and junkies on the scrub. I didn't even know places like this existed.'

Ramsay smiled a little sadly and expertly skimmed another stone out into the water.

'I don't ... This is going to sound stupid.'

'That's all right,' said Ramsay. 'Stupid is a step up from where I am right now.'

In the sky above, two terns were circling one another, rising higher and higher on the updraught. Zoe watched them go, then glanced back at the barely perceptible ripples of another perfect skimming stone on the glass surface of the loch.

'I don't understand how anyone could be unhappy here.'

Zoe bit her lip and felt oddly close to tears.

Ramsay gradually lowered the stone he was holding in his hand. He hadn't been expecting that at all.

'*Really?*' he said.

Zoe nodded, staring at the ground.

'I couldn't ... If you'd shown me just your house and these grounds and this land, and oh my God, you've got your own wood! And the foxes and the birds and the fish and ...'

Ramsay looked at her.

'I know. How could anyone be unhappy here, right? It makes sense, I suppose.'

He heaved a great sigh as he looked around.

'I'd better go see her.'

Alas, Kirsty hadn't ended up being much more help.

'Oh, that's just awful.'

'She needed two stitches!'

'Christ. Another one.'

'Really?'

'Although normally not here – the Highlands and islands are the happiest place for children in Britain, did you know that?'

Zoe felt a pull in her stomach. It confirmed what she'd sensed since she'd arrived, what she'd said to Ramsay. Clean air, clean water, safe places to play. She couldn't think of anywhere better for children. For her own child, who, even though he still wasn't speaking, was more outward-looking, more confident than he'd ever been. Patting dogs, making friends – things she thought he might never manage.

She dragged her thoughts back.

'Yeah, I can see ... Doesn't really help Mary though.'

'No,' frowned Kirsty. 'You know, her being at home, dwelling on things all the time – that's not going to be doing her any good, you know that, right?'

Zoe nodded.

'Totally.'

'We have counsellors connected with the school ...'

'You've used them?'

Kirsty shrugged.

'Honestly, most of our kids ... I mean, if they lose a sheep dog, that's a disaster. And we had wee Ben last year, who had problems with his reading, but nothing I'd refer up. But I hear they're very good.'

'This needs referring up,' said Zoe forcibly.

'Well. Yes. Quite. But, Zoe, listen: she has to be back in school. Get her back after the holidays, and we'll manage.'

Zoe nodded.

'Right.'

She didn't mention it was the very thought of going back to school that had done this to Mary in the first place.

Chapter Seven

Mary needed a few days in bed because the wound was in an awkward place and if she ripped the stitches it could be pretty bad.

But somehow, with Zoe and the boys, it didn't matter.

The squabbling, brattish group she had met only two months before seemed to have changed beyond belief. They made tea, were helpful, fetched eggs. Of course they still squabbled noisily. But it tended to be while they were doing things. Even Hari was useful, ish, man-handling a little broom and carrying his laundry, one pair of socks at a time, up the four flights of stairs to his bedroom. It took a very long time, but that didn't seem to matter.

It gave Zoe longer to spend with Mary – not to talk to her; she had learned her lesson about taking the direct approach, and knew it didn't yield very good results. Instead she showed up at her door with a copy of an old book.

'It's about a girl who doesn't have her mum and is laid up in bed and hates everyone,' she explained. 'So it's probably not relevant to you.'

This direct approach was entirely deliberate on Zoe's part.

She had decided, lying awake long into the night the previous evening, sure that half the rest of the household was doing so too, to stop tiptoeing round the issue. She didn't know where Mary's mother was. It seemed entirely likely that Mary didn't either from the questions she'd been asking. The only person who knew was possibly Ramsay and probably Mrs MacGlone and neither of them were much help.

But Zoe was going to stop keeping up this ridiculous pretence that their mother was simply in another room, busy next door, would be back any minute. She would stop censoring any mention of the word 'Mum' or 'Mummy', stop talking absolute bullshit.

It was a terrible fallacy – and she thought that writers of the past understood this better than writers of the present.

Then, she supposed, to lose a parent was a common thing. You had a five per cent chance of dying in childbirth. Any old disease could kill you. The world was full of motherless bairns and of father-less bairns whose fathers were lost to one war or another. And the world was full of dead siblings, of babies born and left unnamed until the family knew they would survive tetanus or scarlet fever, measles, polio, influenza, dropsy, typhoid and war and horse accidents and deadly childbirth. And they were straight with it. They understood and were clear with children about death and pain; didn't pretend it didn't exist or wouldn't touch them.

Now it was rare to lose a parent or lose a child; and people wouldn't discuss it, in case it invited bad luck in. In case it was tempting fate, or superstition. She thought of how many people wouldn't talk about Hari's speechlessness in case drawing attention to it would somehow visit it upon their own children.

But Zoe had decided to stop with all that. Children weren't stupid, not remotely. They picked up on everything that went on, even if they didn't fully understand it. Hari had known from the earliest times that his father would not come to stay, would not always be there. He wasn't happy about it, but he knew what it was. Pretending there wasn't really an issue about the children's mother had led them straight to the hospital, and Zoe wasn't going to do that any more.

So she said it lightly – this book is about a girl who has no mother – and looked straight at Mary as she did so.

Mary looked back at her warily. Zoe wasn't sure whether she was imagining it or not, but it felt like some of the fight had gone out of her.

'I don't mind,' she said finally. So Zoe sat next to her, and opened up *What Katy Did*.

Chapter Eight

It wasn't so much that the fight went out of Mary. That could never happen. There was a bit of the girl that was wild and she always would be, and Zoe figured she could probably make her peace with that.

But there was something about her not being able to move that made a difference.

For some, maybe most people, being laid up would make them churlish, restless and irritated. For Mary, it seemed to have the opposite effect. Zoe wondered if perhaps it lifted the burden; that the emotional expense of having to be constantly on her guard, defensive, stressed, like a cornered animal, had lifted.

She slept a lot and ate without arguing about the dishes Zoe put together for her. Nothing complicated: thick overnight-steeped porridge with heavy cream you could buy locally and their dense bramble jam, everyone had so much of it; Horlicks (Zoe hadn't had it for years but had found big tins in the pantry); chunky vegetable soup and good bread; even (and more than once, as soon as she realised what a huge hit it was) jelly and ice cream.

And now that her room was cleared up and a bit more organised, Patrick and Hari started going up there to play. Mary made mild objections, but didn't mind really. And every moment when she wasn't working, Zoe would be in there, reading to her.

They got through all the Katys, and straight on to *Little Women* as the days started to shorten and the leaves blew all over the road, blocking the drains and stopping the trains. The fire burned all the time in the kitchen now, and Mrs MacGlone agreed to lay one in Mary's room as well, and after a few days, Zoe was reasonably sure that the wound itself was healed – she was a young girl after all – but also equally sure that having some time as an invalid, staying in bed, was healing something else in Mary, even if she couldn't absolutely pinpoint what it was, and she mentioned as much to Joan when the kindly doctor came to take out her stitches.

'Maybe just say it's not quite ready yet?' said Zoe hopefully in the hallway. Joan harrumphed.

'It's not good for a creature not to be up and walking about.'

Zoe thought of Mary's long lonely walks by the waterside; how far she used to roam, on her own, in her nightie, her mind thinking goodness knows what.

'I realise that,' said Zoe. 'But in this case, do you think you could make an exception?'

Joan blinked.

'I think,' she said, 'I think you're getting rather fond of this place.'

'It's freezing,' said Zoe. 'There's never any hot water, the deer keep eating all the strawberry plants, the children still aren't at school, the house is full of spiders and I'm not making enough money to keep a field mouse alive.'

'Uh-huh,' said Joan.

They smiled at each other as Zoe went back in to Mary's bedside.

'Sorry,' said Joan. 'Four more days in bed.' She glanced sideways at Zoe, who kept her face neutral.

Although she'd normally have started a fight, Mary looked oddly relieved.

'Okay,' she said in a small voice.

And indeed, with night coming in earlier, it was a cosy sight in the bedroom: the heavy drapes, finally cleaned, half pulled so there was still the glimpse of stars beyond; the fire crackling happily in the tiny hearth; the row of books above Mary's bed growing longer by the day; Patrick and Hari pretending to be bears on the hearth rug. Zoe had brought in late flowering plants from the garden, and field scabious and sedum stood there, adding a pretty touch to the large room.

'Then,' said Zoe after Joan had left, 'we really will have to think about getting you some new clothes.'

Mary scowled.

'Stop trying to make me like you,' she said.

'I'm not,' said Zoe equably. 'I'm being practical. It didn't matter in the summer you tearing about the place in a nightie. It's going to matter in the winter.'

'I can wear Shackleton's old stuff.'

'You really can't.'

Shackleton was in his father's old clothes which Zoe strongly suspected had been handed down – or at least just been around the house – through generations of Urquarts. He looked rather dashing in all the tweed, it had to be said.

'Come on, it'll be fun. We'll go to Inverness. They used to have a Zara,' said Zoe, reading off her phone.

Mary looked like she had no idea what a Zara was and couldn't care less.

'Seriously, are you doing this to make me like you?' she asked again sulkily. Zoe figured she must be on the mend if she was getting her attitude back.

'No,' she said honestly. 'It doesn't matter if you like me or not, I'm just the au pair. It does matter that you don't freeze to death while I'm supposed to be looking after you.'

Mary thought about this for a second.

'Okay,' she said finally.

Chapter Nine

Zoe waited until Ramsay was back one evening and in the library, but that he hadn't been in there too long. She didn't want him sunk in some great tome.

She made him a cup of tea and cut some fresh shortbread she and Shackleton had made together that afternoon. Patrick and Hari had also made some but they'd had their own special section, rolled by their own little hands, that they got to eat themselves, because they were so deeply filthy.

Zoe knocked on the heavy wooden door carefully. She still hadn't seen inside the library. The children had paled when she'd said she was going up there.

'It is absolutely quite absolutely private,' Patrick had warned, looking as if she might get eaten by a tiger. It was strange; Ramsay seemed such a mild character, nothing at all like the Bluebeard Zoe had half-expected when she'd arrived. But all the Urquart children were definitely afraid of this.

As she walked down the darkening passage, Zoe told herself not to be ridiculous. But even so, it was in the front of the house, not the wing with the kitchen and Mary's room and the little steps to the servants' quarters where she normally stayed. She wondered if she should have written out a list of things she needed to ask in case she forgot. It was just her boss. She just needed to be brave. Again, she thought rather glumly.

She tapped lightly at first, then, after a moment, a little harder. She heard a voice from inside which she took to mean come in, and pushed the heavy creaking door.

Inside, the room was so beautiful that for a moment she just stood, looking.

Lamps burned everywhere, and the windows were open to the last light of the fading day, a line of gold on the far horizon. The room spanned the entire depth of the house, Zoe realised. It was double height, with walkways around the second storey, and curved metal staircases on both sides.

Books towered over her, up metres in the air to the ceiling – dark reds and golden spines and old green cotton covers. If she had thought the books downstairs in the drawing room were interesting, this was a treasure trove. Zoe stood, transfixed.

He had a little fire too, burning with sweet-scented wood, and at the end of the room under the many-paned window was a huge globe of the world that didn't look like it had all the countries on it yet. In the roof was a large glass cupola through which the night stars were already appearing and popping out. A large telescope sat at the front of the second storey of the library in the window alcove, which had a deep window seat piled high with embroidered tapestry cushions.

Back on the ground to her right were two long desks with piles of books skewed on them, and on her left was a set of map drawers and an apothecary's chest with many tiny drawers labelled with extraordinary things: gentian, sulphur, alumen, boric. There was an astrolabe on a shelf and a skull – was it real? – and a stuffed bird and so many interesting things Zoe immediately wanted to explore them all and turn and flee at the same time. And now she was scared to turn and look at Ramsay, who she had half-thought – and if it sounds ridiculous in this day and age, truly, you had to be there – she half-thought in fact he must be a wizard, and that she had been transported to some other place or some other time.

She gasped and nearly spilled the tea. Then she heard Ramsay say, 'Zoe? Are you okay?'

He was standing up from behind a desk – not, in fact, a wizard; just a shambling, over-tall, slightly bemused-looking man.

Zoe turned round.

'Ah!' she said. 'Sorry! I haven't been in here before.'

Ramsay blinked. 'Yes. I keep it locked, mostly ... There's some exceptional ... well, some things ... '

'The children think you'll kill them if they come in here.'

He didn't smile, and his face suddenly looked severe and rather worrying in the dim light.

'I don't want them to come in here.'

Then it was as if he shook himself.

'I mean, Patrick would be swinging from the rafters.'

Zoe couldn't deny this so handed over the tea.

'It's beautiful,' she said.

'Oh, it probably needs one of your magic clean-ups,' he said. 'I've barely changed a thing, and my father didn't either. The house was built around the library; this part of the building is much earlier. Seventeenth-century probably. All sorts of books were smuggled here during the reformation; too out of the way for the king's men. It became known as a safe haven. That's where the name of the house means – The Beeches.'

'I thought it was after the forest.'

'Those aren't beeches,' scoffed Ramsay. 'Those are oaks, can't you tell?'

Zoe folded her arms.

'Sorry,' he said. 'Not many trees in Bethnal Green?'

'No,' said Zoe.

'Well, anyway,' Ramsay went on, 'it's code. The word "book" comes from the word 'beech'. It's what they were originally made out of. You knew you could store your library here.'

Zoe went closer, brushed her fingers across the ancient texts.

'They're beautiful.'

'Some of them are. Very. Beautiful and important too. That's what I spend my life doing: trying to match them up with a series. With their brothers and sisters. Finding who survived fires and belief system changes and clear-outs over the years . . . '

'Books Reunited,' said Zoe. Ramsay half-smiled. 'Well, yes. Something like that. Did you make this shortbread?'

He looked agitated, as if he hadn't remembered to eat, which he probably hadn't, and devoured two pieces.

'Shackleton did,' said Zoe.

'Good heavens,' said Ramsay. He looked at Zoe with new respect. 'And you taught him that?'

'It's amazing what powers "controlling the internet" brings,' said Zoe, smiling cheerfully.

'Well, I never. Well done, Nanny Seven. I'm kidding, I'm kidding,' he said as he saw her face cloud. 'Honestly, Zoe, thanks. And I wanted to say thank you again about Mary.'

Zoe felt the ground tilting slightly under her feet. Ramsay looked straight at her.

'I have to ask you,' he said. 'Why have you been so kind to her? Mary has been absolutely horrible to you.'

Zoe glanced up at him, amazed he'd asked the question.

'Why is that her fault?' she said. 'Why would that ever be a child's fault?'

Ramsay coloured, and he looked away.

'I don't think it's your fault either,' she added quickly, aware she had injured him deeply.

But he didn't – or couldn't – answer that and Zoe felt the moment slipping away.

'Anyway,' she said quickly, putting a brightness in her voice she didn't quite feel. 'I need to ask you about Mary.'

'What?'

'She needs new clothes. For the winter.'

Ramsay thought about it. 'Of course. I keep forgetting she's getting bigger . . . So much time has passed . . . '

His face drifted away, lost in thought.

'... and I'll need some money to take her shopping.'

He looked up, worried.

'Ah,' he said.

'Not much,' said Zoe. 'Clothes aren't that expensive these days, but she'll need boots and a winter coat. I've had a look ...' she said, pre-empting his objections – she'd been through the boot room already. 'There's lots of old men's coats. There's ...' She wasn't sure how to say this without sounding insensitive. '... no women's clothes.'

The sentence hung on the air, as a log slipped in the grate and crackled into life. Otherwise, the room was incredibly quiet with only some classical music in the background Ramsay had turned down as soon as she came in.

'Yes. I see,' he said, frowning. Then he sighed.

'And there are other things we need?' he said. They both thought back to the dishwasher.

'You're going to need a new washing machine,' said Zoe. 'And a new hoover probably – you could make Mrs MacGlone's life a lot easier; that old upright is her age. And a coffee machine,' she added quickly.

'How could anybody possibly *need* a coffee machine?' said Ramsay.

'How could anyone possibly need a gardener?' shot back Zoe.

Ramsay blinked.

'But Wilby is on legacy.'

'I don't understand.'

'He's ... I inherited him. He got a sum in my father's will – an annuity. So did Mrs MacGlone. It's how servants retire, didn't you know that?'

'Yes, I grew up with a hundred servants on my estate,' said Zoe. 'What on *earth* are you talking about?'

'So I don't pay them. The estate does, from ages ago. They don't have to work for the money – they're both technically retired.'

Zoe frowned.

'And they come and work for you anyhow?'

Ramsay looked rueful.

'Um, it appears so, yes.'

Zoe thought about that.

'Mrs MacGlone comes in ... when she doesn't have to?'

Ramsay looked awkward.

'I have told her to take holidays but ... '

Zoe shook her head. 'That's ... that's ... so you have *no* money at all? Does Larissa know that?'

Ramsay blinked.

'What on earth do you mean?'

'Sorry,' said Zoe. 'Nothing. Pretend I haven't spoken.'

Ramsay frowned. 'What's Larissa got to do with anything?'

Zoe stepped forwards. The room truly was beautiful. Behind the shelving was solid oak panelling that covered the walls and the ceiling too. Circular rough iron plain chandeliers – if you could really have such a thing as a plain chandelier – hung down from the roof, small lights burning in it. There were low green lamps here and there.

She moved forward to the wall.

'There must be,' she said. 'There must be some things here you can sell?'

Ramsay looked pained and lifted his hands.

'I feel ... I feel they're not mine to sell.'

'The books own you?'

Suddenly he looked like an overgrown version of the boy he must have been.

'They built me,' he said quietly. He looked around. 'I've spent half my life in this room.'

Zoe smiled.

'What if I did it when you weren't here?' She looked up. 'Mind you, I'm not sure I'd know where to start ... '

'There's the almanac ... '

Zoe looked at him and he looked like he'd said more than he'd meant to.

'What's that?'

260

Ramsay glanced at his messy desk. 'It's an annual list of rare books ... what they might fetch, whether you have them.'

'So I could go through the list, see what's here?'

Ramsay looked pained.

'Do I have to watch?'

Zoe shook her head. 'I will be very, very gentle with them,' she said. 'And I won't take anything away without permission.'

She picked up the heavy almanac with its tiny print.

'Oof,' she said. 'Maybe I can get the kids to help.'

'No!' said Ramsay suddenly in as sharp a tone as she'd heard. 'The kids can't be in here.'

Zoe glanced up.

' ... Ookkkay ... ' she said.

Ramsay blinked.

'There's ... there's stuff in here they shouldn't be touching,' he muttered. Zoe looked around. It was such a beautiful place. It seemed a shame.

'Okay,' she said decisively. 'I'll do it. I'll find some things to sell.'

'When?' said Ramsay. 'You seem pretty busy to me.'

'Multitasker,' said Zoe, smiling.

Chapter Ten

Which is how, the next few mornings, before the children were even up – they still kept irregular hours; Zoe figured the fact that they were eating better and cleaning up after themselves meant she could save the bed time argument for better days – as the sharp autumn light shone through the bronzed leaves of the overgrown garden, Zoe would spend a neat little hour comparing, filing and tidying up.

She found so much treasure: ancient atlases, when the world was full of pink; gramaryes of spells, as dispassionately laid out as if simply recipe books; recipe books too, some hand-annotated, full of old-fashioned dishes such as mutton jelly, and guinea pig stew. She found, with a cry of triumph, a first edition of *Mrs Beeton*, completely unsullied (Mrs MacGlone, she thought a tad sourly, obviously had no use for it). Some truly ancient *Wisden's*, powdery with lost and impenetrable scores going down the ages.

Ramsay grew used to her there, her dark head bent down over her notebook with a pencil behind her ear, a pensive expression on her face, occasionally a strand of hair falling loose over her face. She moved quietly, didn't disturb him, slipped a cup of instant coffee onto his desk (the coffee was incredibly weak and often half-cold; he had no idea that she was trying to be passive-aggressive about it to lobby for the new coffee machine). They didn't talk, although occasionally she would make a happy exclamation of surprise and he would look up, trepidatious, and she would hold up what she'd found.

Mostly it was the local books she was looking for. Sometimes it was a tourist guide or map of the surrounding areas which weren't valuable in their own right, only in the fact that she'd be able to sell it easily in the van at the visitor centre, in the 'heritage section', and it wasn't really a loss at all.

'And you still have, like, a bazillion,' she'd remind him.

But sometimes – as when she found a first edition of *Peter Pan* by J. M. Barrie, who'd known Ramsay's grandfather, who was from just up the road – she gave a heavy sigh.

'You know,' said Zoe quietly, 'you could probably fix the east wing's roof with this.'

'I think the birds' nests are the only thing holding us all together,' said Ramsay.

'I see this library doesn't have a roof repair section,' said Zoe. 'Did your father never suggest you took a building course rather than English literature?'

'He should have done, shouldn't he?' said Ramsay.

'You'd have made a good builder. Strong back. Big hands,' said Zoe, then she blushed; she'd forgotten for a moment that she was talking to her boss.

Ramsay hadn't noticed and looked at his hands, which were splattered with ink. 'Hmm,' he said. 'Do you think it's too late to learn?'

'I haven't seen you climb up the stairs once without hitting your head on the stag,' said Zoe, grinning. Ramsay rolled his eyes.

'My mind,' he said gloomily, 'is generally elsewhere.'

'I see that.'

And he glanced at his watch and, as he did every morning, frowned and disappeared somewhere much more important – not that Zoe ever found out where exactly this was.

Chapter Eleven

One morning – a crisp day in October with a chill in the air, smelling of bonfires even when there weren't any – Zoe sent Patrick and Hari out onto the lawn in some of the random wellington boots to collect a big bowl of leaves before breakfast; they came back with red, orange and yellow ones, glowing, a big bowl of happiness. They put them in an old polished pewter bowl and set them near the kitchen fire so that they would curl up and dry out and add a lovely smudge of colour to the plain surfaces in the kitchen, even as Zoe had started to cover the walls in colourful drawings the children had done. She whisked them up some hot milk with nutmeg to warm their frosty fingers, and then went upstairs just as Ramsay arrived.

He had also been up to something else, and so they met along the passageway on their way to the library. They smiled at one another, falling into step on the long, faded rug.

'So . . . I sold all those Gaelic tour guides,' she said.

'You didn't?' frowned Ramsay.

'Sure did!'

'Did they know they were in Gaelic?'

'They were delighted! One of them tried to thank me in Gaelic.' She paused. 'I *think* it was Gaelic.'

'What did it sound like?'

'Someone singing a beautiful song then accidentally having to suddenly cough.'

'Yup, that's it. *Tapadh leat.*'

'*Tippa lit*,' repeated Zoe.

'That'll do.'

'Well, anyway. We made a little money . . .'

Zoe leaned over to the library door, putting out her hand for the big old key. Eyes narrowing, Ramsay handed it over and she twisted it carefully in the stiff old lock. The door swung open with its usual creak.

'Ta-da!' she said. Ramsay looked in, blinking in amazement. Zoe had gone down to the pub in Kirrinfief with the money she'd made and asked around for a window cleaner. She'd asked how many windows he'd do for the small amount of cash she had, and was happy that he'd just agreed to come and do the entire west wing (first two floors only), inside and out – although in fact she'd got so anxious about soap and splashes when he was doing the inside that she'd bounced up and down and teetered around him with old towels that she might as well have done it herself.

When he'd gone, the extraordinary change in the light had shown up every cobweb and dusty corner, so she'd ended up getting Mrs MacGlone's feather dusters ('You're in the *library*?' she had said in very disapproving tones and Zoe had smiled as well as she could, and said, 'Just helping you out, Mrs MacGlone!' and run on her way and Mrs MacGlone had given her one of her famous sniffs, which Zoe was learning to ignore one way or the other and Patrick had stoutly put himself in her way, still in his wellingtons, with another feather duster in his hand, and said, 'WE ARE ABSOLUTELY GOING TO HELP,' with Hari nodding his head in agreement and Zoe had said, 'Great, totally, you start downstairs in the drawing room,' which had rather thwarted Patrick's stepladder plan, but Zoe was carrying on with her new policy of just keeping on moving and had charged on).

And now, she looked nervously at Ramsay's face as he saw the room, flooded with light, clear and bright and shining.

'Oh,' he said. 'Goodness.'

And he took off his glasses and put them back on again.

'I haven't . . .'

He rubbed his eyes.

'Well. It hasn't looked like this in a while.'

'I didn't touch anything!' said Zoe. 'Well, you know. Apart from all the stuff I've taken away to sell. Which I've written down! So!'

Ramsay tried to smile.

'As long as you don't leave any holes in the shelves,' he said. 'That I don't like.'

He wandered around, touching things.

'Oh,' he said. 'Thank you.'

'Thank goodness,' said Zoe. 'I was worried you'd be annoyed. Like it was Bluebeard's den or something and no one could go in it.'

'*Bluebeard?*' said Ramsay. 'Is that what you think of me?'

'No!' said Zoe. 'Definitely absolutely not.'

He stared at her.

'Can we change the subject?' said Zoe hastily.

'*Bluebeard?*'

Zoe grabbed the nearest book to her. It was a beautiful golden-edged copy of *The Princess and the Goblin* by George MacDonald.

'Ooh, look at that,' she said swiftly.

'No, you don't,' said Ramsay, carefully taking it from her. 'It's beautiful, this book. I couldn't give it up.'

'I don't want you to give it up,' said Zoe patiently. 'I was thinking for Mary.'

'Oh! Of course!' said Ramsay, handing it back immediately. 'How is my girl?'

'Did you not see her last night?'

He grimaced. 'I got in late; she was sleeping when I put my head round the door.'

'Okay. Well, she's been sleeping a lot. Drawing a bit. Reading. She's very quiet but I think she's ready for shopping.'

'Is this the point where you tell me you've made some money for me and you're keeping it?'

'Yes,' said Zoe. 'I'm going shopping with Mary.'

'Good,' said Ramsay. 'Is she up to it, do you think?'

'Well,' said Zoe. 'I don't believe in girls being quiet and good and all that stupid stuff. None of it. But in Mary's case ... I think she has an excuse for calm, and peace and quiet. And maybe that's just what she needs.'

'But she still needs to go to school.'

'Everyone deserves a chance to be normal,' said Zoe.

Ramsay blinked.

'Thank you,' he said again, looking around the bright, light library. There was a knock at the door. Ramsay grimaced. Zoe went to answer it, poking her head round.

Patrick and Hari stood there.

'CAN WE QUITE POSSIBLY COME IN?' said Patrick.

'I'm afraid not,' said Zoe, feeling totally ridiculous at refusing them. They were holding up, the pair of them, another heavy pewter bowl filled with bright red leaves.

'We did absolutely pick these for Daddy,' said the little boy.

'Well, thank you,' said Zoe bending down. 'I'll take them to him.'

They lingered.

Patrick sighed. Then Zoe had a sudden thought.

'Although,' she said, 'there is something else we could do ...'

And that was how, glowing with the success of her scheme, money in her pocket for the shopping trip, Zoe cheerfully showed up at Hari's nursery with not one but two very excited, cheerful-looking little boys, Hari gazing at Patrick, his one true friend and protector, as if he couldn't quite believe his luck; being, for the first time ever, happy to go to nursery.

Chapter Twelve

Zoe was trepidatious the following weekend when she left the van behind and took the little green car up towards Inverness, Hari in the back, Patrick having complained vociferously all day about being left behind with Shackleton.

Zoe had gone and had a word with Wilby the gardener, pointing out that it was ridiculous that the boys sat around the house all the time and didn't know how to garden. Wilby hadn't found it ridiculous at all; he thought it much more peculiar that the sons of the house would be found working alongside him, very peculiar indeed, and his own father wouldn't have liked it one little bit, but Zoe was a determined person and despite (and slightly because of) Mrs MacGlone's constant complaining about her pushy and vulgar ways, found himself agreeing, which is how Shackleton and Patrick found themselves wrapped up in old clothes and out trimming hedges before she left for the day.

'Get some roses in your cheeks,' she said mischievously, even as Hari's eyes filled with tears. The prospect of a day that involved being outside with Patrick, Best Person in the World, and a pair of gigantic scissors in the garden was absolutely irresistible, and he felt bitterly betrayed.

It was a long way to Inverness, through clouds that seemed to get lower as they went, the colours on the trees still extraordinary but hampered by the low light and the heavy feeling in the air, damp and pregnant, as if the clouds were just waiting to burst.

They parked in the modern town centre car park, a drab multi-storey by the bus station that did no credit to the pretty town around it, nor the dramatic beauty of its setting in the shadow of the high hills beyond, and set off rather anxiously. Mary walked as far away from Zoe as was possible without actually falling off the kerb, and Zoe smiled to herself as she saw so much of the truculent teen she would become, as Hari padded along patiently beside her. She noticed with some surprise that for the first time Hari was keeping up, not pulling and holding her back, or sitting down or looking longingly at other children's buggies.

The short period they'd spent up here already had, it seemed, strengthened his limbs. He was filling out too – his cheeks were rounder and pink – and he didn't look quite so much of a frightened rabbit. There was a confidence about the little lad and Zoe was certain it mostly came from one thing – making a friend. Now he looked around him, curious. She wondered if he was thinking they were back in London. It was a ridiculously long time, she realised, since she'd seen a pedestrian crossing. Mary stalked on ahead of them, looking so grown up. Zoe slightly panicked about the concept of Mary as a teen. And where, she thought, would she even be by then? Who knew?

She realised, as the thin girl walked ahead of her, her limp barely noticeable, scowling at the old ladies who had the temerity to get in her way, that she did have something else to think about: what would happen next. Where she would go and what she would do. There was a bit of her that she tried to keep tapped down: by going away, Jaz would see the error of his ways, realise what he was missing and what he'd lost by giving her up; he would be remorseful, so sorry and try and make everything right again.

It struck her that these days that remorse was very thin on the ground. It seemed nobody had to be sorry any more for anything they did; instead they doubled down, were proud of it, never ever admitted to being in the wrong about anything. If she was to be honest with herself, she was sure Jaz had found a way to blame her – blame her for being stupid enough to get pregnant, to want to tie him down, drag him down, stop him fulfilling his DJ potential. There was an excuse for everything these days. Except it meant someone else picking up the pieces.

But what then? If she wasn't to get back on her feet and go back, what was she to do? She was saving a tiny bit of money from her work with the van and her stipend at the house, but it was perilously small and slow. Although the six-week trial period appeared to be up without anyone mentioning it.

She banished that thought and concentrated on Mary, who was standing in front of New Look with a ferocious look on her face.

'I hate it all – it's stupid,' she said as soon as Zoe suggested they go in and have a look.

'I know,' said Zoe. 'We can start here, hate everything and then see how we get on.'.

In fact, there was a nice selection of teen clothes – the fashion was obviously circling round again, because everything looked to Zoe like outfits her mother had worn – A-line skirts and cord trousers in autumnal colours. They tried a mustard-striped top with striped leggings and a burgundy cord skirt. Mary's long skinny legs and narrow waist made her look lovely, like a graceful raggedy doll, but her face was sullen.

'Okay, next!' said Zoe, and they headed on to H&M. As Hari sat patiently and Mary got changed, Zoe exchanged glances with a woman not much older than her sitting outside the changing room. Her chubby pre-teen was marching out wearing a cropped top that said STARLET on it in silvery lettering and a pair of not terribly well advised leopard print leggings.

'It's HORRIBLE,' the girl was screaming at her mother. 'NOTHING FITS PROPERLY! I HATE IT ALL!'

'I liked that pretty dress in Marks,' her mother said weakly.

'Dresses are stupid! Nobody wears dresses!'

'Here,' said her mother, passing over a larger size.

Mary emerged. She was wearing a purple suede pinafore with a red shirt underneath it.

'That's lovely,' said Zoe truthfully. Mary's face immediately fell. If Zoe liked it, it must be awful.

'No, no, take a look in the mirror – don't you think you look nice?'

'I look stupid,' said Mary, refusing to catch her own eye.

'What are they going to be like as teens!' said the mother conspiratorially to Zoe, who didn't know what else to do but smile back. '*I* think you look lovely. I wish I could get Tegan to wear something like that.'

'Something like what?' came the voice from the dressing room and the girl stuck her head out. 'Oh,' she said.

'It's stupid, isn't it?' said Mary tentatively, looking at the other girl for approval.

Tegan shrugged.

''S'all right,' she said. 'The colours are nice.'

'Do you want to try it?' said her mother hurriedly.

'Neh,' said Tegan coming out. The new T-shirt was even shorter than the one before and displayed quite a lot of stomach, over some very tight jeggings. 'This is fine.'

'Are you sure?'

'Would you like to try something like that?' said Zoe. She didn't like it, but on the other hand she had never liked what her mother had always chosen for her, and was conscious that fashion was both a younger person's game and feverishly important, although the idea of presenting Mary back at The Beeches with a pair of jeggings and a crop top that said STARLET on it rather brought out an inner snob Zoe hadn't known was there until now.

Mary shook her head.

'It looks good on you though,' she said to Tegan, who smiled and said, 'Yeah?'

'They can be nice to everyone but their mothers,' said the mum quietly to Zoe.

271

'She's not my mum!' said Mary, whipping round, her eyes black with fury.

'I was just about to say!' said Zoe. 'Don't get a paddy on! I'm the au pair,' she explained.

'Oh goodness,' said the woman. 'At least you get paid for it.'

'You'd think,' murmured Zoe. Mary was picking up the purple pinafore again.

'Let's take that,' said Zoe briskly. 'And what did you think of the stripes?'

Mary shrugged.

Eventually, they collected large bags full of clothes, particularly from Primark, containing new underpants, tights that actually fitted her, leggings likewise, vests, tops and two big new chunky jumpers that made her look like a student, and rather cute. One had a fox stitched into it that Hari was so obsessed with that Zoe asked if she could buy one for him in a smaller size and Mary shrugged which was as close to a concession she'd got so far.

Finally, as a real treat, Mary took them to McDonald's. Hari's face lit up; it had been a long time. But then it fell again, and Zoe remembered with a start it was where Jaz had often taken him. She pulled him and his chicken nuggets up onto her lap.

'Are you missing Daddy?' she said in his ear. He nodded seriously.

'I know,' she said. 'I know. He's going to come and see you. But I don't know when.'

Suddenly she was conscious that Mary was watching them with great attention. As soon as she noticed, Mary pretended to be doing something else again; eating chips slowly.

There was a silence as Zoe gave Hari a cuddle and wondered if she should just make Jaz come up here. Or at least ask Surinder to do it.

'Where is his daddy?'

The question came out of the blue and chimed so strongly with Zoe's thoughts that for a moment she was confused, until even Mary got embarrassed and tried to look like she hadn't even asked it.

'Well,' said Zoe, going pink. And nervous also. There were two missing parents at the table. 'I don't live with Hari's father; I never really have. Although he loves Hari very much. He's travelling at the moment, which is why I'm here looking after you.'

'Then are you going back?' asked Mary casually.

'Why?' said Zoe. 'Do you want me to?'

Mary shot her a sudden bleak look, and Zoe felt weary and sad.

'I don't care,' said Mary.

'Okay. Well. I have no plans at present to leave, I'm afraid.'

'So when is Hari going to see his dad?'

Zoe would have given anything to get out of the conversation.

'I don't know,' she said. 'It's tricky.'

'Grown-ups always say things are tricky.'

'Things *are* tricky,' mumbled Zoe, going pink. 'Life is tricky.'

Mary let out a great sigh. Zoe leaned forwards.

'Do you miss your mum?'

For a long time Mary didn't say anything and Zoe started to panic, as if she'd done something very wrong. Then eventually Mary pushed the now cold and unpalatable food away and sighed again.

'Yeah.'

Hari looked up, staring at her face intently. He grabbed his mother's chin, then pointed to Mary, then back at himself.

'Yes,' said Zoe, completely understanding. 'Like you.'

The sadness of it, of all three of them sitting there, missing someone from their lives, staring at the congealing chips, was the total opposite of the fun day Zoe had planned.

'She's going to come back for me,' said Mary stoutly. 'She's coming. Soon. I'll probably have to go away with her.'

'Okay,' said Zoe. 'Well then. You'll have some new clothes for when she does.'

Mary seemed cheered by the thought of this, and more cheered when Tegan and her mother entered and sat down. Watching the girls chat – Tegan had a diamanté-studded phone and was showing Mary goodness knows what, but Mary was clearly very impressed – Zoe thought again how deprived of normal girls' company she was. Listening to the friendly woman babble on about Squishies and *Fortnite* and sleepovers and birthday parties and dentists'

273

appointments and all the general mishmash of a child's life, all she could do was smile and agree, marvelling at the gulf between the girls' lives, hoping, as things took on a more even keel, that she could push more of this.

'Where are you?' she asked the woman finally. 'Maybe Tegan could come over and play one day?'

'Stromness,' said the woman. 'We're down for the day. It's only a forty-five minute flight from here! Where are you?'

'Three hours south,' said Zoe, and they both said 'Ah' politely, then went their separate ways; but Mary was definitely jollier as they walked away.

'You're good at making friends,' observed Zoe as they went to look at shoes, and – Zoe insisted – to buy small presents for the boys.

For once, Mary didn't scowl. She looked thoughtful, as if this were a potential characteristic that had simply never occurred to her.

Chapter Thirteen

Buying shoes was so dull that Hari lay down on the floor and fell asleep, but they were eventually done, with a pretty pair of Lelli Kellys (Zoe had slightly baulked at the price of but handed the money over, thinking if you couldn't have a pretty pair of shoes when you were nine years old when could you?) and a pair of smart pale blue Timberlands they found in the sale that would do for literally everything else. Their bags now were weighing them down, and Zoe went and found them an ice cream to keep them going. She noticed Mary out of the corner of her eye, counting and recounting the bags, peeking inside them as if she couldn't believe she had so much treasure.

She looked up.

'We have to find something for you. Daddy said.'

Zoe had completely forgotten – as they'd been leaving that morning, Ramsay had told them both to get themselves something.

'Oh yes,' she said. 'Well, let me grab a jumper. I *really* need a new jumper.'

Mary shook her head.

'No. Let's get something nice.'

'I really don't need anything nice,' said Zoe. 'I'm hoiking books about all day. Or you guys.'

But Mary had already marched into TK Maxx and was rifling through the lines of evening dresses.

Zoe laughed.

'Honestly,' she said. 'I don't need an evening dress. Trust me.'

'You should have a pretty dress,' said Mary stubbornly. 'Everything you wear is horrible. And rubbish and boring. You're just a *bit* old, you're not as old as Mrs MacGlone. And even she wears dresses.'

Zoe wasn't sure which bit of this statement to be offended by first, so she decided to ignore all of it. Mary meanwhile was hard at work, pulling wildly inappropriate chiffon gowns and evening dresses off the rack. Hari was getting excited too, running his little sticky fingers along the bright pinks and shiny frocks. Mary handed Zoe a great bunch of them.

'Try them on!' she ordered.

'You haven't even checked the sizes!' protested Zoe.

'Well, they're all beautiful! You can see what fits!'

They were not, in fact, all beautiful. A canary chiffon made her look like she'd be rejected for even the back row of *Strictly Come Dancing*'s audience and made her slightly sallow skin look liverish. A navy-blue diamanté column made her look like a fierce dowager. But right at the bottom of the pile, crumpled and inauspicious-looking in the way of TK Maxx, was a red parachute silk Katharine Hamnett dress, a name Zoe didn't even recognise. It had a wide circular skirt and a boat neck and a huge silk red sash that tied it up; it didn't even come with a size.

Zoe slipped it over her head, wincing as she did so at the state of her bra. The fabric felt cool and luxurious against her skin, and as it shrugged down she tied the sash around and stood back, preparing herself to look yet again like a ridiculous dolly dressed up for a children's party.

Instead the dress ... She turned to the side. The skirt swirled and settled round her legs. Ooh. She couldn't deny ... She turned again.

The colour set off her dark hair and eyes; complimented them. The fact that she had next to no bust left suddenly didn't matter any more; being flat-chested stopped the dress from looking blowsy or obvious and instead it sat rather chicly. Chic? Really? That was not a word Zoe had attached to herself for a very long time. She glanced back over her shoulder. Every time she moved, it billowed out like a silk cloud, rippling and resettling around her.

'Let me see!' came an impatient sound from outside the fitting room. Impulsively, she felt down to the bottom of her handbag and came across an old nub of lipstick.

'What do you think?' she said, pulling open the curtain. Hari jumped up and ran towards her and gave her a hug, feeling the soft material up and down his cheeks.

'Do *not* get spit on it,' she said, smiling. Mary just stared at her. 'Nice?'

Mary shrugged.

'Yeah. Sure. Get that one.' Hari nodded in fierce agreement. Zoe looked at the price tag – it was heavily discounted, but even so. It seemed ludicrous to be buying a light silk dress in a cold climate going into winter when they needed so many other things ...

On the other hand, she couldn't help thinking, it had been such a long time since she'd had something pretty.

'Oh look,' frowned the saleslady, coming forwards. 'There's a stain there.' She pointed to where Hari's mouth had landed. 'Let me take off another fifteen per cent.'

And to something like that, even Zoe was not immune, as they all snuck back to the car, even Mary giggling. Worn out by the day, both the children fell asleep in the back seat on the long way home, and as darkness fell and Zoe was concentrating on the road, she halted briefly to let some sheep pass and glanced into the rear-view mirror, and saw that Mary's face, drained of all its aggression and fury, looked as young as Hari's in the light from rare passing headlights.

'Goodnight, sweet girl,' murmured Zoe as she took off again, the stars popping out above the car like a dream, soft music playing from the radio, the miles purring slowly away beneath her feet, as the children flew home on dream wings.

Chapter Fourteen

It was Zoe's day to sit in Kirrinfief for the morning, to assuage her conscience. She didn't mind, but it was frustrating knowing how much better she could be doing at the visitor centre.

Sure enough, the first person through the door was Mrs Murray from the shop, looking cross. 'Is Nina not back yet?' she huffed. Zoe considered making a slow 360-degree arc of the little van to check, including looking under the tiny desk, but decided against that level of sarcasm before eleven o'clock in the morning.

'No,' said Zoe. 'She's still got a way to go. You should go visit,' she added, her conscience striking her as she realised she hadn't visited herself in some time, although she had carried on giving care packages to Lennox. She could have, she now thought, popped in when she'd been to see Mary – Nina must have heard about it – but everything had been so panicky and rushed.

'Oh, I wish she'd just have that baby,' said Mrs Murray. 'Can't they just take it out?'

'I think they want it to bake all the way through,' said Zoe. 'Probably for the best.'

'I wouldn't mind six weeks in bed,' said Mrs Murray, a common sentiment by people who'd never actually had to do just that.

Although it had to be said, Nina did seem to be managing better than most.

Zoe smiled sympathetically. 'Hey, I have the new *Blood Roses* in!' she said. Surely this was a no-brainer? She pulled up the eight-hundred-page historical fantasy series – a feminist *Game of Thrones* about an immortal woman who exploded in gouts of blood every time a man was rude to her, razing entire cities to the ground and causing utter devastation. Famously turned down by every publisher in the country, it had gone on to do quite remarkably well with women everywhere.

'Ooh,' said Mrs Murray. 'Yes, I'd love that. Put it aside for me and I'll pay Nina when she's back. Thanks. Also, Nina has to tell Lennox he can't rotate the field.'

Zoe blinked.

'Sorry, you're going to have to run that past me again.'

'He's refusing to do the Samhain because he's rotating the field. Nina can talk him round. Tell her to look sexy or something.'

'She's eight months pregnant.'

'Nothing wrong wi' that,' came a quiet voice behind them, and they both turned round, startled. Lennox was standing there.

'What are you doing here?' said Mrs Murray.

'Well, you asked me about Samhain and I told you you couldn't because I was rotating the field – which I am – and knowing you don't take no for an answer, I figured you'd be down recruiting everyone.'

Mrs Murray folded her arms.

'Well, I wouldn't ...'

Lennox gave the pair of them a firm look.

'Well, count me out,' said Zoe. 'Because I don't have the foggiest idea what either of you are talking about.'

Mrs Murray turned to her.

'Well, fields, you see ...'

'Don't start that far back,' said Zoe. 'What's Savvy Rain?'

Lennox and Mrs Murray looked at each other. 'You explain,' said Lennox. 'I'm busy. Rotating the lower field. Don't get a lobby group together.'

'What about a petition?'

'It's your own time you're wasting.'

'Come on, Lennox, you must have stuff that wants burning.'

'Aye,' said Lennox. 'In my own house, to keep it warm.' And he stalked off.

'He says that,' said Mrs Murray. 'He'll come round.'

'I won't come round,' came the voice from far off.

Mrs Murray turned to Zoe.

'Zoe,' she said, her face looking kindly in the manner of one about to ask a huge favour. 'You have to tell Ramsay he has to host Samhain.'

'I can't do that,' said Zoe. 'I have absolutely no idea what you're talking about.'

'He'll understand. Tell him the committee has it all arranged.'

There was a silence.

'Are you going to burn a man inside a big wicker cage?' asked Zoe suspiciously.

'Noooo,' said Mrs Murray. 'No, they haven't done that for . . . Nooo!'

Chapter Fifteen

She ended up asking him on a day that had gone rather badly, and which she'd thought would be rather fun. Murdo had asked if she wanted to go out on his boat, and she had been delighted and had said yes. They'd arranged to meet down on the dockside by Agnieszka's, who seemed oddly put out but said did they want a packed lunch, but there was no ham and cheese, just cheese and Zoe said not to worry that would be fine.

And she'd got all the children done up in various waterproofs of different shapes and sizes, even Mary, and lined them all up, Hari and Patrick bouncing with delight at the concept of going on a boat.

Then Murdo had turned up wearing a tie and had his hair smoothed back with gel and a bottle of prosecco in the cool box of the boat. And at the exact same moment Zoe had realised that Murdo had in fact been asking her out on a date, Murdo realised that he was expected to give a boat tour to four children, two of whom wouldn't stop jumping in the boat, one of whom asked him several billion questions about whether Nessie was a dinosaur and if so which type, and one of whom had moaned about how boring and rubbish it was to be on a boat, as Zoe had sat in the end, and the rain had hosed down and everyone had tried to pretend they were having a better time than they were, except Patrick and Hari, who were having the best time of all time.

Zoe was mortified as they got home and dried off, wincing horribly at how brattish Mary had been, and how Shackleton had staggered about the place, heavy shoes standing up at the wrong time, and Murdo had tried to ask her personal questions about herself but had had to holler them through the wind at the top of his voice whereupon nine times out of ten Patrick would try to answer them.

'Oh God,' she said in the kitchen.

'What's up?' said Ramsay. It was strange: he seemed to find more and more reasons to pass the kitchen these days.

'Zoe had a date!' said Patrick. 'There was fizzy stuff we weren't allowed to drink.'

'That ... that wasn't exactly ...'

'You took all the children out on a date?' asked Ramsay in consternation. 'You were on a date?'

'I was not on a date,' said Zoe. 'Well. Not after about five minutes.' She couldn't help it; she smiled at the memory.

'Oh God,' she said.

'What?' said Ramsay. 'The poor chap.'

'Oh God,' she said again. 'I'm just ... I'm so used to everyone knowing I'm the au pair up here.'

'Oh good,' said Ramsay. 'People in my business.'

'I didn't ...' She put her hands over her eyes. 'I'm not sure I told him they weren't all my children. Oh God. Oh *God*.'

She giggled relentlessly. 'Oh God. My love life is over.'

'At least you got the fizzy pop,' said Patrick crossly.

'I had one glass,' said Zoe. 'Perfectly competent to drive, thank you.'

But the fresh air and the fizz and the laughter had put roses in her cheeks and Ramsay couldn't help smiling at the sight of her.

'Daddy dates Rissa,' said Patrick glumly, then in a stage whisper: 'SHE'S A WITCH.'

'Now, stop that,' said Zoe. 'Oh!' she said, suddenly remembering. She smiled and went to her bag.

'What's that?'

Zoe drew out a small sheaf of money wrapped in an elastic band. She handed it to him.

'We sold *Lark Rise to Candleford*!' she said in triumph.

Ramsay blinked in surprise. 'You didn't!'

'I know! Whole lot!'

'Oh. The wood engravings editions,' said Ramsay sadly to himself. 'Very special.'

Zoe shook her wooden spoon at him.

'You're wrong,' she said. 'It's what's inside the book that's special. The words you carry with you that are always there. The cover is just the cover.'

Ramsay looked shocked.

'So you're basically dissing absolutely a hundred per cent of everything I do for a living?' he said. 'My entire job, my reason for existence.'

Zoe smiled back at him. 'I still fold over the corners.'

'You don't,' said Ramsay.

'I do too!' shouted Mary from the window seat, waving *Anne of Avonlea* above her for proof.

'Oh God,' said Ramsay. 'What have you done?'

'I take hardbacks in the bath,' said Zoe.

Ramsay covered his eyes with his hands.

'No,' he said. 'You're torturing me.'

'Sometimes downloaded books are better, depending on what I'm doing.'

'You are a witch,' said Ramsay, 'who needs to get out of my kitchen!'

'Is that a verbal warning?'

'I draw on things!' said Patrick hoping to join in, showing a heavily crayoned comic.

'Argh!' said Ramsay. 'Stop!'

But he was laughing as he said it, besieged on all sides.

'I can't believe you have let my monkeys loose.'

'Never look at what I do to cookbooks,' said Zoe, looking at her favourite scribbled-over Nigella.

Ramsay took the money and looked at it.

'Oh well,' he said. And he handed it back to her. 'Here.'

Zoe was surprised.

'What's this for?'

Ramsay dropped his head.

'I just feel ... we owe you. A bit extra.'

Zoe coloured. She had been joking around with him, thinking that they had just been having a nice time in the kitchen. She didn't realise she needed paying for it.

'I'm fine,' she said stiffly, and Ramsay, unclear as to what he'd done wrong, put it away just as his phone rang, and Larissa's tones rang out and he turned away.

Chapter Sixteen

Zoe clean forgot about the Samhain, but the rest of the village hadn't, and Ramsay was equable enough about it, so by Halloween there was, for the first time, a team of people out in the garden, painting and hammering.

Zoe had asked the children about going out trick or treating – or guising, they called it up there – for Halloween (and sold a lot of Scottish ghost books she'd bought in specially) but they'd all shaken their heads firmly.

'Everyone's horrid,' said Mary.

'And nobody wants to come here,' said Shackleton, so she'd shelved the idea. It seemed like this Samhain party, whatever it meant, was a bigger deal around here anyway, and perhaps the children could have fun with that.

She realised quite quickly that she'd underestimated: Samhain didn't seem to be a party; more like a festival. She'd let the boys get dressed up and let them loose but then saw – as the grounds were lit up with flames everywhere; as a great team of drummers, and people on stilts, and slightly raggedy-looking folks started turning up – that this was very much an adult affair, not for children at all.

People were incredibly dressed up too. She was lucky to have the red dress; it was the only thing remotely suitable. At eight p.m., the drums had started and a great procession had begun all the way up the driveway, led by someone painted entirely bright red, dancing and blowing fire through a huge grotesque mask.

People were dressed as witches or the dead, screaming and hollering as the drums played loudly, and heading towards a stage where pipers were skirling, everyone drinking and shouting. The grounds were lit only by braziers. Ramsay was nowhere to be seen, and Zoe realised she'd made a terrible mistake letting the boys out alone.

Zoe ran up and down the party. It was huge. She needed to pause to get her breath, everything was so overwhelming. The night was still but utterly, bracingly cold. The huge bonfire raging down by the shoreline attracted most people, running in towards it and away again, laughing furiously. Some of the girls were wearing next to nothing, dashing like sprites in airy costumes or long tulle skirts lit up by the sparks and the light from the torches. The music sounded wild and furious now; it followed no recognisable patterns, didn't seem to have a start or finish, but somehow, the fiddlers and the bodhran players knew instinctively what they were doing and the music got louder and wilder until your heart beat in the same rhythm as it and you felt it in your blood like a thick pulse.

The dancers were growing wilder and Zoe passed couples dancing and staggering and laughing as she tried to follow the children, who were diving in and out of the crowds of adults, threading hand in hand like a long game of 'In and out the dusty bluebells', and all she could hear was a touch of Patrick's laughter in the air as she tried to follow where they'd gone.

Over in one corner she could see the tall figure of Shackleton surrounded by girls from the village, unrecognisable out of their leggings and fleeces, made-up, their hair long and tumbling, their cheeks pink and excited.

'Is this *your house*?' one of them was asking. 'All of it?'

And Shackleton, looking tall and rather dashing in his kilt, was blinking and smiling awkwardly and saying, 'Well yes,' and Zoe rolled her eyes and left him to it, and carried on searching for Hari and Patrick. She knew pretty much everyone – she'd met the entire village more or less by now – so nothing awful could possibly happen, surely. There was Mrs Murray and the old colonel, and Lennox in a black mask that gave him a sinister aspect, only spoiled a little by the fact that he took his phone out and messaged Nina every fifteen seconds, just in case.

She could still hear Patrick's giggle, rising somehow above the incredible noise of the music and the dancing and stomping and the crackling of the fire, further and further away, and she plunged once again into the melee, her red dress catching smuts from the bonfire, and someone trod on the hem and tore it, but she still didn't notice as it was strewn out behind her.

'Hari! Harrrrriiiiiii!' she screamed through the crowds, pushing past kilted blue-faced men with dreadlocks; girls in long dresses, hair tumbling like mermaids; old and young.

'Hari!'

But still nothing but the sound of a vanishing giggle on the air. Zoe started to get frightened. There were enough people at the fire, but if you wandered off towards the pitch-black woods, or the dark deep water ...

'Have you seen Hari?' she shouted at Shackleton as she passed him again, but he shook his head. She ran up the steps to the front door of the house and then turned round, heart in her mouth, to stare beyond the crowds to the water.

Desperately, she broke through the crowds once more, screaming his name, suddenly utterly convinced that her boy had gone, that while she was getting herself dressed up he had crashed through the waves, down into the depths, all because she dared, all because it crossed her mind to think she might do something as wicked as attend a party.

Away from the crowd, the dark and the cold flowed on the route down to the water as if from nowhere. The wind was howling through the trees which were swishing and moaning of their own accord; the water was splashing and crashing onto the pebbled shoreline.

'Hari! *Hari!*'

'Zoe!'

The voice was clipped and authoritative. It came from behind. Slowly, Zoe turned around.

Chapter Seventeen

As Zoe turned round, her heart was in her mouth. Was it someone bearing bad news? Someone with terrible things to say?

At first she couldn't make out the figure, just a black silhouette with the fire raging behind. It was a strange shape standing not ten feet away. Zoe moved slowly closer, and the shape revealed itself and she nearly collapsed with relief when she realised what she was looking at – Mrs MacGlone, standing bold upright, with a wriggling Patrick under one arm and a beatifical Hari under another. She didn't look like the large weight of either was giving her the slightest trouble, despite her small size.

'I'm just going to put these two to bed,' she said carefully. 'I'm not sure this is the place for children.'

'But we absolutely want to stay!' petitioned Patrick. 'I think we should stay, don't you, Nanny Seven?'

'I absolutely don't,' said Zoe, the relief cascading through her like icy water. Hari stretched out his arms, and she picked him up and held him close, her tears soaking into the flannelette pyjamas.

'Don't run away from Mummy again!' she said.

'We weren't running away,' protested Patrick. 'We were at a party! I had four sausages and Hari had nine.'

'You didn't?'

'Absolutely nine,' said Patrick.

'I'm going to put them both to bed,' said Mrs MacGlone. 'I'll sit with them. You ...'

Just for a second the firelight caught her face, and had it been anyone else, Zoe might have said they looked a bit wistful.

'... you go enjoy the party.'

This was far and away the kindest thing Mrs MacGlone had ever said or done for her. Zoe bit her lip.

'Thank you.'

'Aye.'

And she twisted around as if both children weighed nothing, and carted both of them, Patrick chattering all the time, off round the back door of the house and up the stairs. Zoe watched them go, then realised she was shivering, both from the fright and the cold. She moved closer to the fire, and found she was standing next to Kirsty, who instantly handed her over a glass of hot cider. Zoe gulped it down far too fast, feeling the blood pulse in her ears, and stretched her arm out for another one, feeling the alcohol hit her system. The children were safe – for once, it felt. She didn't need to be worrying.

It was the most unaccustomed feeling. Zoe was used to worrying about literally everything all the time, every second of the day. About everything. The van. The books. The future. Hari. Hari's future. Hari's dad. The children. The house. Money. Everything.

But, she thought, it was as if a huge weight had been lifted off her shoulders. Not tonight. Not tonight. In the crack of the universe, in the tiny glimpse between the light and the plunge into the long months of the dark, on All Hallows' Eve, the Samhain celebrated misrule when the dead came back to earth ...

Except, in Zoe's case, she felt a little like the dead person had been her.

The music was banging to a crescendo, louder and louder, as she moved closer to the centre of the party, a raised stage by the fire near the band.

The frightening red dancers were still coiling with their torches, but something was changing; they were moving the crowds out of the way, creating a passage. Next came ten women dressed in long white dresses, swirling as they twirled their way forwards, throwing leaves in great handfuls here and there, skulls painted on their faces. Then behind them came a procession carrying a litter led by huge men in kilts, shouting lustily. On the top of the platform they had on their shoulders was a chair, a large, ornate throne unlike anything Zoe had seen before. The chair looked part tree, branches and twigs curling out of it quite naturally to form the arms and legs. It must have been carved but looked entirely as if it had been grown straight from the greenwood.

And perched on that, metres up into the air, blocking out the starry sky, was someone in a large cape, obscuring their face.

'MAKE WAY!' bellowed one of the bearded men, his voice like a gravel pit. 'MAKE WAY FOR THE LORD OF THE DEAD, THE LORD OF THE SAMHAIN!'

And from somewhere, bells pealed, sonorous and low as the procession went forward, the violins now playing a mournful song deep and long, and Zoe squinted upwards, half-appalled by the figure. Kirsty came up and stood beside her.

'I know, it's weird, isn't it,' she whispered. 'I get scared every year, and it's only Lennox dressed up like a monk.'

It wasn't Lennox though; Lennox was over in the corner, filming it for Nina to watch.

The party made it to the stage and gradually set the litter down. The tall figure rose from the chair, facing the crowd, who roared its approval, and the Lord of the Dead raised a great bony finger in the air and everyone went quiet. He stepped forward, Zoe watching him, realising at last who the tall, overbearing figure was. He stood, the hood over his neck obscuring his face, and lifted up a great book from the chair, bound in

thick leather, with heavy gold inset lettering on the spine, and
began to intone, clearly and loud enough to reach the very back
of the dancers:

> *But pleasures are like poppies spread,*
> *You seize the flower, its bloom is shed;*
> *Or like the snow falls in the river,*
> *A moment white – then melts for ever;*
> *Or like the borealis race,*
> *That flit ere you can point their place;*
> *Or like the rainbow's lovely form*
> *Evanishing amid the storm.–*
> *Nae man can tether time or tide;*
> *The hour approaches Tam maun ride.*

Zoe didn't understand the words, but caught their meaning well
enough as the pace of the recital picked up.

> *And, vow! Tam saw an unco sight*
> *Warlocks and witches in a dance;*
> *Nae cotillion brent-new frae France,*
> *But hornpipes, jigs strathspeys, and reels,*
> *Put life and mettle in their heels.*

At this, the band struck up again, slowly starting a waltz. Turning
round, Zoe saw the crowd automatically form a circle, and before she
knew it, she was dragged into it, a boy on either side, pulling her as
they started to leap in a circle.

> *As Tammie glowr'd, amaz'd, and curious,*
> *The mirth and fun grew fast and furious;*
> *The piper loud and louder blew;*
> *The dancers quick and quicker flew;*
> *They reel'd, they set, they cross'd, they cleekit,*
> *Till ilka carlin swat and reekit,*

293

And coost her duddies to the wark,
And linket at it in her sark!

First round one way, then the other, then they split into couples and Zoe found herself waltzed around, pushed and pulled one way and the other, moving into the centre and back again, as the circle went around, broke, reformed and never stopped moving and the music spiralled ever upwards, and Zoe found she was exhausted and laughing hysterically and dancing maniacally all at once.

And how Tam stood, like ane bewitch'd,
And thought his very een enrich'd;
Even Satan glowr'd, and fidg'd fu' fain,
And hotch'd and blew wi' might and main;
Till first ae caper, syne anither,
Tam tint his reason 'thegither,
And roars out, 'Weel done, Cutty-sark!'
And in an instant all was dark:
And scarcely had he Maggie rallied,
When out the hellish legion sallied.

At this, the violins all screeched at the same time, and midnight chimed from a great bell held by one of the band, whereupon, to Zoe's absolute shock, one of the women in white with another great hooded death robe came through the party from the back of the floodlit forest riding a horse, and galloped around the party with a large woven basket from which she discarded great handfuls of golden-sprayed leaves behind her.

The dancers immediately stopped and charged after her, grabbing at the floating, flying golden leaves as she vanished into the dark forest and they followed to get up to who knew what mischief in the greenwood.

Completely out of breath and utterly disorientated, Zoe stood glued to the spot as everyone thundered past her, chasing the horse, laughing and shouting moving further and further off.

The musicians changed to a more sedate waltz for those few left behind. Zoe's eyes landed on Ramsay who, laughing to himself with the full ridiculous magnificence of it all, had collapsed back onto the huge throne, one leg dangling over the side as he drank deeply from a large ornate goblet someone had left there.

Suddenly, in the light of the fire, on the stage with the house behind him, on the oversized chair made from the forest, he ceased to look like the slightly absurd, apologetic figure he made around the house, where he had to stoop to enter most rooms, where his feet were too long for the treads on the stairs, where he constantly looked distracted, as if wherever he was, he truly needed to be somewhere else, glancing at his watch, vanishing to his library, disappearing from the house.

Here, the cloak thrown back, a rumble of laughter in his chest, he looked like what he truly was for the night: like a lord of misrule. Zoe moved forward, hypnotised. He looked like someone totally different – powerful and in command and ... dangerous? But not in the way she had ever thought before. Rather he looked – as the flames licked the side of the big red sandstone house, as the shadows flickered on the walls – elemental and at home in this place.

And she felt a jolt deep inside her – something thick and visceral, that she hadn't felt for a long time, that she had thought she might never feel again. In the heat of the flames and the sharp bright noise she felt, as if from nowhere, an absolute bolt of desire.

He couldn't see who it was in front of the stage; the fire was crackling in his eyeline. Her dress, she noticed now, was almost entirely torn away below the knees, and she was completely filthy – mud up her legs from looking for Hari at the shore, smuts from the fire in her face, her hair blown everywhere by the wind. She was very pink and without even thinking, held up her arms.

Ramsay, carried away, rather drunk on the spirit of the night as much as anything else, without thinking for two seconds reached down his long arm, and scooped her up on stage, pulling the gorgeous girl into a dance, spun her around – he was tall enough he could do this while still sitting down – and pulled her close.

'*Weel done, Cutty-sark*,' he said, pulling her close and tight to him and Zoe suddenly felt the oddest sensation: she realised she was feeling desperate to be in his arms, desperate to be held by him. He was so very large and broad, she felt herself practically disappear inside him, as if she herself was folded into something very small and very safe. She felt his heartbeat, his great chest pressed against her small one, and found herself moving her head to bury herself in it. He smelt of burning wood, of whisky, of books, of everything Zoe wanted most in the world.

Then the violins and the pipes crashed in and he spun her out and then realised – Zoe saw – to his absolute horror that the girl he had picked from the melee was— Well, it was her.

His face, which only a moment before had been proud, wild, not a little frightening as he had spoken the strange language of the poem he was reading, instantly adjusted as if he was coming back down to earth, as if the fire was dying down and he instead remembered everything that was real, and real life came flooding back to both of them, and he blinked and wrinkled his forehead in a way she recognised incredibly well and said, in a very different voice, apologetic and somewhat stuttery, 'Ah, Nanny Seven . . . I mean, Zoe . . . '

And Zoe went from feeling like a whirling dervish in her red silk dress and wild hair and inflamed heart dancing like the wind in bare feet in front of a great fire, to feeling like a rather dirty London au pair girl in a torn dress, her make-up everywhere – she must, she realised, look absolutely ridiculous.

'Sorry, I . . . '

'I didn't mean to grab you,' said Ramsay, dropping her hand as if it were hot. 'Oh God. I'm so sorry . . . I got a little carried away . . . '

He suddenly looked terrified, as if she was about to accuse him of something.

'Of course it was completely inappropriate, I . . . '

Zoe shook her head.

'It's . . . it's fine,' she said, her brain too fizzing with disappointment and embarrassment to say anything else. She realised suddenly how cold she was in the light dress, and as the revellers started to return from the trees, laughing and clutching the gold-sprayed leaves, and a queue started to form where they were turning the huge roast pig, she suddenly felt utterly absurd.

'I'll ... I'll just go check on the children,' she stammered.

'Um, of course, of course,' said Ramsay, and he gently gave her his arm to help lower her down from the stage, and even as she leaned against him, Zoe couldn't get away from how ridiculous she felt, what a fool – what an *utter* fool – she had nearly made of herself. Her heart pounded as she walked, head down as if disgraced, telling herself over and over again she had got carried away with the alcohol, with the night. Nothing had happened. Nothing.

Ramsay watched her go, feeling more of a clot than ever. What on earth was he thinking? What a ridiculous ... Oh God. For a moment, before he'd realised it was her, he had simply thought she was ... he felt embarrassed to even think of it. A beautiful apparition. A dark-haired, scarlet-clad witch conjured up on Halloween night, lovely and liable to slip away; free and wild and so sexy ...

What had he been thinking? He had suddenly wanted to ... his children's nanny. Christ on a bike, he'd end up in the papers. He rubbed his forehead wearily and turned back to the revellers, but the high point of the evening had been and gone, and there was little to do now except mingle politely with those of his guests still sober enough to stand up straight, and thank the local boys and girls who'd turned up with the bin bags.

He didn't realise they had been observed, the flickering long white dress and long dark hair of a girl who could have been a ghost or a spirit child in the halls; a thin girl sitting alone in her room, staring through the curtains in the dark, sleepless, waiting, who had seen it all and was now sure that the worst would happen.

Chapter Eighteen

The oncoming winter weather hadn't halted the flow of tourists at all. Zoe had thought that tourism in Scotland, like most places, would be seasonal, but had found out that on the whole it was fairly constant – nobody expected good weather any month of the year, so it didn't really make much difference when you came. And it added to people's joy if they got one of the glorious, bright clear autumns, or bursting, frenzied springtimes when they were expecting heavy rain.

So in fact there were rather more tourists, as the weather grew darker and many people quite liked the idea of sitting in a coach for lots of the day rather than having to walk about. And news of the van had started to grow; the coach driver (out of shame, Zoe was convinced, for his lying over the accident) had spread the word about the book van, and now there was quite the parade of bibliophiles, so much so that the coach driver (whose name was Ross) was considering launching a reading tour, and had actually bought several books himself and made a little library corner just next to the toilet, a rather unfortunate placement, but space was highly limited and it was better than nothing.

Meanwhile, Zoe had also started bringing Shackleton down on

the weekends (to avoid inevitable questions about why he wasn't in school) and setting him to work for a few hours in the kitchen with Agnieszka.

The joy he got from managing to turn out some immaculate scones made them incredibly happy, and from then on a steady stream of delicious baked goods was provided and Shackleton earned some money for his efforts, and it touched Zoe greatly when he spent the first lot on two Superman costumes for Patrick and Hari, although it got slightly more wearisome when the boys refused to take them off under any circumstances and, when finally peeled off, would both sit in front of the new washing machine until it was done and would run about in front of the fire in their tiny underpants until their costumes had dried, teaming up to fight crime that normally ended up in them kicking Mary (although to be fair they mostly tried to aim for her good leg).

One evening, Zoe was watching them do this as she stirred a risotto on the stove and trying to protect Mary – who was refusing to move from the window seat where she was reading *The Secret Garden* or to stop dangling her leg down which frankly would have minimised the amount of damage the boys could do and was generally acting as more of as a provocateur than anything else – and shoo away Porteous, who would scamper in and out of the boys' games, then pop back to see if Zoe had dropped any rice, then the tail would be off again. Everyone was trying to get Shackleton to stop playing the new Drake song on his laptop by making fun of it mercilessly which was making him angry and riled, defending his idol.

Ramsay popped his head round the door as he came home, cold and tired after a long drive, with a lot of work to do and, remembering well the bleeping, angry, cold evenings of the past, was surprised and amazed to see the noise and laughter emanating from the kitchen, the warmth and good smells and good heavens, was Shackleton dancing? Even Mary was smiling! Then he remembered the night of the Samhain and, beside himself with embarrassment, was about to withdraw when—

'DADDY!' hollered Patrick, who for some reason was wearing

nothing but his underpants, which appeared to have holes in them. The little boy tore towards him, followed by, Zoe noticed, her heart slightly breaking, Hari, both running towards the tall figure kneeling on the ground.

Oh please, she thought. Oh please. She hadn't heard from Jaz for so long. She knew it was awful – he had to come visit, he had to. She texted him, sent pictures on WhatsApp, but nothing.

And she knew it was bad for Hari. Everything else was better, she kept telling herself fiercely. The house, the companionship, the fresh air, even the nursery. Everything. She was doing the right thing.

But oh, he needed a dad. She turned her face away, unable to watch, but Ramsay, unprompted, without even a pause in what he was doing, simply took Hari's curly head under his huge hand, pulled him in. 'Hello, little man,' he said.

Zoe looked up and didn't realise how desperately anxiously she was looking at Hari until Ramsay noticed it and released the little boy, straightening up from everyone.

'Um ... supper smells good,' he said. Zoe blinked.

'You want to eat with us?'

'Well ... if that's all right?'

'It's your house,' said Zoe a little shortly. 'Of course it's all right.'

She was still embarrassed by the visceral reaction she had had to him; how in an instant it felt – unfairly, horribly – that everything was different, and they both blushed.

'Right then,' said Ramsay at the exact same moment as Zoe's phone pinged, and she glanced down and saw that it was Jaz.

The first thing Zoe realised, as she went out to read the message, was that at some point – she couldn't remember when – she'd stopped following his Insta. That was odd. She had been poring over it every day for so long, examining every picture, trying to see who was in the background, whether it was the same person, the same girl ...

When had that stopped? When had she stopped thinking about him like that, worrying away obsessively at the thought of him, like picking a scab she knew she should leave alone? And now ...

'Coming to see boy, yeah,' it said. Then: 'Where the FUCK are you?'

'Scotland,' she typed cheerily. 'Get to Inverness.'

'You in Inverness?'

'Three hours away.'

'FFS.'

She sent him a happy emoji. 'H. desperate to see you.'

'Is he talking?'

'No.'

'Right. Well, least it wasn't my fault.'

Zoe stared at the screen. Leave it, she told herself. Leave it. He didn't know what he was saying. He never did. That was the problem.

'When will we see you? Will send postcode.'

'What's house number?'

'Doesn't have one. It has its own postcode.'

'You've landed on your feet then.'

Zoe felt her own feet freezing through the cold stone of the kitchen floor and told herself again: don't fall for it. Don't. Don't react. Just think about Hari. He's the only one who matters.

'When?'

'Landing 11.15. Tomorrow. Will rent a car.'

Zoe swallowed back the bitterness of that blithe statement. Just renting a car at random. Throwing down a credit card without looking at it.

'Good,' she sent back. 'Text me when you land.'

And then, all thoughts for the day flown, she turned and stared into the room, her heart beating fast, wondering what the hell to do now.

Would he want to stay over? She hadn't thought to ask. Maybe she'd leave it. She didn't want to prejudice him one way or the other. Where? There were a million empty rooms ... What would Mrs

MacGlone say? Oh God, would Jaz be rude to her? Or expect to stay in her room . . . No. He wouldn't.

She banished those thoughts from her mind, paced up and down, threw cold water on her face. When should she tell Hari? He'd go nuts, presumably. Although she would enjoy telling him. But then again, what if Jaz changed his mind? Or the flight got delayed or something went wrong? That would be worse than anything. She'd leave it, and then pick him up early.

Oh God. She . . . Damn it, why did she only have that stupid red dress to wear? She badly needed a haircut; she'd given up on her nails altogether; she had absolutely nothing at all to wear . . . dammit dammit dammit. Not that she wanted to impress him – she'd passed that stage a long time ago – but she wanted to show him she was doing fine. Not so fine that she didn't need money but . . . okay. Fine.

Could she just ask him straight out? She'd text Surinder, see what the situation was maybe?

Oh *God*, why did he have to do this to her? She stomped down through the quiet house, her arms wrapped round her – *why* did it have to be so cold? – and into the blessedly heated kitchen. She could have hugged the stove. She barely noticed that Ramsay was already in there, dressed in a checked shirt, reading the TLS, the kettle boiling.

'Shackleton, could you finish supper?' she managed to ask, then beat a retreat until they were done and she could put the boys to bed.

Chapter Nineteen

'I never thought,' Kirsty said as they sat sheltering inside the van in Kirrinfief the next morning, 'that I would be giving beauty tips. I am quite proud of myself.'

'I know,' said Zoe. 'I've just completely given up.'

'What does he look like?' said Kirsty. 'I'm genuinely interested. I've been married for six years. He picks his nose.'

'When?'

'ALL. THE. TIME.'

'Oh,' said Zoe.

'So. A bit of excitement is definitely worth it. Let me have a look.'

Zoe pulled up Jaz's Insta.

'Ooh,' said Kirsty. 'Ooh, look at him. He's very handsome. I like his beard.'

'These are *very* flattering photographs,' said Zoe.

'I realise that. I've already taken off the Instagram thirty per cent. I look like a size eight in all of mine.'

'Why?' said Zoe.

Kirsty sighed. 'I do not know. Probably to bamboozle an evil girl I went to school with who lives in Australia now.'

'Okay,' said Zoe, nodding understandably.

'Anyway,' said Kirsty, 'here's the full sample range.'

'I can't take all this,' said Zoe as Kirsty opened up a full Avon box.

'You *can*,' said Kirsty. 'It's Mum's. Her best mate got divorced and became an Avon lady and my mum felt sorry for her and bought up absolutely everything and now her house is full of it. I'm doing her a favour really.'

'You mean you stole all of this?'

'Teachers don't steal! Speaking of which, you know the time is approaching . . .'

'I don't. Your term times are weird.'

'Okay. Well. It's half-term. And then that's the limit of the deal. They need to be back after that.'

'I cannot imagine it,' said Zoe. 'I've been trying to get them to do a bit of schoolwork but Mary won't do anything except read and Shackleton won't do anything except bake.'

'Are you kidding? That's brilliant!' said Kirsty. 'They'll be miles ahead of all of my kids. Seriously. If Mary's reading she can catch up everything else. Once you can read, the door is open. Everything else is just colouring in.'

'Mathematics is colouring in?' said Zoe doubtfully.

'Of course it is! That's why they use all those funny signs!'

She frowned.

'Have you heard from CAHMS yet?'

'Well, Ramsay hasn't mentioned it,' said Zoe.

'It wouldn't be this fast,' said Kirsty. 'Ach.'

'Or maybe there's nothing wrong with her and she's just an early teenager,' said Zoe.

Kirsty smiled as old Ben came in.

'Have you no' got that blue book yet?'

'Yes!' said Zoe, remembering in triumph. 'Nina says it is absolutely definitely this history of the Spitfire.' She picked it up from behind the small desk, where she'd hidden all the history of Nessie books in case the villagers started picking fights with her about it and telling her it wasn't real.

Ben looked at the handsome navy-blue volume carefully.

'Aye!' he said suddenly. 'It *is* about spitfires!'

'Brilliant!' said Zoe. 'A blue book about spitfires!'

His face looked sad suddenly.

'I don't think it's that one though.'

'Nina says it is.'

Ben frowned.

'I'd just . . . I'd just need to be sure.'

And he wobbled off down the steps.

'I don't know how you do this without starving to death,' said Kirsty.

'I have my methods,' said Zoe, looking out into the quiet street. 'Although, brilliantly selling books to local people doesn't appear to be one of them.'

She glanced at her phone again.

'Oh crap. The plane's landed.'

'Were you hoping it had crashed?'

'Noooo! Well . . . if he was insured . . . nooo. Well. No . . . '

Kirsty smiled. 'Tell Ramsay, okay. Tell him to come down and talk to me about school please. We worry about him. I'm glad he's got you.'

'He hasn't "got me",' said Zoe instantly and without humour

'You know what I mean, you idiot. I'm glad you're there. Mrs MacGlone is cold company. And those poor sad girls didn't help him much.'

'Do you think . . . is their mum ever coming back?'

Kirsty sighed.

'Nobody has a clue, love. Nobody knows.'

If she hadn't been so nervous, it would have done her heart good to pick up the boys, who came charging out, both dressed up as pirates with, behind them, a rather sorry-looking 'prisoner' Zoe identified as Rory.

'Absolutely walk the plank!' squeaked a small familiar voice. Tara dashed out looking exhausted.

'They have,' she said gravely, 'been *quite* the handful today. You know they encouraged the other children to break the song circle!'

'I thought Hari wasn't allowed in the song circle,' said Zoe equably.

'And that one talked all through meditation.'

'Because meditation is absolutely stupid!'

'And I believe they hurt Rory's feelings.'

'NO, THEY DIDNAE,' hollered the small prisoner.

'Well!' said Tara.

'Well,' said Zoe. 'See you after the weekend!'

She put the boys in the car nervously.

'Daddy's coming,' she whispered in Hari's ear. His face lit up.

'Not my daddy but Hari's daddy?' said Patrick, who missed nothing. 'Ooh!'

Hari was smiling broadly and clapping his hands together. Oh God, thought Zoe. Maybe it wouldn't be too bad. She'd WhatsApped and suggested Jaz meet them in town but he'd said immediately he wanted to see where his son was living, in a slightly pompous imperious tone that didn't sound remotely like him.

She drove back quickly, worried that Jaz would get there before her. As it was, she barely had time to get in the house, throw on some more make-up and pull on a black top even though it wasn't quite warm enough the second you stepped out of direct sunlight. It still looked halfway okay.

Zoe didn't realise – although Jaz spotted it as soon as she stepped out of the car, as would have any of her London friends – that actually, she looked a million times better than she had for a long, long time.

The fresh air and utter lack of pollution had brightened her complexion; the late summer sun had graced her with a couple of freckles on her nose. She fell into bed exhausted every night from her two jobs, and was sleeping better than she had done in years – as was a properly exercised Hari, who no longer woke her, upset and churning in the middle of the night. The sparklingly clean and soft water and the fact that she was no longer dyeing it made her chestnut hair soft and luxuriant, and the good plain food had cleared up her skin.

But there was something else there too – the stress of day-to-day living, of finding rent, of worrying about the future. It had not gone, of course not. But it had lifted. The fine lines around her eyes and the furrow in her brow had all evened out. She was still skint of course, and still worried about what was to come. But not the way she had been. Not the terrible all-encompassing three a.m. worries about the future. Not the waves of anxiety and panic that used to roll over her when she was least expecting it; the nervousness of standing at the cashpoint machine, waiting to see if it would work. There was nothing to spend money on here anyway.

She was looking, Jaz thought, as he got out of his tiny red car – there hadn't been a lot of choice – amazing. Almost as she had when they'd first met. If he had been a rather clearer thinker, he'd have thought that this place was doing her good.

As it was, he thought she was trying to look hot on purpose for him. Which was kind of true, but not in the way either of them thought.

'Hey!' She waved at him. 'Hang on.'

The wind blew her hair to the side as she bent back into the car, heart beating wildly. Jaz looked again at the house. It was absolutely the dog's nuts. Not as fancy when you got close to it as it looked from far away, obviously, but still, he was going to take a lot of pictures of himself standing in front of it. Cool. As he stared at the house, two small faces poked out of the downstairs window, staring at him oddly. Jaz stared back at them. He wasn't going to wave. He didn't give two shits who these posh kids were.

Zoe was leaning over Hari who was kicking his legs in a desperate effort to free himself from the car seat.

'Daddy,' she said, and he squirmed and wriggled in delight. It's worth it, she told herself. To make him happy. It's worth it. Everything is worth it.

And, trying to compose her face, she finally released the car seat, and the little boy scrambled past her, turned round and jumped down.

They watched – Ramsay too, who was upstairs in the library and had heard the cars draw up – the tiny figure of Hari tear across the crunching gravel, with weeds shooting up among it, as Jaz knelt down and opened his arms wide.

Ramsay noticed the way Zoe pulled her arms into herself, hugged herself, as if trying to hide away; trying to stop her emotions coming to the surface. In the huge driveway, the grass behind, she looked very small down there, vulnerable in a way he hadn't noticed before.

'HARRRRRRRRI!' Jaz picked the little boy up and spun him around, as the child threw his head back in joy.

'Good to see you, bro!'

You're *not* his bro, thought Zoe for the billionth time, but she stayed silent. She started walking towards him. Hari was squirming in Jaz's arms, and Zoe realised he wanted Patrick to come and meet him. She turned and beckoned the children. Patrick emerged from the car and Shackleton from the house; Mary was having none of it.

Zoe walked across the gravel.

'Hi, Jaz,' she said. Ramsay found himself watching to see if they embraced, then wondered why he was doing that (they did not) – then turned away, feeling he was spying, that he was doing something wrong, wondering why he cared and why his mind was leading him places it absolutely could not go.

Chapter Twenty

'Wow,' Jaz was saying. He kept taking selfies of himself in the drawing room or posing next to the suit of armour or one of the swords on the wall, and every time he did so Mrs MacGlone would harrumph loudly from the kitchen.

'What's up with her?' he said loudly. 'Is she racist?'

'Jaz,' said Zoe urgently. 'This is where I work. Come on, let's go have a cup of tea – do you want a scone?'

'A *scone*?' said Jaz, bursting out laughing. 'Oh, a *scone*. Is that what we do now? *Eat scones?!* You've changed, man. A *scone*.'

Zoe scowled.

'Do you want one or not?'

Hari was nodding happily.

'Oh, sure I'll try a *scone*,' said Jaz, as if it were the funniest idea he'd ever heard in his life. Zoe knew his bluster was overcoming how out of place he felt, and she understood it – she'd felt exactly the same when she'd first arrived. She'd always assumed that Scotland was just a slightly windier outcrop of England really. She didn't realise, had never seen how different it was, to its very bones, in the stones of its walls and the trees and the earth itself.

Not to mention, neither of them were from houses like this.

Nothing like. For them both, the word 'estate' had very difference connotations.

'Scones are good,' she said.

The kitchen was cheerily warm and cosy, even with Mrs MacGlone fussing over the dishes and keeping her back to them.

'This is Jaz,' Zoe said as brightly as she could. 'Hari's dad. He's visiting.'

Mrs MacGlone looked round, her mouth a small line.

'Well,' she said grudgingly. 'You didn't need to tell me he's Hari's dad. Two peas in a pod.'

Hari stuck his head against his father's beard and they both smiled, and Zoe felt her heart wobble.

'I'll make tea,' said Zoe. 'Mrs MacGlone, I'm here all afternoon . . . I can take over . . . '

'Want to get me out the way, do you?'

'No!'

'You know I don't gossip.'

'I do know that,' said Zoe, who could have done with a bit of gossip on the many long evenings, even about people she didn't know.

'Well then.'

But she stepped away from the sink and put her coat on.

Patrick had been following them around and now couldn't wait a moment longer and stood right in front of Jaz.

'I am absolutely Hari's best friend,' he announced.

'Oh. Well. Good,' said Jaz. 'Can you teach him to speak?'

'Jaz!' said Zoe. He knew fine well he wasn't meant to discuss it.

'I absolutely like Hari how he is,' said Patrick, and Zoe could have kissed him.

'Come on,' she said suddenly. 'I'll put a film on for you.'

There was mass cheerfulness at this rare treat. Hari, though, looked miserable, torn between two wonderful things to do: a film, or be with his dad.

'You can watch it too,' said Zoe. 'We'll be right here, okay? Just for a little while, while we talk?'

Hari nodded and clambered down from Jaz as Zoe went and put

the video on. There was a very timeworn video of *The Wizard of Oz* and an ancient VCR which she sorted out for them; even Shackleton didn't mind watching *The Wizard of Oz*.

Then, finally in the kitchen, they were alone.

'So, who's this weirdo boss you're working for then?'

'How much do you know?' said Zoe.

'Just what Surinder told me. Some posh gigantic weirdo whose wife left him.'

'Um, good afternoon,' said Ramsay, who'd materialised in the kitchen door, figuring it was rude to leave it any longer and wanting, for some obscure reason, to get it over with. He was carrying a huge pile of books, over which only the top of his head could be seen, towering up to the ceiling.

Zoe jumped up, puce.

'Jesus,' she said. 'I didn't hear you come in.'

Ramsay blinked and looked for somewhere to set the books down, then decided against it and remained standing, stranded in his own kitchen doorway.

'Clearly.'

Jaz wasn't in the least perturbed.

'Sorry, man! Nice to meet you. I'm Jazwinder.'

'Ramsay Urquart,' said Ramsay, putting out his hand. Several books fell down and Zoe ran over and grabbed half of them.

'Nice house,' said Jaz, looking around. 'Reckon the missus has fallen on her feet.'

Ramsay blinked and looked at Zoe, who was still bright red.

'Oh. I'm sorry, I didn't realise you were . . .'

'We're *not*,' said Zoe fiercely.

Jaz laughed.

'She loves it really.'

'So, are you staying?'

'Nah,' said Jaz. 'Got a room in the city. Early flight home innit.'

The fact that, once again, Jaz would do something so very casual – book a hotel room rather than stay overnight for free – and still wasn't giving her any money truly stuck in Zoe's craw yet again.

'Oh nice,' she said sarcastically. 'Staying in a hotel. How lovely.'

'A hotel in *Scotland*,' said Jaz. 'Come on, it's hardly Ibiza.'

'I wouldn't know,' said Zoe, hating the bitterness in her voice. To stop herself, she went and filled up the tea, automatically handing Ramsay his, who took it without saying thank you. Jaz eyed them both curiously. Ramsay muttered something about going out, grabbed his books again and tripped over his feet on the way up the steps, Jaz sitting watching him go.

'What a lanky drink of water,' he observed. 'God. Seriously.'

'Why are you being rude in his house?' said Zoe, rounding on him. 'I don't think there's any need for it.'

'There's no need for *this*,' said Jaz. 'God, I come a billion miles to see the lad and all I get is abuse.'

Zoe took a deep breath.

'It's good you've come to see him. You should take him out in the grounds – it's lovely out there.'

'I will,' said Jaz. There was a silence.

'So, you look like you've landed on your feet,' he said again eventually.

'Is that what it looks like?' said Zoe, torn between the desire to show that she'd been doing all right and not wanting to let him off the hook. 'Thank God for Surinder.'

'Yeah right.'

He blinked and looked away.

'Look, right. I wanted to tell you. Just . . . I've gone into the firm.'

He meant his uncle's textiles firm that Surinder worked for in Birmingham.

'You're moving to Brum?'

'No. I'm going to run the London export office.'

'Right,' said Zoe, wondering where this was going. 'Well, that's good.'

There was a long pause.

'So . . . I mean. You could come back if you liked.'

Zoe blinked.

'What do you mean?'

'Come back to London.'

He ran his hand inside the collar of his rather ridiculous satin bomber jacket. Zoe screwed up her face.

'I don't understand. You want me to live with you or what?'

'Oh Christ ... I mean. Well. I was kind of thinking you'd find a place and I could give you some cash. Pay maintenance properly.' His voice dropped. 'Do it right.'

He was fiddling with his cup now, staring at the table.

'I know I've not ... I mean. Come on, Zoe, help me out here.'

Zoe couldn't have been more surprised.

'But ... I don't know what you're saying. I thought you were touring festivals, being a DJ.'

'I'm saying ... come back to London. Get your old job back. I'll take Hari every second weekend or whatever, pick him up from nursery. Live near. Give you money.'

'But you didn't do any of those things before! When we lived right there!'

'I said to you, I've changed. Things have changed.'

'What's changed them?'

Jaz shrugged. Zoe took a long drink of tea, her heart sinking, even though, of course, she didn't want him back, of course not.

'You've met someone,' she said finally.

He shrugged again.

'Well, we was over, right?' he said, trying to make it into a joke, although it wasn't remotely funny.

'You've met someone ... who knows about Hari,' said Zoe, trying to put it together. The truth struck her like a punch in the guts.

'Oh my God. You're in love.'

Jaz looked embarrassed as a schoolboy.

'Weeeeelllll ...'

'You are, aren't you?'

He half smiled.

'She ... she makes me want to be a better man,' he said, as if he was trying to be noble in a film. Zoe snorted.

'Well, I might need a bit more to go on than that, if that's all right.'

Chapter Twenty-one

But Jaz was completely serious. Once the floodgates were open, he wanted to talk about this new girl non-stop. Her name was Shanti, she was ravishingly gorgeous, totally amazing, ran her own business and was, Zoe noted with just the hint of an eyeroll, twenty-three years old. He even showed her pictures – she was undoubtedly ravishing: long dark hair, wide green eyes. Zoe felt like his aunt.

'Well, this is great.'

'You don't mind, do you, Zo?' he said, slightly apologetically. 'Only, I mean. You and me. That's ancient history, yeah?'

Ancient history was sitting next door hiding behind Shackleton whenever the Wicked Witch of the East showed up, but Zoe didn't say that.

'Sure,' she said. 'I'm glad you're happy.'

'I mean, we started talking about, like, everything. We watched the sun come up in Goa, and she's just so spiritual, you know?'

Zoe thought there was a strong connection between people who were spiritual and people who had never had to forage underneath the sofa cushions to find enough coins to feed the meter key, but managed not to say so.

'And she just made me see everything differently – about how it's a privilege to have a child, and how I had to show him how to be a man and how a real man takes care of his family.'

Zoe's bit her lips together tightly and thought of their son, her pride and joy, and doing what was best for him.

'Well then,' she said, keeping the sarcasm out of her voice, or at least, making a good stab at it. 'I'll look forward to meeting her.'

'You'll love her,' said Jaz again. 'Everyone does.'

Zoe wondered if he'd ever spoken about her with such enthusiasm. She knew he hadn't.

'Okay,' said Zoe. 'But actually . . .'

She looked around. The fire was crackling in the grate. She could hear a faint giggle from next door, which probably meant the Cowardly Lion had just appeared. She ought to be getting on with supper.

'I mean, it's not *all* bad here,' she said, grabbing the chopping board and an onion.

Jaz looked around. 'Are you kidding me? We're, like, a billion miles from . . . well. Everything. I mean, you might as well be dead.'

He stood up.

'And I thought the house looked posh, but look at it.'

He pointed to another overlooked spider's web in the pantry entrance. 'It's falling apart, isn't it? Look at that oven! And it's freezing in here. I mean it looks posh, but really it's shit.'

'I don't think so. It's actually really beautiful.'

'Come off it. And those spooky kids, Christ. And that old tall geezer, I reckon he's got the hots for you.'

'Don't be ridiculous,' said Zoe. 'I'm the au pair!'

'Yeah, blokes always shag the nanny, well known fact,' said Jaz. 'And he's gross. Killed his first wife, having a go for the younger one. Textbook.'

'*Shut up!*' said Zoe with far more vehemence than the stupid comment deserved.

'Ooh, all right,' said Jaz, putting his hands up. 'Touchy! Come on, don't be daft. Come back to London. I'll find you a place near us. Help with the rent. Pick up Hari. Come on, it'll be good. Back with your mates, where you belong. Get your mum back over. Not in the middle of nowhere and not where it's absolutely blinking freezing. You've had your fun; you've made your point. Come home.'

Zoe chopped onions to stop herself having to answer straightaway. She didn't even know what she thought.

'Hari's happy up here,' she said.

'Well, he still ain't talking, is he? So he's obviously not that happy.'

'That will happen in its own time.'

'Yeah, at *home*, in London, near some real doctors. And some kids that look like him,' he added pointedly.

'There's loads of kids that look like him,' said Zoe stoically. Loads was overstating it, but he wasn't the only mixed-race kid in nursery by a long shot, so Jaz could stick that in his pipe and smoke it.

'And anyway, I can't,' said Zoe. 'The book van owner is in hospital. I'm her cover. I'll have to stay.'

'That's all right,' said Jaz. 'That'll give me time to get sorted. Shanti's got a nice place in Wembley. So I might move in with her, find you a place nearby.' Zoe still looked worried. 'I'm . . . Can't you see what I'm offering? For Christ's sake, Zo. I've come all this way. To do the right thing.' He ate his scone moodily. 'I thought you'd be biting my hand off.'

'I . . . yes, I know. I mean. It's very generous.'

'I just want to—'

'—do the right thing, yeah, I get it. Better late than never.'

She smiled weakly.

'Well, you have to come back sometime.'

Zoe nodded rather bleakly. A silence fell.

Hari's little curly head poked around the door, and he beamed with happiness to see both his parents there. It was as if he was checking they were both real.

'Hey, bro!' said Jaz, standing up. 'Come show me around, yeah?'

'I can absolutely come too,' said Patrick, his head appearing above Hari's.

'No, Patrick, I need you to help me with supper,' said Zoe in a tone that brooked no argument. The child looked hurt. Jaz ignored him and put his hand out to his son. Hari took it as if he were meeting Santa Claus. The look on his face was rapturous.

'Thing is,' said Jaz, as they turned to go out into the garden, where the wind was blowing the leaves into spirals. He lowered his voice. 'Also, you can't. You can't take a man's child out of the country. You know that, Zo. It's not legal.'

'We're not out of the country!'

'What, this is England?'

He snorted and pointed at the loch, shadowy and forbidding-looking.

'No,' said Zoe. 'But it's part of Great Britain.'

Jaz looked around and raised his shoulders.

'Neh,' he said. And even if he didn't mean to sound threatening, he did, somehow.

He led Hari out, bouncing with glee, staring up at his father, the hero, and Zoe watched them in the slow fading light, running through the leaves, Jaz spinning the little boy around, both of them so similar, even in the way they walked.

It should have been a touching scene; a reunion.

Instead, it filled Zoe with fear, something akin to panic. Patrick came towards her.

'You're shaking, Nanny Seven.' He lowered his voice. 'Did you see the monster?'

'I don't know,' said Zoe.

Chapter Twenty-two

When Jaz and Shanti came in, worn out and cold from the frosty evening, they were out of breath and cheerful (Patrick was sulking manfully, doing a jigsaw puzzle by himself in the corner). Zoe was making bets with herself as to how long he could actually keep silent. Shackleton was watching her as she pan-fried chunks of local beef until they were brown, then poured them into an ancient cassoulet pot with red wine, cloudberries, stock, wild mushrooms and rosemary, letting it slowly melt down together. The smell on a chill autumn's evening was absolutely heavenly.

Jaz stood in the door frame.

'You want to eat?' said Zoe. Jaz shook his head. 'Neh,' he said. 'It smells weird. I'll grab something in Inverness … They must have a KFC, right?'

'I don't know.'

Hari looked up at his dad.

'Look, bro. I'm going now. But you'll be back soon, okay? And then I'll see you all the time, all right?'

'Jaz,' said Zoe. 'I have a job here. I can't just walk away from it.'

Patrick's ears were pricking up.

'I'm here. You left.'

'I didn't leave *here*,' said Jaz. 'I went travelling. And now I'm back. In London. And *you* left.'

'Before we starved to death!' said Zoe. Jaz rolled his eyes. 'Don't be dramatic,' he said. 'You'll upset Hari.'

'What happened to you being a changed man?' Zoe couldn't help herself asking.

'I'm here, telling you to come back to London with me where I'm going to find you a place to live and look after my son,' said Jaz. 'And somehow I'm the bad guy.'

There wasn't much more to say after that. He left, going into the darkening garden, then starting up the ridiculous tiny red car. Hari stood at the window in the kitchen door, staring at the car until it disappeared from sight.

'I don't like him,' whispered Patrick to Zoe, who couldn't help smiling even as she said, 'Don't be silly – that's Hari's dad.'

'Yes, and now Hari is absolutely sad,' said Patrick, with which Zoe truly couldn't argue.

Supper was delicious, but Zoe could barely touch a thing. Hari just stared longingly out of the window and occasionally let out a sigh. Mary was in one of her picky moods. Only Shackleton ate with appetite and evident pleasure. Zoe cleared up mechanically, making the children rinse their plates, and put an overtired Hari to bed as soon as she was able, finding it very difficult to read from *Up on the Rooftops*, with its London settings and London landmarks and Patrick constantly asking if that's where Hari was going and where did they live and could they climb up on the roofs and how he would climb up on every roof in London when he came to visit him.

The house felt so empty when everyone had gone to bed. Normally Zoe fell straight asleep five minutes after the children, her life was so full now, but tonight she couldn't. She padded around the kitchen, made tea that she let get cold, considered texting a friend. But what would they say? Her London friends would just say, 'Great! See you soon!' Finally Jaz was facing up to his responsibilities; finally he was coming home. Her mum would be pleased because her girl would be in London, among her own sort, back where she belonged, none of this running off to Scotland nonsense. She could call Kirsty, she supposed, but she didn't even know Jaz.

She felt so alone. Upstairs was a little boy she would protect with her life. But what was the best way to protect him? Here, with companions, and wide open spaces? The difference in him, his outlook, how much he smiled, how much he was learning, the trees he climbed . . . to go back to a little studio in the city. Not that there was anything wrong with the city but . . .

The thought of commuting to work, squeezing into an over-crowded tube or bus, waiting for hours, crushed up against everyone else, being an hour away from home . . . compared to now, her daily meander through the great hills, where she could see the whole glory of nature spread out below her, changing every single day, often it seemed simply for her benefit. Changing the smell of hot dirty trains for the bonfire breezes of the west way, the clacking of rats on the tube tracks for the majestic soar of an eagle over the hills, the funny wobble of a partridge out for a stroll, or the wild geese on the water, or the heron, or the seals, sunning themselves on the rocks.

Another cup of tea went cold and she put the kettle on again. Did Jaz have a case about her moving? She knew you couldn't take a child out of the country, but Scotland was the same country. Well, for now. She knew though that even if she could legally move here with Hari, deep down she was indeed taking him far away from his dad, and that a court might see things very differently, if it came to that.

The thought of court clasped at her heart. To go from being terrified of Jaz never returning to see Hari to suddenly being scared of having to go see him all the time . . .

Oh God. What a mess. What a mess. What if she had to drag

Hari into court? The very idea of it made her shiver. What about if he had to stand there? What if they had to make him talk to a judge and he wouldn't answer? Would they blame her? Would they take him away?

She was terrifying herself now, her thoughts spiralling out of control. What if they thought she was unfit? What if Jaz's new girl-friend was amazing, and Hari loved her and liked being back in London and . . .

She dropped her head onto her arms on the table so she could – as she always had to, sharing a room with Hari – cry without making a sound, even though nobody could have heard her in the vast stillness of the great house, only the ticking of the grandfather clock Patrick had started winding every day (it was one of his jobs; if they all had to have chores, Zoe had tried to make at least some of them fun, and he took it very seriously), even as the kettle on the stove started to whistle.

And that is how Ramsay found her, half an hour later, as the fire burned low and he was letting himself in the back door; on the brink of sobbing herself to sleep.

He started when he saw her – it looked like she'd passed out – and she jerked awake in that way you do when you're falling asleep and feel like you've missed a stair, and for a moment wasn't at all sure where she was, then scrubbed at her tear-sodden face, but in that moment she had looked to Ramsay, who until this moment had thought of her as incredibly capable and positive, and had been bowled over by her plucky attempts with his tricky children, at how she let nothing stand in her way, in how she had literally let the light in. He wouldn't have admitted it in a million years, given she was well over a foot shorter than him, but he found her intimidating and so capable. So used to dealing with very little; unfazed by the noise and fuss around her. There was something indomitable about her.

And now she was completely undone and he felt a rush of

tenderness towards her, like a bird with a broken wing. He put down the heavy box he was carrying and rushed over. His first instinct was to scoop her up in his arms; she realised, looking up with a shock, that her first desire was for him to do that. He stopped.

'Are you all right?'

Zoe blinked, then her face flamed. She jumped up and ran to wash her face, trying to cool herself down. What must he think of her?

'Sorry ... yes, just ... must have drifted off ...'

She rubbed furiously at the mascara which was running under her eyes. Ramsay stood there, his large hands waving around rather nervously.

'Are you absolutely sure you're all right?'

It was the concern in his voice that very nearly set her off again. She stayed at the sink, not quite trusting herself to turn around.

'Um,' she said, testing her voice. A definite wobble. She swallowed hard.

'It was just ... it's always tricky ...'

'Seeing Hari's dad?'

Zoe nodded.

'Well,' she said boldly. 'You know.'

She still hadn't turned around and therefore didn't see Ramsay's grimace.

'Mmm,' he said non-committally. 'Well, it's nice he's coming to visit your lad.'

'Oh, it's a bit worse than that,' said Zoe, finally turning round. Then she saw the box.

'What's that?' she said suspiciously, still scrubbing at her face. Ramsay's lips twitched.

'I was ... I was going to keep it as a surprise,' he said. Zoe walked forwards.

'Is that what I think it is?' Her voice was surprised, even as she'd thought the day didn't have much more to throw at her.

'I was going to set it up for you tomorrow ...'

'But how ... why?!'

'I've ... well ...'

He rubbed his face awkwardly.

'Ever since you started ... you know. Clearing out the library a bit. It's ... well ... ' He coughed. 'Given me a bit of inspiration really. I've been working on selling a lot more.'

Zoe moved towards the precious shining vision: a new coffee machine.

'Ooh, I love it!'

'It has ... pods?' His brow furrowed. 'I didn't really understand what they were trying to get me to do.'

'I know!' said Zoe, jumping up. Her ability to retain her equilibrium surprised him. She knew how to perk herself up; not, he realised, for the first time. She wasn't a wounded bird at all. She had resilience.

She was plugging in the machine, exclaiming with delight when she saw it came with two dinky cups and a milk frother, and he watched her as the extraordinary device warmed up.

'Any decaff?' she said, checking the clock. It was late. 'Ah,' she said. 'It doesn't matter. I won't sleep anyhow.'

She served them both up perfect tiny macchiatos with a little squiggle on the top.

'Look at that!' she said. 'Isn't that better?'

In his huge hands, the tiny cup looked hilarious, like a giant's plaything. He couldn't get his finger through the hole in the handle to lift it.

Zoe realised she had drifted off looking at his enormous hands, was wondering what they would feel like on her body, wondering ...

'I know,' Ramsay was saying. 'You never quite sleep the same again once the children are born, do you?'

She flushed and came back to herself, realising he was asking her a question.

'Oh no,' she said. 'And when you're on your own ... '

'Well, quite ... '

They both sat down at the table.

'What happened with you and your wife?' she found herself asking.

'Married too young,' said Ramsay quickly, as if by rote.

'Me too,' said Zoe. 'Well, not married. But.'

Ramsay took a sip of his coffee and grimaced.

'Don't tell me you don't like that?'

'It's ... different.'

'Yes because it's actually coffee. It's how coffee is meant to taste.'

'Well, what have I been drinking then?'

'Brown water.'

'I like brown water.'

'Well, hooray for you.'

They smiled.

'I don't think you are ever young again,' mused Ramsay, setting his ridiculously tiny cup back on the table and looking at it. 'Not properly. After children. Do you?'

'Not in the same way,' said Zoe. Outside, an owl hooted, but otherwise everything was very still.

'Not in the same way you can do anything, go anywhere. I remember the first time I realised it would be a catastrophe if I died. Not for me, but for him, you know.'

Ramsay nodded fervently.

'What ... what you wouldn't do for them.'

It was so quiet and still. A certain magic seemed to have settled over the kitchen: the glowing lamps, the waning fire in the stove, that liminal line between sleep and wakefulness in the lowest part of the night, when anything seems possible.

Zoe was torn between wanting to ask Ramsay everything about the children's mother, everything she needed to know, and an absurd desire to take that hand and boldly place it on her. She realised he was left-handed. No ring. Oh God, why couldn't she take her eyes off it? It was a beautiful hand: slender but strong, a thin covering of pale hair that vanished in a line up his wrist band. The nails were broad and square, cut short, the fingers ridiculously long. They looked like the hands of a pianist. She had to take her eyes off them. Or go to bed before she did something absolutely ridiculous that would get her fired, something that would be fuelled solely by sadness and caffeine, and the fact that her boss was the only person in a very long time who had shown her a tiny bit of kindness.

'So ... your husband?'

He was still speaking.

'Not my husband. My ex-boyfriend.' She sighed, snapping back to reality. Oh God. Jaz. 'He wants me to move back to London.'

He raised his eyebrows.

'I said I couldn't,' she added hastily. 'You know. Well. Until Nina's back.'

'And then ...?'

He reminded himself he was disappointed simply because she was the best au pair they'd ever had. The children would miss her, he told himself.

Zoe shrugged. 'They'll be back at school by then ... I ...'

She sighed.

'Can I not think about it right now?'

'Of course,' said Ramsay. 'I don't think we could handle a Nanny Eight.'

She smiled. Of course she was just the nanny to him. Of course she was. She was just an employee. She was Mrs MacGlone, give or take forty years.

She's a member of staff, Ramsay was telling himself. She works here. Au pairs come and go, of course.

As one they tipped their coffees into their mouths and downed them.

'Right!' said Zoe, trying to be breezy and preparing to jump up. 'Time for ...'

But just then came a set of headlights careering on the gravel and the sound of a car screeching to a halt.

Chapter Twenty-three

There was a loud banging at the back door, but whoever was knocking didn't wait for it to be answered and instead stumbled straight in. Zoe and Ramsay both jumped up in a way that looked rather guilty. Standing in front of them, the lights of the car still on behind her, music blaring out of it and the engine running, was Larissa.

Zoe noticed two things straightaway: that she looked absolutely beautiful – she was wearing a tight cerise dress, necklace and, OMG, was that a tiara set in her tightly coiled blonde hair?

And secondly, she was clearly very, very, very drunk. She was wobbling precariously in heels on the flagstone floor.

'Darling?' she said. She looked dizzy and sad. 'Darling?'

Ramsay started forwards.

'Oh crap,' he said. 'Oh, Larissa. I'm so sorry. I'm so, so sorry. I totally forgot.'

'I've been there . . .' she said, slurring. 'I've been there . . . with all those horrible men making remarks . . . making remarks about *you*, Ramsay. And me.'

She sniffed dramatically.

'Do you want some tea?' said Zoe quickly. 'Or a glass of water?'

Larissa turned round as if she'd noticed Zoe for the first time, as indeed she had.

'*Oh!*' she said, her voice cracking. 'Oh. So *this* is how it is.'

'This isn't how anything is!' said Zoe.

'Larissa, sweetie, calm down. Come on, let me drive you home,' said Ramsay.

She looked at him, mascara running down her face.

'I was ... I tried *so hard with you*, Shackleton Ramsay Urquart,' she said very, very loudly.

'Oh, there it is,' said Zoe. 'Seriously, why make Shackleton have it? I'm sure he's got a nice middle name.'

'Sssh,' Ramsay was saying. 'Come on, sweetie, I'll take you home.'

'I tried *so hard*. I was nice to your *horrible fucking kids*. I come round here *all the time*. I call you, I take you out, I ... I ... Are you fucking her?'

'What?' said Ramsay. 'Come on. I'm taking you home.'

'Fucking the au pair! Of course! Don't tell me – she used to be a nun and she plays the guitar.'

'You don't know what you're saying. I'm taking you home right now.'

Zoe was bright red and made to get out of there.

'Don't you move!' shouted Larissa. 'Get me a whisky!'

'She's not the help,' said Ramsay.

'I can speak for myself, thank you,' said Zoe, flaring up.

'Of course she's the fucking help!' said Larissa. 'You're banging the help. Always did fuck down, didn't we, darling?'

It was as if she'd torn off a mask. Everything was coming tumbling out.

'You're drunk,' said Ramsay. 'You don't know what you're saying.'

Zoe privately thought rather the opposite; that this was what she had wanted to say for a long time.

'Larissa. Please. Let me drive you home.'

'How on earth will you have the energy after spending all evening fucking the au pair?'

'I'm off,' said Zoe, absolutely puce now. Ramsay shot her a pained look but she ignored it.

'I had to sit there ... everyone asking after you ... everyone looking pityingly at me. At *me*! I forgot to tell them you prefer poor little girls ... '

Zoe got up and headed for the kitchen door. Standing there were all four of the children. Even the great house couldn't block out the screaming.

'Oh great,' said Zoe. 'Come on, you guys, let's get back to bed. It's nothing.'

'NOTHING?' screamed Larissa. 'Ha! Meet your new mother, children. There she is. You think she's the nanny, but no. She's moving in! And doing your dad. Hope you enjoy it, nanny! It's the one thing he's good for.'

Zoe stiffened, but didn't turn around. The children's faces were stricken.

'It's all right,' she said. 'Come. Come with me. Now. Shackleton, help me. Listen. It's okay. Sometimes grown-ups drink too much alcohol and say silly things they don't mean.'

Now Larissa was singing 'Here comes the bride' in a high voice.

'Make her absolutely stop,' said Patrick.

Ramsay put his hand out to take Larissa outside.

'DON'T YOU TOUCH ME!' she screamed. 'DON'T TOUCH ME! DON'T TREAT ME LIKE THE FIRST ONE.'

At this, Zoe pulled the children out of the kitchen and slammed the door.

Chapter Twenty-four

Zoe was shaking with fury as she dragged Patrick and a tear-stricken Hari away, and Shackleton gently led his sister up the stairs. From behind them came Larissa's screeching, followed by Ramsay's quiet, murmured tones. Eventually, at last, the car drove out into the night.

Zoe ushered everyone into Patrick's room and sat them all down on the beds, then went to the sink and drank a glass of water down in one gulp, trying to get hold of herself.

That Larissa could behave like that in front of Ramsay's children – in front of her own child – Zoe was so furious she wanted to scream, throw things, hit stuff. Obviously the woman was upset and drunk and dejected but even so. Even so. Who could do that in front of children, drunk or sober?

It took many deep breaths and was with an exceptional effort of will that she managed finally to turn around to a row of worried and upset children. She didn't want to tell them they'd been right in their analysis all along.

'Now,' she said, feeling her heart racing. 'Sometimes adults ... drink too much ... and behave in ways that ... well. Aren't ideal. And in this case, Larissa was ... very tired. And got the wrong end of the stick. And said some things I'm sure she didn't mean, that definitely aren't true and I'm sure she'll feel awful about them in the morning. And that,' she added with a flourish, 'is why you shouldn't ever drink.'

They stared at her, except for Mary, who was staring out the window.

'I think,' said Patrick eventually, breaking the silence, 'she absolutely does not like you.'

'Well, not everyone likes everyone,' said Zoe automatically. 'And that's okay.'

She went and knelt down by Mary. 'Darling. I know you understood some of those words. You know it's not true, don't you? Larissa was just being ... highly strung.'

Mary's face was icy.

'She wants to marry Daddy. But she can't, because you're going to marry him.'

'Oooh!' said Patrick.

'No!' said Zoe. 'Jesus! No! That's not it at all. I promise.'

Mary shook her head.

'It's true! It's true! I saw you!'

Zoe blanched with guilt. Saw what? There was nothing to see, there had been nothing, nothing ...

'At the Samhain! I saw you hugging!'

Mary blinked. Oh Christ.

'We were dancing, Mary. For two seconds. That was all! Nothing ... nothing like what you think.'

But her face was bright red because it hadn't been nothing to Zoe, and Mary, her dark eyes burning into Zoe's face, knew it.

'YOU'RE LYING!' screamed the girl. 'YOU'RE LYING! EVERYONE LIES TO ME! EVERYONE LIES!'

And she stood up and charged out of the room.

PART FOUR

'The ravens are gathering,' the Beefeater told them, pounding his pike on the turret floor. 'They're getting ready to fly. And when they do, they shall turn the sky black and the river red and the stones will crumble and the earth will crack and weep for all who are lost. So. Who would like a Tower Bridge tea towel to take home?'

Wallace stared at him. 'What did you just say?'

'I said, "Who would like a Tower Bridge tea towel to take home?"'

'Me!' said Francis loudly.

From *Up on the Rooftops*

Chapter One

It took for ever to settle the boys, and Zoe knew she had to get to Mary. She calmed them, told them it was just an upset lady talking and eventually agreed to let Hari sleep in Patrick's room, just this once. The boys got into the same bed and she stroked their heads.

'It's not true,' she whispered. 'Go to sleep.'

Shackleton had slouched off and Zoe was worried about him; he kept things so bundled up. But she had to deal with Mary.

'Go away,' was the answer to her knock. 'GO AWAY!'

'I just want to talk to you.'

'I don't want to talk to you. Ever. EVER.'

Zoe went and grabbed a large blanket from a chair at the end of the hallway.

'Okay,' she said. 'I'm just going to sit here until you're ready. I'm not going anywhere, Mary. I'm here for you.'

'I hate you!'

'That's fine too.'

Unfortunately, a long emotional day had taken its toll, and lying on some surprisingly comfortable cushions from the sofa on the long landing, Zoe found herself without any fight left in her, the events of the day too huge and stressful to take in all at once. When Zoe had a small problem, she could lie awake and worry about it for hours. Here, with a big one, she was too overwhelmed, and sleep overwhelmed her.

Ramsay, arriving back two hours later, having had an entirely unsatisfactory drive back to Larissa's during which he had planned on telling her a few home truths and instead had had to put up with Larissa refusing to get in the passenger seat, then, when he'd basically had to lift her in, she'd fallen immediately asleep with heavy snores. He had covered up the beautiful dress with his big coat, and had driven the deserted country lanes in complete silence, seething and upset, not even realising how fast he was going until he almost killed a deer and realised he was likely to kill Larissa and himself and leave the children in an even worse state than they were in now, and so he had pulled over and given himself ten minutes to calm himself down.

He finally deposited her at Lochdown Manor where, to his horror, several of her loathsome posh hunting, shooting and fishing friends were still up, killing a bottle of whisky. They had been his crowd too, once upon a time, and they were delighted to see him and seemed to find Larissa's little interlude absolutely hilarious.

'Oh Christ, knew you were in for it, Rammy boy,' said Crawfs. 'She was fuming all evening.'

'Remember when she slut-dropped with the waiter to make you jealous? And you weren't even there?'

'Christ, she was a mess.'

Ramsay realised he was at severe risk of feeling sorry for Larissa and so took her upstairs, took off her shoes, if not her tights, and put her to bed in the vast Laura Ashley bedroom he had come to know on nights when he had felt so lonely he couldn't stand it one second more. He had thought she was so sweet.

He filled a large glass of water and put it next to her and, as he turned his head to look at her blonde head one last time, shook his head. He had the worst taste in women. The worst. No more. He was done with it.

The boys ragged him out of the house and he took her car home.

She could sort it out later. He sped back to The Beeches, along the dark side of the loch, the setting moon illuminating long wakes across the chop, the depths as mysterious as ever. The weather was getting up. It looked like their run of crisp clear autumn days was coming to an end. Storms were forecast, although the only forecast you ever needed around here was 'changeable'.

He was staggering with tiredness by the time he got back to the house. Zoe would, he assumed, leave in the morning. She had said she was going home. This would do it.

Oh God, what a mess. What a bloody mess, the lot of it. It was four in the morning. He might as well try and get a little sleep.

He was astounded to find Zoe lying sentinel in front of his daughter's room. He realised that he had been absurd; his first thought had been that she would leave. Her first thought was for his only daughter.

He looked in on Mary. She was lying there breathing steadily in a way that seemed slightly suspicious to him so he said her name very quietly, but she didn't answer, and after a moment or two went up to the bed, crouched down and kissed her on the forehead.

'I love you,' he said quietly.

Mary lay as quietly as she could in the bed. She knew it. He had proven it. He was apologising to her. He loved her. She tried to keep her eyes still so the tears didn't leak out on to the pillow.

Ramsay almost tripped over Zoe on his way out of the room. Her face was so open in sleep, it felt intrusive to stare at her too closely. His hand went up to stroke her hair, then he grabbed it back again. Enough. Enough bloody trouble.

She was the second sleeping woman he left that evening. His feelings towards them were very different.

Chapter Two

At first, when she woke, Zoe didn't know where she was, only that she was freezing and upset and felt absolutely horrible.

Secondly, she realised that she was lying on the floor, and it was morning, and rain was hitting the windows. All of this was awful. Oh God. What had happened?

Gradually the events of the preceding day came back to her, and she sat up in the long corridor, groaning.

Oh God! She hadn't meant to fall asleep! She was meant to be checking on Mary! Oh God! She leapt up, all her senses on fire. Oh Christ. Was there an adult in her life who didn't let this child down? She knocked, and on getting no answer felt icy water plunge through her veins.

'Mary? Mary?'

She rattled the door, which opened. The room was empty; the window was open. A freezing gusty wet wind blew in.

She's downstairs getting breakfast, Zoe told herself. She's just downstairs with Hari, getting breakfast.

The idea of Mary helping Hari out with anything was profoundly unlikely, but she clung to it regardless and tore down the stairs.

The kitchen was empty. Everyone, it seemed, was having a long lie-in after their dramatic late night. The two little coffee cups were still sitting by the sink. Zoe stared at them as if she couldn't work out what on earth they were. It felt like months ago.

'HARI!' she hollered, then tore up the stairs.

'Patrick? Have you seen Hari? PATRICK?!'

Her voice now had a tone of panic in it. The little boy came to the door, wiping his eyes. He glanced back at the now empty beds.

'I have absolutely not seen Hari, Nanny Seven,' he said.

'Christ,' said Zoe, trying not to panic the little boy. 'Where is . . . Hari? HARI!'

She ran up to the servants' quarters, banged open every single door, little identical rows of metal beds one after the other, but no Hari. He always, beat a rhythm in her heart, came when called.

Nothing.

She tore back down again. By this time Mrs MacGlone had arrived, and Ramsay was downstairs.

'Mrs MacGlone! Coming in . . . have you seen Hari? He's not here!'

'Have you checked everywhere?' said Mrs MacGlone. 'I mean, there are a lot of rooms.'

'Yes!'

'All the cupboards? You're sure he's not playing hide and seek?'

Zoe shook her head. 'He can't. We don't play that game.' Her voice shook out to a sob 'He can't shout out when he's found.'

'I'll check the other rooms,' said Mrs MacGlone.

'Well, *do it* then,' said Zoe, a tightly coiled wire. 'And Mary too.'

Mrs MacGlone frowned as Zoe ran to the back door and threw it open. The wind blew in and tried to slam the door back in their faces. There was Mrs MacGlone's tread on the flattened grass – and, just visible, on the frosted grass across the lawn – two more sets of footprints.

'She's taken him,' said Zoe, going white.

'What?'

He was there so suddenly, so utterly, filling the doorway, pulling on jeans and an old fisherman's sweater over a striped pyjama shirt that looked as old as the house.

'Where is he?'

'Mary ... Mary's taken Hari ...'

Ramsay swore.

'Are you sure? They haven't just ... gone out to play together?'

The wind roared through the trees.

'That ... that is not really the kind of thing they do,' said Zoe through chattering teeth.

'Christ,' said Ramsay. 'Oh Christ. Come on. Bugger, where's my phone?'

It was lying dead on the counter, Larissa's repeated calls having utterly exhausted it.

'I've got mine,' said Zoe, her voice shaking. 'Mrs MacGlone, stay here and keep ... watch the boys ...'

The boys she didn't take was the phrase left unspoken in the air. Mrs MacGlone nodded, mouth a thin line, and turned round.

'Don't scare them!' shouted Zoe rather pointlessly, as both of them were down in the kitchen, watching her and Ramsay dive out into the overgrown lawn. Shackleton caught them up in moments.

'I'll check the woods,' he said, and his voice, suddenly low, made both Zoe and Ramsay turn back briefly as he seemed so much older than his age.

Outlined in the grey morning light, Zoe suddenly got a flash of the house behind her. The trees were bending in the wind, the sky was full of grey scudding clouds and the windows of the house were blind, like eyes that couldn't see.

'HARI!'

The rain was swirling, throwing leaves here and there; the fierce rustling in the trees and the eerie whispering grasses and the house which had began to look like home suddenly looked like the most frightening place she could imagine.

'MARY!' Ramsay was calling too, desperately, neither of them able to believe that the children were gone – they couldn't, they couldn't be gone.

In her mind, Zoe ran through the world they were living in. The

338

hills, freezing now, a real risk of exposure. The rough scrub of the hillside, so easy to get lost.

The loch. The loch.

Ramsay came to the same conclusion at exactly the same time and suddenly they were both running against the wind, crying out names that got lost in the wind, faster and faster.

They reached the shingle beach at the same time, the waves pounding on the shore, and looked at each other in disbelief.

The little rowing boat was gone.

'She wouldn't,' Ramsay muttered to himself. 'She wouldn't. Why would she?'

Zoe's trembling fingers were dialling the phone. She dropped it on the shore and Ramsay picked it up and dialled quickly.

'Coastguard,' he said in a clipped voice. 'East side of Loch Ness.'

He stared at Zoe, both of them unable to believe what he was saying even as he said it.

'I think two children have taken a boat out, and we don't know where they are.'

Zoe barked a little sob as Ramsay gave them more details. She walked towards the very edge of the water. There was nothing to be seen and the water was choppy; the grey water and the grey sky made everything look the same.

'Yes, I'm sure!' Ramsay was saying, clearly doing his best to keep under control. 'The Beeches. Check it.'

He waited. 'Okay. Yes.'

He handed the phone to Zoe.

'They can't send a helicopter. It's too stormy'

Zoe suddenly felt her knees gave way, and Ramsay caught her just before she fell to the ground.

Chapter Three

Ramsay held her up but she shook him off. She didn't have time, she couldn't be weak. She couldn't. She grabbed her phone, her hand shaking. Ramsay would have carried on supporting her, but she backed away, not even realising she was shaking her head at him. She fumbled again but managed to find Murdo's number.

'Oh hello!'

Murdo was his cheerful self – had been, in fact, since Agnieszka had come over to comfort him over his abortive date – and Zoe found herself clinging to the normality of his voice.

'What have you got for me? Yes, I loved the Cherry-Garrard. I loved it. Every day it wasn't zero degrees and I wasn't trying to kill penguins for food. I told Agnieszka to try making some penguin but—'

'Murdo,' said Zoe desperately and he finally caught the tone of her voice.

'What's wrong?'

'It's Hari ... he's disappeared. On the loch.'

'The lad?'

'Yes.'

'What ...?'

'We don't know. We think Mary took him out …'

'But there's a storm coming in.'

Ramsay was staring at her desperately. Zoe fought back her rage and terror.

'She … she didn't know that,' she said finally.

'Where … where are they?'

'They can't have got far,' said Zoe. 'It's a rowing boat.'

'Aye, but there's currents out there on the water …' said Murdo, and Zoe whimpered in terror.

'Aye, right, don't worry. I'm on my way.'

Murdo sent out an APB then shot across the loch in the boat that went faster than any of his guests could ever have imagined. It pitched and bounced in the heavy water. He picked up his binoculars and looked around. He knew every inch.

Zoe was standing, looking out alone, on the shore at the foot of The Beeches, her arms wrapped around herself, her face utterly desolate, Ramsay some distance away.

Murdo peeled off, the boat bouncing from side to side in the choppy water, veering from side to side. He was soaked through, the water getting in between his oilskins and down the back of his neck. It was a gnarly day, there was no doubt about that at all. This time of year, the weather barrelled in from the west and you never quite knew what it would be until it hit you – but when it hit you, oh boy. Squalls pitched here and there, never quite all in the same direction, and it was as much as Murdo could do to keep the boat level and scan for the children at the same time. The idea of children being out here in this chilled him to the core. He would never ever come out in this with guests.

He looked at the radio again, but suddenly it became unnecessary as, through his thick hat, a noise hit him: an old, stuttering motor boat. Turning round he saw that it was Alasdair from the pub, accompanied by old Ben, both with worried expressions on their faces.

'We'll take the north,' said Alasdair, shooting round.

Behind him were, as it turned out, the cavalry, and, to Zoe standing on the shore, it was astonishing: an array of every type of boat – weekend yachts, small tubs, rowing boats, sleek pleasure boats. Hamish McTavish had to be dissuaded from bringing down his canal barge.

It was a flotilla. Murdo was keeping the channels clear to coordinate and be in charge.

Zoe couldn't believe who was out there. The colonel, who had done nothing but complain about how Nina knew what he liked, was puttering along in a tiny little tub with an outboard motor. And there was Wullie, who had sold Nina the van in the first place and done nothing but complain about it. The water was choppy, the sky was tearing itself apart, but there was Lennox in a rowing boat of all things, his muscles straining against the ferocity of the tide. The entire village was there.

Murdo reached her first, and she scrambled aboard, not tripping this time.

'They can't have got far,' said Murdo, 'if they took the wee boat.'

Nobody said the awful inevitable: you didn't have to go far. If there was a fault in the boat, the riptide would pull you down soon as look at you. You could drown ten feet off the shore. If the rip didn't get you, you could die from exposure in half an hour or so this time of year. The loch was the worst kind of dangerous: beautiful and tempting.

'Can he swim?' said Murdo.

'He's four!'

Murdo would have liked to have said or done something comforting at that point. But he knew what Zoe didn't: people died in the loch. Not every year. But it happened. He looked at her pale drawn face, every nightmare scenario playing out on her features, and could think of nothing else to do but take off his own coat and put it round her, as if it could stop the shaking, as if it had a chance.

Chapter Four

Murdo coordinated the boats as they separated; they crossed the loch in strictly organised areas. The helicopter soon added its stuttering noise to the crashing wind. In Murdo's boat, Zoe and Ramsay were not near each other; both trying to block out the worst thoughts in their heads, the worst of all possible worlds.

Everything was grey and the rain swept in off the mountains and visibility dropped to almost nothing, and now Zoe stared about her in despair: you couldn't see three feet in front of you.

A powerful police launch had joined the force and it had a high light beam in front of it, but it still felt as if they might be in the middle of the night, not eight o'clock in the morning. Noises across the lake, across the storm, took on a strange otherworldly power. It was impossible to tell how near or far you were from the rest of the boats. Time lost its meaning as they moved slowly in among the rushes of the shore or around the tiny islets that appeared at low tide. Only Zoe stood defiant in the prow of the boat, hollering over and over, 'Hari! Hari! Hari!'

And every bit of her little boy was suddenly in her head at the same time: him chuckling to himself as he learned to walk in the little bedsit, and the sleepy little face as she breastfed him in the early deep endless hours of early motherhood, shocked and bamboozled by the fierce strength of her love, even as she could see him, flashes of him, pale, washed up on the shore, pulled down by the mermen deep beneath the sea, fish eating his eyes ... no.

'HARI! HARI! HARI!'

She would remember him dancing to music on the television; remember the happiness on his face the first time she had let Patrick go with him to nursery; the look as he intently caught red leaves in the late autumn sun; the extraordinary life in him; his surprisingly heavy, intent little body; the weight of his head as he slept in her arms; the scent of his hair, stuck up in the bath with shampoo like a tiny Mohican.

'HARI! HARI!'

And Ramsay hollered, 'HARI! MARY! HARI! MARY!' staring out in every direction.

Chapter Five

All of a sudden, something swelled beneath them. Murdo swore. Zoe, knowing nothing about boating, didn't realise anything was amiss and carried on shouting the name of her lost boy, the name she would shout for evermore.

The boat lurched suddenly to one side, all of them instinctively grabbing on to the port side.

'Bugger,' said Murdo again.

'What is it?' said Zoe. The pressure was immense, the engine whining as it felt the strain.

'Um ... it must be an undertow,' said Murdo, seizing the tiller. But it was no good; the boat was caught and would only bend in the way the water seemed to be forcing it to go. He pulled the tiller again, and his hand was knocked off, stung.

He glanced around. There wasn't another boat anywhere near them and the rain was pounding harder than ever. Visibility was terrible.

'HARI!' Zoe screamed, using her phone as a torch, a useless pimple of light in the deep grey.

'Shit!' said Murdo suddenly. Out of nowhere, a large rocky outcrop had appeared, right in the centre of the lake. 'The water is low. Shit!'

He tried to work the tiller, again to no avail.

'Shit!'

They were heading closer and closer to the rocks at a high speed. 'Oh God,' said Murdo. 'Put your lifejackets on . . . We might have to abandon ship. What the *hell* is going on . . . ?'

He threw the lifejackets to Ramsay and to Zoe, who was staring terrified at the large rocks bearing down towards them, high and sharp and ready to dash them to pieces, whether, Murdo thought in horror, they jumped out of the boat or not. The current was dragging them there regardless. Drenched through, they could do nothing more than stare at the cruel waves crashing at the base of the rocks and brace themselves for impact.

It was impossible to hear anything over the noise of the engine, the pounding rain, the helicopter overhead. The noise was deafening. It took Zoe a while before she realised in the maelstrom, just as they were about to hit and she was coming to a terrible realisation, that one) Mary and Hari couldn't possibly be alive in this, and two) that she too was going to die and, that being the case, she didn't really care.

So it took a moment. And even when she heard it, she didn't believe it. Assumed it was a trick of the wind and the water, or even the sprites – some malevolent spirit under the water who would do this to add to the horror, or something her imagination was conjuring up in its very last moments, something of a dream, as if the whole thing were a dream . . .

She turned to Ramsay and screamed at him to make herself heard.

'Can you hear that?'

He went still, stopped trying to control the uncontrollable boat, and stood stock-still. And she saw from his face that he had heard it too.

'M-mmmm-mummy.'

Chapter Six

Zoe stared at Ramsay in anguish. Ramsay didn't think twice. He grabbed the rope out of the bottom of the boat and did a very brave and foolish thing. He dived straight into the water and headed straight for the rocks. He was pushed against the first one pretty hard but, undaunted, he took the rope between his teeth and disappeared underneath the water until he found what he was looking for – a twist of rock to tether the boat to.

He burst above the waves to grab a breath, then disappeared again. The storm had stirred up the sediment which made it almost impossible to see, but there had been boats and buoys on this loch since time immemorial and sure enough, down here he found a hole in the rock that he could slip the rope through, make a tight bowline and signal to Murdo, who tied it tight the other end. Then he jumped up on the rocks, bare-footed, oblivious to the cuts and bruises covering his body, and held the boat, actually held it, pulling it one direction or another when it got too close, swinging it away from the rocks; all the while Zoe could hear 'Mummy! Mummy!'

She had to see. As Ramsay, who now looked nine foot tall to her, held the boat off the rocks by, it seemed, sheer force of will, she had to know. With her lifejacket on, and before Murdo had the chance to stop her, she too dived into the freezing water and made a desperate doggy paddle for the rocks. Ramsay, incredibly, was able to keep one hand holding the boat and one grabbing her out of the water when, as soon as Zoe left the boat, the engine roared back into life and Murdo could move out after all. Murdo unhitched the bowline from his side as Ramsay knelt down to help Zoe out onto the rock side, and he accelerated away, calling all the other boats at the same time.

Together, Ramsay and Zoe scrambled up the harsh side of the rocks, Zoe's feet slipping, Ramsay's utterly bloody. At the top they looked down the other side, and what they saw changed everything, all at once, in a heartbeat.

Chapter Seven

Water is a living thing. It moves; it flows; it cannot be contained. Water is stronger than anything in its way. It can wear down mountains, bring down houses, turn everything to slush and mush. Water always gets its way.

And at low tide, these stones were revealed, but only for a few hours a day until they reclaimed their position once more in the mysterious depths. And here was an upflung rowing boat, its paint peeling, not remotely seaworthy, flung by chance upon a tiny shingle beach, the smallest lick of sand, a shallow outcrop in an area so deep, it couldn't be measured until they invented satellites.

And next to the rowing boat, cowering, shuddering, were two children staring up as Ramsay and then, being heaved up, Zoe, who clambered over the top and stared back in amazement, in absolute disbelief at the found children.

And the voice came again: 'Mummy.'

Zoe gaped, the wind and the shock already having knocked the breath from her. Ramsay thought she might fall. Instead, she slipped and slithered down the other side of the shingle, weighed down and soaking.

'Hari. HARI!' she shrieked.

'Mummy!' he said brightly.

Mary jumped up immediately, and Zoe was terrified of how furious she felt.

'What were you DOING?' she shrieked. 'What the hell were you DOING?'

She had never felt a fury like it. It came from a deep, primal place, from the depths of her lizard brain, and she couldn't possibly have controlled it.

Mary was shivering and sobbing in her white nightgown, her hair drenched around her shoulders, looking once again like the ghost that had haunted the corridors and pathways when Zoe had arrived.

'Christ, Mary,' said Ramsay, walking down towards her. 'You could ... you could ...'

He couldn't even finish the sentence.

Zoe had Hari in her arms. She was choking up seawater, and his little body was soaked right through and utterly freezing so she pressed any warmth she could feel onto him.

'Ma sister she found me,' he announced so confidently that Zoe's jaw dropped open. 'We go boat.'

'Hari,' said Zoe, shaking. 'Oh my God. Hari. You're talking.'

But it was more than that. As he beamed up, all fear forgotten and nothing but pride on his face, Zoe clocked something she would only realise later: Hari had the most Scottish accent you could possibly imagine.

'I's going on boat,' said Hari. 'Bit cauld.'

Zoe shook her head.

'Oh my God. Oh my God.'

Suddenly the lights of the police boat illuminated the tiny, implausibly narrow spit they had landed on. The helicopter, as soon as it heard, sheared off to land on the nearest part of the coast to take them to the hospital, its clattering a welcome sound.

Zoe burrowed her face in Hari's little shoulder. Something else plucked her coat and she twitched round.

Mary was standing there.

'I'm sorry,' she was saying over and over again. 'I'm sorry. I'm

350

sorry. He went and found the boat, and I was trying to stop him. I promise, I was trying to stop him!'

'I go on yon boat wi' ma sister,' said Hari proudly.

'It was his idea,' said Mary. 'It was! He'd pushed it off! I was trying to stop him!'

'Jesus,' said Zoe. 'But you let him! You let him!'

Mary shook her head.

'I was getting him!'

'Oh God,' said Ramsay, and Mary stared up at him, terror in her eyes.

'You hate me,' she said.

'Oh Christ, Mary,' said Ramsay, opening his arms. 'I love you. I love you to distraction. I just don't know whether that can possibly be enough.'

'I loves ma sister,' said Hari charitably, and Zoe blinked again in utter astonishment as the welcome, comforting tones of the police boat ordered them to stay where they were, even as the waters of the loch were rising again, tapping round their ankles. Had it taken much longer ... had they slept in even another twenty minutes ...

But that was not something Zoe could think about for the rest of her life.

The police made them pull off their wet clothes and wrap themselves in silver blankets and sleeping bags. Ramsay, Zoe couldn't help noticing, was utterly covered in bruises and cuts. He had been very, very quiet, holding Mary and saying nothing.

Hari, by contrast, suddenly couldn't stop talking. He loved the police boat beyond everything and wanted to have a look, which the nice police lady was very happy to let him do. Eventually Zoe grabbed him as the boat took them in to the little Beeches shore. All the other boats had rendezvoused there, Murdo at the head, and Zoe threw her arms around him as soon as she saw him and burst into tears, and he patted her on the shoulder and held her up when she couldn't stand.

They were all despatched to hospital – the helicopter was there, after all – but in fact, only Ramsay needed a couple of stitches in his feet. Regardless they spent the day getting tested and doing interviews and being fussed over and, finally, the hospital insisted on keeping them in overnight. Zoe found the room Hari was in, cosy and warm, and climbed into his bed. He lay there, breathing happily.

'Oh my God,' she said, covering her face. 'I am going to have to call Jaz. Shit. I don't know what to say. He might not even have left yet.'

'I loves mah daddy,' said Hari sleepily.

Zoe was terrified of making too much of Hari speaking in case it was an accident, a one-off, something that would vanish again if she spoke about it. She held him. It was … it was something else. He sounded utterly and totally born and bred in the Highlands.

'What happened, darling?' she said. 'What happened this morning?'

'Mary wanted to play,' he said. 'She's ma sister.'

'I know,' lied Zoe. One difficult thing at a time.

'And I go in the boat.' He pronounced it *bo-at*.

'Uh-huh.'

'I loves bo-at.'

She buried her face in his neck, unable to get all her limbs around him; if she could, she'd have gone back to being pregnant, absorbed him right back into her body where she could keep an eye on him.

She felt herself falling asleep, drifting off in the warm room in the hospital, nothing to hear in the room but a faint electrical hum, the scent of her child in her nostrils.

'Monster took us,' said Hari, yawning.

Zoe blinked.

'What?'

'Monster did pushing,' said Hari. 'Well, good night.'

And he reached out his little hand and managed to turn out the bedside light as Zoe lay in the darkness, suddenly wide awake.

Chapter Eight

Zoe had missed Jaz the previous day and so called him first thing in the morning. It is amazing quite how good a gloss you can put on things when you've had a decent night's sleep. It also helped that down in London – where Jaz had already returned – the weather was climate-change nuts and it was still sunny and twenty-two degrees every day, and so it was hard for Jaz to imagine quite how bad it could have been. He wasn't best pleased to find he had to come back up to Scotland, but was cheerful that she knew now that she had to be in London.

Zoe sighed. She couldn't in any conscience stay in a home where things like this could happen; it was definitely something of a deal-breaker. Although she didn't tell Jaz anything about that.

She looked up from the call to see a vast shadow in the doorway of the little room. It was Ramsay, and Zoe wondered how to delicately announce that possibly, due to attempted homicide, would he mind paying her up till the end of the month.

It also occurred to her that Nina was still in hospital and she'd have to see her too to explain. She hated to leave the van in the lurch, but she didn't really have a choice.

Hari was still out for the count. Ramsay had a nurse beside him.

'She can watch him,' he said. 'Could you ... could you come with me?'

Zoe looked up at him. His face looked haunted and exhausted.

They left the paediatric building. Outside it was, astonishingly, a lovely, calm day. Bloody Scotland, Zoe found herself thinking. It could not make up its mind day to day.

Ramsay didn't say anything, just kept hobbling. Zoe glanced at him. She was expecting an apology, which she was also planning on accepting, but would tell him that obviously it was impossible for them to stay and that if anything would make a difference, he had to – *had* to – get Mary the help she needed. She had tried. It hadn't worked. It could all have been so very, very different. From various garbled accounts, they'd put together that Mary had pretended to be playing hide and seek with Hari, intending to lose him in the woods and give him a fright – malicious, but not dangerous. Hari had instead grabbed the boat, and Mary had done her best to save him. Of course he wouldn't have been out at dawn at all if it wasn't for her.

Ramsay's flushed face and hangdog expression seemed to have anticipated this and they trudged round a grassy perimeter, littered with leaves, round the low pink-brick hospital buildings.

At the very back of the hospital, out by the bins, nowhere most people would come or see, was another low building with its own separate parking. Out in front was a surprisingly beautiful garden made, Zoe read, by the local community. It had gravel pathways and knot hedges and benches situated just where they were best placed to catch any rays of sun that might appear. Here and there were people in wheelchairs, talking to their relatives.

Ramsay, still silent, led Zoe to one of the empty benches and asked her to sit down. Then he went to the main door and buzzed on the bell.

It was, Zoe realised, a security bell. He entered and she watched him through grilled glass, talking to hospital staff who obviously knew him well. After a time, something happened and another figure appeared, and the main door was buzzed open once again.

Zoe could barely make the figure out as the bright sunlight was pouring into the low garden. It looked incredibly old; bent over, with wispy hair. But as Ramsay led her over, Zoe realised with a shock that it was a woman, not much older than herself. She had missing teeth and a gaunt haggard appearance and she was extraordinarily thin.

Zoe stared for a long time. Then she glanced at Ramsay to confirm what she thought was happening was happening. He simply nodded.

Zoe stepped forwards.

'Hello,' said Zoe. The woman didn't answer. There was nothing in her eyes to suggest that she'd seen Zoe or was even looking at her on the same plane at all. Her hands were shaking.

'Sit down, love,' said Ramsay, and when the figure didn't respond, he gently touched her shoulder and lowered her into the seat, where she stared straight ahead, not looking at either of them, one hand stroking the other.

'This is Elspeth,' said Ramsay, his low voice a rumble. 'The children's mother.'

Chapter Nine

'Hello, Elspeth,' said Zoe, gently taking the woman's stroking fingers, which then started stroking Zoe's own hands. They were thin and papery, as if she were a hundred years old. 'Your wife?' she said, looking at Ramsay.

He nodded.

'Common law. You couldn't tie down Elspeth. "You might be lord of half the world, you'll not have me as well",' he quoted wryly. 'That sounds like you, doesn't it?' he said to Elspeth.

Zoe stared at her.

'What happened?'

He sighed.

'All of it?'

Zoe shrugged.

He leaned over, tucking Elspeth's cardigan over her shoulders. She ignored him as if he weren't there.

'Sorry for talking about you,' he said to her. 'I ... I promised I would never talk about you. But something happened. Something happened.'

He blinked, his voice wobbling.

'When I met her ...'

'In the village they say she was very beautiful,' said Zoe.

'She was. Don't tell me – they also say she was fey.'

'They do,' said Zoe. 'I don't know what it means.'

'I do,' said Ramsay. 'I think they're right too. She came from a faerie hill and got stuck ...'

'But ...'

Ramsay rubbed the back of his neck.

'She was very young ... maybe too young for children. Shackleton was a difficult birth ... She was never quite ... She had post-natal depression, for sure. Maybe worse than that. She wouldn't see a doctor, get help. I was going out of my wits.'

He grimaced.

'My family weren't pleased I was with her ... which is putting it mildly ... and I was trying to get on with everything ... I was away.'

His voice lowered.

'I was away. Too much. She'd wander. At night. Into town. Leave Shackleton with Mrs MacGlone, and just ... vanish. For longer and longer periods.'

'Where was she going?'

Ramsay shrugged.

'Anywhere with drugs, as it turned out. Anywhere else. And I came home, but it didn't help. Didn't make her any happier, any more settled.'

An incredibly kind nurse came out with two cups of coffee; Zoe clutched hers. Even with the warming sun, she still hadn't got over her chilling dousing the day before.

'She was just wild,' said Ramsay. 'Couldn't be tied down. It was like I was trying to domesticate her, trying to cage her. But I wasn't. I just loved her.'

Elspeth's fingers were still stroking Zoe's hand.

'Every time I came downstairs ... the front door would be wide open, and she'd be gone.'

'Is that why you like it shut?'

Ramsay shrugged.

'How did you manage to stay together to have three kids?' said Zoe.

Ramsay stood up then, stared out of the boundaries of the hospital, through the garden, out past the walls and the houses and straight to the mountains beyond, where the sun was glinting off the wing of something circling, only barely visible to the naked eye, so very far away. He let out a great sigh as if letting down something very, very heavy.

'Nobody ...' he began, then clenched his fists. 'Oh. What the hell,' he said to himself. 'Only Shackleton's mine,' he said quietly.

Zoe blinked. 'What? What do you mean?'

'We were together – just about – long enough to have a baby. Then she'd vanish. She hated me by then. She'd go who knows where? Ireland once, I think. Then she'd come back. One time, pregnant.'

'With Mary?'

'What could I do?' said Ramsay. 'She'd broken my heart and needed help and I was the one person in the world she wouldn't accept it from. I thought ... I thought she might come home if we settled down, if we raised Mary and Shackleton together. But she was worse by then. Getting worse all the time.'

'So she left you with Mary? What about Patrick?'

Ramsay sunk his head. 'I can't ... I can't explain how bad it got. Patrick, she barely came home at all. Left him on the steps like a foundling.'

'You're kidding.'

He shook his head.

'I wish.'

'But in the village ...'

'Oh, they say a lot of things. She'd turn up from time to time. I made out she was working ... Ha.'

He touched Elspeth.

'Oh, my darling. Imagine you ever having a boss.' He paused. 'We just ... kept ourselves to ourselves.'

'And what about social services?'

Ramsay gave her a look.

'Why don't you think they're round every second? They know

358

all about it. She had no family we know of . . . If I was happy to take them, they were happy to sign off on the paperwork.' He winced. 'I think that house still means a lot.'

Zoe blinked. She couldn't bear the thought of Patrick being left . . . or Mary.

'She did try. She'd clean up for a few days, a few months, come back. She used to sew for the children, make the most beautiful things. Then something would happen . . . something would trigger her and . . . '

Zoe suddenly realised something.

'Mary's scar?'

Ramsay nodded.

'Two years ago. And after that . . . she couldn't see them any more. She couldn't. It was bad for them anyway, her bouncing in and out. And then she hurt Mary so badly. And I have never known a child who so needed a mother . . . '

Zoe swallowed hard, thinking of all the unpleasant thoughts she'd had about the difficult girl.

'The police got involved . . . I had to take out a restraining order and, well, that did it. God it was so, so horrible.'

'What happened?'

'She found some drugs. Took them. She'd been clean for a long time, didn't know . . . didn't know her own limits. Overdosed. stopped breathing for nine minutes. Heavy brain damage. It's a commoner problem than . . . well. So they say. It doesn't feel common to us.'

He patted Elspeth on the arm.

'She . . . she might regain some function some time. Well. They thought that. A while ago. I come here a lot. We don't know what she knows.'

'This is where you are when you go away all the time?'

He nodded.

'I keep thinking she might get a little better.'

'And when you're working?'

He laughed ruefully.

359

'This place costs a fortune.'

Zoe nodded. The cash in the biscuit tin; the lack of anything in the house. Well.

'I was trying to hold it all together.'

Zoe leaned forwards.

'Nobody can hold it together on their own. Nobody.'

He turned round and looked back at the main hospital.

'But I see it now. I've tried to deny it for so long. Mary needs help. This kind of help. Psychiatric help. Christ, she's so like her. Up until now I thought it was maybe because we had trouble keeping people to look after her – Mrs MacGlone hated Elspeth, absolutely hated her, and found it hard to get close to the children. She didn't think we should take in Patrick at all.'

'Not take *Patrick*?' said Zoe in disbelief. 'Who wouldn't want Patrick?'

Ramsay shrugged. 'And I thought, well, it's because we can't get a good nanny so that's obviously why ... I just couldn't bear to see her mother in her.'

His voice drifted off.

'And then we got you. And I realised the nannies weren't the problem.'

Zoe bit her lip.

'Oh, I don't think ...'

Ramsay looked at her, his eyes so weary.

'You did,' he said. 'You've changed everything. You don't realise what you've done. You've turned it into a home. For ... for all of us.'

Zoe shook her head.

'But you don't realise –' And as she started to say it, she understood for the first time that it was true. '– this is ... the first real home Hari and I have ever had. *You* made a home for *us*.'

And the awfulness of that and what it meant and the fact that it wouldn't change a thing, that they would still have to leave, regardless, made tears sting Zoe's eyes.

Chapter Ten

They wandered back wearily. Ramsay had gently patted Elspeth on the hand, but she'd shown absolutely no sign of noticing. Zoe stared at her; she couldn't help it. What strange mercurial creature had she been, bewitching Ramsay so? If you looked closely enough – and it was very odd being able to stare so intently at another human being without their reacting or caring – you could see in the bones stretched under the skin that there must once have been a beautiful girl in there somewhere, who had bewitched the young Ramsay, still reeling from the loss of his father. She could see Mary's high cheekbones, her firm chin. She couldn't see anything of Patrick at all. That child really had come out of a fairy hill, she found herself thinking, then she banished the thought immediately.

They walked quietly, sadly, back to the ward.

Hari wasn't in his room. Zoe was about to swear vociferously before Ramsay grabbed her and showed her into the next room. The sheets were off the bed and had been made into a tent that covered the whole room. Underneath could be heard giggling. Ramsay pulled it up. Hari and Mary were laughing their heads off, playing with Hari's tablet.

'HULLO, YOUSE THERE,' shouted Hari cheerfully.

Ramsay took Mary off – she was scheduled to have a meeting with the CAMHs nurse with a view to what would be the best next steps. Before she left, she apologised once again to Zoe so wholeheartedly and desperately that Zoe had managed to nod. She knew it was churlish but it was hard to go further, not when things could have so easily – *so* easily – have been all over the Sunday papers.

She swallowed hard, thought of the poor mite's mother, whom she could never see again, took a deep breath and patted her on the shoulder.

'Okay,' she said, inexpressibly weary. 'I think the doctor is really going to help you, sweetheart. We just want you to feel better. That's all.'

Mary nodded gravely and let her father lead her out by the hand. Zoe turned the television on for Hari. They found an old repeat of *Balamory*, and Hari happily recited the lines one after another while Zoe stared at him, wanting to gobble it up with her ears, unable to believe it was true, until she finally found a minute to lock herself in the bathroom and empty out her tears.

Chapter Eleven

The nice paediatrician didn't really know how to help her, except to encourage her to be pleased. 'Well, it *is* an anxiety disorder,' she'd said, and Zoe had grimaced and said she'd known that.

'And you know Einstein . . .'

'I don't think he's Einstein,' said Zoe gently but firmly.

'Has something happened to him to relieve his anxiety?'

Zoe would have thought rather the opposite, even as she heard him giggling next door at a cartoon.

Could Hari ever tell her? Ever explain the strange quiet world he had trapped himself in, the walls closing in around him every day, until something had breached them – the shock, perhaps? The bracing chill of knowing how close you came to losing everything, and how important it was to use everything you had? Hari, when questioned, simply and cheerfully said that it was the monster, and Zoe assumed he was talking in metaphor or had got confused in the wet and the noise when you couldn't see two feet in front your face.

'Are you pleased?' said the doctor, as Zoe started to cry again, but she nodded a lot through her tears.

The drive home was slow and would have been quiet were it not for Hari, who said, 'Tree!' 'Stones!' 'Birdie!' every time he spotted something, wonderingly, and Zoe had to fight back tears every single time. She had decided not to tell Jaz; to surprise him.

She hadn't told Hari they were leaving. She didn't know how. As he got out of the car, he dashed towards Patrick, shouting 'PATRICK! I KEN TALKING!' And Patrick jumped up and down and then stopped, a frown on his little serious face, and said, 'Yes, Hari, but absolutely you must let me talk the most,' and Ramsay turned to Zoe, his face aching and said, 'Is there no way you could . . . ?' and she felt herself choking up again.

The CAHMs nurse said Mary was going to start with sessions with a psychiatrist straightaway but if things didn't improve, they may have to consider medication. Ramsay had told this to Zoe as if this might work in his favour, might mitigate things. And in other circumstances, it might have done. But there was no way – absolutely no way when Jaz found out just what exactly had happened – that she could stay here with his boy.

Zoe had avoided seeing Nina at the hospital, which made her feel horribly guilty, but she was about to have to do something awful and leave her in the lurch and she already had too much to worry about.

But here, back home – back at The Beeches, rather, of course – it was a perfect autumn day; all the colours brightened up the sombre look of the house, the oranges and yellows and bright reds of the leaves covering the lawns, the wind picking them up and whirling them around. Wilby had started raking them up, and Patrick and Hari had wasted very little time in running into the pile of leaves and bouncing full length in to it. Eventually Shackleton had come out to see what they were doing and decided to join in, totally under-estimating his own size and girth, and had completely demolished the pile, so Zoe had sent them to find rakes (there were a jumble in the ancient hut) and help Wilby clear the leaves up properly which resulted in a perpetual motion of leaves being swept up and jumped into.

It was unseemingly mild and was warm enough, just about, if

you were wearing a cardigan, to sit outside, and Mary was doing just that in her new fox jumper. She was nervous around Zoe, who had decided that whatever happened now, she had to get over it. She was the adult; Mary was the child, and an unwell and markedly unlucky child at that. So she went straight up to her and sat down.

'Whatcha reading?'

Mary held up *The Magician's Nephew*.

'Splendid!' said Zoe. 'Oh, you lucky thing. I wish I was reading it for the first time.'

'Nobody,' said Mary thoughtfully. 'None of the books you give me have mothers.'

Zoe blinked and thought about it. Narnia, Katy, Alice, Anne with an E. Mary Lennox. Mary was right. None of them did.

'I think that's just what makes stories,' she said. 'If a child is to go off and have adventures, that's how it's done.'

'I think I've had enough adventures,' said Mary.

'I do too,' said Zoe, and they sat near each other watching the boys charging about like happy deer in a bright red field.

Ramsay stood by the car watching them all and realised the horrible truth with a lurch: he wanted her to stay. So much. Not for the children – although yes, for that. For her. For everything about her: the way her hair fell across her face; her pealing laugh; the music she played in the kitchen; her fierce love for her son; her way of getting on with things, which had, he knew, been his terrible failing as he had been drifting along, hoping on some level that Elspeth would come back, or things would change.

He had, he realised, been waiting to be saved like a princess in a fairy tale. And she was the handsome prince.

And how he wanted her. But now it was too late, for even as he thought this, a familiar small red hire car was rattling up the drive.

Chapter Twelve

Surprisingly, three people got out of the little rental car: Jaz; a very pretty girl Zoe realised must be Shanti, and one more.

Surinder walked towards Zoe and the girls hugged.

'I don't know what to say,' said Surinder. 'I . . . I really hoped this would be a good thing.'

'It was,' said Zoe, swallowing hard.

Hari came rushing up, his hair everywhere, panting and out of breath.

'Hiya, Auntie!' he said casually.

'What?' said Jaz. Zoe couldn't help grinning as she saw his face. 'WHAT?'

'Och! Hiya, Daddy!' said Hari turning around.

'WHAT?!'

Jaz was so surprised he looked like a cartoon.

'You're talking!'

'Aye,' said Hari.

Jaz stared at Hari then back at Zoe and then at Hari again. Surinder burst out laughing.

'I absolutely taught him,' said Patrick.

'He's my brother,' said Hari.

'Yes, we met ... Hi, bro,' said Jaz rather awkwardly.

Patrick looked at him severely.

'Thank you for coming to visit. But Hari and I have very important things to do with leaves. BYE!'

He turned round and went back to the garden, Hari in his wake. Jaz stood, dumbfounded.

'Why don't I make us all some tea?' said Zoe. She came down and shook Shanti's hand. She was, as Jaz had said, extremely beautiful.

'Hello. Sorry. I'm Zoe. I realise it's a lot to take in.'

Shanti was staring up at the house, absolutely hypnotised.

'Wow, what a place!'

Surinder was taking pictures of the boys darting about in the low sun.

Shanti followed Zoe into the house. The polished wood smell of beeswax hung in the air; Mrs MacGlone had obviously been busy. The sun streamed through the windows onto the grain.

'Oh my God,' she said. She peeked into the drawing room, which had the sun shining in and was currently filled with a huge construction of an aeroplane that Shackleton and Patrick were working on. Pieces of balsa wood and old cut-up sheets were laid on the large table.

'Look at this place,' she said. The children's voices could be heard on the air, laughing and chattering.

She followed Zoe through into the kitchen, and Zoe put on the kettle.

'Or we've got coffee,' said Zoe, remembering that night. When all she had wanted was to feel his hand on her ... she shook the memory away.

'Nice machine,' said Shanti. 'Cor. I don't know what I was expecting, but it wasn't this.'

She turned to Zoe.

'I'm ... I'm really ... I hope it didn't seem weird that Jaz started going out with me.'

Zoe was about to bat it away and say no, not at all, but she decided she might as well be honest.

'Well,' she said. 'You're the first woman I've known about since . . . me, but we've been broken up for a long time, really.'

'But you're the mum of his . . .'

'Yes, all of that.'

'He looks like an amazing boy.'

'I don't know about amazing,' said Zoe, then she reflected. 'Well. Yes. He is.'

Shanti nodded.

'Thank you,' said Zoe, 'for making Jaz step up to his responsibilities.'

Shanti rolled her eyes. 'I grew up without a dad,' she said. 'I threatened to kill him if he didn't get his shit together.'

'Well . . . thanks . . . So did I. I should have threatened him with that.'

Shanti grimaced.

'I wouldn't thank us just yet. He's been to look at some flats . . .'

Zoe let that hang there in the air and busied herself with finding enough mugs and whether or not there was any shortbread to be had, which fortunately there was.

Chapter Thirteen

Ramsay looked like he was about to disappear into his library – he couldn't bear to sit and listen to this man discuss how to take Zoe away, stick her in some awful hole in London somewhere, how he'd never see her again.

But Zoe gave him a look that said, more or less, 'Manners!' and he came and joined them on the wrought iron chairs she'd made Shackleton drag out and wipe down – when, Ramsay thought, had she even found the time to find out about those? And when did his grunting, incommunicative pre-teenager turn into such a smart, willing boy?

Once they'd all settled down, no one was quite sure how to start, until Jaz, sitting with his legs splayed out, one foot on the other knee, which Zoe knew he did when he was nervous and trying not to look it, asked how on earth Hari was talking – and what on earth did he sound like?

Ramsay shot Zoe a look but she didn't return it. Instead she blinked and said, 'Well. Mary and Hari got themselves into a bit of a scrape on the loch. Where they are absolutely forbidden to go.'

Shanti turned her head.

'Where is it?'

'Just at the bottom of the garden,' said Zoe.

'Oh my God ... you really have everything here,' she said, eyes wide.

'Anyway. Hari got a fright and ... the doctor says something seems to have broken through.'

Jaz shook his head.

'I thought I was coming up here to look after my traumatised little boy. Instead he's listening to Proclaimers records and eating haggis pies.'

Nobody said anything after that.

Jaz kicked at the ground. Then he stood up.

'I'm going to get him. He can show me the lake.'

'Loch,' said Zoe automatically.

'Christ's sake, Zo, not you as well.'

He walked away, his attitude sullen, and Shanti winced. Surinder watched the entire thing shaking her head.

'Oh God,' she said. 'You're worse than Nina. Speaking of whom ... '

She glanced at her watch. 'I'll need to go if I'm going to make visiting hours.'

Zoe jumped up too.

'Hang on, I've got some books in the van for her.'

Surinder walked up to it happily.

'Oh look, there she is,' she said, patting it happily. 'Oh, we had some good times in this old thing.'

She grinned. 'Now there are a few people I need to look up while I'm here ... Boys mostly.'

'How long are you staying?'

'It depends when Nina pops,' said Surinder. 'They owed me some time off. And Lennox will be busy with his hands up sheep's arses or something.'

'I don't think it's their arse,' said Zoe.

'Oh thanks, James Herriot ... '

Surinder climbed up the steps of the book van and turned the handle.

'Oooh,' she said in surprise. 'You've changed it!'

'Um ... I don't think so ...'

'What are all these Loch Ness monster books? And stuffed toys?'

'People seem to like them,' muttered Zoe.

'Cor. Colouring books! And these touristy things – does Nina know you're selling all these?' Surinder narrowed her eyes. 'I mean, it's just not what she normally does, that's all.'

Zoe winced. 'You mean I've gone downmarket.'

'Noooo ...'

'Look,' said Zoe. 'I couldn't sell enough of the other stuff. I'm not Nina – she's a bookselling genius. But there's a huge market here – absolutely massive, full of people interested in the history of Scotland and the area – so we've been selling loads of atlases, and they're beautiful. And the monster books are just something for the kids to colour in when they're on a long bus tour, that's all.'

Surinder blinked. 'Hmm. Maybe you're right. Nina isn't much use with the figures.'

She picked up one or two of the beautiful big map books, which had large price tags.

'Wow! You're selling these?'

'Yeah ... from Ramsay's collection. Stuff that doesn't get a lot of traction in London.'

Surinder nodded.

'I feel like I'm being inspected,' said Zoe awkwardly.

'Ha,' said Surinder. 'So do I.'

Zoe smiled.

'Jaz seems a lot ... calmer.'

Surinder nodded. 'Shanti is good for him. Definitely. Although you know Jaz – always has lots of good intentions. May not necessarily stick with them in the long run.'

The girls popped their heads out of the van. Shanti had gone over to join Jaz and Hari by the lochside.

'Looks like she's quite taken with this place,' said Surinder. She sighed and looked around. 'Me too. I forget in Brum that there are places like this. It's just ... it's just so free up here ...'

As if to back her up, a flock of wild geese passed low on their journey south, flicking their white wings into the slowly setting sun, the deep autumnal light.

'Yeah, yeah, all right,' said Surinder. She narrowed her eyes.

'I wonder if Lennox has still got those tenants in ... Right. Better go and see Nina.'

'Don't tell her about the colouring books,' said Zoe quickly.

'Yeah, okay.'

Surinder regarded her.

'Coming back home then?'

'Mmm,' said Zoe.

Chapter Fourteen

Some decisions happen for you. Some creep up. But some you can pinpoint.

That evening, as the sun went down, Ramsay marched down to the cellar where he rarely touched the dusty old bottles his father had stocked there and grabbed two with the oldest-looking names. Then he came upstairs and, finally getting the transfixed boys to stand well back, lit the pile of old wood and bracken they'd all gathered from the forest along with some of the leaves from the garden. Zoe wrapped potatoes in silver foil and popped them in at the base, and brought out long forks for the adults to cook the sausages, the fat popping in the heat. Jaz found some music on his phone and they kept warm, the children running around laughing, the old wine slipping down from mugs and tin cups gathered from the kitchen. Surinder returned from the hospital saying Nina had reread the entire Val McDermid back catalogue and now thought everyone was a potential murderer but was otherwise perfectly well, and Jaz and Ramsay had to sit near each other as the boys wanted each to sit on their knees – Hari just loved having his dad there to show off – and Zoe watched as Ramsay caressed Patrick's head, answered his obscure questions about fireflies and satellites, and the huge clear weight of his love for the boy, who was someone else's boy, came crashing in.

It was in stark contrast with Jaz's carelessly leaving his own boy behind. If it hadn't been for her, she realised, and Surinder and Shanti, Hari could be fatherless right now. Jaz caught her eye and as if he knew what she was thinking, winced slightly.

But otherwise it was, given the awkwardness of it, an exceptionally pleasant evening, and when they set off, Shanti driving, for the hotel, everyone stood at the end of the long gravel drive and waved them all the way down.

'I like it when Daddy comes to visit,' said Hari thoughtfully. 'It's braw.'

Zoe smiled and took his and Patrick's hands to take them upstairs.

'Wait,' said Hari. And he scampered over to where Ramsay was stretching his too long legs out towards the fire, clambered up his leg and gave the very surprised man a hug.

'Night!'

Zoe and Ramsay looked at each other in amazement and Zoe led him off to bed – with her, nowhere near Mary, and no more staying over with Patrick – pondering the situation.

Was she making things worse for Hari by letting him getting so attached to everyone here? On the other hand, what did she want – him to be miserable?

She was still deep in thought as she went to pick up the glasses and forks from outside. Ramsay hadn't moved and was still staring into the fire, the glass in his hand, his big navy fisherman's jumper on the side, still with leaves caught in it.

'Here,' she said, plucking one and handing it to him. 'You can keep it as a memory of a happy day.'

He turned to her then and his face was so full of longing she couldn't bear it, and he gently encircled her tiny wrist with his huge hand.

'Please,' he said. 'Please. Stay.'

Chapter Fifteen

The book bus was incredibly busy by the loch the next day. The whole site was bobbing with half-term families spotting seals and eating soup, and Agnieszka was delighted. Murdo came in and Zoe hailed him.

'We have – Ramsay and I – I mean – not us – not together, ha! Nothing like that!'

She blushed deeply remembering the night before when she had stuttered and made her excuses and run to bed, deeply confused, deeply frightened, and lain awake all night imagining, just imagining what it would be like if he had picked her up in those huge strong arms of his, if he had grabbed her, hauled her into the house ... or worse, the woods ... and what it would do to the household, and how impossible it was.

'Anyway ... I'm babbling. I just wanted to say. We owe you everything. Ramsay wanted to give you ... I realise it's not much ...'

She hauled out the great crate of ancient whisky the cellar had revealed.

'Oh my,' said Murdo. 'Oh goodness. I wasn't ... I mean anyone would have done it. Anyone *did* do it – it was like Dunkirk out there.' He smiled. 'Och, look at this. It's too much.'

'It's nothing like enough,' said Zoe in a serious voice.

'And,' said Murdo, 'it wasn't me anyway. Something pushed me across that loch . . .'

'Stop it,' said Zoe. 'You've worked here looking for the monster for too long. It's addled your brain.'

'Aye, mebbe,' said Murdo. 'Mebbe not.'

Together they took the whisky to the boat.

'Well now,' said Murdo. 'That is a nice thing. Are the two little ones all right?'

'They are fine,' said Zoe, not wanting to go down that road any further than she had to.

Kirsty came to join her over lunch with Agnieszka's excellent cock-a-leekie soup and some rough-hewn bread and Zoe told her the whole story, or some of it, rather. Kirsty whistled through her teeth.

'What's the diagnosis?'

Actually Ramsay had . . . before he had . . . Well. They'd discussed it. The doctors were adamant that medication was required. A very low dose, just to steady her mood. Ramsay had been fiercely against any kind of drug. 'A nine-year-old on medication?' They'd both been outraged, and then even more surprised when the doctor had told them precisely how many nine-year-olds in Scotland were on medication. It was a lot. Then Zoe had simply asked, would other children be safe under the same roof as Mary if she was taking it and they had assured her that they would, and that was enough for Zoe. It wouldn't be for ever. Just a calmer Mary. So they could get through to her; so they could help her. Zoe asked Kirsty about this; she agreed.

'It'll be okay,' Kirsty said. 'There's absolutely loads of kids on it. Honestly. It changes lives.'

'She nearly changed ours,' said Zoe glumly. 'I have to keep telling myself it's not her fault.'

'I genuinely think,' said Kirsty, 'you're going to find the meds really help. And it means she'll probably adapt a bit better to school.'

'Yes. A lot less biting,' said Zoe, smiling sadly. Then she said, 'I was wondering . . . I was thinking . . . we need to thank the village for what they did. And the kids . . . they didn't get a proper dress-up Halloween. They feel too unpopular and weird to go out.'

'That's a shame,' said Kirsty, meaning it.

'And I thought the Samhain party would make up for it but . . . ' Zoe blushed at the memory.

'It turned out not to be remotely suitable. Well, anyway, I was thinking . . . I know it's past but if we had a Halloween party, could we ask everyone? Then the kids could . . . kind of get back on board with everything? Or would that be mad?'

'Everyone? That's sixty children!'

'I know.'

'But,' said Kirsty, 'I can't imagine any child hating having two Halloweens, no.'

'Great,' said Zoe. 'Spread the word.'

Chapter Sixteen

It took her a lot of looking. She did it at night. Ramsay was away, and Zoe knew why. But at least she knew where he was.

She needed to find something. In the library. Something that would let them put on a party; something that could get the children ready. For school; for the normal life waiting out there for them.

She discarded books not in the almanac such as ancient encyclopaedias that didn't know what atoms were made of and beautiful golden treasuries of the lives of the saints that only the most hideous sadist could ever have bought for a child. She needed something good. Something she could sell right away.

Up on the mezzanine level, beneath a pile of church hymnals, she finally found the kind of thing she was looking for. And whistled.

The pale grey cover of the rooftops of London; the two little boys scampering down the side of St Paul's Cathedral. She checked the date on the inside cover. It was a second edition, not the first, but still worth an absolute fortune: an early edition of *Up on the Rooftops*.

She let the children see it, rather reluctantly, and explained that they were selling it.

'But that's the book we're reading! And we haven't finished it!'

groaned Patrick. 'We don't even know if Delphine is on the Queen of the Nethers' galleon! The Corsairs took her!'

'I have it,' said Zoe. 'I have it on my Kindle. Don't worry. You can have lots of copies of one book.'

'But! I do worry!' said Patrick, blinking.

'I know,' said Zoe. 'But trust me. It's going to be worth it. We're going to have a Halloween party!'

The boys gasped.

'Are ... can girls come?' said Shackleton.

'Everyone can come,' said Zoe.

Mary looked at her. The meds made her sleepy, slow to respond to things.

'What kind of party? Like the Samhain?'

'No,' said Zoe emphatically. That had got right out of hand, that one. 'A children's party. I thought we could do up the house nicely and get lots of spooky things and do bobbing for apples and so on.'

'And have absolutely lots of sweets?' said Patrick.

'And absolutely ginger,' added Hari.

'Ginger what?' said Zoe.

'He means fizzy drinks,' explained Patrick.

'Oh. Okay,' said Zoe. 'Well. Yes. All of that. I thought we'd invite people you were going to go to school with.'

'OOH!' said Patrick.

'They're horrible,' said Mary. Shackleton was watching now too from the fire.

'Well,' said Zoe confidingly. 'I thought what we'd do is get you the most amazing costume and invite everyone and make the house look absolutely brilliant and have the best party ever and then everyone would realise you were super-cool and the girl who you bit ...'

'Stephanie,' snarled Mary. 'She said my mum was crazy.'

Zoe had been about to suggest conciliation. But now she decided to go the other way.

'Stephanie. Well, we could snub her.'

'What do you mean?' said Mary, looking interested.

'Well, obviously *normally* we try to be nice to everyone.'

'Mary doesn't,' said Patrick. Mary was about to scowl, but let it pass as if it didn't matter to her. This was lost on no one.

'... but in *this* case I think we could be super-nice to everyone else, and then when she comes ...'

'She might not come,' said Mary.

'Everyone will want to come,' said Zoe. 'Trust me. So you are really pleased to see everyone, but then when she comes you can just be like, "Oh hey." And *I* could be like, "Oh, *you're* Stephanie," but in, like, a really mean way.' She did it again. '"Oh, so *you're* Stephanie." I mean, I know that is very nasty and horrible ...'

'She told me my mum was a loony.'

'Exactly. Extenuating circumstances.'

'And I could bite her!' said Patrick.

'No,' said Zoe. 'This is my point. We don't bite anyone any more.'

'Stenuating circumstances,' said Patrick.

'Still, no.'

'What costume could I have?' asked Mary shyly.

'Whatever you like! Zombie princess? Terrifying witch?'

'And we're going to get money from a *book*?' said Shackleton.

They gathered round as she took photographs and listed it on eBay. The bids came in thick and fast and it was extremely exciting to watch. By the time it was bedtime, there was enough for a very jolly party. By the time Ramsay got home, there was enough for ...

'Well, goodness,' said Ramsay, staring at the screen. 'Goodness me.'

'Thank you,' said Zoe, who had texted him earlier and asked if she could list it. 'You're good to let us spend it.'

'Well, I wouldn't have known it was there if it wasn't for you.'

Zoe stood up, standing shyly away from him. He was grimly aware she was doing this and frowned.

'I'm ... I'm sorry about the other evening,' he muttered.

'No ... I am,' said Zoe before she could think about it. Then: 'Sorry. I mean. That's fine. Forget it.'

He nodded sadly.

'Well?' said Zoe gently. 'How was tonight?'

He took a deep breath and they moved away from the children. This was new, being able to talk about it.

'There's some ... Well. Good news, I suppose. Hard to know. I heard from the police. They let me lift the restraining order.'

He shook his head. 'She's ... she's no longer a threat apparently.'

'Good,' said Zoe. 'Is that good?'

'It means the children can ... '

He shook his head, staring at the four heads laughing around the computer.

'Oh,' he said. 'Oh. Those fucking drugs. The price she paid.' He tried to stop himself crying. 'I'm so sorry, I'm being ridiculous.'

'You are not,' snorted Zoe. 'You could all have done with a bit more of this a long time ago.'

She handed him some kitchen roll and he thanked her.

'Are you going to take them?' she said.

Ramsay sighed.

'Shackleton absolutely refuses. He ... he remembers. He saw her at her absolute worst, and she let him down again and again. And Patrick doesn't know her at all. He's never had a mummy.'

'Mary?'

'Yes. Yes. Perhaps I'll take Mary.'

He ran his hand through his hair.

'It'll be a big shock to her.'

Zoe thought of the placid woman with the long stare who had been quite happy to sit and stroke her hand.

'You never know,' said Zoe. 'It might be enough ... just to be near her.'

'Do you think?'

'No,' said Zoe. 'But I think in this life sometimes you have to take what you can get.'

Chapter Eighteen

teen

They had a hard day's work decorating the house, but there was no doubting it did look magnificent. Even – wonder of wonders – Mrs MacGlone got stuck in, and helped to adorn the house with cobwebs and pumpkins and scary plastic skulls with tiny flickering lights inside them, and some of Mary's old dollies, including several that were broken and quite horrifying. They put coloured paper over the lights and Mary was busy putting grapes into a bowl to act as eyeballs when Mrs MacGlone came in and looked around and folded her arms and then unfolded them and said, uncharacteristically pink in the cheeks:

'Well now. Well.'

Zoe smiled at her. 'Are you staying for the party?' she said. 'Have you got a costume?'

'Oh,' said Mrs MacGlone. Then she glanced away. 'I didn't think I was invited.'

Zoe went up to her.

'Of course you're invited!' she said. 'Mrs MacGlone you're ... you're the bones of this place. It couldn't run without you.'

Mrs MacGlone shook her head.

'Och, that's not true.'

'Well, come, please,' said Zoe. 'And bring your husband.'

Mrs MacGlone looked pleased as she took down her coat.

'Aye right then well. Maybe.'

Then a thought occurred to her.

'You know. We havnae done this for a long time. Probably trip all the fuses in the place. But Wilby keeps it up to date … costs a fortune in electricity of course …'

'What?' said Zoe as Mrs MacGlone went into the kitchen and pulled open a cupboard that contained the fuse box and the boiler. She ran her hand down to a switch.

'Well, here goes nothing,' she said, and pressed it.

At first, Zoe couldn't understand what the orange glow was coming through the windows. The children all leapt up, led by Shackleton, charged through the front hall and opened the front door, letting in a sharp blast of freezing air. Zoe followed them outside and gasped. The entire front of the house was illuminated, lit up to make it spectral and entrancingly beautiful.

'Oh wow,' she said.

'Good old Wilby,' said Mrs MacGlone happily.

Zoe had given up trying to keep the children calm, and had let them get dressed up and put on a Halloween compilation at high volume and, mindful of the time, had gone upstairs to get dressed.

Ramsay was standing at the library door.

'Just locking up?' said Zoe.

'Ah,' he said. 'Well. I suppose …'

He looked down at the keys in his hands.

'I could lock it tonight and then …'

'What are you thinking?'

'Well … the reason I keep the children out of there …'

'Is because they get into everything and would destroy your stock? Because it destroys your concentration? Because you have to get away from them?'

He looked up, surprised.

'Christ, no. Books are meant to be read. They *want* to be read. No. It's not ... It was never anything like that.'

He turned the key over in his hand.

'No. God. It's where I keep all my correspondence ... all the news and information about Elspeth and social services and ... you know. Everything. Everything they don't know.'

'So you're thinking of opening it? Letting the light in?'

He shrugged. Zoe bit her lip and lowered her voice.

'Do Mary and Patrick know ... know everything?'

He looked alarmed suddenly.

'But I am their dad.'

'I know. But ...'

He nodded.

'I know what you mean. I just always figured ... they have enough to bear already.'

Zoe sighed. It was wrong, but it was right too.

'What about Shackleton? Doesn't he know?'

Ramsay shook his head. 'Of course not. It would just ... it would feel so unfair.'

Zoe nodded. She understood.

'He's a good boy, you know,' said Ramsay, pondering.

'I do know!' said Zoe. 'I love all your children!'

It was meant, Zoe told herself later, it was meant to come out as light and breezy, like 'I love grapefruit!' or 'I love *Brooklyn Nine-Nine*!'

But that was not how it sounded. That wasn't how it sounded at all, and Ramsay stared at her, hunger in his eyes as if desperate to find someone – anyone – who felt for his children. And Zoe felt the terrible ties tighten once again – her dear wish to stay, and the fact that she couldn't. She couldn't.

'I'm going to go get changed,' she muttered. Then turned back.

'Maybe lock your filing cabinet,' she suggested.

He nodded.

'Yes. Yes, of course.'

Chapter Nineteen

By five p.m., the lights of the cars had started to come up the drive, and it was almost fully dark. Zoe put the grey tulle dress on. The fairy wings were ridiculous but somehow rather fetching. Mary popped her head round the door and Zoe did her hair in the mirror and added pale white face make-up and dramatic black mascara.

'I look *awesome*,' said Mary.

'You do,' said Zoe.

There was a clamour of noise from downstairs.

'Right,' said Zoe. 'You're going to have to go be a hostess.'

Mary looked nervous.

'Will you come with me?'

'I will.'

And for the first time, Mary took her hand and they walked downstairs together.

It was something to see how quickly Mary's fears were dispelled. Zoe grinned at Kirsty, who made a fabulous witch. She'd obviously done an excellent marketing campaign – everyone was there, the house a maelstrom of tiny gremlins, superheroes, one robot who kept falling down the stairs and some rather loud vampires as well as two dinosaurs.

'Wow, Mary, your house is *awesome*,' one green-painted sprite was saying.

'We miss you at school,' she heard another one say. 'It's boring. Everyone is really well behaved all the time.'

Zoe smiled and passed on through the throng. To her utter amazement, she saw a vision in a vast French ballgown, brocade at the neck, which stuck out either side, a vast grey wig and a massive beauty spot, with a red line painted across her throat. It took her a few seconds to realise it was Mrs MacGlone as Marie Antoinette, and that she was cheerfully organising the apple-dooking. She waved in a jolly way to Zoe, who headed over.

'This,' she said, waving about her cup of cider. 'This is how the house should be.'

Over in the other corner, children were trying to eat treacle bread off a line in some kind of race, manned by Agnieszka, who waved furiously. She was wearing a large witch's hat with a green wig on it and was standing next to a burly man in a full skeleton costume, including mask. They were holding hands. Zoe couldn't tell, but she had a reasonable supposition just who was under that mask, and why a certain boat seemed to have taken on a permanent mooring on a particular side of the loch these days.

The children all knew exactly what to do. It occurred to Zoe that Halloween was rather different up here. Outside, a small girl dressed as a lizard was loudly singing a Taylor Swift song as the older parents watched appreciatively.

'What's going on?'

'You have to do your party piece,' said Mrs MacGlone, 'before you get any sweeties. Didn't you know that?'

'I didn't,' said Zoe, conscious that the smaller of the two dinosaurs was standing next to her.

'I dinnae hae a party piece,' it said.

Zoe glanced down and picked him up.

'You *are* the party piece,' she said, 'and this is your party. So. I say you don't need one and you're perfect.'

'Or!' said the taller dinosaur. 'You could tell a hilarious joke.'

They conferred in loud whispers for a little while, then turned to face Zoe again, who tried to look attentive. Patrick nudged Hari.

'WHY,' announced Hari, then looked to Patrick again.

'Why did the dinosaur ... ?'

'Why did the dinosaur ... ?'

'Why did the dinosaur say "moo"?'

'Why did the dinosaur say "moo"?'

'I don't know,' said Zoe. 'Why did the dinosaur say 'moo'?'

The small dinosaur just shrugged.

'Because he was absolutely learning a new language!' shouted out the tall dinosaur, and they both burst out into fits of laughter even though Zoe was ninety-nine per cent sure that Hari had absolutely no idea what the joke was about. Then they darted off and started telling it in stereo to Mrs MacGlone.

Idly, Zoe picked up her phone to take some photographs and noticed an email from Jaz.

Her heart started to beat rather fast as she opened it. When she sent him pictures of Hari and any news, they always used WhatsApp. An email was very unusual.

Sure enough, she saw what it was. Estate agent listings.

She went outside to look at them, into the freezing cold and the dark, not wanting anyone seeing what she was looking at.

'This is what's available,' Jaz had typed. 'I spoke to the council but they said because you moved out of your last place by choice it would be a really long wait.'

Zoe scrolled down. Tiny dank studios on main roads. Large rooms but in shared houses with strangers, who knew where. And all of them, so, so expensive.

She turned round and gasped. The house, every room lit up, the illumination of its beautiful old walls – how could she ever have thought it was gloomy and strange, instead of wonderful? How could she ever have found this place cold and lonely?

Well, all right, it was cold. She shivered in her grey tulle dress.

Suddenly, a dark shape appeared from behind the trees, where it had been directing parking. Ramsay hadn't got an outfit – it had been a big day – but then he'd suddenly remembered an old phantom mask that was kicking around the house somewhere – there was always something kicking round the house somewhere – and he'd put it on. He rather liked it, he found. People were just happily saying hello because they didn't recognise him, rather than giving him those awkward looks they did on the rare occasions he wandered into town.

Everyone was here now and so he was going back to the house, freezing in his black suit when he saw her, silhouetted against the lights of the house. She suited the dress she was wearing, thought Ramsay, not even realising it was a costume until she turned slightly and he saw the wings. Her cheeks were pink in the cold and he smiled; she looked beautiful. Then he realised she was resting her head against the wall, somehow desperately sad, and he started to run.

Chapter Twenty

As soon as she saw him, the mask oddly sexy, she decided something. If she had to go, if she had to leave, go back to her small, panicky London life, drag Hari away from this life he'd made with Patrick and Shackleton and even Mary, then hell – she was going to have something. Something for her. Because everything she was doing was for someone else, and worth it, yes, but suddenly she just felt the injustice. Why did she never get what *she* wanted?

She made a shushing face at Ramsay, and beckoned him over to the trees, where the light faded.

Among the forest, away from the lights and noise of the house, it was quiet and freezing, and the stars were ice chips overhead and the trees made their gentle swishing noise in the wind, and an owl hooted, and she didn't say a single thing, just stopped by a tree, refusing to say a word, to discuss all the difficulties, all the problems.

Tonight, she wasn't going to be the au pair, and he wasn't going to be the boss. She was going to be the girl from the fairy hill. He was going to be the handsome stranger.

He understood immediately and completely, and ripped the mask off, hurling it to one side.

She had to reach up so far that in the end he simply picked her up and pressed her against the tree so he could kiss her better, and she didn't even notice the rush of the bark, the swish of the gently tumbling leaves, the bite of the wind. She was conscious of nothing else when he kissed her, as carefully and intently as in daily life he was clumsy and hesitant. It was a revelation. His mouth; his huge hands in her hair and round her waist; his empowering chest. He was utterly overwhelming; to kiss him was everything, everything she had ever wanted to do.

She stopped, looked up at him in the moonlight.

'To think I thought you had a wife locked up in the attic.'

'Oh, I do,' he said. 'That's my *other* wife.'

He stopped when he saw her face.

'Oh please,' he said. 'Let me make a joke about it. Just once.'

'I think,' said Zoe. 'You're better at kissing. We should probably do that again.'

Chapter Twenty-one

Zoe couldn't have said how long they'd been there. She'd lost all sense of space and time and the world, and Ramsay was hurrying nothing, even though they were both profoundly aware of their growing excitement; the heat rising between them in the dark wood.

She heard her name from far away and gradually came to, even though she couldn't bear for them to pull apart.

'ZOE!'

'It must be one of the children,' she said, realising she was panting, and his mouth was stained with her lipstick. The looked at one another, the spell breaking. He pulled back with a deep groan, but put out his hand and caressed her cheek.

'Ohh!' She gave a sigh.

'ZOEEEEEE!'

'You stay here,' said Zoe. 'I can't . . . We . . . You know.'

'Oh Christ, I know,' said Ramsay bitterly. She gave him an apologetic look, then darted out of the woods, rubbing her mouth. Her heart was racing. Oh God. Oh God. She wanted him so badly.

'ZOEEEEE . . .' Surinder pulled up short. 'What the hell are you doing out here?'

'Um, lanterns,' said Zoe pointlessly, but Surinder didn't care. She was clearly quite tipsy.

'Zoe! Nina's in labour! She's having her baby!'

'Oh wow,' said Zoe. 'That's amazing!'

'And everyone's had too much cider. Have you?'

'I have had no cider,' said Zoe, although she felt completely intoxicated and light-headed.

'Good. Right. Fine. Can you drive me to hospital?'

'What? No! We're in the middle of a party!'

'Not really,' said Surinder, and sure enough, the children had had their fill of dooking and sweeties and dancing to the 'Monster Mash' and were heading off down the hill.

'They had a great time,' said Surinder, who was dressed as a sexy vampire nurse, which Zoe couldn't help think might be a bit confusing at the hospital. 'Everyone was wondering where you were.'

'Never mind that,' said Zoe. 'Seriously?'

'MOVE! BABY COMING!'

'Right, okay,' said Zoe. 'Come on. Let me grab a coat at least!'

'No time!' Surinder pulled her along. Zoe fumbled with her phone and quickly told Ramsay to get back to the house and look after the children. Then they went to the little green car, only to find it was completely hemmed in on all sides by people who hadn't left yet. Ramsay hadn't done such a brilliant job of directing the parking.

'I'll go announce . . .' said Zoe.

'No!' said Surinder. 'We have to go! She needs us! Her mum won't be able to make it till tomorrow!'

'Lennox will be there.'

'Yeah, treating her like it's a calving. She needs us!'

There was only one solution. They jumped into the little blue van.

The drive was surreal, Surinder babbling away, Zoe concentrating on the road ahead, her mind racing as she thought of everything that had gone on.

The little hospital Zoe felt she was getting to know rather too well was quiet at that time of night. Surinder jumped out of the van and dashed through the door, Zoe following more quietly, wishing against anything she wasn't dressed as a fairy (and would have wished, had she but realised it, that she didn't have a head full of twigs), although when she walked through A&E and saw a mummy on crutches and a very drunk young vampire vomiting in a bucket, she figured it wouldn't be anything the staff hadn't seen before.

Surinder burst into the maternity ward she'd already spent much time in, full of drama, ready for excitement, only to find Nina sitting up in her usual bed, head buried in a Ngaio Marsh, Lennox wandering about looking for change for the coffee machine.

'What?!' she said. 'Where's your baby?'

'Ah,' said Nina sadly.

'False alarm?' said Surinder.

'No,' said Nina. 'I'm in labour. But apparently . . . Well. The midwife came and took a look at me and said, "Gonna be a slow one."'

'Oh!' said Surinder. 'Oooh, I am guessing you do not want to hear that from a midwife.'

'That's what I thought,' said Nina. 'I have seen a jillion women have their babies in the last eight weeks. And really you want that thing shooting out. Ideally two seconds after the epidural. Because I have now been here for a *lot* of them.'

She looked glum and sighed.

'Oh God. Don't tell me it's going to be okay.'

'I won't!' said Surinder. 'I've heard it's like being in a car crash.'

'Uh. Thanks.'

The midwife bundled in.

'There you are! Now, what you should do is get yourself moving. Get yourself around and about.'

'You've just spent two months telling me I'm not to move at all! Are you sure this isn't a terrible idea?'

'Nope. Not any more. Get moving.'

'I've forgotten how,' groaned Nina. 'Just like how I suspect I may have to wear pyjamas for the rest of my entire life.'

'I thought like that,' said Zoe, smiling.

'And look at you now – you're a fairy,' said Nina, smiling back at her. 'How are the monsters?'

'Tonight,' said Zoe thoughtfully, 'they're only dressed as monsters.'

Nina raised her eyebrows, then, with some difficulty and some help, got up off the bed.

'Okay then. Let's go for a wander. I'm nearly finished my book anyway.'

'That's okay – we've got the van,' said Surinder.

Inside, Zoe winced. Oh God. She really didn't want Nina to see the van. Not how it was; not now.

But Nina's face lit up.

'Oh God! Yes please! I miss her so much!'

She stood up uncertainly, her belly so ridiculously large it looked absolutely absurd and impossible that she could be standing up sat all.

'Would you mind,' she puffed, as the midwife took the monitor off, 'taking an arm each?'

And the three girls marched out into the car park.

Chapter Twenty-two

It was freezing outside. Zoe couldn't believe she hadn't noticed before.

'I should have had another contraction by now,' said Nina gloomily. 'Seriously. If these were Victorian times, it would take five days and everyone would have to heartily mourn me.'

'Won't they induce you?' said Zoe, shivering again at the cold air, which Nina welcomed.

'They want to give him a chance ... OH!' said Nina.

'It's a boy!' said Surinder. 'OMG, you liar! You gigantic big fat liar!'

Nina smiled shyly.

'I just ... I didn't ... I didn't really want to know. I promise I didn't. But they had to scan me *so much*! I got *so bored*!'

'But why didn't you tell me?'

'Because ...' Nina's voice trailed off. 'I know. I'm sorry. But ... it felt like ours. Lennox and me. Something so special that was just for us. Sorry.'

'Yeah whatevs,' said Surinder. But Zoe, with a great sigh of longing, understood completely. Something between her and Lennox; something so private, so precious.

They needed to help Nina up the steps. Zoe's heart was in her mouth. Maybe the fact that Nina was about to undergo a seismic event ... perhaps that would change it? Maybe she wouldn't really pay attention?

'WHAT THE HELL?'

'But the van,' Nina was saying. They'd had to get her seated on the steps, but she kept twisting her head round.

'It's ... it's "curated"! Ugh, I hate that word. But it's ... it's books I love, and that I know people will love. There's a limited amount of space, and I wanted to fill it up with wonderful, wonderful books!'

She looked like she was about to cry. Zoe felt absolutely horrible.

'I mean ... who can love a Nessie colouring book?'

'Every five-year-old who came in,' said Zoe, but her voice sounded weak.

'I mean ... it's just ... it's like tat! Stupid Scottish tat you can get anywhere!'

'It's ... it's what people wanted!' said Zoe. 'I'm not you: I couldn't automatically spot what people want! You've got a magic power for that! I ... I just ... I just thought my job was making sure you could make money.'

Nina shook her head.

'But it won't! Maybe in the short term, but in the long term ... you need clients that come back! Who trust you, who know you'll find the right book for them!'

'But on the loch, there's an endless supply of new customers! Who want a memento of their trip, to remember lovely Scotland!'

'By selling them whisky-flavoured crap? Is that what you think of this country ... aarrgh!'

Nina doubled over.

'Oh lord,' said Surinder. 'Now what have you done?'

'Nothing!' said Zoe, stung.

'WOAH!' said Nina, then breathing hard, leant over on the step. 'Balls!'

'Well, good, surely,' said Surinder.

Nina looked at Zoe as she gradually straightened up. Then another contraction seized her.

'Oh God,' she said.

'Come on,' said Zoe. 'Let's get you back in hospital.'

Nina shook her head fiercely.

'I can't move ... ohhh ... BUGGER.'

'We'll get you a wheelchair.'

Surinder jumped up.

'No ...' said Nina as another contraction racked her.

'Well,' said Surinder. 'They're not wrong about giving someone a shock for labour.'

'You stay with her,' said Zoe. 'I'll get help.'

'And Lennox!' croaked Nina. 'Ah, bugger bugger BUGGER.'

Zoe ran into the hospital, returning armed with a midwife, who got Zoe to start the van, then turned the lights on to examine Nina.

'Ah,' she said. 'I ... I ...'

Nina screamed.

'This appears to be happening rather more quickly than we anticipated ...'

After that, it was a blur. Zoe hung back, not feeling as if she was a part of this, and all she remembered were members of staff running back and forth and hearing Lennox's low coaxing voice, soothing Nina, telling her she was doing brilliantly and Zoe realised he was talking to her – as Surinder had predicted – exactly as he talked to his sheep, and his calm way with animals seemed to communicate itself, even as Nina made all sorts of noises and swore. Zoe went off to stand in the freezing moonlight and stared up at the sky and remembered the night Hari was born, and the fear and the joy and the sheer amount of goo – but even though she knew Nina was in pain, she couldn't remember the pain, couldn't bring it back.

All she remembered was the fierceness of the joy. Jaz had been taking stupid pictures for his stupid friends and she had known, even then, even as soon as she got pregnant when she hadn't even met his parents, that this was wrong, this was all wrong – but as soon as Hari had arrived, they had both coalesced somehow, not with each other, but with the baby. He had found him as wondrous as she did. Still did. There was no denying that.

Zoe suddenly heard a great piercing wail; a brand-new soul, entering the world.

She checked her watch. Midnight, exactly midnight. The tiny gap where spirits can creep through; where the living and the dead can meet; where worlds collide.

Tears sprung to her eyes.

And something else; a reminder. That when Hari had been born, she had sworn, over and over again, that she would do nothing – nothing – but the best for him. Ever.

And here, on a freezing autumn evening, in a little hospital in the middle of great dark hills silhouetted against a starry sky, she remembered that vow.

To do what was best for him.

And then she turned and went to greet the new mother, who, safely back in a warm and cosy hospital bed, a tiny wrapped bundle in her arms, had forgotten all rancour. She had earned that badge, the stripe of women who have gone through labour, blooded in the same war.

And Nina could do nothing but cry and stare at the tiny face and hug everyone (and occasionally lean over the side of the bed and throw up).

'Go on then,' said Surinder. 'Darcy? Heathcliff? Rochester. Willoughby. Definitely Willoughby. Lawrie. Gatsby. Ooh, I like Gatsby.'

Nina looked at Lennox, who looked back at her and smiled.

'Don't be ridiculous,' said Nina. 'This is John.'

Chapter Twenty-three

Zoe had left them to it, driving home alone in the van to a silent house.

Ramsay was waiting for her in the kitchen, sitting in the dark doing nothing, simply waiting for her to come home. He knew she would have time to think about things; have time to think things over.

He looked at her face. She wasn't smiling.

She came over, clambered up on top of him and curled up on his chest, and they both cried.

'I have to go,' she said. 'I have to. A child needs a mother and a father.'

Ramsay nodded, sighing.

'And it's not good for Mary and she's going to need a lot of support, you know that. She's not going to get "fixed".'

He nodded again, stroking her head.

'We could ... we could visit?' she said hopefully. But she felt strongly that somehow, once she was back in London, commuting on the tube, struggling to make ends meet, to pay her bills as the way money vanished through your hands in the city was terrible, the spell would be broken. They both knew it.

'Of course,' he said.

'I think Nina is going to be just fine,' said Zoe. 'If Lennox ever puts the baby down.' (Zoe was oddly prescient about this: Lennox never did put the baby down.)

Ramsay nodded.

'She wants it done her way,' said Zoe. 'I get that.'

They didn't kiss again. Not with the children's pictures a bright cheerful display around the new coffee machine. They just lay, her on top of him, the two heads together, one big, one small, for a long time.

Down in London, in a small pretty kitchen in Wembley, things were incredibly loud.

'What the hell?' Shanti was yelling. 'What the hell is this shit?'

She was reading his email.

'It's all we can afford, darling. This is all I'm making.'

Shanti looked down them.

'These are awful! I wouldn't put my dog in a place like this!'

'But . . . I want to have him near me! Especially now he can talk! We can hang out, and go to the football, and I can teach him how to DJ and we can be buddies . . .'

Shanti gave him a look.

'Darling,' she said. 'You know how we said. You know how we said it was about what was best for your son.'

'Being near me,' said Jaz stubbornly.

'You saw him up there.'

Jaz stared at the floor.

'You can see how good it is for him up there.'

'But it's *miles* away.'

'Not as far as Ibiza, babes.'

Jaz stared at his shoes.

'Tell her,' said Shanti. 'She'll be so upset.'

'It's two a.m.'

'Tell her,' said Shanti. 'If it was me, I wouldn't be sleeping a wink.'

Chapter Twenty-four

Zoe sat up in the kitchen, Ramsay making coffee, as her phone was buzzing. Who was texting at this time of night? Oh, of course, DJ Jaz didn't keep the same hours as everyone else.

'I don't need to see it,' she grumbled out loud. 'You've won already.'

But she opened it of course.

'Look. Those flats are all crap. Let's leave it for now, yeah, babes? You seem happy. Just stop him speaking Scottish and teach him to love Tottenham.'

Zoe's hand flew to her mouth.

'Oh my God.'

'What?'

'He ... Oh my God! Oh my God!'

She frowned.

'He is never going to support Tottenham.'

She stared, breathing heavily, for ages, then she sent back a stream of emojis: a pouring out of endless hearts and kisses.

'Hearts and kisses?' said Ramsay, peering over her shoulder. 'Can I have some?'

She looked at him. The house gave out not a creak as if it too were holding its breath. Outside the trees swished gently in the deep dark. It was a very quiet moment.

Zoe looked at him, huge, at home, looking at her with lust and hope. He was absolutely irresistible in the dying light of the kitchen fire.

'I suppose . . . you could . . . visit the maid's quarters.'

'You'll have to tell me where it is.'

'*Stop* that!' she said as he pulled her close to him.

'You really are,' he said, 'quite impossibly short. I've been thinking that a lot.'

'*Have* you?' said Zoe as he swung her into his arms.

'Go right,' she said. 'Back stairs.'

'Christ,' said Ramsay, pausing to kiss her. Then he put her down, picked up the two coffee cups, rinsed them in the sink and put them in the dishwasher.

'Well,' said Zoe. 'I think you would be amazed to know how much that turns women on.'

'Would I?' said Ramsay, taking her by the hand as they turned the lights out in the kitchen, shushing each other.

Back in London, Jaz put down his phone.

'Did you hear back?' said Shanti, rubbing his back.

He shook his head.

'She must think I'm such a dickhead, messing her about.'

'I reckon,' said Shanti, 'you're the least dickheadish she's ever felt about you in her life. And *I* am very, very proud of you.'

Tears formed in Jaz's eyes.

'I just . . . I just miss him.'

'We can visit,' said Shanti. 'You know he's better up there. You know it's the right place for him, in the open air, surrounded by other children; not some shitty bedsit on his own. You saw what was best for him. You've done the right thing. I am so, so proud of you.'

Jaz sat down and nodded, the tears sliding down his face, while she buried her face in his back and held on tight.

Chapter Twenty-five

Mary was standing looking awkward as Zoe plaited her hair in the mirror. She had a new school uniform, which looked scratchy on her and too big, and the tie was wonky. She grimaced.

'You look good,' said Zoe. 'And Dr Wainwright said you could come and visit your mum after your session.'

'She likes to brush my hair,' said Mary thoughtfully. She looked at Zoe. 'But I don't know if she'll ever talk. Will she ever talk?'

'I don't know,' said Zoe honestly. 'But I think nothing could make her happier than having you there.'

Mary nodded as if she was taking this in.

'Okay,' she said, taking a deep breath. 'School.'

Mary nodded sadly. 'Shackleton says he's up for it and Kirsty is going to come out and meet you.'

Mary sighed.

'All those books . . . all those adventures. None of them happened in school. I don't think there are adventures in schools.'

Zoe smiled.

'Ah, Mary,' she said, finishing off the plait with a smart tartan ribbon. 'Do I have some books for you.'

Chapter Twenty-six

And now it is nearly Christmas, and there's a bright hoar frost running right across the lawn, and Patrick and Hari are wrapped up like little skiers, waiting anxiously on the steps.

Shackleton and Mary are waiting indoors, not desperate to go out in the cold. Mary is doing her homework and Snapchatting her friends constantly. Shackleton is making scones. They chat occasionally.

Ramsay is upstairs in the library, door wide open, working with a fire on. The boys were running about earlier, but now everyone is a little nervous.

Also, Zoe and Ramsay aren't much closer to telling the children, having convinced themselves that the children haven't noticed, which is odd because if there is one thing Zoe knows, it's that children notice everything. But they have kept it till late at night, and used one of the many, many unused guest bedrooms (they thought they were getting away with it too until they met there one night and realised that Mrs MacGlone had laid a fire, changed the bedding and put a vase of fresh flowers next to the bed). It is their very private haven and they are keeping it to themselves as long as they are able.

Wullie from the village turning up with an extra second-hand van made Zoe feel an absolute idiot for not thinking of it before. She was tempted to paint the van tartan just to shock Nina, but has wisely decided against it for now. Nina is back in Kirrinfief with her beloved regulars. John sometimes accompanies her, but Lennox has a Baby Bjorn and rarely goes anywhere without him, so in fact she hasn't found maternity leave the trial she was dreading. And Zoe goes to Loch Ness and they meet regularly and let Agnieszka try out her new sandwich on them – ham, cheese *and* tomato – and talk about books and babies. Zoe doesn't go over to the farm much. She really does hate that chicken.

At The Beeches, the large white car draws up slowly. Zoe steps forward, the front door, for once, wide open.

Jaz jumps out first, and gallantly opens the door for Shanti behind.

From the passenger seat emerges a stooped, slightly balding figure wearing a smart suit with a tie.

Jaz jumps around the other side, still, Zoe thinks, with a slight grin, slightly showing off. From the other side emerges a sweet-faced woman in a sari and heavy coat. Zoe worries she is cold.

'Daddy!' yells Hari and jumps forward, then freezes at the sight of the older people. He knows, thinks Zoe. He knows. He just can't quite square it in his little head.

So she steps forward, takes his hand in hers – and takes Patrick's hand in her other hand – because families come in all shapes and sizes – and steps forward, and says hello.

Acknowledgements

Thanks: Jo Unwin at JULA; Maddie West and Rachel Kahan at Sphere and William Morrow; Milly Reilly, Joanna Kramer, Charlie King, David Shelley, Stephie Melrose, Gemma Shelley, Liz Hatherell, Hannah Wood and all at Little, Brown; Jake Smith-Bosanquet, Alexander Cochran and the brilliant team at CW.

Also: Rona Monroe for gently suggesting something very important; Shirley Manson for backing me up on the whole Loch Ness Monster thing; the beautiful Betsy hotel in Miami (www.thebetsyhotel.com) who lent me their Writer's Room to finish it; Muriel Gray for flower names and generally being awesome; Agnieszka Ford, who bid for her name to be included in this book at a charity auction – thank you so much, Agnieszka, and hi, Sophia!

Plus: the Board, Lit Mix, Laraine, and my lovely Beatons.

Jenny Colgan is the author of numerous bestselling novels, including *The Little Shop of Happy Ever After* and *Summer at the Little Beach Street Bakery*, which are also published by Sphere. *Meet Me at the Cupcake Café* won the 2012 Melissa Nathan Award for Comedy Romance and was a *Sunday Times* top ten bestseller, as was *Welcome to Rosie Hopkins' Sweetshop of Dreams*, which won the RNA Romantic Novel of the Year Award 2013. Jenny was born in Scotland and has lived in London, the Netherlands, the US and France. She eventually settled on the wettest of all of these places, and currently lives just north of Edinburgh with her husband Andrew, her dog Nevil Shute and her three children: Wallace, who is twelve and likes pretending to be nineteen and not knowing what this embarrassing 'family' thing is that keeps following him about; Michael-Francis, who is ten and likes making new friends on aeroplanes; and Delphine who is eight and is mostly raccoon as far as we can tell so far.

Things Jenny likes include: cakes; far too much *Doctor Who*; wearing Converse trainers every day so her feet are now just gigantic big flat pans; baths only slightly cooler than the surface of the sun; and very, very long books, the longer the better. For more about Jenny, visit her website and her Facebook page, or follow her on Twitter @jennycolgan.